EDITH'S
RETURN TO
DEVON

DANIEL PITT

EDITH'S
RETURN TO
DEVON

A LIFE CHANGED BY AUSTERITY
AND PURSUED BY REGRET

Copyright © 2013 Daniel Pitt

The moral right of the author has been asserted.

Apart from any fair dealing for the purposes of research or private study, or criticism or review, as permitted under the Copyright, Designs and Patents Act 1988, this publication may only be reproduced, stored or transmitted, in any form or by any means, with the prior permission in writing of the publishers, or in the case of reprographic reproduction in accordance with the terms of licences issued by the Copyright Licensing Agency. Enquiries concerning reproduction outside those terms should be sent to the publishers.

Matador
9 Priory Business Park,
Wistow Road, Kibworth Beauchamp,
Leicestershire. LE8 0RX
Tel: (+44) 116 279 2299
Fax: (+44) 116 279 2277
Email: books@troubador.co.uk
Web: www.troubador.co.uk/matador

ISBN 978 1780884 325

British Library Cataloguing in Publication Data.
A catalogue record for this book is available from the British Library.

Printed and bound in the UK by TJ International, Padstow, Cornwall
Typeset in 11pt Adobe Garamond Pro by Troubador Publishing Ltd, Leicester, UK

Matador is an imprint of Troubador Publishing Ltd

*This book is in loving memory of my grandparents;
Ted and Marjorie and Ted and Pat
who are still dearly missed.*

*This book is dedicated to my parents and to all my family who I am
truly blessed to have.*

Chapter 1
Abandoned and Forgotten

December 1929

I brushed past the honeysuckle which had scrambled and engulfed the red brick wall and had begun to meander down around the warped and flaking perpendicular door. As I approached the entrance, flanked on either side by two spiral shaped topiary trees, with a tentacle of dormant honeysuckle grasping at my hair; I looked back behind me, down the gravel path that ran back to the house, to check that no one had followed me. As I approached the door and the garden that lay beyond it, I felt conscious that someone or something had been following me and that they had been observing my stiff and nervous strides away from the empty house, along past the lawn, down the path, into the obscurity of the garden.

When I was satisfied that there was no one behind me, I turned back to face the door. The air now smelt like a night on the fifth of November, with a stench of rustic smoke and burning paper, coming over from the other side of the door. Originally, the door that lead into the kitchen garden had been an ornamental wrought iron gate that allowed one the opportunity to see what lay beyond. Then the Great War came and Father demanded that the gate be taken down and used for scrap metal, to help with the war effort. Ever since then, a wooden door had blockaded the entrance and had been painted and repainted so many times that now the gate looked terribly chafed and stale, with the paint beginning to crack and peel off its layers, like dry unwanted skin.

I reached out a hand to the cold, black iron handle and after a moments' hesitation, I pushed up the handle and pressed my weight up against the door, causing a fleck of white paint to detach itself from the door and land on the arm of my long black coat. As the door tiredly opened with a creaking groan; I brushed the flake from off my arm and wearily entered the garden. The smell of burning, the crackling and spitting of the fire, was the only sound to be heard, and the only feeling of warmth and comfort on that cold December day.

The kitchen garden's experienced and dedicated team of staff had all gone. They had all been dismissed weeks ago after the funeral. Now only two servants remained in the house, my loyal butler and the housekeeper, who had promised to stay with me till the end. I too, had also promised them something. I had promised them, that when the time came for us to leave Devon, I would take them both with me. That I would keep them both employed in my service and give them both some much needed security, which now after the financial crash, so many people did not have. That promise however, I was forced to break, after Mr Cuss, my solicitor, advised me that when all was settled up, I would be lucky to have enough money to live upon myself, let alone pay the wages for two servants. So today was the last day for all three of us, but at least we would be leaving together.

I walked along the terracotta coloured paved path, now littered with a dishevelled litter of leaves from the apple trees' and made my way up towards the sundial elegantly placed in the centre of the garden, with the herb border running along next to it. At each corner of the garden was a cone shaped topiary bush, which were always trimmed and manicured to perfection. Several forcing pots were on the right of me nearest the wall, next to the path that ran all along the perimeter. The kitchen garden was surrounded on all sides by a red brick wall. Fans of pear trees were secured to it, along with fragrant roses that rambled up diamond shaped lattice panels, which now all slept in silence for winter. There were also a few bee boxes hung to the wall, creating apartment blocks for the bees during the winter months. The vegetable plots were nearly all empty and exposed, but had not been dug or trenched as they normally would have been. The curly kale was still looking healthy, lime green sky scrapers of brussels sprouts and a neat terrace of golden parsnips. On the left, the runner beans had all been harvested, their remaining foliage stripped off and heaped up to wither and die down, while the metropolis of bean canes had been left standing, like a dead carcass. In a plot cleared up by the attractive Victorian greenhouses, a rusty, dark brown oil drum was smoking and puffing away, sending out a column and swirl of smoke that reached up over the garden and escaped over the wall. I walked towards the bonfire, passing the sundial and shrivelled herbs. The smell of smoke and intensity of the fire already beginning to warm me up and I coughed at the smell of the fumes.

*

I glanced over through the cloud of smoke to the green houses, full by now with golden barrel cactus showing off their charming emerald green skin, with vanilla coloured sharp spines. Narcissi and begonias were all potted up in terracotta pots, neatly labelled and stacked in well positioned rows, all housed on sturdy varnished staging. The grape vines had spiralled up the poles that held up the middle of the glazed span-roof of the green house. The door into the green house was shut, with a metal galvanised watering can left in front of it, where the last gardener had abruptly put it down after being summoned to the house to be told that he and his colleagues were dismissed, and that the house and estate would now have to be sold. Behind the green houses the tool and potting sheds had also been left with their pots and tools downed and never to be picked up or used again. I noticed a digging fork plunged into the soil by what was left of the marrow plants. The fork had been left frozen and locked into place, not pulled up, washed and cleaned as had been the custom and then hung up away in the tool shed for the next day.

As I approached the clearing with the burning oil drum in its centre, shooting out ash and sparks into the air, I once again felt that I was not alone in the garden. That same, uneasy presence had once again made me shiver and pause on the path. I listened, closely looking to the right and left of me. There was no one there, it was just my nerves and my mind playing tricks on me. A fluttering pigeon suddenly flew overhead and landed on top of one of the cold frames. I reassured myself that it must have been the pigeon that had made me feel uneasy. I moved off the path, away from the sundial, and on to the cold December soil, my heels sinking into the ground, making me feel a little unstable.

I noticed by the side of the bonfire, a few steps away, was the cream tea chest that I had instructed Mr Tucker to bring over from the house, and place here for me to burn its contents. Mr Tucker had kindly offered to burn my unwanted old family papers, letters and numerous copies of black and white photographs himself, but I declined his offer, as I did not want him to see the photos I was burning. Mr Tucker had probably overheard enough bad feeling in the house as it was, and besides I wanted Mr Tucker to remain in the house and supervise the removal men loading up all my belongings into their lorry.

I carefully walked over to the tea chest where Mr Tucker had left it. Feeling the heat of the fire to the side of me, I knelt down to the open box, my long black coat trimmed with thick, black fur dragged and brushed the ground. I reached into the box and scooped up the final pile of papers and photos into my hand and made my way swiftly back to the oil drum. The fire warmed my cold numb face and hands as I threw the bundle into the flames.

I stood on my tiptoes, being careful not to get too close to the cylinder, and watched as the flames began to burn the corner of a photo that had once been so special to me, but was now beginning to burn away, like an old unwanted grocery bill. The orange flames began to cause the black and white photograph to curl and shrivel up, its colours began to smudge and stain with a chocolate, milky grey colour, before the photo began to fragment and disintegrate. As I looked over into the bonfire, feeling its brilliant heat intensify on my face, I caught a final glimpse of that photo, and the face of my brother, before the flames reached. Then, that kind gentle face, that I had loved so much and been so close to for so many years, disappeared and was erased. It was as if I was watching myself die, for everyone in the village had said that no sister and brother had been closer than Eddie and I. Yet that was all over now. Eddie was gone. He had packed a few of his things after our terrible argument in Fathers study, and had abandoned me to my fate of moving from everything I had known, loved and treasured, to a strange and foreign city, into a poky, one bedroom flat.

I realised then that I had known nothing about Eddie, everything I thought I knew about him had been a mask. I thought I had known my family, that there had been no secrets between any of us, especially Eddie.

Yet Mother had known all along about Eddie, for what must have been years, and not told me, nor Father. She had taken the secret with her to the grave. Father too, had lied to me, and been in utter denial about the state of our finances. If only he had acted when the first sign of trouble in the financial markets appeared. If only he had heeded the warnings his broker had sent him, and not shut the warning letters away in the drawer of his desk in the study. Unfortunately, Father, like many men of his age and stature had done what he had always done when things looked bad. He had held his nerve and not become cowed by the pressure. Yet sometimes in life, holding your nerve and ignoring the bleak events you see around you and doing nothing about them, can be like signing your own death warrant.

With the last of my unwanted papers, letters and photos gone, I turned my back on the fire. Stepping back on to the paved path I walked back towards the sundial, and back towards the door, knowing that when I went through it and closed it, no one would ever come here again. I would be the last person to see the garden as it had been. As I returned to the vale of twisted and dead honeysuckle, and ducked under it into its tunnel to push back open the flaking door, I checked that within my pocket the envelope that I had rescued from my Queen Anne writing desk, just in time before the removal men picked it up to take to the lorry, was still safely with in the deep recesses of my pocket. For the hour had come, when finally I had to hand the envelope, and what lay inside it, to its rightful recipients.

Before leaving though, I looked back one last time, to witness what I was about to leave behind. The garden was frozen, lost in time, left exactly as it had been on the day the gardeners had begun their day, desperately hoping that life would continue as it always had done, despite the sudden and tragic changes that had come upon us all. But life did not, and could not go back to how it had been. The crash of '29 had changed everything, and the garden lay frozen, abandoned, and very soon would be forgotten.

Chapter 2
The Spectre Had Arrived

I never did return to Devon. Nor did I re-enter the garden I had abandoned all those years ago. For how could I go back? My world had ended. There would never be a revival. Only in the safety of my dreams did I return home. For only in the security of my sleep and thoughts did I go back to Devon and once again enjoy the sight of my former home set high on the Jurassic peaks of the north Devon coast.

How I loved to remember the joy of entering the avenue of hydrangeas and pines that lined the drive to the house so superbly. I can still recall the pleasure and fragrance of the brilliant red and pink Bourbon roses covering the trellises and arbours of the rose garden. The soothing smell of the English lavender potted in classical urns adorning the grey stone, lichen covered terraces that lead up to the tennis court. I can still remember the feel and texture of the gravel paths. The sound of the seagulls calling out above the bay. The horns and bells of the boats and crafts entering the harbour and the merry tinkle of the cliff railway bell. Even Mrs Goodwin's seed cake I could still taste and her delightful ginger scones with dollops of clotted cream drizzled with golden honey, enjoyed at a table under the drooping wisteria.

My years of exile from that safe and tranquil world were spent far away in isolation with only regret and remorse for companions. I cannot, however be ungrateful. For my grief and trials have thankfully paused. I have found happiness in the simple things. I crave only peace. I accept the things that cannot be changed. Yet Devon continues at times to taunt me and I confess that the peace and quiet that I have such a desire to hold onto here in rural Wiltshire often does lapse into a darkness and depression of the past. Even now in 1952, I still fear the coming of a spectre from my past that will at long last catch up with me and shatter the simplistic life that I crave to keep.

*

I blame Thelma's letter that arrived from Devon only a few days ago. Ever since that wretched letter came my thoughts of the past have steered back to Devon again. They were normally red letter days when post and news arrived from Thelma. I had, up until now, been satisfied and comforted from tales and general chit chat from Thelma. Her letters had become a joy to read and I had enjoyed reading them, yet this time I found that her letter distressed me. It had started like any other letter and I had been lured into thinking that it would be like all the others. But as I read line by line, a strange, uneasy feeling came over me. A feeling of bitterness and even danger. I blame not only Thelma's letter for my uneasy spirits but also this blasted rain that arrived mid-afternoon and spoilt my plans for picking the runner beans and removing the withered heads from off the roses. At around three the sky had turned a strange devilish red, almost the same colour of North Devon's soil. It should have pre-warned me that a change was coming. Within a few hours a melancholy grey sky had swept in a cycle of rain, which had begun to patter on my sitting room window but now lashed it with a fury that I had not seen for many years.

Thankfully I had gone out to the privy ages ago, well before the storm set in and thank the Lord I had for I would have got drenched. I decided to have my customary evening drink of cocoa, play a little on the piano and end the evening listening to the wireless whilst enjoying a good book. It may sound humdrum but it suits me and for a while the evening past as most evenings did. The warn pages of my novel and it's leather binding reassured me and brought me to a slumbering state of mind, falling asleep against the mutterings of the late news bulletin. I had paid little attention to the news of late being dominated by the power struggle in Egypt. I rose from my chair with my empty stained cup of cocoa in hand and was about to retire for the evening. That's when it came. That's when it happened. I ceased my plans for bed and stopped dead. It felt like a bullet had past through me. My body was being slowly drained of life and energy. I felt a coldness come upon me and my hand lost its grip of my cup and it fell to the floor. The drastic change that I feared had arrived. I sat down on the rest of my arm chair utterly stunned with what I was hearing. Not since the outbreak of war and Pearl Harbour had a news broadcast given me such a shock. I listened intensely wanting to stand and move closer to the wireless to guarantee that I would not miss out on hearing any vital information. I however felt too weak to stand and I started to shake. I wanted so much to interrogate the well-spoken news announcer. How many had been rescued? How many had died? Had Thelma survived? Yet my Bullet wireless could do little to help me.

My questions were not answered. Even as I reached my bedroom at well past eleven I found I was unable to stop fearing the worst. I dashed and jumped from rug to rug, attempting not to step on the cold bare floorboards as I climbed into my bed. I read a passage from my well-handled Bible and then attempted my normal routine of prayers. Not that there was anything normal about my prayers tonight. The storm outside was shouting at the window and causing my privy door to bang like a gun was being fired. My normal steady concentration for praying was utterly broken, for I found myself climbing into cold sheets without having completed my nightly devotions. As I listened to the howling wind, the thud of the privy door and the clatter on the window from the rain, my mind and thoughts once again returned to Devon.

*

Sally's tea room had shut up early with only five people in during the whole day. Two of the customer's had been sisters. Two young, happy-go-lucky Australian girls, taking the stormy weather in their stride. The sign board that had been placed outside to attract custom had been drenched and the green chalk menu from the day's specials run away to nothing, leaving only green trails of chalk to run down the board. Along opposite the harbour, three drunken male students staggered and swayed out of the Rising Moon tavern, still gorgeously lit up with a heartening glow of warmth and amber colour, its light illuminating through its small pokey windows and was a stark contrast to the dark ghostly harbour, with its treasure of masts and boats all waiting in silence for the storm to pass. The three young student's had been up at the bar all evening, enjoying rather a few fortifying pints of ale, surrounded by the amused locals. The alcohol the three young men had consumed to great capacity had made them oblivious to the wild weather and the three were laughing and joking, getting soaked to the skin in the pouring rain. One of the students brought out with him his beer glass, downing the last frothy drop. He placed his glass on a flat stone seat, cut deep into the wall of the tavern and left it out in the night to re-fill with rain. He then burst into song, singing in a rather off key and raucous rendition of the latest song from the wireless 'Come rain or shine', sending his chums into more fits of laughter. The three linked arms round each other, and went off down the road looking like they were about to perform the cancan. As they went by, a few bemused villagers twitched their curtains to see who was making all the rumpus. The villagers however were, on the whole, tolerant of the student's misdemeanours, as it was the students who seemed to have all the money to spend. The students made their way past a parked Humber car safe in its space on the road, a little worse for wear from the droppings of the retreating sea gulls who normally congregated round the harbour area, scavenging for unwanted fish and chips that had been dropped by the careless tourists. Yet tonight even these gulls had fled to safety. The Humber's owner, a rather fanatical fern collector, was down for the holiday season as well, deciding to take advantage of Devon's exotic ferns, collecting rare specimens up in the woods by the mineral water factory, before returning to his natural history department at Oxford, where he worked as a professor. A newly retired couple had left the shelter of the grotto-like hole of the lime kilns in the wall of the cliff by the Victorian dance hall, discarded their vinegar soaked, empty fish and chips newspaper, and were huddled together briskly walking back to their hotel room in the grand Bath Hotel. The wind continued to gain power, pounding the outstretched peninsular of the quay, sending the waves to spill over in to the harbour, sending a shock wave of water to smash into the city of boats and masts. The armies of lobster pots were all huddled together, like a family of penguins trying to keep warm. The propped up deck chairs were waiting patiently, folded up tightly against the safety of the quay wall like clams, in the hope that tomorrow the sky would clear and that they would be back in use.

The fishermen had now all abandoned the harbour. The only sound to be heard above the relentless rain, wind and choppy sea was that of a fishing trawler's bell, ringing for its skipper to return. The boat was aggressively rocking from the large waves, causing its brass bell to ring desperately for assistance. The bells chilling sound rang out like a bell of a ship about to crash in to an iceberg in the Atlantic. It could see the danger coming, but could not do a thing to prevent a collision. As the fishing boat continued to bob and sway, its bell continued to ring and ring, trying in vain to warn its captain that danger was coming as the harbour was no longer safe. The sea continued to pound at the harbour steps, washing in pieces of seaweed and drift wood. A family of barnacles had secured the lowest flooded steps, their downy feelers spread out looking for food. The brown, green sea-wrack floated on and off the steps, with their life guard poppers keeping them on top of the surface.

*

After what had been a long and weary day the shadowy and wet figure of Mr Cuttlefish, the harbour master, crawled up Neptune Hill passing on the way The Rising Moon tavern. He had been so tempted to call into the tavern on his way home. The tavern had looked so inviting from the bleak harbour where he had been working all day. He would have loved to have gone into the tavern and ordered a pint like the rest of the locals but he lacked the confidence to do such a thing. He knew too well, that the locals still after all this time, would not accept his presence in the tavern. No one in the village had really forgotten his family's shame. No one ever called him by his real name now. He had gone by the name of Cuttlefish since returning to Devon back in February, thinking it was for the best to assume a new identity. He had hoped that everyone in the village would have forgotten him and his family, after all it happened so many years ago, and he had been away from Devon for many years. Most in the village had forgiven and forgot. One or two people, like his friend who worked as head clerk in the mineral water factory, had never judged him from the start. Then there were the new comers to the village, like his neighbour and her daughter, who he got on so well with. However many of the diehard locals, the old school, still knew who he was and although they made no trouble for him during his daily work in the harbour, they shunned him the rest of the time and made it clear he was not welcome in the tavern. When he finally reached his cottage door, he fumbled about for his key in his long, slippery wet coat with the only source of light from his only companion, his trusty hurricane lamp that he always took with him to work. After an irritating search he finally retrieved his key from his pocket and after unlocking his front door, pausing only for a few minutes to watch his jangling mobile of whelk, clam and top-shells dangling from a frayed rope hanging by his door, he and his lamp moved into the dry conditions of his home. As the evening wore on high above in the depths of the hills above the village a normally calm, forgiving River Lyn was becoming swollen and bloated. The river could not take any more pressure. The never ending days of torrential rain had caused an erosion of the steep banks causing water, mud, rock and soil to run down all sides of the valley to meet the already full basin of the river. The river was about to have a severe break down and sever its confines, and without warning the River Lyn was becoming a raging torrent. As the water rushed down the valley and gorges, picking up speed and strength, uprooting all in its path, mud, trees, stones and boulders were pulled along unable to withstand the mighty rush.

A little further down the river, not far from the village, a tired, depressed clerk was working away at his Davenport desk, trying to make sense of his factory's accounts. The small mineral water factory was a Swiss style building, placed on a sturdy bank next to the running waters of the River Lyn, enclosed by the alpine woods and ferns. The small factory had been producing mineral water for decades, taking advantage of the natural, crystal clear, sparkling water from nearby springs. The water had been highly praised by all in the village and soon people from all over Britain came to buy the factory's bottled water. The factory claimed that its waters could clear and rid the body of the effects of anaemia and rheumatism, to name but a few ailments; the factory's reputation grew and brought in many tourists and visitors. The factory had even survived the great crash of 1929, when its founder and owner went bankrupt and the factory was sold on. However, after the Second World War the factory began to fall into decline and obscurity. The last few years had been hard, and the strain was proving too much for its owner and small work force. The owner asked his loyal clerk to stay late into the night if he could, to bring the books up to date and prepared to be inspected by the accountant the next morning. The clerk was hunched over a pile of ledgers and figures, becoming more heavy hearted by the hour. The cold, wet, wild weather had forced him to remain in his box of an office full of cabinets and records. The clerk had been given a bottle of Bristol cream sherry by his boss as a consolation for working so late into the night. Another desk lay empty and bare next to his. His former fellow worker and friend had packed up her desk days ago now, after being made redundant, due to the ever increasing financial crisis now rising up against the factory. The clerk took another sip of his sherry and then continued on with his work, pausing only for minute to smile at the black and white photograph of his wife and daughter.

The slender clock on the wall ticked away, preparing to strike nine, as the clerk continued to write. He suddenly paused his writing and put his pen down next to his fat ledger. He stood up over his desk and listened. He could hear a noise, the sound was like a roaring train travelling at top speed, only with no sound of a cheery shrill whistle. The clerk bent slightly to make a closer inspection of the view outside through his biscuit tin-size window; the view disappearing due to condensation caused by his heavy breathing. After wiping his hand over the glass to remove his breath he peered out more closely. He could see very little, just rain, the slight trace of a dry stone wall shielding the factory from the river, and to the left a wiry looking bridge, popular with crossing hikers and groups of children playing pooh sticks. He straightened up again. As a new sound could be made out through the roaring train noise. A bone shattering cracking noise, the sound of wood and timber snapping. The noise grew with more intensity and he began to get flustered looking round his office to ask for advice, but there was

know one there to give it. He turned back to
crystal cut sherry glass shuddering, the remaining
the glass. His desk lamp also had caught the shake
calendar toppled over, down to the bare floor boards. Sudde
warning, the factory's electricity failed, and the poor clerk wa
darkness, without any time to do anything but give out a trauma
scream, but a scream that came out distorted like that of a dream, as the
clerk's wooden office wall broke open. A mass of water, rubble, timber
and wood came crashing in, and within a second the other walls of the
office, along with its roof collapsed. The whole factory of pipes,
machines, bottles, timber and tiles went down, like a house of cards
being flattened. Mercifully the poor clerk was killed outright by the
masonry and wall that had blasted its way in on top of him, and would
have drowned with the wall of water which would drag his broken body
down the river. The mass of water continued on its course, drowning
the exotic ferns and woods on the banks. Huge boulders the size of
engines were being uprooted where they sat and dragged along down
the valley for the ride. The wooden bridge would be the next casualty;
it was removed with no effort, snapping and splintering into shreds,
debris being swept down like match sticks. The tempest continued to
gain strength and vigour, and had now finally arrived down into the
village, plunged into sudden darkness like the factory had been. The
tempest headed first into a simple terrace of fishermen's cottages, its
residents unprepared for what was about to happen. As the danger fell
upon the village, many of the villagers had little idea that their lives were
about to change for ever. The change had come. The spectre had arrived.

CHAPTER 3

Faith and Prayer

I awoke with a shock, nearly launching myself out of my bed with a sudden shake. My heart was pounding and I felt like I was having a heart attack. I held my chest for a few minutes, panting for breath and sweating with fear. *It was only a dream,* I reassured myself. *It was just a dream.* My imagination had run away with itself.

Turning to my round-faced clock with its copper body and tiny legs: I read the time, 3.25am. The prospect of sleep until six would not be possible and I was too fearful to try in case any more images of the disaster sailed into my mind. Rising up from out of my bed, I fetched my dressing gown which was draped over the stool at the dressing table. The dressing table was cluttered with the normal womanly things: jars of face cream, two perfume bottles; a glass dish holding a string of pearls, a gold watch and my gold ring with a red ruby stone in its centre.

After fastening my gown and walking out on to the landing, trying not to cause any disturbance, I crept down the stairs like a spirit, with the time ticking away in the deep bowels of a grandfather clock, which stood masterfully in the corner of the widest step of the stairs. My left hand slithered down the cold, wooden banister until it slid off the end, as I reached the bottom down into the dark hall. Shuffling into the long galley kitchen I felt for the light switch, locating it with a few slaps of my hand. I slid open a small box of matches and lit the stove to boil a pot of water. After scooping some tea into my tea pot and waiting for the water to simmer, then when the water was boiled, I combined the tea hot water and tea placed the lid on with a clink, and allowed the pot to stand for a few moments. I turned the electric light off. The kitchen was full of white natural light from the full moon, which seemed to be suspended above my kitchen garden. The light of the moon was magical and relaxed my stressed spirit.

I looked out of the window, my eyes squinting over my garden towards the paddock which ran behind my property. I looked further on at the sombre head stones and cherub statues in the village cemetery. How ghostly they all looked. Appearing like a gathering of the dead; the moonlight granting them a diminishing time to appear alive before they would return to simple unassuming tributes again. In the paddock closer to home, I could make out the scampering shadows of rabbits jumping about on the sodden grass. They were keeping well out of sight from the barn owl that was patrolling further up the paddock and had made a home for itself in the roof of the chapel cemetery.

I went back over to the light switch and switched it back on, only to strain my tea and add a splash of milk and a tiny tea spoon of sugar. After collecting the cup and placing it onto its matching saucer, I headed over to my breakfast table with the box of matches, ready to light a lamp that I hoped would help calm me better than artificial light. After lighting the lamp standing in the middle of the table, I closed up my friendly looking box of matches. The picturesque scene of a steam ship, sailing a turquoise sea, set against a mustard-yellow sky. I loved this picture on the box of England's Glory matches. It was a reassuring picture to me. One of peace and tranquillity and a box I had kept for years, simply buying ordinary boxes of matches and transferring them into my own special box. Turning off the electric light again, I found my way back to the table and sat down. A dark wood Welsh dresser stood by the side of me, littered with empty cordial bottles, blue and white willow patterned china and enamel plates and cups. A huge jug of red roses, cow parsley and lemon balm stood in centre of the dresser. As I sipped my tea, I paused to look out through the window at the moonlit garden, and noticed the dew and wet of the past two days of rain, glistening like diamonds on the grass and shrubs. The fur trees were over laden with moisture and looked as if they had suffered a perm. Glancing out at the wet damp garden, my thoughts continued to drift away back down to Devon. The disaster continued to haunt me. I could not get my old home of Lynrock out of my mind. Two days had passed since the disaster and I had heard as many up to date bulletins on the wireless as possible. Five bodies had been found in the wreckage already and the death toll was still expected to climb. I had read page after page of the special coverage in the papers, as every national newspaper was dominated by the news of the disaster. The more I read and the more I listened, the more my dreams turned to nightmares. I was becoming more frantic with worry for Thelma, who had a cottage down by the harbour. I had rang and rang her phone number since the news broke, trying desperately to reach her, hoping that either Thelma or her neighbour who she shared the phone line with would answer and reassure me that she was safe. But the lines were dead and unavailable.

My worrying thoughts were suddenly interrupted by a sharp bark from a fox that rang out from the darkness of the garden. I stood up and went over to the window scanning the garden, peering in the direction of the onions in the vegetable patch where I thought the bark came from. The onions had their necks bent completely down ready to start the ripening process and the broad beans were now well over. I squinted even harder, my face almost touching the glass, causing the glass to steam up with my shaky, exaggerated breathing. I wiped away my breath from the window just in time to catch sight of the intruder that had gained access into the garden. A long black creature scampered out of its hiding place by the runner bean tunnel, dashed across the garden dragging its long bushy tale behind it. The shifty creature reached the hedge and dashed out into the open field of Farmer Richards paddock, causing the rabbits to retreat to their burrows. Mr, or Mrs, fox had vanished into the night.

As my Broadway clock next to the dresser struck four, I sat back down and sipped some more tea. The lamp continued to offer a comforting glow. Yet the reassurance from the lamp could do little to stop my mind from worrying. What had become of Thelma and the other villagers who I had grown up with? My mind raced again and I was becoming desperate for answers. It was the not knowing that was proving so painful and not being able to do anything. I pondered over the last letter that Thelma had sent me at the beginning of the month. Leaving my lamp and my cosy warm kitchen, I went back into the hall and into the sitting room which was silhouetted with the light of the moon that was seeping through my thin summer curtains, draping the room in shadows and mystery. Switching on the light my eyes blinking wanting to shut with the sudden brightness of the light, I walked over to my Queen Anne writing desk and riffled open one of the small drawers and retrieved the very last letter that Thelma had written to me at the beginning of August. With the letter in hand I returned to my kitchen and sat down again at the table, with the lamp providing adequate light for me to read the letter.

Opening up the envelope again and shifting the letter out from inside it holding the pages shakily in my hand, I attempted to read Thelma's letter dated 9th August 1952. The letter was full of news about Lynrock, telling me about the people who were down there on holiday. There was some bore of a professor who was obsessed with plants who had rather tested Thelma's patience. Two Australian girls had also arrived and were enjoying a summer holiday in Devon before returning to Australia on the 17th. The holiday season sounded as if it had gone well so far, thanks to the wonderful start to August. I read and re-read the first page, checking every detail of Thelma's words. The first page had been focused on Lynrock news and then about Thelma's unfortunate redundancy from her job as a secretary at the mineral water factory. But she went on to tell me the wonderful news that she had been offered a new position in the village as a waitress in Sally's tea room.

After finishing the first page I placed it under the second and attempted to try and continue reading. However the second page proved too much for me, as once again Thelma's words and the dreadful things they said brought a wave of shock and despair over me. I still could not believe what Thelma had told me. How could the village do it? After all my family had done for them? Self-pity is never flattering but that is how I felt. My already shaky nerves felt even worse as I attempted to drink the last drop of my tea. I picked the cup up with a trembling hand but discovered that the tea had grown cold and stale and did nothing to ease my worry.

Still trembling and feeling rather unsteady, and beginning to feel rather sick, I rose from out of my chair, went across to my larder and rummaged around until I located the bottle I needed. With the bottle in hand I fetched a glass tumbler from the dresser and poured myself a brandy. I drank the brandy quickly, gulping it down, the sting and sharp taste made me cringe with shock and revulsion. Falling back down into my chair, still feeling bitter like the brandy I had just drank, I sat in a dazed state staring at the glazed, domed shade of my lamp. I tried to concentrate on the lamp and its light, trying not to allow anything else to enter my mind. I could not bare to feel so down and so low. I hated the feeling of bitterness which I had found never did anyone any good. Still Thelma's letter disturbed me and I could not let go of the anger I was feeling. Clasping my hands together like a cockle shell, lowering my head and closing my eyes, I began to pray and hoped that my mind would be put at peace.

After many minutes past with only the sound of my Broadway clock ticking, and a far off bark from the fox again, I opened my eyes. The brandy and prayer had done their job. By five I was feeling a little calmer, full now of nervous expectation. It was the type of feeling you get when you're about to make a journey or go on holiday. I knew now what I had to do. I did not want to go. Nor leave home. But there was no other way. I had no choice. Folding up Thelma's letter and placing it back into its envelope, I rose determinedly from out of my chair with the letter in hand, ready to return it back into the desk. I would shut it away and forget it. Outside the dawn chorus was beginning. The birds were proclaiming the coming of a new fresh day and their place and mine in it. Hearing the birds singing that dawn was coming and that the rain clouds had gone, helped me to focus. I had a long Sunday ahead of me. There was much to do and plan. For tomorrow on Monday morning I would set off to find Thelma. She had been my friend now for well over a decade and once again she needed my help. I did not allow myself to think the worst. I was sure that Thelma was alive. Now was not the time to give up on her. I needed to re-engage with the spirit we all had during the war.

*

Outside in the sodden wet garden, the bird's singing was becoming louder and stronger, as more birds had joined the chorus. After making sure the lamp was safe to leave I went back into the sitting room and sealed Thelma's letter back into its compartment in the desk, locking the drawer to keep the letter safe. I would not take the letter with me. I would leave it in the desk. What Thelma had told me I had to try and put to the back of my mind. There was nothing that could be done. I could do nothing to prevent what the village were deciding to do. All I could do was to look to the future and try to forget the past. So, trying to feel determined, trying not to doubt and to think about nothing else but finding Thelma, I forced myself back upstairs to wash and dress and prepare for my return to Devon.

Chapter 4
No Rest on Sunday

I still had no news regarding Thelma. According to the wireless the number of dead from the disaster had now reached thirteen and was unfortunately still rising. Power and water were down in the lower village. Drains had been destroyed, giving an additional problem to the villager's living by the harbour of no sanitation. The army had been called in and an immediate evacuation of the surviving villagers was now well underway.

The normal routine of church in the morning, a small roast for lunch followed by an afternoon snooze and a nice cup of Camp coffee, then later attending the evening service had all fallen by the wayside. Instead of resting on the seventh day I ended up cleaning my entire house as if I was going on some sort of Biblical exodus. Making extensive travel plans (a story in itself), checking the bus and train timetables as if I was about to take an examination on them.

My plan was this. If I left home by ten thirty, caught the eleven o'clock bus that came to its stop opposite the village war memorial, that would get me down as far as Bath. I would then have to take another train to Bristol, and from there to Barnstable in Devon. All I had to do then was find transport to take me over Exmoor, and then down to Lynrock. What could be more simple?

After checking timetables, re-checking then checking again, I telephoned five different hotels in Lynrock to try and book myself a room. All to no avail. All the hotels in the upper village were full of traumatised survivors. Every receptionist I phoned spoke to me as if I was mad wanting to stay in a hotel overlooking a disaster zone. One receptionist even accused me of being a member of the 'damned press' and told me I should be ashamed of myself trying to sell a story for my paper, when so many had lost their homes and lives. With my hand almost locked into position from holding the phone for so long, and with my ear feeling red hot and still ringing from the sharp scorn from the last receptionist I had spoken to, I finally managed, with some difficulty, to book myself in to The Chough's Nest Hotel located along the costal path. It apparently overlooked the bay and the bleak disaster zone. Being granted the booking had been no easy task. I practically had to beg the manager's wife of The Chough's Nest, a rather curt Mrs Barns, to arrange my accommodation, who informed me that all non-essential travel was either discouraged or banned by the authorities. I listened with good grace to her rather lengthy speech about how terrible things were down in Lynrock and her recommendation that if I wanted a summer holiday it was best to go to Cornwall. I explained that I had no desire to come down on holiday but wished to look for a relative who had been living down by the harbour and who I was unable to contact.

Mrs Barns was a little more civil, but still hummed over my request for a room. By now I had been on the phone for well over fifteen minutes and knew I was getting nowhere. I interjected Mrs Barns in mid flow, grumbling about the lack of power, the phone lines only just being restored and what a terrible inconvenience it all was to her.

"Look, my dear Mrs Barns," I said in a polite but forceful tone. "I used to live down in Lynrock I was born and raised there. I still have a relative living down by the harbour and I need to find her. Now would you do me the kindness of taking my reservation?"

I was now desperate for a resolution. *If only she knew who I was or who I used to be*, I thought smugly to myself, *that would put her in her place*. I knew I had told an untruth telling Mrs Barns that Thelma was a relative, but I thought that it would give me more hope of being allowed to travel down and get a room if she thought I was searching for a relative and not just a friend. My final forceful words finally did the trick and Mrs Barns took my reservation. Mrs Barns went on to inform me that they would have to put me on the top floor of the hotel, as the other rooms were either booked by holiday makers or being used for survivors. After going through the formalities of reminding me to bring my ration book and identity card as one lady who had booked in last week had forgotten both much to Mrs Barns' disgust our conversation ended. I at long last was able to put down the phone, giving my hand and warm ear some much needed peace and rest.

Thankfully one worry I did not have was to take a leave of absence from school. With the summer holidays in full swing I had no work or professional obligations to attend to. I did not return to school until September. Most of my planning and children's progress reports were now done, so I was free from the joys of teaching for a short period.

*

When Sunday evening eventually came I wondered up to bed, still feeling despondent from not hearing any news of Thelma. Out of sheer tiredness from all that I had done during the day and the stress of hearing the depressing news from Devon, I completed my Bible and prayers, crawled into bed and thankfully fell into a deep sleep.

*

I was glad to greet Monday morning, the day of my departure, in time to see the sun rise over Farmer Richards' paddock, with its grass sparkling with dew, enticing the swallows to fly low to find their breakfast. I left instructions with my elderly neighbour Madeline that I would be going down to Lynrock to look for Thelma. I would be gone for about four days, and would, God willing, return on Saturday. I placed my case in the hall ready to go. I was not taking very much, just the basics. I packed my brown leather walking shoes wrapped in an old *Telegraph* newspaper, a waterproof mac, a few other items of clothing, a few toiletries my Bible and current novel and only one evening dress. After all this was not a pleasure trip.

If I was to keep to my timetable of eleven o'clock departure I would have to get my skates on. I looked around the house and double checked that lights were turned off, taps in the kitchen were not dripping, the back bedroom curtains pulled and my Streptocarpus on the kitchen window sill was watered. Hopefully Madeleine would come in on Wednesday to revive it, and place any post on the companion table in the hall. I had given the house a good clean the day before although very unbiblical of me to do this on a Sunday I know. The Eubank cleaner had certainly been well used and I had dusted and polished all morning. I always enjoyed polishing the special furniture, like my father's art deco style book case. It was filled with his dark blue, black and brown leather bindings of the classics like *Jane Eyre* and *Bleak House,* along with a rather warn copy of Shakespeare's works with its cardinal red cover nearly thread bare with over use. There was also a collection of '*Tales of Mystery*' by Edgar Allan Poe, which was a great favourite of mine and my father's. Books had been an important part of my life as my father had at one time been a publisher, and was always to be found in his library or study reading some manuscript or new novel. When opening Father's walnut bookcase, which was beautifully engraved with two glass windows at the front revealing the library of contents, the smell that came from that collection of books was one of the past. A musty, rich woody smell, like a bottle of sherry. It was a smell that brought back to me my father's old library and the past. The happy days of childhood and the exciting times of the twenties; they were memories I was glad to look back on. I closed up the bookcase and locked it with its small key, thus securing the smell I loved so much, like putting a stopper on a bottle of perfume. I had removed the red-satin like roses from off the top of the piano, which had been scarred during the Blitz. The roses had looked lovely for well over a week, but they were now starting to drop and I knew I would have a fresh arrangement to replace them with next Sunday from church. I was always lucky to be given a bunch from the weekly flower arranger.

  I left my current project of music on the stand of the piano and scolded myself that I would try to master the 'Moon light Sonata' before the end of the year. I had played the piano since childhood. In the days before the war it was a requirement for a debutant to be able to play the piano to perfection, and be able to perform for guests at the drop of a hat after dinner. But that world was over now. It had almost vanished and eroded away. I then went over to de-clutter my Queen Anne writing desk of obsolete correspondence, old tradesman's bills and receipts that I had paid but not yet put on file. I then remembered to make a note to employ the chimney sweep for the end of September to clean out the fire and chimney in case we had another hard winter. I closed my larder journal which was full of my previous grocery lists along with the ever increasing bills for everything. I checked my larder. It was looking considerably bare due to the impact of rationing which had still not come to an end. I went on from there with the kitchen tasks, requiring me to remove my ring from my finger, which I placed on the window sill under the protection of the Streptocarpus. With the kitchen sink cleaned, a trip to the privy was required. I knew it would be a while before I got the chance to go again. Afterwards I got back to the house and locked up my kitchen door and hung the key up on the hook. I briskly walked into my dark hall to collect my awaiting bag, which looked rather tired and battered now after decades of use but it still suited my purposes perfectly. After all I was one of the 'make do and mend generation' and only replaced something if it was broken or beyond repair. I never got rid of anything because it was considered out of fashion. I suddenly realised I still had my cleaning apron on so I quickly removed that and replaced it with a tailored jacket that hung up on the coat stand. After inspecting my appearance in the long hall mirror, checking my blue jacket and matching skirt were correct, I pulled my blue slanting hat with a smart black band on to my brunette hair and secured it with a hat pin. My appearance I thought looked elegant and coordinated but not too dressy for travelling. I looked at my mother's old gold watch, now always firmly strapped to my wrist and read the time of 10.20 am exactly. The only other item of jewellery I had secured for myself was my mother's string of pearls which were now packed in my case. My mother had enjoyed an expansive jewellery collection with some beautiful pieces. I recalled one occasion when she generously loaned me one of my grandmothers jewels; a necklace of red diamonds set in a gold setting. My father had also bought at an auction, a set of diamonds belonging to a relative of the Russian Royal Family which I had also been fortunate enough to wear. My mother's jewellery had passed down to me when she died in 1927 and I had hoped as no doubt my mother had, that the collection would have remained in our family. Sadly my circumstances had forced me to part with them. My train of thoughts suddenly came back from the past to the present, finding myself standing in the hall ready to depart. From there I went into the study which was a very small, masculine looking room. The dual aspect room contained a heavy looking bureau, complete with a Victorian office chair, where I did my school work during the evenings. Beside the desk was a comfy armchair with a high supporting back, a small sideboard with a few photos displayed in French silver frames and a ticking French clock.

I looked out the front window which looked into the loggia. The sun was out and beginning to dry up the saturated garden. It was certainly nice to have some August sunshine at last. I closed the door on the study, collected my handbag off the companion table and picked up my case from the floor. With a hearty sigh and a deep breath I opened my front door and stepped out on to the terracotta tiled loggia. The sun was a welcome visitor to the garden and the air was sweet with the smell of lemon balm. With a quick action, I slammed the front door behind me, giving the small knocker a shudder and knock against the green wood of the door. I brushed past a scarlet coloured geranium which was growing productively in a black classical urn next to the door.

Although I felt a little apprehensive about making this trip down to Devon and to the past, I knew it had to be done. I had spent far too many years allowing my secret past to lie dormant inside me, so with my case in hand I reluctantly set off on this mountain of a journey.

Chapter 5
Returning Home to Devon

As arranged, Madeleine was at the bottom of the garden standing by my warped picket gate, shaded from the sun by a twisted looking oak tree. She was waiting to see me off and collect my key. She gave me a royal looking wave and I reciprocated. With case and clutch bag in hand, I stepped off the loggia, and proceeded down the gravel path, inspecting my garden as I walked.

My garden was a reasonably sized plot; full of Lady Silvia roses with delicate prawn coloured petals and dark green leaves. Lemon balm grew like weeds and were intermingled with carnations, sweet peas, fox gloves and lupins. The flowers had taken a bit of a battering with the days of rain, but I hoped that with a day of August sunshine it might revive them. The rest of the garden consisted of a large magnolia tree in full leaf to the right of the loggia and Madeleine's hedge which partitioned our two gardens giving me perfect privacy. This created a sort of court yard to the side of the house nearest the study. Although it was a confined space it allowed room for a garden bench, a bird table and a raised bed of flowers which changed with each season. The rest of the garden was laid to lawn with long stretches of rose beds shaded by cherry and apple trees, and a boundary surrounded either by hedging or trees. My secret garden gave a sense of peace and seclusion.

*

I reached Madeleine at the end of the gravel path, bordered on both sides with my cottage garden plants. She kindly opened the gate with its black painted letters of Folly Lane Cottage set on a faded white sign. The sign and gate closed behind me with a firm pull from Madeleine. I heard the Tudor handle and lock snap back into place as if to tell me: You are now committed on this journey, Edith. There is no turning back and we will not let you enter again until your journey is completed! Madeleine greeted me warmly.

"Good morning Edith! What a lovely day you have chosen to return to Devon."

Madeleine was a small, kindly looking lady who had lived with her unmarried daughter, Victoria in the house next to me for over five years. She was an unassuming, well-mannered lady and one of my very best friends, despite our differences in age as I was in my early forties and she was approaching seventy in October. Madeleine and Victoria were very much like me. They enjoyed a peaceful existence in Wiltshire and had found the last few years hard and difficult to adjust and change to.

"Yes," I replied. "It's glorious! What a difference from the last few days."

The weather was now at its best and was beginning to dry up the damp grass. The fir trees were also beginning to recover from the wet conditions and settle back into their rightful shapes.

"Yes indeed my dear. Those poor souls in Devon. If only they had had this weather last week, the disaster would never have happened. I've been praying so hard for them, especially your friend Thelma. Have you heard any word from her?" Madeleine said, with a hint of desperation in her voice.

"No," I said sadly, "still no news. I have tried to contact her but no one seems to answer. A lot of the lines are still down. The last I heard from her was a letter which came at the beginning of the month."

Talking about Thelma's letter again caused my stomach to churn. It was now tucked away in a compartment of my handbag, along with a letter destined for Gloucester which I needed to post before the end of the day.

I had debated about taking Thelma's letter with me. I had shut it back in the drawer of my desk, trying to move on and forget what she had written. But last night before retiring I had found myself retrieving it from the desk, clasping and almost crumpling it up before snapping it into my handbag. I decided I wanted something that had recently been in Thelma's own hand with me on the journey. I consoled myself that it had been a hard letter for her to write as indeed it was for me to read it.

Madeleine then said, "You might find things have not changed much. It strikes me as a sleepy sort of place from what the papers have said."

"Yes it is," I said with a slight quiver in my voice, secretly thinking to myself that places like Lynrock, small and gossipy, never do change.

"Now Edith!" Madeleine said in an impetuous and concerned tone. "Have you got a good place to stay down there? So many of the hotels are being used as relief centres, according to the wireless this morning."

"Oh! Yes," I said, brushing off her concern, "I'm staying in The Chough's Nest Hotel in upper Lynrock which is part of the village above the affected area. I had a lengthy chat with the hotel manger's wife, a delightful woman," I added in a sarcastic tone.

"That's all right then," Madeleine said with a sigh of reassurance, "only I read in the newspaper that the Bath hotel down by the harbour where Mrs Snail stayed with her late husband years ago has collapsed. Most of it got washed out to sea!"

At the mention of Mrs Snail, Madeleine turned to the other side of the lane to look at the house opposite mine. The house was one of the biggest properties in the village and the most sought. It was a timber framed Tudor cottage with decorative framing, elaborate wooden beams, multiple chimney stacks, and decorative diamond lattice windows. A wisteria had interwoven itself along many of the front walls by the porch and gave a glorious display of colour each summer. The house was set in beautiful park land gardens, overlooking one of Farmer Richards' fields.

The house, as you may have gathered, belonged to Mrs Cynthia Amelia Snail, wife to a junior cabinet minister in the last government. After the Conservative Party returned to power and Mr Snail lost his constituency and seat in parliament, they both left London society for a quiet country life in Wiltshire. Mr Snail unfortunately died in 1951 after suffering a stroke, following only a few months of enjoyable retirement with Cynthia. Some villagers had meanly said it was probably a blessing, as she had a reputation for being strong willed and unflinching in any domestic argument. She did, I must admit, have a way of lording it over every one, and had a slight Lady of the Manor attitude. However every villager recently was doing everything in their power to find favour with Cynthia, as she had made it known down at the post office (the heart that pumped the blood and gossip round our village) that she was going to purchase a television in readiness to watch Her Majesty the Queen's coronation next year. Madeleine went on to say that Cynthia had summoned her round for coffee tomorrow. She hoped that in accepting it would gain her favour in readiness for a possible invite to the coronation viewing.

Madeleine added rather artfully, "I will have to say how much you and I are looking forward to the village coronation party next year. With any luck my dear, we may get a viewing of the coronation on Cynthia's new television!"

It was true I was looking forward to celebrate the great event. I have always been a proud and loyal royalist. But I could not think about it at that moment, for I was too worried about Thelma. Madeleine suddenly resumed our talk of Devon.

"My dear Edith," she said in a determined manner, "how on earth will you cope with getting up and down the cliff every day? It's such a drop I hear and you know what the roads are like. They're so steep! They will be even worse now with the disaster. Even some of the rescue and relief efforts are being hampered. I hear some of the area has no sanitation or power!"

"Don't worry Madeleine. I do know how to rough it for a while. I did survive the Blitz of Bath in 1942! Getting down from the hotel to the harbour won't be an issue as they have a cliff railway which runs from the top of Lynrock all the way down to the lower village. If that fails I can walk. I love walking. I will be perfectly safe. If I take the railway down I will just pray the cable does not snap!"

I laughed and looked at Madeleine, whose jaw and mouth had dropped. She looked startled and horrified at my joke. I could see my little attempt at humour had not gone down well, so I immediately said to cover myself, "Don't worry Madeleine, I was only fooling. And I will not be going alone, the Lord will be going with me. As for the living conditions I will just have to make do and mend like we did in the war. It is only for a few days. I will be far better off than the poor residents down there." *You can't argue with that,* I thought to myself.

"I keep forgetting, my dear, that you used to live down there. Although you never speak much about it? You will be like the prodigal son returning home. Who knows you might not want to come back!"

I felt rather unsure of myself on the mention of me being like the prodigal son. Not the most tactful thing to say to me, but in fairness Madeleine was not aware of my past and life before Wiltshire. I let the comment go over me. There was no way I would ever want to live back down there again. I cheerfully responded, trying to change the subject and get away from the mention of my past with, "Well I guess I should be making tracks or I will miss the bus."

At this point I was becoming aware that time was not waiting for me. I advanced quickly off the path and on to the wet muddy conditions of the lane, left in part by the heavy rainfall and by old Farmer Richards' new tractor!

"Yes my dear, I suppose you had better go."

She then slipped out from her red jacket a vanilla envelope about the size of small book. She pressed it into my hands. The content's was heavy and I heard and felt the sliding about of money.

"Here you are Edith. This is an emergency fund from church, along with prayers and regards from Reverend Harmer. We hope you can pass it on to the church down there."

I was very touched at the kind, yet practical gesture of Christian love from everyone in the village. "Please do thank Reverend Harmer for me and the congregation. It's such a wonderful gift. I will certainly pass the donation down to the vicar of the Baptist church. I may try and help myself with anything that needs doing down there. Perhaps I could look after the injured or misplaced children."

I unclasped my handbag and placed the envelope inside, making sure it was secure, before sealing my bag. The clasp shut with a sharp snap.

Madeleine laughed, "Well my dear you have had plenty of practice looking after children. I saw one of your pupils yesterday afternoon playing Cowboys and Indians in the allotments. I think Adam thought the runner beanpoles were Indian Tepees!"

I laughed, picturing Adam running in out of the bean poles dressed in buckskin and eagle feathered headdress getting plastered with mud.

"His mother said in church yesterday what progress Adam had made last term in your class. She said what a dedicated teacher you were."

Madeleine spoke full of pride, as if she was my mother, proud of her daughter's excellent achievements. I too was pleased with the comment and I felt a little happier with the prospect of returning to school in September.

Madeleine then came towards me, kissed me goodbye and gave me a light hug.

"Look after yourself, Edith. God bless you. Don't worry about the house. I will take care of it until Saturday. I hope the journey won't be too testing for you and I do hope you find your friend in good health. I will continue to pray for her. All the village will."

I was glad to hear that Madeleine and the rest of the village would pray for me and for Thelma. There is no substitute for the power of prayer.

I gave my goodbyes to Madeleine and followed the lane past her immaculate garden, with winding drive to a romantic looking door with a rusty old horse shoe set under a gothic arch. A large weeping willow dominated the garden and brought shade and cover to a small side sun room full of geraniums of every colour. A snug wicker chair was in the corner with a small cushion embroidered with tulips. Madeleine often had a nap in there during the afternoon while Victoria set about cooking dinner. I walked out of the peace of my lane and turned down to the left. The lane took me past Farmer Richards' back yard which ran along the back of mine and Madeleine's properties. It went up a slight hill to his own farm house. Farmer Richards was, shall we say, a typical farmer. A very nice man, but always rather in a muddle. Indeed his whole farm was one big expanse of muddles. Looking into his yard full of slushy mud and puddles, I wondered how he ever found anything of importance in the soggy mess and jumble of the yard. Old tyres of every size and thickness had become constant fixtures. Grubby looking trailers covered with old straw, dust and redundant sheets had now been smothered by the brambles and thorn bushes. A redundant rusting

Ferguson. A. Tractor in pre-war battleship grey was surrounded with weeds of cow parsley and dandelions. An empty paddock, void of its former occupant Primrose the horse who had been moved to a new stable by the farm house, was now becoming corrupted with piles of rubble and rubbish, looking like a bomb site from the war. Two metal sheds full of agricultural artefacts and tools were rusting away to a dark brown consistency, but to the left of the shed was a portioned off area to house Benny the bull when he was no longer serving the cows. However, to Farmer Richards the chaos I have just described was his paradise and his reason for living. I found I rather liked Farmer Richards'. He did however have an unfortunate bad habit of interrupting my weekends free from marking, when I was enjoying pottering round the garden, to stop and tell me the most graphic reports of one of his Friesian herd having trouble giving birth. Or he would recount the most boring tales of woe about the trouble he was having with the hydraulics of his new Fordson Major tractor, which was responsible for the mud on the road.

As Farmer Richards' domain left my view, I hurried on past the allotments. They were all well-kept in our village and hosted a family of skittish speckled hens searching for a meal. Occasionally one might catch a glimpse of Adam Berry dressed as an Indian chief doing his rain dance before rounding up his braves, although no sign of him today. A Victorian greenhouse ran down the back of the plot with sturdy, solid wooden staging which was always cleaned and painted annually. In front of that were a few seedling boxes and frames. In each patch of vegetables was an occasional terracotta rhubarb pot, no doubt protecting some exotic-looking rhubarb plant. The whole plot was then surrounded by a typical dry-stone wall and access granted by a wide picket gate, with a large sign reading 'private'.

It was at this point, seeing the allotments and the Victorian green house, adorned with its span roof, that I was reminded of my old kitchen garden back in Devon. How grand it had been. I suddenly started to worry about my decision to go back to my former home. I had not been in the place of my birth and childhood since I fled the county in December of 1929, and swore I would never go back. For how could I, with all that had happened? With my stomach starting to churn I carried on walking up the road, past the black secretive gates of the cemetery flanked by two conifer trees, which led to the chapel of rest and villagers' last resting places.

*

As the church clock struck eleven, in the high street I came alongside the war memorial and stood opposite the designated bus stop and royal red phone box. I gingerly crossed over to the right, watching the village high street now bustling with the ladies of the village, all clutching wicker baskets along with their irritating ration books. After crossing the road I stood at the bus stop next to the vacant phone box and waited. While standing silently for the bus to arrive I spotted a few of my girls from school playing hop scotch down by the stone market cross. They seemed to be enjoying the freedom of the summer holidays as I had been doing up until the news came about the disaster. Observing their play gave me pause to reflect on my own youth and an intense longing to be their age again, to enjoy the bliss and ignorance of carefree summers that when you're young seem to go on without end. Ahead of me at the top of the village I caught a glimpse of the green Great Western bus coming down past the school, causing the girls to abort their game of hop scotch and to shout with excitement of seeing a bus! The bus passed the bustling post office and was headed directly towards me at the waiting stop.

*

I quickly rummaged through my bag looking for the tiny silver flask of brandy I had placed in one of the compartments along with my smelling salts, two letters, my purse, ration book, my brown identity card and a handkerchief. After locating my brandy flask I spun round on my heels, having my back towards the high street and the approaching bus. The phone box thankfully concealed my pleasure of taking a quick slug of brandy. The rich dark liquid stung my throat and caused my face to crease in revulsion. Taking brandy, I found, was a required taste, but the effects of the drink for calming the nerves far outweighed the unpleasant taste. My thoughts still raced away, for the brandy could not work that quickly to calm me. I began to wonder what state I would find Thelma and my other former neighbours in? Many villagers had turned against me when my family scandal broke back in 1929, and as I was forced to sell the estate and dismiss the servants. Most of the village had shunned me or done little to support me in my time of need. My bitter memories were suddenly put to a halt. Not with the numbing effect of the brandy, but by an abrupt shout from behind me.

"Come on love! We've not got all day!"

My bag was flung into the boot of the bus and I boarded it, scowling at the rude, beastly bus driver who had so commonly shouted at me (*probably a socialist,* I thought). I handed over my money begrudgingly and told him my destination. As I walked I was aware of a slight sway, caused either by the effect of my brandy or the fact that the bus was preparing to move off. I sat in my seat and shuffled about, trying to get myself comfortable. I opened my handbag to check its contents and as I was pushing the church donation money lower inside I then saw Thelma's letter. "Oh blast, blast!" I had forgotten to post my other letter to Gloucester. I was highly irritated with myself, but then thought I could post it in Bath. However that would cause confusion and anxiety to the recipient.

*

The village cemetery still looked grey and depressing, as I suppose most such places do. As we sped past it, the way I had come, the rest of the village disappeared quickly. We moved down past the allotments, busy with clucking hens, past the vortex of muddles and mud of farmer Richards' yard. Then finally the tranquillity of my own lane and home which soon disappeared from sight. We moved along the road by the side of Cynthia's expansive gardens. In the field at the back, farmer Richards' herd of Friesian cows were grazing on the luscious green grass and yellow buttercups. The bus finally turned the sharp bend and halted at the stop sign. Whilst waiting it suddenly hit me what I was about to embark upon. All the build-up of sorting, cleaning and making arrangements, were over. My climb up the mountain had begun. The bus suddenly pulled off the lane and on to the newly built road, heading towards the city of Bath. As I adjusted my position once more in the seat I realised that after years of living in exile I was finally returning to Devon.

Chapter 6
Doctor Carrot

Bath 1942

"*Don't sit under the apple tree with anyone else but me, anyone else but me, anyone else but me. No, no, no. Don't sit...*' Gosh it that the time? My happy singing at the Belfast sink came to a sudden halt as I switched off the pleasant company of my wireless and the catchy new number by Glen Miller. I was brilliantly happy. April so far had been such a cheerful month, we had enjoyed countless days of cold, but gloriously sunny, weather. The trees in Victoria Park were beginning to shower us with light pink and strawberry blossom. The yellow trumpets and orange cups of daffodils lifted the heart and gave us all a much needed boost of confidence. The weekend was only a day away now and like most people I had that Friday feeling! Only one more day of work and then two days of freedom.

As much as I loved my job which I had now enjoyed undertaking for well over twelve years since moving to Bath from Devon, I was looking forward to a weekend off. It was going to be such a nice change to be at leisure and not to have to keep looking at my New Gate London clock ticking away and having the frantic scrabble of getting ready for work every morning. *Tomorrow morning Edith*, I thought to myself, *you can enjoy a lie in but best not to dilly dally today or you'll be late.* After quickly washing and dressing, I finished by breakfast of warm brown toast, made from the national loaf, tangy marmalade, ever decreasing butter and a nice pot of tea. It was rather funny how quickly I got used to rationing. White bread was no longer available only the national brown loaf. I and every one in my office at the Guildhall nearly went hysterical with excitement when Spam came out. I still found the packets of dried egg substitute rather ghastly, and even the government must have thought it was pretty revolting as they had just published a pamphlet of what to do with it. Dried milk was just about bearable. I did wake up nearly every day longing, craving for a banana or an orange, or any fruit for that matter. Fruit was something you could not get hold of for love nor money.

As for clothes, well don't get me started! I was desperately sewing and mending each evening, sat in my leather chair whilst listening to the wireless and praying that I would not look like a scarecrow when I tried on the jacket or dress I was mending or fixing up. My skills at making do and mending were not the best, but I did have a go. Plus any woman who did look smart, dressed up to the nines, was given severe looks by onlookers as they thought you were not being patriotic. God help you if you had too many buttons on your clothes, people looked at you as if they wanted to stone you! Everything did seem a challenge and a struggle, but there was a war on and we all had to do our bit. Our suffering was nothing compared to what our troops were going through.

The sun was pouring through the twelve panes of the window in my kitchen, all taped up safely with masking tape to prevent them shattering in the event of Hitler dropping a few bombs on us. However, according to my neighbour, a rather overzealous acting air raid warden, Mr Jim Randle, who seemed to have his metal helmet on permanently every time I saw him, apparently Hitler was not interested in us and all the bombs were headed for Bristol. "Don't worry," he would say to me nearly every flipping day I saw him. "They won't fall on us, Edith." I think Jim must have thought me a very nervous lady to think he had to reassure me every time we heard the moaning of the air raid siren. Sure enough though, Jim was always correct; Bath so far had been spared the terrors that Bristol, London and the other major cities were enduring. After clearing away the enamel plate and cup from my breakfast table and, placing them back on to my rickety looking dresser, I went in to my cosy sitting room to pull aside the blackout curtains that barred the April sunshine from entering the room. I pulled the curtains back and observed the view through the taped up panes of glass. In front of my terrace was a smart straight road running past an open square with a fountain. I was extremely lucky to have opposite me, beyond the other side of the road, the beautiful sunken Parade Gardens which were always spectacularly kept and manicured. Above, at road level, a classical stone balustrade ran along the top of the gardens connected to a grand sweeping staircase which lead down into the sloped gardens. A stone ramp by the steps allowed access for mothers with prams. The garden paths meandered down to the banks of the River Avon. One could then proceed along a roofed colonnade of sandstone Tuscan pillars which continued along the River Avon and ended at a bridge, which I always thought would have looked better in Venice than in Bath. Above the gardens and roof of the colonnade, and just to the left of my terrace, was the mighty looking Empire Hotel. It was a great Everest of a building, which like the Grand Pump Room Hotel by the abbey, had been requisitioned by the government to house parts of the admiralty and Ministry of Defence personnel evacuated from London. My place of work for the last twelve years was the Guildhall, which was located a few streets from the Empire Hotel. Turning left from my terrace one could find one's way down past the orchard and tennis court to my Baptist church, by the train station which I attended each Sunday. I was housed on the second floor of Sheila's Parade terrace in a modest but comfortable flat. My flat consisted of a sitting room with a typical Georgian fireplace and terribly crazed framed mirror, with two brown leather chairs either side along with my work basket of material and sewing. Sat in the window was a Queen Anne writing desk with lovely little drawers and cubby holes, which I had salvaged from my former home in Devon. I also had a beautiful bookcase, another inherited piece from my father, full of musty leather bound books with beautiful marbling detail. My best friend, my round black Bakelite wireless, sat on top of the bookcase giving me much enjoyment during the lonely evenings. On the wall opposite my fireplace was my very much loved piano. It was covered in old black, white and grey photos in French silver frames. Pictures of my parents during happier times. The walls were a rather dusty green colour with a few prints hanging from a picture rail. One was of Venice, *The Palace of Doge* I believe. Through a small door, partitioned with some dark grey curtains, was my poky kitchen. The rest of the flat comprised of a small bedroom which housed my sewing machine waiting for me to try and alter my rather tired looking grey jacket. To the right across the hall was my bathroom which was a real luxury. That was my own little home.

With the curtains drawn back, the flat was now full of sunshine and looking far more cheerful. Content with the appearance of my flat I was ready for the off. I picked up my handbag, collected my coat from the hall pegs along with the brown wooded box containing my gas mask. I put a black hat on, stepped out into the dark communal hallway, locked my flat door and shot off for work. On the ground floor of my terrace was Jim's busy newsagent and tobacconist shop, run mostly by his wife, Jane Randle. Their flat was situated above the shop and under mine. Jane was a rather stern, well covered looking lady, who shall we say was not exactly wasting away with the shortages in food and reduced diet in rationing. I stepped off the stone platform of my front door, now bare of its railing around it which had been taken down for the war effort. The streets were a hive of activity. Mostly snooty admiral officials and civil servants, who marched about like they owned the city. The civil servants and top brass were not that popular with the citizens of Bath. You had to practically fight your way on to the bus or trams which were now always hogged by the mass of black suits, attaché cases and newspapers belonging to civil service persons, who all looked like undertakers carrying briefcases.

*

I walked past Jane Randle, giving her a wave as I passed. She responded, and as always she wore a rather gold fish expression. I always tried to be neighbourly and keep on good terms with her as it was her shop basement I fled to during an air raid. I went in to the square, past the spraying waters of the fountain and cooing, stuttering pigeons that were congregating around it looking for their breakfast. The streets were busy, packed with children off to school cradling their satchels and gas masks. Two soldiers briskly overtook me and headed towards the abbey, probably heading for the Grand Pump Room Hotel. The undertakers were also out in force, swaggering off with their morning papers, cases of documents and gas masks underarm.

*

The air was fresh and vibrant, perhaps a little chilly, but at least it was bright. The merry sound of the tram bells rang out from the next street, and a fluttering and flapping of wings from pigeons erupted behind me, startled by the bells and chimes of the churches ringing out for nine o'clock. *The Bath Chronicle seller* in his rather broad Somerset accent could be heard drumming up trade against the rustle of people heading for their various destinations. A few men peddled past on the road, tinkling their bike bells as they past me and waving to friends and acquaintances. Everybody looked like I felt, they were thanking God that it was Friday!

I crossed the road and turned the corner, passing the Empire Hotel, with a wall of sand bags protecting the entrance and reception windows like the walls of an igloo. All its windows were well taped up, and two soldiers were guarding the double doors of the reception area now bustling with undertakers.

*

I then walked along a crowded street more busy with the humble citizens of Bath going about their business for the day. A caterer's van went past along the road with the Sainsbury's wine merchant's van not far behind it. Two shabby looking girls went by on bicycles with flowery patterned scarves tying their strands of ebony and blonde hair in place. Father Tim from St Johns church was also on his bike, with his Bible safe in the deep wicker basket on the front of his bike.

I paused at the end on the pavement next to Smiths, a shop which made the most smart looking leather bags and cases. The smell of fresh, clean leather meandered in the air. I stood on the pavement along with several other women, undertakers and a postman, waiting for a medical van with its massive red cross to pass, heading for the hospital, before crossing the road to take refuge on the paved island with a royal red phone box located on it, then crossing again to the other side. I waited again with another lady who was far too busy examining a dishevelled list of things she had to undertake to talk or acknowledge me. In front of me, beyond the road, was my place of work.

*

The Guildhall was an impressive, rather grand looking building, built in a classical Roman / Georgian style with an elegant pediment in the centre and an impressive dome above it on the roof, surrounded by chimney stacks and classical urns on pedestals. In the centre of the dome was a slender white flag pole, bare of its Union Jack. Two sweeping wings of offices ran off the main building, with large Venetian windows all taped up now. Stone pillars decorated with spirals and scrolls were set into the walls, along with carved friezes depicting classical scenes.

*

I had been working in this building for well over a decade, but even after all that time I still felt special and rather important, walking in through its grand lobby and reception room and stepping onto the ruby red carpet of the grand stone staircase. From there I could look up at the massive gleaming chandelier hanging above me from the centre of the cream and gold painted domed roof decorated with Rococo mouldings. As I went in that day, I still had that same feeling of wonderment and privilege to work in such a building. Although my place of work did look a little more bare than usual. Most of the paintings depicting Georgian ladies in beautiful silk dresses, powdered wigs with caps and hats, and the pictures of the men with Bob-wigs had all been taken down and placed in the basements until the war was over. Apart from two pictures of the King and Queen. Many of the chandeliers in the building had all been removed to places of safety in case of bombing, however the chandelier above the stairs in the dome had been left. The carpet had also been taken up, which made the lobby and downstairs offices very cold. Most of the paintings had been replaced with war posters like 'Dig for Victory', or 'Keep a Pig'. The worst poster (which I hated) was a poster of a rather creepy looking carrot, dressed in black tie and wearing spectacles with the words next to him: 'Doctor Carrot the children's best friend!' *Heaven help any poor child having a creepy looking carrot like him for a friend,* I thought as I signed in at the clerk's desk. I collected some internal memos from Ann at the desk for my department and carried on up the stairs. My hand glided up the polished brass handrail adorning the top of an elaborate black and gold iron balustrade.

*

I reached the first floor, to a very open landing of white and grey tiles all beautifully laid in a diamond and star design. The landing was lit thanks to our remaining seventeenth century chandelier and one of the large Venetian windows secured with tape. A few carved chairs with red cushions littered the corners of the landing along with large, gold-coloured candle stands. This floor was where the treasurer and his department were housed, along with the town clerk in the next wing. Also on this floor, through impressive panelled doors was the Banqueting room, which was one of the grandest rooms I had ever been in. It boasted gold and white walls filled with large portraits of important historical local people. The room enjoyed an impressively high ceiling but its three chandeliers had been taken down and many of the paintings covered up with sheets. The hall was only used for important occasions like a ball or Lord Mayor's dinner. I went along a corridor of panelled doors, until I reached the end of the wing and came to another open landing and stairs. I proceeded up the stairs to the second floor where the Education Department was located. I walked along a poorly lit corridor of empty plinths which did have busts on but like the other valuables had been removed for their own safety. The walls had terribly bad square stains where paintings had been hanging but taken down, and there were a few nasty yellowy damp patches that had gathered strength in the petal mouldings in the apses. All along the corridors and stairwells were war posters of 'Keep Calm and Carry On', and a rather smug looking lady hovered over a sewing machine saying 'Make do and Mend'. Every time I saw that poster I felt highly strung knowing my own attempts at sewing were so bad. Red fire buckets were positioned along the corridors as well as buckets put in strategic places to hold the rain water from the leaking roofs.

*

I finally reached my office and opened the six panel door. The office was dark and empty. As usual, I was the first to arrive. I went over to my desk which was nearest the window and pulled back the blackout curtains and wooden shutters. The streets outside had become more bustling, with a lot more navy personnel larking about on their way to headquarters. Several women with sparse looking baskets trudged along, looking rather depressed, probably trying to think what they could cook for their families that night. A few M.O.D personnel all in uniform pushed along the crowds of women and workers, looking rather in a hurry. I saw the postman with his post bag heading in our direction. Thankfully this meant I would not have to go to the sorting office like I did the Wednesday before to collect it. The post seemed to get later and later, and sometimes it did not come at all. Like the day before. I took off my coat and hat and hung them up on the coat stand along with my gas mask. I moved across the office which was reasonably big, with a high ceiling and ormolu lantern hanging from the centre. The glass in the lantern had been taken out of the sides, in case of a bomb. Underneath lay a round table in the centre of the room with three French Empire style chairs arranged around it. Three desks, one of which was mine, occupied the rest of the space. The other two desks belonged to Eileen and Thelma who I shared the office with. There was a row of filing cabinets, sorting, pending and out-going trays, and a large pin board with all the local schools in our cluster area marked on; a large book case with government documents, binders and publications; a Georgian fire place with a gold rimmed mirror over it. There was also a safe for putting any important documents or money in. I uncovered my typewriter from its cover, and pulled off the day before's date from my calendar to reveal the date of 24th April 1942, all in large red font. *Just today*, I thought, *then it's the weekend!* I got a few letters out my pending tray from head teachers that needed answering and had to be ready to be posted off that morning. I looked through my appointments diary to see if I had any schools to visit the next Monday. To my shock I saw I had four, so all the paperwork regarding school budgets would have to be done that day. I also had a stack of paperwork to plough through regarding claim forms and documents for the evacuee children. I would also have to submit yet another maintenance form to get someone to fix my filing cabinet door, which had stuck and the wooden handle had been prized off. All in all it would be a typical day, with an occasional air raid warning, which would mean a scrabble down to the basements. I was just about to get the post from the mail room when Eileen, my friend and colleague, came in. Eileen was a quiet, shy girl; she was kind and thoughtful and a joy to work with as she was always most efficient and a tidy worker.

"Good Morning Edith!" Eileen came in as she always did, hung her coat up next to mine but placed her gas mask under her desk, as she was always worried of a gas attack.

"Morning Eileen! How are you this morning?" I said, shuffling some papers round as I spoke.

"I'm well thank you, Edith. Mum's had a bad night with her rheumatism again, so I said I would go and get her some mineral water later and drop it in at lunch time."

"That's a good idea", I said "Your poor mum, I do feel for her having that. Least we have had some nice spring weather so far, and it's the weekend."

"Yes, it makes you feel so much brighter having some sunshine." Eileen went over to our wall of wooden and metal filing cabinets adorned with rows of black box files, with white crisp labels. Eileen scanned the box files and selected the one she needed.

"I know what I meant to say to you," Eileen said suddenly with surprise, "Are you going to that dance with Thelma tomorrow night at the assembly rooms? Only Thelma asked me if I was going, but we don't really hit it off much so I told her if you were going I would tag along with you."

Eileen looked at me longingly, hoping I would say yes so she would not be stuck with Thelma, who was a nice girl but a bit too forward and head strong when it came to men. Particularly now the city was swarming with officers and flashy civil servants.

"I was not planning to go," I started, "but, being its Saturday and as its been ages since you and I went out..." I paused and then said with a burst of excitement, "Alright! Yes. Let's both go together. If you like we could stop off at the Red House and get a bite to eat before we go to the dance. My treat."

Eileen's face lit up and she sounded delighted at the invitation,

"Oh that would be lovely Edith, what a good idea, I've not been to the Red House since I went with Mum last December, I know it was December because it was just before Pearl Harbour." Eileen went on looking through her chosen box file, looking through at the papers and heavy bundles tied up with blue ribbon.

"If the foods good," I said, "We could always cry off from the dance and spend the evening there. Let Thelma enjoy the dancing with all the navy officers."

Eileen laughed, "Thelma won't need any help from us, she's already on officer number two. She dropped the last one last week. Speaking of Thelma, she seems very quiet, you would not know she was here."

I looked at Thelma's desk, looking like a bomb had exploded on it. Thelma was the complete opposite to me and Eileen. We both kept our desks immaculate, while Thelma left her desk in a state of devastation. Yet somehow she always managed to put her hand on anything she needed. I looked at the tall mantelpiece clock on the marbled fire place. "Yes Thelma is rather late." I paused again. "I'm going down to the mail room, I will probably bump in to her on my way down."

"Right you are," Eileen said in an up-beat tone, "I will go and get us our morning coffee, if you can call it that," Eileen added in a dry, depressed manner.

*

I shot down the corridor passing other colleagues in the education department, greeting them as they arrived, dealing with queries and hearing the sound of phones starting to ring and typewriters tapping away. After dealing with two queries regarding evacuee paperwork and a leaking roof in the office two down from mine, I reached the stairs and went down heading towards the grander main stairs back to the lobby and then to the mail room. I collected the packages, tubes and letters, and staggered back up the stairs with the bundles, the job which used to be done by our mail boy and assistant, Bobby, who came to us in 1938 at the age of eighteen. Bobby had been such a lovely young man, very polite, quiet and had a wonderful sense of humour, but tragically he was killed in France, the year after his brother. I often wondered how his poor mother was coping to lose both sons to the war. I got back to my office, still with no sign of Thelma, but a nice warm cup of watery coffee from Eileen, who was already sat at her desk typing away.

"My word! That must be two days' worth of post there," Eileen said, looking mystified at such a large bundle of post.

"Yes," I said. "I suppose this must be the post we did not get yesterday, as well as todays. I put down the post on the round table in the middle of the room and started to divide it into piles, allocating letters addressed to their recipients in each pile. I then opened up a log cardboard tube with a white plug on it. "Oh what is this we've been sent now?" I said to Eileen, as I pulled out the roll from the tube. I unrolled the paper roll, like a pirate's treasure map and studied the poster.

"Oh look! Just look at this!" I said in a horrified manner, "This just takes the biscuit!"

I turned round to Eileen and showed her the poster. Eileen snorted, a broad smile came over her face, and her cheeks went red. Then she burst out in to fits of laughter. "Just my luck to be sent five posters of flaming creepy Doctor Carrot!"

"Well he is the children's best friend," Eileen, said choking back laughter and wiping away tears, before finally adding "It could have been worse Edith, the government could have sent you that 'make do and mend' poster, with that nice lady on the front you love so much."

I looked at Eileen with a drab expression on my face, then looked back at Doctor Carrot and then back at Eileen. Eileen had slightly composed herself, before an artful smile crept on to her face again, and we both erupted in to shouts of laughter. An attractive rich voice from behind us interrupted our fun.

"You two must have already started on the gin to be this bloody happy first thing in the bleeding morning!"

Thelma swept in, looking like the Queen of Sheba swinging her long chestnut hair about. She flung her bag and gas mask on to her already messy desk and took off her long brown coat to reveal an impeccably well cut brown skirt and jacket with a black top underneath, a creation she had annoyingly made herself with great perfection. She was an excellent seamstress.

Thelma then said in a rather stressed and warn out manner, "Oh fetch us a cuppa would you Edith dear! I am absolutely shattered. Couldn't get on the bloody tram with all the undertakers, had to walk all the flaming way!"

Chapter 7
Much Needed Advice

1942

Friday morning soon went as quickly as it had begun. Eileen went out at twelve-thirty to get some bath Buns, and to get a bottle of mineral water for her mum from outside the Roman Baths. Eileen going to get mineral water reminded me of a factory my father had helped to establish down in Lynrock. It had the same reputation as Bath's waters, for being able to help rid the body of impurities, and helping with painful conditions like arthritis. The last time I was in Lynrock the factory was booming, and a proud testament to my father.

With Eileen out for a while, I continued on with typing the last two letters for two headteachers ready for my meeting with them on Monday. All my evacuee's money was now chased up and in place, and Thelma was just typing up a covering letter to go down to the treasurer. My tummy was starting to rumble and I was really ready for some lunch. So I finished my letter and placed it in the pending tray, ready to prepare for posting when I returned.

I placed two box files back on the top of the filing cabinets and then picked up a memo to go down to the maintenance department, asking them to please get the filing cabinet handle and drawer fixed before the end of the day. We desperately needed to retrieve some records out of it, as access to the records had ended when the handle was pulled off. I was just about to put my coat on and get ready to go to lunch, when Thelma returned from the lavatory again! It had been her sixth trip so far that morning. She came in looking a little flushed, her eyes looked stained as if she'd been crying and dabbing her mouth with a hanky. She came in through the door like a naughty school child who had played hooky from school. "Are you alright Thelma?" I said, as I put my coat and hat on. Thelma flung herself in to a wooden swivel chair and looked stunned and rather bothered about something. "I say Thelma?" Thelma had not heard me the first time I enquired after her health, so I asked her again. I walked over to her desk, covered in a jumble of papers, books, pencils, two cups of cold half-drunk coffee and a few cosmetics and magazines.

"Thelma!" I said, "Are you feeling well? You look a bit hot and bothered?" Thelma suddenly acknowledged me, she smiled and brushed off my concern in a blasé manner

"Oh I'm fine thanks Edith, just over did the drink and fags last night. You know how it is." Although Thelma tried to diffuse my concern with a not bothered with anything or anyone attitude, her eyes betrayed her. Her eyes were full of a deep, gut wrenching fear. A look I had seen before many years ago in someone else.

"Thelma, I am not a fool. You have hardly done any work at all this morning. You made four mistakes on letters, you snapped at poor Ann down in reception, when all she said to you was she found no trouble getting on to the tram this morning, plus you've been in and out of the loo all morning. I know something's wrong, now what is it, are you feeling ill? If you are go home, put yourself to bed and enjoy the weekend and then come back on Monday."

Thelma looked at me, her eyes still full of fear and her hands looked a bit shaky.

"I said I'm fine Edith, just drop it please, it's probably something I ate, or too much drink last night." She spoke with a slight quiver in her voice and her lip had trembled as she began to speak. "Thelma this is more than a hang over, I know there's something going on, please tell me. You know what they say, a problem shared and all that."

Thelma got up shakily from her seat and barked at me with a fierce tone.

"Look Edith, just mind your own business, stop nagging me, you're worse than my mother!" Thelma stormed out the office and marched down the hall.

I was a bit taken back by Thelma's attack. In all the years we had worked together I had never heard her shout like that. Yes Thelma was a bit rough and ready, some would say common. But she was an attractive, feisty spirited young girl and she did have some fine qualities like kindness and rallying round when there was a problem.

*

I collected my memo, put my gas mask box around my shoulder and closed the office up for lunch. The corridors were busy with my fellow workers of secretaries, administrators and visitors from other departments in the building. An occasional piercing ring of a telephone could be heard behind the closed office doors but they would soon pause for lunch.

I walked down to the grand polished landing opposite the doors to the Banqueting house. A group of secretaries were gathered by the stairs, all carrying massive bundles of papers and ledgers. The head of the health department was coming up the stairs with a group of official looking people trailing behind him. I looked up and down the corridor looking in vain for Thelma, but there was no sign of her. I greeted Mr Rustle who was the head of the Health department which was housed in a separate building next to the hospital. We both spoke for a few minutes, talking about the weather, the war, and how his department was coping. Then I walked down the main stairs. The light from the chandelier hanging in the dome, poured down into the cold reception area. I paused at the desk to give Ann my memo regarding my filing cabinet, put my gas mask and bag behind her desk for a minute while I went to spend a penny, as I knew the lavatories would be cleaner in here than in a café. The ladies, was empty with all the cubical doors left open wide, except one which was bolted. After spending a penny, I came out of the loo and went to wash my hands with the palm oil soap. Just as I was adjusting my hair and hat in the mirror, I heard the lock and door of the closed cubical open. I looked in the mirror to study who was coming out, and to my surprise the reflection was of Thelma. She staggered out and headed over to the wash basin next to me. I pretended to be looking at my own face, but I was observing her. She looked terribly ill. Her hair was a mess, her face looking a rather sickly white, and she had the look of someone who had been violently sick. Thelma and I were both now standing in front of the mirror observing each other.

"Not a pretty sight is it," Thelma said in a glum, downtrodden way.

"I do the best I can with what the Lord gave me," I said trying to joke with Thelma, hoping that using some humour at my own expense might lighten the mood, and help her to come clean about whatever was on her mind.

Thelma did give a small, blink and you'll miss it, smile. She carried on looking into the mirror, as did I, until I finally asked her again, "Thelma, what's going on? Trust me, I might be able to help?"

"You can't help Edith no one can, not unless you can… " She paused and looked rather tearful again. "What's up?" I said. "What's wrong?"

"Got myself into a bit of bother Edith, you see, well, the thing is. Oh! God Edith, I'm in real trouble." Thelma finally dropped the hard girl routine, and I could see she was beginning to crack under the strain of whatever it was she had been keeping to herself. "Tell me what the trouble is Thelma and I will help you." I paused and then gave Thelma the reassurance she craved. "Thelma, I'm not easily shocked, whatever it is, you can tell me." Thelma was now looking at me with even wider and more penetrating eyes. Finally, after a long pause, seeing Thelma unable to release the pressure from herself, I asked the thing that I had suspected as soon as I had seen her come out of the cubical door.

"You're pregnant aren't you?"

My question finally pushed Thelma over the edge, as she broke down and whimpered like a dog. Her hands came slamming down on the wash basin surround. Her gold ring tapping sharply against the marble. She began to bend her back and head like a dolphin, with her head almost touching the cold tap of the sink.

I turned round to face her and pulled her up close to me, giving her a much needed hug and a blessing that someone was there for her. "It was a one off", Thelma began her voice sounding panicky "It was that M.O.D officer who I was going out with. We met in the Assembly rooms a few weeks ago and we got on really well. We only did it the once."

Thelma sounded like a child who had gone in to a sweet shop without any money, stole a gob stopper, and then been mortified with surprise when the manager barred her exit and summoned the police. She continued to weep, desperately, her fingers digging into my jacket like a crab. "I am afraid Thelma, sometimes it only does take the once. Have you told him, the father, this officer, that he's going to be a father?"

"Yes!" She began to howl now, like a wolf and sputtered out in desperation, "He told me he knew someone, who would do away with it quietly."

I was at this point a little more horrified, not in anger towards Thelma, but anger and shock at the advice she had been given by the man who was partly responsible for this problem.

Thelma continued to become more agitated by the minute

"What will happen when it starts to show? Mum and Dad will go ballistic with me, they really will. I haven't got the money to pay for the baby to be got rid of anyhow, and if I had it, what would happen? Women die giving birth!"

Thelma continued to sink in to me, and it felt like the longest few minutes while I tried to gather myself and prayed I would give her the best piece of advice.

"Are you absolutely sure you're pregnant Thelma?" Thelma picked her head up and looked up at me crestfallen.

"Yes it's was confirmed this morning, I saw the doc, that's why I was half an hour late. It wasn't the tram that was late at all."

That explained her outburst at Ann. I collected my thoughts together, and looked about at the ceiling as if the answer to this problem was painted up there. I could hear one of the taps dripping in the rather stuffy loos, and the flapping of pigeons perched in the porthole window outside. After like what seemed hours, but was in reality only seconds, I finally spoke.

"Thelma, listen to me. The first thing you must do is to keep calm, and not get yourself into a state. It won't do you or the baby any good. You take the rest of the day off. I will cover for you. When you're calmer and in a better frame of mind, then you must think what you want to do. This is going to be the biggest decision you'll ever have to make. I am sure if you tell your parents they will stand by you, and support you."

Thelma suddenly cut me off from my sermon, she stood up tall and away from me, and fired at me for the second time that day. "What bloody planet are you living on Edith? If my parents found out they would kill me! They would send me away. They would throw me out into the gutter. Mum always told me if I got myself in any trouble I would be on my own."

Thelma had become jittery, and looked like a rabbit struggling in a trap.

"My life isn't like it was for you in Devon playing Lady of the Manor. I'm a working class girl, I can't buy myself out of trouble. You Lords and Ladies are all the same. You don't live in the real world!"

I was stunned by Thelma's words, and my face must have shown it. I staggered away and turned my back on her, trying not to show her I was upset by her catty remarks. That flipping tap was still dripping only it now sounded much louder, and it was so stuffy in the loos. How little Thelma knew or understood. How little anyone understood or realised what happened to me and my family. I was no longer a Lady. That title, I had left behind after '29. My old, carefree existence and pleasant life had died when Father had died. I was as much working class as Thelma was now. I had tried hard to give kind, Christian advice, not judgmental and yet, somehow I had found myself in a deep hole and under attack. I tugged at my coat, feeling hot and bothered and very stressed, and that ruddy tap was getting on my wick.

Thelma suddenly retrieved herself, took a deep breath and then spoke more softly.

"Edith I'm sorry, that was unforgivable of me to say such a wicked thing, I didn't mean it really. I was angry, not with you, more with myself for getting myself in this terrible mess. You're not snobby, not one bit. I think you're a lovely kind woman. One of us. I didn't mean what I said."

I continued to study the wall and looked back up again at the ceiling. The altercation between Thelma and I and the fear I saw in Thelma's eyes was the same fear I had seen in someone else's eyes a long time ago in my father's study. The circumstances had been different but the principle had been the same. Someone who had trusted me, who I had been so close to and came to me for help, desperate for me to help them, but because of my upbringing, my lack of experience in the world, and my own self-importance, and perhaps that the person had been so terribly close to me, I gave him the wrong advice. Advice that had disastrous consequences, and cost me my one remaining relative to walk out and leave me behind.

I had made a mistake back then, and I had vowed I would never be so judgmental again. I gave a deep breath and looked up at the small porthole window of the ladies loo. The sun was streaming through it, betraying and unmasking a funnel of dust dancing in the light. I turned back round to Thelma, who looked crushed at the words she had said to me. I then gave her what I hoped was the best humanly possible advice.

"Look Thelma, if the worse comes to the worst, and your parents do abandon you, then don't go to anyone else but me. You have my address. If you need anything, or a place to stay, then you can come and stay with me, for as long as you need to, until you get yourself sorted. I would be very happy to help you. Yes, it's true what you implied, I did have a very sheltered life in Devon, and yes you may be right, I perhaps don't really know what goes on in the world. But I do know that if you make a quick, snap choice and decide to…" (I gave a deep gulp) "get rid of the baby you could regret it, and you will mourn the loss for the rest of your life. You would have to be able to live with the choice you made. Please don't do anything without thinking carefully. I don't know whether you believe in God, but I find when I am stuck and in a hole and don't know what to do, I find prayer is the best thing to do. Ask God to help you, talk to him, use him as sounding board."

Thelma was quiet, humble and took what I said on board. She came over to me and kissed me on the cheek, her strong perfume of dark roses smothering me like a wave of material.

"Thank you Edith, you're a good friend. One of the best." She smiled sweetly, her red lips curved up, and she looked and sounded calmer and more resigned to her condition. She looked again at herself in the mirror and held her head up. She removed tears from her eyes and fiddled with her hair. "I will take your advice and take the rest of the day off, if I may. I can get my head together, try and talk to my mother."

Thelma sounded worried at the mention of her mother, her voice quivered. "I will see you on Monday Edith, won't I?" She sounded worried that what I had said, I had not meant. Her lip quivered again. I put my hand on hers and gave it a light rub, she gripped it and wrapped her fingers round mine. She was still frightened.

"Of course you will," I said reassuringly.

"I think I'll give the dance tomorrow night a miss," Thelma said wisely, "I have a lot to think about, and it's my endless parties, dances and drink which have got me into this trouble."

I was relieved by Thelma's words, and I thought she sounded more responsible, as if perhaps for the first time she was going to start taking charge of her life. She then came over to me and kissed me on the cheek quickly, and said in a thankful tone, "Thank you for what you said I won't ever forget it, and thank you for not condemning me."

*

Thelma slid out of the lavatory before I had chance to say any more to her. Her long brown coat brushed past me and as the door shut behind her a welcoming blast of fresh air came in and hit me in the face, I had become very hot and bothered during the last ten minutes. I was left alone in the lavatory, the tap still dripping away, and the sound of ringing phones outside in the reception. I felt rather bemused, rather tired. All my energy seemed to have departed. My happy Friday morning seemed like it had happened a year ago. So much had happened since Eileen left for lunch. I came out of the ladies' the bright light of the reception made me blink and I felt disorientated. I half expected to find the reception room full of Germans, and find Bath under occupation. So much had taken place in that ladies' loo during the last few minutes that I could not believe the world outside had not changed, or been shaken in some way. However, the world was still the same. The Germans had not invaded. All was as it should be, or as best as it could be with a war raging. I went out through the reception, collected my bag and gas mask from Ann's desk, and walked through the lobby with my shoes making a prominent click on the marble floor. I came out of the double doors and stood breathing in the fresh air, taking refuge by the wall of sand bags. As the people of Bath went by, I considered the advice I had given to Thelma. I hoped her parents would be forgiving and help their very frightened young daughter. I understood how hard it would be for them as a family, but felt sure after the shock had warn off that they would stand together and remain a united family; something I dearly wished my own family could have done. I wished that we could have stood together. Sadly I had not been there for my brother when he needed help. I had judged him too harshly and this had resulted in us both never to speak or see each other again. The much needed advice I should have given him I never offered.

Chapter 8

Don't Worry They Won't be Hitting Us

1942

I was running late for my meal with Eileen and was scrabbling about trying to get myself looking presentable. The day had gone so quickly. I had enjoyed a much needed Saturday lie in, and not got up until gone nine-thirty. Friday, and all that had happened with Thelma, had taken its toll. I had spent most of Friday evening, after getting in from work, sat in my leather brown chair listening to Vera Lyn on the wireless, whilst trying to patch up a dress for my meal out with Eileen and wondering how Thelma was, and what her parent's reaction had been.

I thought myself rather stupid, brooding nearly all of Saturday morning over Thelma and the baby. A problem which really was nothing to do with me, But somehow I had become involved. I felt so frazzled that after a quick bit of lunch I wandered down into the Parade Gardens to listen and watch the gypsy band that always played in the park on a Saturday. I hoped that the nomadic and romantic music might help take my mind off Thelma, but it didn't. The gardens had been busy, most of the deckchairs taken with wounded soldiers dressed in their blue suits and red ties, some with white bandages to their hands and splints over their arms. The gardens were a nice place to go down to as they were beautifully kept, and one could walk down to the banks of the River Avon or just meander down the paths admiring the gorgeous cherry trees, now just coming into their own. The pink blossom looked like tissue, and there was a beautiful magnolia tree opposite the band stand, with flowers becoming so perfect it did not look real. I promised myself that if ever I was lucky enough to have my own garden I would plant a magnolia tree in it. I listened to the gypsy sisters' both with long jet black hair and red and gold dresses, which moved so gracefully as they sang and danced to their father's catchy tunes round the band stand. After a few hours I left my deckchair sat under the safe canopy of a willow tree, and wandered round the gardens to admire the borders of daffodils, and hyacinths woven with polyanthus. The roses were not out in bloom yet but when they were it was a lovely show of colour and scent. It would be something to look forward to, I thought to myself, as I continued dreaming of having my very own garden filled with sweet smelling roses and a vegetable plot. I then tried to be realistic. It would probably never happen. I had made plans and dreams before and ended up disappointed, but it was nice to dream. I seemed to do nothing but dream these days, trying to escape reality.

*

As I climbed the steps out of the gardens I went round to the shops, busy now with families and young injured soldiers out with their nursing teams, who were trying to do the best they could to help take their minds off their conditions for an hour or two. A number of people I passed were complaining to each other about the endless shortages and rationing, and the point of having a blackout at night. I went into Stones, one of the most aromatic shops you could ever go in, all panelled with oak shelving like my father's old study. The smells of tea, mint, nutmeg and ginger was an enticing rich velvet smell, and the shop had wonderful china tea pots and porcelain. I purchased from Mrs Stones whom I knew from church as she sat in the pew in front of me, my rationed bag of tea. We exchanged a few words about the lovely spring weather, how nice the gardens were, and how much we admired our troops and now the latest arrival of the American troops into the country. Mrs Stones went through the paperwork of my ration book and coupons, then stamped the book off and handed it back to me. I wished she and Mr Stone a good evening and said I would see them in church tomorrow, then I carried on up the street, passing the hospital that specialised in Rheumatic problems where Eileen often took her mum to. The high street ran downhill containing shops protected with tape and sandbags. Carters was not exactly run off its feet, nor was McElroy's ladies fashion shop, full mostly with the civilian clothing designs, all very practical and hard wearing for the hard times we were living in. As I got closer to the centre of the city, the streets seemed more over run by the undertakers, now all off duty but swanking about smoking and patronising the Pump Room and surrounding tea shops. The street finally levelled off and I was walking between the grand terrace and steps of the Grand Pump Room Hotel, now under occupation by the M.O.D on the right and then on the left through a colonnade towards the abbey. Before the war the Grand Pump Room Hotel had been the place to be. Anybody who was anybody went there. All the urns along the terrace had been potted up with flowers, a red carpet had adorned the steps and two porters always stood outside ready to offer assistance to guests. The hotel's suites and rooms had been the most magnificent. The hotel even had its own bus, that went to collect guests but the war had put a stop to all that. The hotel was now under occupation under the military's control. The porters replaced with armed soldiers, and the bus replaced by staff cars and military vans. The beautiful building was now scarred by fortifications of sand bags and taped up windows. As I passed through the colonnade of Tuscan pillars and sculptures of two Greek sphinx above in the cornice, I reflected whether, if when this dreadful war ever did end, if the hotel would ever open again.

*

Through the colonnade was the forum of Bath set in front of me. The abbey was directly ahead. The Gothic building, with its great west door set in a Tudor arch along with its flying buttresses and the many beautiful stained glass windows, was the jewel of Bath. I carried on walking with tea bags and gas mask in hand, walking past the elegant Pump Room. The Pump Room by now was full of suited civil servants sat in Chippendale chairs around tables covered in stiff white cloths, covered in sparking silverware and china, enjoying afternoon tea. A soothing orchestra was playing in the corner sat around music stands, and the grand piano was being played by the talented young pianist. As four o'clock approached I came along past the right of the abbey, into another paved square full of people, and down a dark side street. Out of the darkness of the alley, I came out by my spraying fountain and reached my flat overlooking the gardens that only two hours ago I had sat in. I was glad to get in, put the kettle on for a cup of tea and sit down before getting ready to meet Eileen for dinner. After sitting down in my comfy leather chair, with the wireless on and sipping my cup of tea I paused for a minute trying to think what I should wear for I imagined going through my wardrobe, looking through my small collection of outfits. I gave a yawn feeling rather sleepy and decided that a quick cat nap for ten minutes would do me good. I put my half full cup down, shut my eyes and fell asleep.

*

My ten minute cat nap turned out to be more like an hour and a half, and it was gone half past five before I awoke and threw away my cold tea, with the slight skin formed on the top. I went in to the bedroom to select my dress and prepare a bath before dressing. After having my shallow bath I dressed in a light red evening dress, along with my mother's pearls, fixed my hair and used a little beetroot to paint my lips. I was really running late.

I turned off the wireless, checked the blackout curtains had no gaps in, though some people were becoming a bit blasé about the blackout. I could hear Jim saying "Don't worry Edith they won't be hitting us!" But I still thought it was better to be safe than sorry. I went into the hall and put a black coat on over my red dress and secured up my coat. I collected my gas mask and handbag, and went out of the flat door locking it up.

The evening was cool but clear. There was hardly a cloud in the sky. I went round past my office window of the second floor of the Guildhall, thinking to myself I was glad I had tomorrow off before going back on Monday. The Guildhall was silent and deserted as were many of the buildings. I got to Eileen's house which was only a few terraces away, and after saying a quick hello to her father, who was off on his air raid warden patrol, I collected Eileen and the two of us made the short journey to the Red House for dinner. On the way I explained to Eileen that Thelma was unable to see us tonight, as she was still ill from the tummy upset she had on Friday. Thankfully Eileen did not question it, so for the time being Thelma's secret was safe. Although had Eileen known, she was not the sort of girl to go gossiping or condemn Thelma.

*

We arrived at the Red House and stepped up on to a marble pillared porch and through some double doors into a black and white tiled landing, with a closed up bakery up at one end. There was a solid, tall wooden desk, with two desk lights perched on the top, and several ferns in blue and white urns on wooden pot stands stood placed along a black iron balustrade which ran along opposite. Three steps lead down into a sea of tables and chairs, covered in white table cloths, silver candelabras and their flickering candles. A smart waiter dressed in black trousers, white shirt and tie, with a matching black waistcoat, came up from the dining room to great us. He escorted us down the three steps, passing two black cherubs holding up electric lights made to look like candles in candelabras that stood either side of the stairs.

Our charming waiter, who spoke fluent English with an attractive French accent, made us comfortable at a neat table and presented us with menus. As the evening progressed we eventually learned that our waiter, Charles, had got out of Paris before the Germans had marched in. He seemed extremely polite and had the gift of the gab, but you could tell by the way his eyes sparkled when he spoke of France, that he was deeply missing his country and beloved Paris. The Red House was rather peaceful, Eileen and I virtually had the place to ourselves. The whole restaurant had a comforting glow of candle light, which reflected across the dark wood-panelled walls. All the tables were covered in shining cutlery and salvers, and the crystal flute glasses were spotless. We chatted over a rather watery wine about family, friends and work. We both wondered that now the Americans were involved, how much longer the war could go on for. We both said how lucky we had been not to be involved in any air raids, and we both craved to eat an orange. As we talked and mulled over old times, Charles came back and forth with our courses and took away empty plates. Our main course had been Rabbit pie, although as Eileen said there was not much rabbit in it but we both agreed that the gravy was nice. Charles, in his smart waiters uniform with golden coloured buttons on his black waist coat, kept giving Eileen the most adorable smiles. Then he would dart through a pair of swinging doors with ornate iron work and glass in. Dessert was rather nice, rice pudding, and we had a pot of watery coffee to follow. We continued chatting for ages after. The candles in the silver candle sticks were nearly half way down by the time we rose from the table to settle the bill. After our bill had been paid at the tall polished desk on the landing, Charles helped us into our coats, fetched from the cloak room paying great attention to help Eileen into hers.

Charles kindly showed us out and wished us both a good night, and invited us to come again. As the door closed behind us, I could see Charles put a hand round the blind of the door and change the sign from open to closed, and I observed Eileen turn round to give him an admiring look and a good bye wave. Somehow I thought we, or should I say Eileen, would be seeing Charles again. Eileen and I walked along the reasonably quiet streets. The sky was so clear, and all the streets seemed lit up by the white glow of the moon. I parted with Eileen round the corner from her home and kissed her goodbye, saying I would see her at work on Monday. We both said how much we enjoyed the evening and Eileen said we should go again in a few weeks' time. As I walked back home, guided by the bright silver coin of the moon, I could hear the exciting, toe tapping, finger clicking music coming from the dance in the Assembly rooms. I was glad I was not there, and glad Thelma had the sense to stay at home with her mum. I hoped she and her mum were having a peaceful evening, and were able to support each other once Thelma had told her about the baby. It of course would be a shock to her mum, but I was sure Thelma's parents would look after them both

*

I came in to my square, empty now of people and pigeons, and walked through my front door feeling rather relaxed after the enjoyable evening I had had with Eileen and the dishy Charles. I hung up my coat and gas mask and went along into the kitchen, securing the windows with the blackout curtains before putting on the lights.

I prepared myself a hot drink of Camp Coffee, and was about to sit down with a good book from my father's book case. I had not yet read *Tales of Mystery*, which had a brown leather binding with engraved gold letters on the cover. I wanted a few hours to relax before I started my blasted sewing and mending. As I began to relax and settle with my book in hand there came a light tapping on the front door. The tapping stopped me in my tracks, and my heartbeat quickened and sounded like a drum from the band in the Assembly rooms. I looked quickly at the curtains on my way to open the door to check it was not Jim on his round to tell me off about the slightest tad of light showing through. I unlocked the door cautiously, I knew it must be Jim, what did the silly old fool want now? As I pushed open the door slowly, just about to say "good evening Jim", I saw to my shock it wasn't Jim with his metal helmet with the silver painted *W* on the front, ready to tell me off, it was Thelma!

*

Thelma stood in the door way snuggled up in her brown coat. Her face was pale and tear stained. Her lipstick was smudged, and she had a slight reddish mark like a bruise across her cheek. She had a very heavy looking case, jam packed, almost bulging open. Thelma looked at me with a tired and desperate look. "Thelma!" I said astonished and surprised to see her. 'This is a nice surprise!" I studied her closely. She looked like an evacuee; lost, scared, and unsure who to trust.

"Mum's chucked me out Edith! I got no one else to go to."

Thelma suddenly broke down, tears pouring out of her eyes and down her cheeks. I pulled her in and hugged her tightly, rubbing her back with my hand, reassuring her.

"It's alright Thelma, I told you yesterday, you can stay with me as long as you wish. It won't be a problem." My words seemed to make her more upset and her breathing became jumpy, like a fish gulping for air on a bank, beached by retreating waters. I took her heavy case from her and pulled her in. She seemed very shaky, and a little disorientated. She could barely see she had so many tears in her eyes. Her eye make-up had run down with her tears, leaving black smudges and stains across her face. She continued to splutter and gulp. I helped her out of her coat, sat her down in my leather chair, and put a patchwork blanket over her. I went into the kitchen and got out a rather dusty bottle of my remaining brandy and poured a small drop in to a glass tumbler from the dresser. I went back to Thelma and put the brandy in to her hands. She looked up at me, looking like a panda, with pale complexion and black smudged eye make-up.

"But I'm pregnant Edith! You're not meant to drink with a baby are you?"

"This little drop won't do you any harm," I said. "Come on, you drink it up please, it will do you good." Thelma clasped and wrapped her hand round the tumbler, feeling the cut indentations of the glass. She then drank the brandy down in a quick fashion, and put the glass down on the side table. She could take her drink far better than I could.

"Thank you, I needed that," Thelma gasped at the sharp, quick shock of the brandy.

She sat back in the chair, still looking over done and warn-out. After a few minutes of her saying very little, apart from thanking me again for putting her up, she told me what happened

"I told Mum tonight. I told her everything, but she went mad! She came over to me like a soldier about to bayonet me. She started to shake me, and said what a stupid girl I had been, and then, when I tried to tell her that I wanted to try and keep the baby she got even worse and ranted on and on about what my father and the neighbours would say and what they would think. Then she said they would have to move away. She said I had been nothing but a wretched girl, she told me that I had been a mistake, and then she slapped me, and she said I was a common little slut. She said I had brought shame on the family and that she would never forgive me. I tried to explain, I really did, I told her I was going to do the right thing, but she just wouldn't listen to me. She told me to pack my things and leave before Dad got home from the factory. Then she stormed out the room. I tried speaking to her again in the kitchen. I begged her to talk to me, to help me, I told her I was so scared, but she just ignored me as if I wasn't there. So I went upstairs and packed my things and came here."

*

Telling me what had happened brought her to even more pitiful tears. She put her hand to her cheek, which looked terribly red where her mother had struck her. I went over to her and knelt down beside her, putting an arm round her.

"You can stay here as long as you need to. You don't need to worry. Your only worry is to look after yourself and the baby." I paused, considering the baby. "Are you going to keep the baby?" Thelma looked at me stunned and said in a spirited, and more determined way, spraying me with tears and spit.

"I might be common, but I'm not getting rid of this baby but I'm so scared of having it and what people will say and I was so hoping mummy would help me."

I knew how hard life was going to get for her. Women who had children out of wedlock were severely frowned upon. Many girls were often sent away in disgrace. Thelma desperately needed her mother. But her mother clearly had washed her hands of her, and her grandchild. I knew I would have to look after her. Thelma needed me. I patted her hand and smoothed it gently.

"You have got me Thelma. I'll look after you, I promise you and the baby. I am sure your mum did not mean what she said. She was angry and probably very scared for you. She probably knows how hard it's going to be for you, and that's why she was angry."

My words about Thelma's parents were meant to give her hope. But I knew deep down, her mother probably had disowned her. I always got the impression in the past that Thelma had been born on the other side of the sheets. She had not been planned by her parents. Perhaps that's why her mother had acted like she had. Her daughter had made the same mistake she had. History had repeated itself.

*

By quarter to eleven, Thelma was curled up like a cat, asleep in the chair. She looked like a girl of seven, not the nineteen year old woman that she liked to play and flaunt to people. I put her case in my room. She would have my bed until I could get a smaller bed for myself. We would have to share the room, which would not be easy, but I had made a commitment to her and I was in no way going to throw her out like her mother had done. I wondered what her father would say when he found out. I imagined that he would take the same approach as his wife, calling his daughter a slut and saying that she had made her bed and would now have to lie in it. They were very black and white sort of people.

I switched off the main lantern light hanging from the ceiling, and put on a table lamp. The sitting room looked cosy, tranquil and at peace. Shadows draped over my picture of Venice giving it a rather spooky look. I looked over at the pictures of me and my parents. I wondered what they would have done if I had landed myself in Thelma's trouble. I hoped they would have supported me, though I was a little doubtful as it was not the done thing to have a child out of wedlock. But I consoled myself to think that my parents had loved me very much, and if I had ever got myself in trouble, I knew they would have supported me in the end. They were not like Thelma's parents.

*

I went into the kitchen and put out two white enamel mugs to make cups of tea. *What would us British do without our tea*, I thought to myself. Whenever there was a crisis, we always seemed to have a cup of tea on the boil. I suppose it was a relaxing and mind numbing exercise, a brief pause from the trouble facing us. I put the Camp Coffee away back on the shelf by the cooker, smiling at the Scot and Indian on the label.

My ticking clock, set in a heavy wooden frame by the dresser, ticked away silently, preparing to strike eleven o'clock. Outside the kitchen window, I could hear the ringing chimes from the churches outside, and I could just about hear the band of the Assembly rooms still playing away. I thought to myself ironically that the same band I could hear playing now, was the same band Thelma had enjoyed listening and dancing too, surrounded with nearly every man in the room with not a care in the world. Now, a week later, she was curled up in a jittery sleep, abandoned and disowned by her mother and told to fend for herself by her boyfriend. She knew that she would be given the cold shoulder, and given disgusted looks from many other people as soon as her baby began to show. *What a lot can happen in a week*, I thought. I also wondered, as Thelma worked at the Guildhall, whether she would be allowed to retain her position. I removed a rather sick looking daffodil from the vase on the kitchen table, its orange cup and petals shrivelled up like a prune. I started to pour some water in a small saucepan to heat up, when I paused and put the pan down. I could hear something from above. I listened carefully. It was a noise that sounded like a rumble of thunder.

*

The rumble continued and got slightly louder. I thought it might be a train or a rumble of an army truck from outside by the Empire Hotel. I then realised that it was the blasted Germans flying over us, headed towards poor Bristol. I carried on preparing the tea and looked for my matches. A smile came across my face thinking of Jim outside on his patrol with his large grey metal hat on. Then there came the air raid siren with its high, chilling moan that we had all become so used to that it no longer bothered me. We had all heard it so many times, without anything dangerous happening. I could hear Jim's friendly voice in my head now, as I located my box of 'England's Glory' matches,

"Don't worry Edith my love," I could hear him say, "They won't be hitting us, there headed for Bristol."

The rumble of planes in the oily sky seemed to get louder and deeper. It vibrated around the whole of the kitchen. I heard Thelma get up and call out in an unperturbed voice

"Do you think we should go down to the basement Edith?"

I thought for a minute and then replied calmly just as I was about to strike a match. "No don't worry dear, my neighbour Jim has told me I don't know how many times, the Huns are heading for Bristol. Don't worry they won't be hitting us."

*

There then came a massive high pitched sound, like a sharp continuous whistle. My heart felt like it had stopped beating. I suddenly called out to Thelma in a desperate voice of terror, "Thelma… get down!" Then all hell descended on us. A massive explosion, like a volcano blowing off its rocky crater top shattered the peace of the evening. The whole of my flat seemed to wobble, and shudder like a jelly. Then there came another sharp whistling sound followed by a huge explosion. My glass jar of Camp Coffee fell from its shelf along with the HP Sauce. They both smashed on the floor, along with my dried egg tin. A white light like that of the sunrise seeped through into the kitchen, giving the appearance that dawn had arrived. There then came another explosion, followed by another and another. I could hear the contents of the flat become disturbed, I could hear breaking glass, objects falling from their positions and Thelma's terrified screams.

I was so startled I staggered backwards, my hands stretched out like a traffic conductor looking up at my green glass pendant light, which was swinging back and forth like a clock pendulum. My willow patterned plates began to fall off the dresser and smashed on to the kitchen table.

Another massive explosion went off, rocking the whole terrace violently. I could hear another sharp whistling sound which seemed to go on and on before it fell and exploded on to its target. Another bomb came rushing down and rocked the terrace again. I heard from the living room more terrified shrill screams from Thelma, and could hear her shout my name. "Edith, Edith, we better go…" The light above me began to flicker and blink, then another bomb came down and I heard its explosion. I heard something heavy fall down in the sitting room and hit the piano, causing the musical instrument to call out in panic and pain along with Thelma's desperate screams.

I could hear the sound of breaking glass and china, and cracking noises all around. My copper pots and pans began to fall off the pan rack as it leant over and went crashing to the floor. My pink and white china on the dresser became unsteady and started bouncing off it and then shattering on the peach coloured tiled floor. My wall clock dislodged itself, and went smashing down on the floor, hitting the side of the dresser as it fell. My last remaining bottle of brandy that I had kept since the war began, slid off the sideboard by the Belfast sink and smashed into pieces. The brandy splashed out like a fountain, soaking the floor and sink. Thelma suddenly gave out another scream, and called out my name again sounding desperately panicked. I called out to her and turned to go and protect her, and to try and make it down to Jane's basement. But as I turned another explosion went off and hit the building. Without any warning I saw my huge old warped dresser lunge forward, lean slightly and then continued to lean. China cups, plates, jugs, glass tumblers and enamel ware slid off their shelves. Draws slid open and rocketed down, throwing out their contents of cutlery and utensils, along with old receipts and government war recipes which fluttered out and gracefully fell to the floor like parachutes. Then the whole contents and dresser came slamming down on top of the kitchen table. The crystal vase of daffodils went smashing into pieces, sending water, flowers and shards of crystal across the table and on to the floor.

Another bomb and explosion followed, and plaster came crumbling off the ceiling sprinkling me with dust. The next bomb came down with such a force that I lost my balance, I could feel myself begin to sway, and I put out my hands to prevent the fall but it was in vain, I went smack down on the tiled floor amidst the broken glass and china.

I lay, lying on the floor feeling small shards of china and glass under the side of me. I seemed to have fallen into the foetal position. I felt shocked, and dazed. I could hear Thelma come rushing in and screaming my name. "Edith! Edith! O God Edith!"

I felt disorientated and I could hardly see a thing. Although I could just make out the colour of orange floor tiles, shattered fragments of glass and the broken remains of HP sauce; the bottle now in several pieces but still with its picture of Big Ben intact. I felt suddenly a little strange, and I could feel the room begin to close in on me. My whole body seemed to go numb, as if a mist was covering me and everything became very dark and black.

*

When I awoke from my faint I was still on the floor. I felt suddenly cold and unsure of what had happened. My eyelids flickered wildly, adjusting to the strange red glow which seemed to flood the room. I could still see the fragments of the HP sauce bottle, with Big Bens picture still visible. There seemed to be chalky dust and fragments of ceiling covering the floor. I felt a black shadowy figure hovering over me, and a cold small hand across my forehead. The noise of bombs seemed further away now, but the air was full of dust. I could hear crackling noises' like the noise you hear sat in front of a fire. Every now and then there were crashes of rubble and breaking glass. The electricity had gone off, but the room seemed alive with a red glow. I heard Thelma's voice sounding a little calmer.

"Edith are you all right? You fell and hit your head. Don't try to move, not yet."

Thelma no longer sounded panicked as she had when the attack began. I still felt a bit foggy but I could feel the rest of my body, I could feel my legs twitching and I slightly shifted, feeling an uncomfortable fragment of pottery beneath me.

I slowly began to gather myself together, and pulled my head up slightly to look around. The tiled floor was a debris field of broken china, glass, kitchen utensils, copper pots and grey metal pans. A great deal of plaster and Georgian moulding had come down over the sink. The sound of explosions continued joined now with the sound of machine gun fire. The air raid siren was still moaning away but even that was like white noise, present, but part of the normal daily routine, like the sound of a telephone. I continued to lie on the floor, with Thelma looking over me. I suddenly remembered why Thelma was here, and all that had happened before the raid.

"Thelma! Are you alright and the baby?" I said in a worried voice

"I'm fine, a few scrapes but we're both alright. How do you feel now?"

"I feel a bit dizzy, but I think I will survive."

I started to pull myself up with a helping hand from Thelma and got to my feet, still a little dazed. We both staggered towards the sitting room door, now partly blocked by a beam and wreckage of the dresser. We had to bend down through the damaged door, dodging the brass curtain pole which had come down on one side, and was now bending over the door frame.

*

The sitting room was lit up like a red filtered stage light from the theatre. The room was badly disturbed. Smashed frames of glass and photos lay strewn across the floorboards and shards of glass covered the piano, which had been hit by the Georgian mirror that had prized itself off the wall above the fire place and hit the top of the piano as it went down. My father's bookcase thankfully remained unharmed, along with my Queen Ann writing desk, but both were now covered with glass, dust and plaster. The window had been blown in and torn down the blackout curtains allowing the hellish glow to illuminate the room.

We both walked towards the remains of the window with glass crunching under our feet. We could see the blacked-out buildings, church towers, chimney stacks and terraces of the city, now flashed up in a red and orange glow so bright and brilliant like a lighthouse or brazier. The city was alive with flickering flames and the sounds of crumbling buildings, cracking timber and the rumble of falling masonry. The Huns' evening work must surely soon be over. Their death bombs and guns had rained down now for what seemed like hours. The sky was turning a dark red, mixed with the black oil of night. Across the road beyond the blackness of the sunken Parade Gardens we could see the long silver track of the River Avon like a sheet of glass, which the Huns must have used as a guide to target the city. The Empire Hotel was in darkness, isolated by the burning buildings behind and around it.

Black, thick smoke erupted and slithered across the sky as more parts of the city fell under attack. Thelma and I just stood in silence, still clutching each other, dumbfounded by the scene. We looked across towards the hotel, but all we could see was red flames and the tortured remains of chimneys and church steeples.

Many of the Georgian terraces had been hit, and St Andrew's church roof was on fire. A mass of burning beams and timber were being engulfed with jumping orange and red flames. One could even see the flames leap from building to building and then lurch on to trees enveloping them. The sound of breaking glass seemed so loud and splintering with the sound of roof tiles and chimney pots crashing to the ground. Buildings to the left of us continued to burn, and a black, choking smog began to obscure the view of St Andrew's. It now looked like a shell of gothic walls, with empty windows free of glass and a massive fire in the centre, looking like a fire ready for the 5th November.

*

Below us in the square, the fountain was surrounded by shards of sparkling glass, tiles, rubble, bricks and guttering. The top of the fountain was also covered in shards of glass and chips of masonry. We suddenly noticed a figure peddling frantically along the road on a bike, followed by another heading across the square towards the Pump Room. An air raid warden, which I prayed was Jim, was running down the road sparkling with shards of glass and rubble. Several women and children ran frantically along the road with sack bundles and one woman was pushing a pram. They appeared as if they were heading down into the gardens for safety. Another man on a bike with a cap on, came along past the Empire Hotel in a rush, but then suddenly came to a halt. He got off his bike, flung it down on the pavement and ran off. The shards of glass must have punctured his bikes tyres. Flames continued to thrust in to the air as if they wanted to catch the stars. The siren was still howling away, but now a new noise could be heard; the reassuring bell of a fire engine in the distance.

Thelma stepped further into the bay and stuck her head out of the empty window frame. She looked up and down the street, then looked back down into the square and said in an attentive, jittery tone, "Listen! Listen what's that man shouting about, there's somebody coming down by the hotel. What's he shouting? I can't hear him."

I stepped a little closer into the bay window, hovering in front of the upset contents of my writing desk. I listened closely and stared out into the street. By the hotel, a rushing figure, followed by five or six others, holding what looked like buckets, seemed to be heading directly towards the fountain in front of our building.

"What are they doing?" Thelma asked, rather bemused.

The group of men came in to the square surrounded the fountain and plunged their buckets into the basin of cold water. One man, after filling his bucket rushed off down the alley trying desperately not to spill the contents. He was followed by another two men. I joined Thelma and gingerly popped my head out to observe the scene. Thelma found a sudden confidence to shout down to the men to gain some insight into the situation.

"I say! Hello! What's going on? What's the situation down by the Baths?"

Thelma seemed remarkably calm, speaking clearly, with authority. A caped man looked up at us revealing a black sooty face, visible with the brightness of the fires raging all around us. He shouted up at us in a charged, nervous voice.

"The abbey's safe Miss," he said, "and the Pump Room and Baths, but St Martins' a goner, and the Assembly rooms are ablaze! Bloody Huns even hit the hospital. We're trying to put the fire out in the west wing, you two alright?"

"Yes", I said, "We're a bit shaken but alright thank you. Would you like us to help you? Can we do anything to assist?"

"No miss. You two girls had better stay where you are. Don't go out into the streets yet. Some poor souls have been gunned down!" *That explained the machine gun fire I had detected earlier.* We agreed to do as he advised and would stay put. The gentleman gave us a doff of his cap and rushed off with his bucket full of water, on his way ready to try and save the wing of the hospital.

The sound of the fire engines and activity of M.O.D personnel came from the abbey square. It was becoming louder against the burning timbers and smashing of breaking glass. More people, women and children, were scampering out of their homes, rushing to the gardens in fear that more bombs would drop. Thelma and I brought ourselves back into the shaken room.

"I can't believe it!" Thelma said sounding shocked, "The Assembly rooms! They were only just restored two years ago!" Thelma suddenly paused. She looked at me with her blackened face with a scratch to her head, and she had chips of plaster and dust in her hair.

"We were both going to the Assembly Rooms tonight. Don't you remember Edith? We were going to that dance." She rubbed her tummy and looked out in to the burning city.

"If this baby hadn't come along, we would have been there tonight."

Thelma looked shocked and a wave of relief came over her face. She became emotional and tears rolled down her cheeks, clearing away a trail of grime and dust from her face. I put an arm round her. She appeared almost beautiful with her features covered by a make-up of dust, but with a lovely smile across her face and her eyes sparkling with tears, yet she spoke with almost joy in her voice.

"Don't you see Edith, My baby has saved me! It saved us! If I didn't have this baby inside me we would have been in the Assembly Rooms tonight like we planned."

She laughed out in thankful tears, and I too had tears come to my eyes. It was a strange moment to feel such reassurance and comfort in an evening of such devastation. The worry and fear she had felt over the last few days was beginning to subside. Thelma's baby was no longer a burden, but a blessing. She was rising to the challenge the Lord had given her. Thelma would overcome the setbacks that might lie ahead, as I knew, in time, so would the city of Bath.

Chapter 9
Walking Around the Underworld

1942

The morning after the attack, the city rose from a tortured night of little sleep and frayed nerves. Even as dawn came, fires across Bath were still burning and smouldering. The sky was grey and reflected the mood of the city. Everything seemed to be covered in a black sooty grime. Terrace after terrace looked like grottos, as plaster and brickwork had been gutted by fire storms from the Huns' bombs. Many of the city's buildings had been dive bombed and strafed with machine guns. High explosives from the incendiaries had bombarded the city. The streets were covered in a litter of rubble, glass and masonry. The abbey had survived but lost one of its beautiful windows. It got off lightly compared to the Assembly Rooms which were now gutted. The Pump Room was unharmed along with the hotel. Four of the city's churches had been completely obliterated. The west wing of the hospital had taken a direct hit, but the patients had thankfully fled to the safety of the basement. The gas works had also been hit which had caused a fire storm around the surrounding area. Consequently, gas and electric was down across the city.

Thelma and I began our clear up operation after just a few winks of sleep. We had lost most of my china and glassware, along with my prized bottle of brandy. A lot of plaster and the beam around the door into the kitchen had fallen down, but thankfully most of the repairs would be cosmetic. After sweeping up most of the glass and broken china, and clearing up HP sauce, Camp Coffee, my brandy and other cooking ingredients from the kitchen floor, we then moved into the sitting room. With a bit of a struggle we managed to lift and then push the broken mirror off the piano. Thelma swept up glass, china and plaster, as I did not want her doing any heavy lifting in her condition. I moved my writing desk and bookcase out into the middle of the room, for Thelma to come along and sweep up the glass from the window.

We were both feeling pretty parched, but with no gas we could not boil any water, so we made do with a cup of tap water. All my kitchen chairs had lost either legs or backs, so we sat in the cleared window seat of the bay window and took in the scene from outside. The square and street were covered in glass, and the front wall of one of the flats in my terrace, five doors down, had collapsed into the road. Pieces of charred furniture were thrown out into the road and an air raid warden and two other men in army uniform were surveying the scene. A group of two women and five young children were staggering up the road, with a dusty pram filled with belongings and items they had saved from their home.

Thelma looked out into the square observing the family walking up the road and said, "I wonder what happened to my mum and dad, and Eileen? I best go round home later and see if they are both alright. They are still my parents after all." I knew Eileen was probably safe, but I felt apprehensive with the mention of Thelma's parents.

"That's a good idea," I said, "And as you say, they are your family, perhaps after all that's happened they may have changed their minds."

We carried on trying to clean up, and by half past ten we both decided to attend my church to thank the Lord we were both safe and had been brought safely through the raid.

Thelma had never been one to attend church, apart from the odd Christmas service and Baptism, but she seemed pleased to go and I lent her a hat to wear. The walk to church was like walking through the Greek underworld. Even buildings not bombed looked black and grey from the smoke and dust. Rubble covered the road like litter, and we could hear the constant sound of cracking glass from under our feet as we walked along the street to the Baptist church. The church was full of nervous, shaky looking people. It was a highly emotional congregation. Many were crying and blowing their noses. I too was feeling lost, seeing lots of empty pews and Mr and Mrs Stones missing from the pew in front of me. I later learned that both Mr and Mrs Stones had been killed, along with Bobby's father who had been on air raid watch by the Assembly Rooms. I cried silently behind my green covered hymn book, thinking that Bobby's mother had not only lost both her teenage sons, but now also her husband. My only comfort was hearing Thelma singing and saying prayers with a deep sound of conviction in her voice. The service itself was of course highly emotional, and by the end I counted seven members of the normal congregation absent; their empty pew seats looking vacant and forlorn. Our final hymn 'Jerusalem' was sung with far more resolution and vigour than I had ever heard it before, despite our depleted congregation. As our lovely minister said at the service's conclusion, "We will carry on. The Lord will deliver us out of this evil, but it would be on his timetable and not our own". As the service ended and our last hymn 'Abide with me' was sung, many including myself were choking back the tears, disguising our distress with the occasional forced cough.

After the service Thelma and I walked home together. Thelma had never been to the Baptist church before and many church members had come over to her to give her a warm word of welcome, and to say how grateful they were that we had got through the night unharmed. Everyone looked like they had been through it. Many of the congregation, including myself, looked dusty with grubby faces, scratched legs and burns.

Somehow personal appearance did not seem to matter. All that mattered was being together with fellow friends and worshipers, to give thanks for those that had survived and mourn those that had tragically been killed.

Thelma said how peaceful the service had been, and I got the impression that it had done her good. We walked along the dust, rubble and broken glass of the road. Many of the buildings had been hit along by my church, though the church itself was unharmed. The tennis court near the church was littered with shards of glass from the Majestic Hotel. The hotel was utterly gutted. The orchard looked like an oasis, not a tree had caught fire or been scarred. As we passed along the beginning of Sheila's Parade terrace, which was built in a letter L formation, I noticed that the end two flats had collapsed. They were no more but a pile of timber, rubble and bricks with only a remaining wall of the next flat standing. The three fireplaces were all that was left on the wall where there had been rooms and upper floors.

"Gosh! We have been lucky," I said to Thelma, "that's only five flats down from us."

*

We carried on up the road, looking to the opposite side which looked a complete mess. The whole Georgian terrace was gutted with great mountains of bricks piled high in gaping holes above the remaining bent roof rafters, ridge tiles and jigsaw pieces of tiled roof. In one house, one of the back walls was still covered in rather grubby gold wallpaper. A large painting of a bishop set in a gold leaf frame was still hanging on the wall as if nothing had happened. How the painting had survived through last night and was still on its wall was any ones guess. The next house had a large, fluttering black and white chequered flag outside it, to warn everyone of an unexploded bomb crashed inside the ruins.

"That should deter anyone wanting to go scavenging about," Thelma said with a cynical tone in her voice. We both paused to look at the wreckage that had once been peoples' homes. We were both just about to carry on, when Thelma looked on ahead and suddenly bounded up the road towards a man coming towards us.

I went after her, being careful not to brush up any glass from off the pavement.

"Thelma what's wrong?" I shouted, trying to keep up with her.

I stopped a little way off and paused, as I could see who the figure was that Thelma had now halted to speak to. Her father was a tall man with a warn, weathered face, with smoker's lines around his mouth and terribly bad frown lines. As I approached I noticed Thelma's peaceful mood had depleted and once again she was in tears. Her father too looked as if he had been crying, but he looked angry. I decided to re-introduce myself to her father, as I had only met him a few times and that was not much to go on. I also wanted to try and mediate what looked like a few fraught words between an angry father and daughter.

"Hello again Mr Time's" I began, "I am pleased to see you, though I am sorry it is not under better circumstances."

Mr Times doffed his cap and greeted me with a good morning; he spoke very cut and dry and in a rather gruff manner.

"Yes, it is Miss Parfitt, in more ways than one. I am told you know about the shame my daughter has brought upon me?"

I could see this was going to be a difficult conversation and in the middle of a war torn street, this was not really the place. "Thelma, your daughter," I began in a calm steady voice, "is staying with me, as your wife forced her out of the house last night. She has explained to me her situation. I do appreciate it is not what you and your wife wanted for her, but it's happened. It's always easy to be wise after the event, but I support Thelma as she is my friend and wants to be a good mother to her baby."

Thelma's light crying still continued and she beckoned me closer to her, away from her twitching and angry looking father. Mr Times looked at me with his blood shot, angry eyes, and spoke with a frightful tone, spitting from his mouth.

"Who and what this girl does is no longer any concern of mine. She's brought shame on me which will cost me dearly my reputation and standing in Bath." He continued to spit out his words like a lizard, with nicotine hands twitching and extending."

"I warned this girl time and time again about men and the way she made up to them. And because of her, my wife's now lying half blown to bits outside the Assembly Rooms." Thelma looked as if she was going to be sick, she heaved slightly; but brought nothing up.

"Mr Times, I am so very, very sorry about your wife, however it was your wife came to be outside in the middle of an air raid, you can hardly blame Thelma for the bombing and her mother's death. It's a cruel wicked charge to lay at your daughter, who may I remind you, like it or not, is carrying your grandchild."

Mr Times seemed unbothered by my speaking up to him. He had lost his wife, and I suppose his daughter, and he was only consumed with bitterness and wanted to blame someone for all that had happened. He had one further blow to shatter Thelma's already shaky new confidence in having a baby with no husband, or family, apart from me to support her.

"I don't care what this slut does, so long as I never have to lay eyes on her again. As far as the world knows' my wife and daughter were both killed last night in the raid. This girl" (He pointed his chubby finger at her) "no longer exits as far as I am concerned. I will never forget the look on my poor wife's face when she told me what this madam had been up to. Then my stupid wife ran out into the raid to go and get her. It's her fault her mother is dead."

By the time he had finished, Thelma was on the point of fainting. The shock and realisation that her mother, who must have relented and gone to try and find her, thinking Thelma had gone to the dance at the Assembly Rooms as planned, was now dead. I was filled with anger looking at this man who was blaming his daughter for his wife's death, when it clearly it was no one's fault. He wanted someone to point his finger at, and Thelma had fit that bill. I gave a very angry and frank response, now nearly spitting myself.

"Mr Times your daughter is innocent of this wicked charge you have set against her. The fact your wife left the house in the middle of the raid to find Thelma speaks volumes to me. She still loved Thelma, and wanted her and the baby back home with her. Furthermore, Thelma will not be leaving Bath, as she will be living under my protection, herself and the baby. If you tell people your daughter was killed with her mother in the raid that's your choice, but people will soon discover the truth and realise you're a lying, bitter old man that wants to lay the blame at everyone else's door but his own."

By this time, Thelma was practically hanging on to me, Mr Times was even more angry and shouted an obscenity at us both as he charged up the road toward the rubble ahead.

*

I recovered from the encounter and thought that Thelma had been more sinned against than sinned with having a father like him. She was looking like she could faint again but I staggered back up the road, supporting her to the safety of the flat. We were greeted by Jane Randle who was concerned for us both, as she said an ill-tempered man who had the smell of strong liquor came to her shop looking for us both. Thankfully Jane had pleaded ignorance of where we lived and that she even knew us, and with Mr Times living the other end of the city he had no cause to come this way again. Jane was a great tower of strength and helped Thelma and I up to the flat. I got Thelma into a leather chair and put her feet up on the foot stool. Jane returned with a tray of orange squash and biscuits. Thelma took ages to calm down but Jane's firm but loving words reassured her and helped her to sleep. I was very grateful to Jane and for all that she had done. Jane informed us of some good news: aid from Bristol was on the way, including hot meals and urns of tea. Jane had also heard some of my conversation to try and calm Thelma down and consequently she now new that Thelma was expecting. I think she guessed what had happened regarding her parents. Jane Randle was a woman of the world and she did not condone or condemn Thelma, which I appreciated greatly. I suddenly remembered about Jim and enquired if he was alright. Jane looked crestfallen and informed me Jim was missing, and his fellow wardens including Eileen's father were out searching for him. I felt miserable for her and was ashamed of the way I had mocked Jim behind his back for just doing his valuable job of being an air raid warden. Jane quickly left us and said if we needed anything to let her know. I reciprocated and asked her to tell me if there was any news regarding Jim and that if she needed anything to pop up and see us.

By half past two Thelma awoke, and I got her to come with me to the Pump Room where an emergency canteen had been set up. She hardly said two words and was clearly in shock to hear of her mother's death, despite the harsh words she had spoken to her. I also thought she must be grieving for the loss of her father who no longer accepted her or, at the moment, loved her. We both entered the Pump Room which was filled with dishevelled, tired people and families, and found a seat by a large grand clock ticking away in an alcove. Warn out mothers with crying, grizzling children and impatient men either queued up at the canteen or sat down at the re-arranged Chippendale tables and chairs to enjoy a hot cup of tea and bite to eat. The orchestra were banished into the corner of the room, rather like the orchestra playing on the sinking

Titanic trying to keep people calm and not to panic. One grand Lady even applauded when they had finished and said in a posh, well to do voice to a friend. "Not up to their normal high standard, but still it's nice they played. Can you believe that some of these people have erected their clothes lines on the statues outside! I mean, I ask you, where are people's standards today, and it's not even fine quality material they are hanging up!"

The snobbery of this grand lady brought a smile to Thelma's mouth and to mine, so at least the aristocratic woman had done us some good. After our meal Thelma and I, arm in arm, wandered home together. Sure enough, outside the Pump Room, several people had put up washing lines across the Roman statues on the wall. I found this rather amusing, but also reassuring, that all formality was being put aside to help us all get through such a difficult day. There was no class structure today; everyone rich and poor were all in the same boat together. By now sweepers were about trying to sweep up broken glass from the paved streets. Shop keepers were surveying their shops to see if there was any damage. Many women and children clutching bags, prams and gas masks headed off towards temporary relief centres. They would be housed in the Salvation Army centre and the wings of the hospital which had not been hit, as well as the remaining churches and public rooms. A few smartly dressed nurses were pushing medical trolleys around to give first aid to anyone that needed it. Many people had simply crashed out on benches outside and even on the paved streets, looking warn out and in shock.

Everyone seemed to be helping each other, even people who had lost their homes and everything they owned. They were all trying to be cheerful and grateful. The British spirit had not yet been crushed by the Germans.

*

Thelma and I checked in with Jane to see if there was any news of Jim, but there was no answer so we both wearily proceeded up the next flight of stairs to the next landing and reached the welcoming sight of my front door. Thelma still said very little. I thought about everything that a happened over the last two days and realised it was best not to push her about how she was feeling. We both continued on with the clearing. We managed to move the kitchen table out from under the fallen dresser, and allowed it to fall to the floor enveloping the room with yet more dust.

Thelma suddenly spotted a small tiny box on the floor. She picked it up and blew on it to reveal a picture of an old fashioned steamer afloat on a green and blue sea, against a mustard coloured sky. "At least I found the matches! We'll be able to light your two hurricane lamps tonight."

I was grateful that Thelma had spoken an actual sentence in what had seemed to be a prolonged, melancholy silence. I took the box of matches out of her hand and I stared at the picture, smiling with delight. I twisted the box in my hand with its contents moving from side to side.

"What's so special about those matches? You look as if I found the crown jewels! " Thelma said in a bemused tone.

I smiled and said, "My brother gave me this box of matches many years ago, so that I would always remember the time we spent down in Lynrock harbour. When we were there we would sit on a wall overlooking the harbour, sometimes just watching the fishermen for hours and listening to their singing. We would spend hours talking and laughing about such silly things. My brother always said he would have liked to have been a fisherman. I think he liked the idea of freedom and being out on the open sea. That's why I love this box of matches. The picture always reminds me of the time I spent with him watching the ships go by and planning our hopes and dreams for the future."

Thelma looked at me blankly and said in a quizzical manner "You never told me you had a brother!" She looked over to the piano where my family photographs had been displayed. She picked up a broken picture frame with a photo of me and my parents in. "How come he's not in any of the photographs. Whatever happened to him?"

I suddenly felt myself stiffen and become tense. My stomach churned and I could feel my chin tighten. I did not know how to answer her. I knew I was going to start babbling. I could feel my heart quicken and my forehead began to feel moist with sweat.

"He went his own way after our father died. I never heard from him again."

My reply was sharp, quick and to the point. I had not told her a lie, but it had not been the full truth. No one knew that. Only I and my father knew the truth and he took it with him when he died.

Thelma looked surprised and was about to question me further when I briskly said, "Let's get the bedroom window open and try and get rid of some of this dust."

We opened up all the grimy windows that had remained intact and tried giving the rooms yet more dusting. Thelma retrieved the remains of my family photographs with broken glass frames. Thankfully the contents of the frames were unharmed. By 6 o'clock Thelma and I were shattered. She seemed a little brighter now and more talkative. We both sat in the leather chairs at either side of the fireplace, looking at the badly dented piano with a broken mirror propped up against it. Thelma started talking about the future and said something I was not expecting.

"Edith, if possible I want to have my baby here with you, so that you can help me. However after I've had it, I want me and the baby to have a fresh start elsewhere. I don't mind where it is. I just want to get away from here and Dad. A place where the baby and I can live quietly."

I was taken aback by Thelma's plan. I knew it would be a squash for us all to live in a one bed room flat, but I had got used to the idea and almost welcomed it. Now Thelma was on about starting afresh away from Bath and away from me.

"Is this about what your father said? If it is you don't need to worry. It was not your fault what happened to your mum. It was an accident. Your mum was a victim of this war…"

Thelma cut me off

"It's not that Edith, but you heard what Dad said. He's so full of hate and anger. I don't want that for my child. I want this baby to have the best start in life and for us both to be happy. I don't want my child to one day bump into a grandfather carrying all that hate inside him, and for him to take it all out on them. It wouldn't be healthy for the baby, or for me."

I could see that Thelma was talking sense and deep down I knew she was right. It would be best for the child to live away from Bath. Yet I still wanted to help Thelma. In a way I felt responsible for her. She was like a sister to me. So I put a proposal to her.

"Very well if that's what you want and how you feel, then of course you must do what you think is best. How would you feel about living by the sea? There is my old home of Lynrock in Devon you could go to. It's peaceful, quiet and no one will know you there. I may be able to write to the clerk at my father's old factory, and see if there are any vacancies for a secretary. At least the possibility of gaining employment would give you and the baby some hope for financial security."

Thelma looked pleased.

"Why don't you come with us? You're like a sister to me now. We both get on well don't we?"

I was deeply touched by the offer, but knew it was impossible. My time in Devon had ended. I could not go back. Too much had happened. Once you had left, you could never go back.

"Thank you Thelma. That means a great deal, but I don't think it would be a good idea. There are too many memories for me. I will do as I said and write to my father's old clerk, Alexander."

*

So Thelma's fate was sealed; after giving birth she would move down to Lynrock, the place I had been born and raised and called home. Thelma said that she wanted me to be the child's godmother when it was born. I said I would be delighted to accept that role. Whatever happened, Thelma and I would remain in touch. We had both grown close in the last few days. I found I had a new respect and warmth for her. I was thrilled with the idea of becoming a godmother and being part of a child's life.

When I had been younger I had always thought I would have a family of my own. I dreamed, even planned, to have a husband, home and children. It had been another dream that had not happened or come to pass. After what had happened with my brother I somehow could no longer trust men. Both my father and brother had told so many lies and covered their tracks in so many areas that I felt I had no wish to believe in men or be taken in by them.

*

It was strange to think that whereas I had left Lynrock for Bath, Thelma was now leaving Bath for Lynrock. We both had a lot in common.

The next few hours were spent with Thelma and I mending the blackout curtains and batting down the hatches. Jane was organising a carpenter to temporarily patch up the sitting room window and he was due to arrive later. In the meantime we both sat undertaking our tasks in the exposed bay window, overlooking the still smouldering city. If there was another attack, this time we would all be ready for it.

Chapter 10
A Discarded Telegram

1942

After all our work of fixing and mending, Thelma sat down in the chair by the fireplace and fell asleep. The day had been long and difficult for her. I also was feeling a little on edge like most people were, but the confrontation with Thelma's father and learning about her mother's death, and the deaths of so many other people I knew had greatly unsettled me.

I felt rather claustrophobic in the flat, everything seemed out of place or broken and I felt the need to see some green grass and flowers. I left Thelma, who was still sleeping like a log, a note to say I had gone for a walk in the Parade Gardens and wouldn't be long. The main road was still littered with rubble and broken glass though the M.O.D were now doing their best to clear it up.

I headed down the grand stone steps to the Parade Gardens and the memorial of Edward VII guarding the bottom. The gardens seemed busy with small groups of people talking and chatting in deck chairs and drinking from white and blue enamel mugs. Some people were sleeping with thick blankets over them, many perhaps wondering what the night to come would bring.

*

I went along the path leading to the ornamental arcade wall of Tuscan pillars ahead of me, with enclosed bays of sandy coloured stone. Scattered along the path were reserved blue and white striped deck chairs with gas mask boxes and items of clothing. Seeing the chairs brought back happy memories of times spent by the harbour in Lynrock. No matter where I looked, the past always resurfaced. I proceeded down the path slowly, still feeling charged with worry and concern. I followed the wall all the way round heading in the direction of the river.

On either side of me there were patches of lush green grass and daffodils swaying about in the light April breeze. I decided to keep on the main path and walk along the sandstone wall to meet the sloping banks of the River Avon. A queue of people were waiting by a refreshment stand, hoping to get a cup of tea or cocoa.

I carried on up the path, passing a few soldiers walking arm in arm with their sweethearts, looking so in love and probably just enjoying each special hour they had. With so much in the world going wrong and turning to what seemed an unstoppable evil, it seemed the worst time ever to fall in love, let alone get married. The magnolia tree was still looking lovely and the weeping willow's wispy branches swayed about in the breeze above my head. I passed a few women and children with sacks of clothes and homely items they had saved from their houses. All were looking shattered and rather displaced. I gave them a weary smile and then continued on my walk, trying not to think about the question Thelma had asked me regarding my going with her to Devon. It was out of the question. However that night, I would draft a letter to my father's old clerk, who now ran the mineral water factory down in Lynrock, to try and secure her a position of employment. I passed an urn sat tall on a decorative pedestal filled with spring flowers and reached the open sloping bank which ran down to a path by the river. A few children were laid out on the grass fast asleep under blankets with pillows for their heads. Many were cuddling dollies and teddies (perhaps all they had in the world now).

*

A poor looking woman with two children, one plodding along carrying a teddy and the other a baby safe and cosy in its pram, walked along the path in front of me and then sat down at a park bench looking warn out and tired. Her oldest boy was sat down nestled into her side, hugging his teddy and playing at the corner of his mother's coat. Her youngest made no sound from the safety of the pram which was behind her, facing back toward the garden steps. As I walked past the little family, I could see that all was not well with them. The woman's eyes looked heavy and red with large bags draped under each eye. She was dressed in a shabby looking black coat, black skirt and injured looking hat. She seemed to be clutching at a small brown piece of paper that she had pulled out of her coat pocket. The lady looked rather dusty and dirty, as did her son.

She stared ahead looking like a waxwork figure with no expression of any emotion and apparently oblivious to everything and everyone around her. Even her two children seemed distant and removed. It was such a contrast to the spring like gardens she was sat in.

I normally would not have ever gone up to a complete stranger, but it looked like the family had lost their home and were destitute and in shock. I felt I had to see that she was alright and offer a word of support or advice. I crept back a little gingerly and approached the family. The eldest child looked up at me and gave me a heart-warming smile. He was a dear little boy with a round, chubby face. His cheeks were red and he had brown eyes with eye lashes to die for. He wore a small cap on his head and had on a dark jacket. It had three holes and was rather frayed and worn at the sleeves. His trousers also had holes in and were grey with dust.

"Hello," I said in a happy but shy manner. The little boy greeted me with a hello, but the mother said not a word. She continued gazing out, not even blinking her nose was streaming from crying. Yet she made no attempt to wipe it away.

The little boy continued to look up at me. His lovely chestnut eyes looked full of love and yet there was something rather sad about them. "I like your bear," I said to him hoping that by talking to her son it might bring his mother into the conversation. "I hope he is not too much trouble."

The little boy shook his head and said, "No he's a good teddy. He loves to eat biscuits!"

"Does he?" I said, my voice sounding more lively seeing the little boy look so happy to have someone to talk to. "What's your teddy's name?" I enquired.

"His name is Frank, after my daddy!"

The little chap sounded full of pride and excitement at the mention of his father. He continued chattering in a relaxed manner.

"Daddy is away at the moment, but he's coming back soon!"

As the little boy spoke of the great news of his father's return home, I could see his mother's heavy eyes flood with tears. Her lip quivered. I moved over to the redundant side of the seat and sat down right next to the boy's mother, her hands still desperately clasping at what appeared to be a brown envelope. Her son continued playing with his teddy and he began humming an offbeat tune. I decided to speak to his mother, wanting to try and comfort her in her state of sadness. I could not think of a suitable introduction so I reached out and held her wrist. She finally turned to look directly at me, as if noticing me for the first time. Her face was pale, as white as a can of condensed milk. Her lips were shaking along with her hands which were now beginning to lose their tight grip on the envelope. Her eyes were now full of tears and she began to speak, spluttering and spitting in my face as she did so.

"My husband... My husband was... He was on the *Repulse* off Malay in December last year. He wrote to me. He said how well he was doing. Then he was killed by those bloody..."

She stopped, quickly realising she had sworn in front of her son. I knew as everyone else did that back in December last year the *HMS Repulse* and the *Prince of Wales*' battleships had been sunk by the Japanese off the Malayan coast. I thought that perhaps the shock of last night, and what sounded like the recent death of her husband, must have pushed her too far. The lady then resumed her talk.

"I found the telegram in my coat this morning. I think I must have worn this coat for Frank's memorial service. I've been trying to tell Jack."

She nodded at her son still playing with his teddy and humming. She looked out across the river; its sparkling waters were dark green, lime and pink courtesy of the reflection from the shrubs and willows and cherry trees. Silver, shimmering ripples of light ran across the river reminiscent of an impressionist water colour painting.

"But how do you tell your son that his father has been killed? Jack is only five. He needs his father to come home. I need Frank. I don't understand this war. It doesn't seem to end. It just seems to get worse and worse. How can God allow all this to go on?"

I could see Jack's mother was in great shock and grief. Her loss was still recent, only five months earlier. She looked as if she had no home, and had two children to bring up alone. I pondered on her statement about how God was allowing all this evil to go on, seemingly never to stop. I got up and went round to look at the baby, who had been so good and quiet tucked up in the pram. Jack looked up as I went round to see his baby sibling sat behind him.

"There's a lot there!" Jack said as I got to the front of the pram.

I looked in, and then looked at Jack, who looked back at me. I looked back in to the pram, full of bewilderment and confusion. The pram was full of clothes and not a baby as I had naturally assumed. Inside were two jackets, one brown, one dark green, two pairs of trousers, a few bundles of socks and an old battered flat cap. The collection of clothes looked so neatly folded and lovingly placed in the safety of the pram.

"I don't understand!" I said sounding confused. "Why are all these clothes..."

His mother then interjected and sounded annoyed and weary.

"They were all Frank's old clothes. I wanted to try and take them to the Salvation Army Centre, to give them to anyone who needed them, so many have lost their homes. It's taken me all this time to sort them out. Frank would have wanted them to go to someone who really needed them, instead of just sitting in the wardrobe. But I, I..."

She sounded a little angry and desperate. She began to cry again, an uncontrollable wail erupted from within her, alerting the pigeons that were plodding about on the bank to fly off with fright, also giving several people cause to turn round and look startled in our direction.

"Even after five months, it's still not any easier. It's so bloody hard. I just don't get it any more. Why? Why did my Frank have to die? What's the point of all this? This bloody war."

She was distraught. I walked back over to her and hugged her. I felt desperately sorry for her. She had tried to part with her husband's things, but found the ordeal of parting with them too much. She must have left the telegram lying silently in her coat up until now, and having discovered it today it had once again brought back the day of losing her husband. Almost hysterical she seemed to sink in to me. Her whole body was now shaking and jumping about in my arms.

Little Jack looked over at me, still smiling and hugging his teddy tightly. He then patted his mum's back and said in a sweet voice "Don't cry Mummy. Daddy be home soon. He will be so pleased with us giving the poor people some of his old clothes."

A few minutes later Jack's mum seemed to go all numb and limp. She could release no more tears. She let go of her telegram. The brown paper of sorrow fell to the path with a flutter. I looked at Jack, who had been fascinated with his teddy, but was now looking at me and his poor mother, full of concern.

I turned to Jack's mum giving some thought before I spoke.

"I know you probably think it's easy for me to say, but you will come through this. It is still very early days for you. Unfortunately other people expect you to move on after the funeral. They hope somehow you will get over it with a 'pack up your troubles and smile attitude.' Grief's not like that. The loss is always with you. However, in time you do find a way to cope and accept that life does go on. I know I am a stranger but I am sure Frank would want you to keep going. It's up to you to make sure that Jack remembers him, and never forgets his father. I know you're still mourning. Believe me I do know. I… "

I suddenly paused my words of comfort. The memory of Father dying so suddenly, the shock of finding all his lifetime's work shattering to pieces had been too much to bear. I could see myself standing in father's study on that final afternoon of 1929 begging, pleading with my brother not to leave me alone. I had implored him to think about the consequences of what would happen if he left and to consider what our parent's would have thought. The memories of that afternoon stung me like a jelly fish. Like Jack's mum, too much misfortune had fallen on me so quickly. What with my brother and his problems, I found too much had gone wrong at the same time.

I wept myself as I held this poor, broken-hearted woman. My tears were not just for her and her desperate despair, but for myself and my own malingering grief. A grief that came flooding back. I then resumed my helpful words fighting back my own tears.

"I do know what you're going through. I lost someone I loved very much, You never ever think you will get over it, but in time life does have a way of picking up the thread again."

The gardens seemed so peaceful now, as if every person was deliberately not speaking, so as not to upset or disturb Jack's mum in her grief. Even the birds had gone silent. The only sound was of the willow and cherry trees shivering in the slight spring breeze.

*

Mother and son left the slumbering gardens together, hand in hand, walking past the young soldiers arm in arm with their girlfriends. I too decided to leave. I strolled past the tired looking families who had now sat down exhausted in the striped deck chairs, enjoying a little break from the destruction above them in the city. Jack and his teddy looked back at me and waved me goodbye. I waved back, wiping away tears that had now run from my eyes.

Jack's mother had thanked me for talking to her and said how kind I had been, but I felt wretched. I wrote down my address for her and said if she needed anything to come along and see me. The truth of the matter was I knew deep down that she would probably never fully recover. She did at least have her son, and he was her reason for carrying on. But the loss of her Frank would always be there, as the loss of my brother is still always with me. I had promised to take Frank's clothes to the Salvation Army to save her the upset. As I left the bench pushing the pram, I noticed that innocent looking bit of paper which contained the life shattering news fluttering across the grass, like a butterfly. Jack's mother had treasured it for over five months and had now discarded it. The telegram settled on the grass for a moment but then was whipped up from its resting place and the breeze swept it across the gardens and into the air.

I pushed the pram of clothes up the stone ramp by the steps, reached the top of the terrace and moved on to the pavement opposite the Empire Hotel, still guarded by officers and sandbags. I continued along the pavement trying to avoid glass and rubble. Jack's mum had said I could keep the pram as a thank you for being so kind to her. I at least now had something to give to Thelma ready for her baby. I wondered if what I had said had helped Jack's mum. What comfort can you give someone who has lost so much and was unable to see any hope for the future? I thought that at least I had held her hand and made her feel someone was willing to listen to her. I reached the end of the pavement and waited for a large bus to pass by before crossing the road. When the bus sped past I straightened up and continued on my way, pushing Frank's old clothes across the road towards the Salvation Army Centre.

Chapter 11
The Red House

The peace and tranquillity of Wiltshire had departed quickly as our bus, being driven by that horrid driver, was now approaching the city of Bath. I wondered what Madeleine would be doing now? Perhaps she was preparing for lunch or out in the garden pottering about. Probably by now Farmer Richards would be back on his tractor, or tinkering away on his plough.

The bus went along roads and lanes at a reasonable speed, creeping through small villages, and past the grand entrances of big estates. Many of our large country houses had been requisitioned as either hospitals or M.O.D barracks during the war, and were trying to regain their high standards of upkeep that had lapsed in recent years. We headed up steep hills passing beautiful silent fields of green lush grass, with only the sight and sound of Friesian cows and white, fluffy, black-faced sheep grazing peacefully. I had not really paid much attention to my fellow travellers. I had spent half the trip remembering my old flat in Bath opposite the sunken Parade Gardens. Remembering my lovely old office in the Guildhall and the friendships I had built up with Eileen and Thelma. Then, after we drove out of the village of Box, I had recalled the terrifying nights of the blitz, the endless rationing and food shortages. Poor Jim Randle who had been my well-meaning air raid warden, his body was recovered late Sunday afternoon in the rubble of a school. Jane took the news of his death very badly indeed. The Germans attacked Bath again on the Sunday evening, thankfully resulting with not so many casualties. As soon as the air raid siren had sounded everyone had fled quickly to the shelters. We had all learnt our lesson from the first attack.

*

I now looked about at my fellow travellers. Most of them appeared to be happy children enjoying the summer holidays, although their constant singing of 'You are my sunshine' was beginning to grind on my nerves (after the seventh time). The other passengers consisted of two elderly women, who were both busy knitting and gossiping, and an elderly devoted looking couple sat behind them. They looked highly excited about going down to Bath for the day. Sat directly in front of me were two students reading the newspaper. The two young men were discussing in great depth the revolution that was going on in Egypt. Colonel Nasser had overthrown the playboy King Farouk back in July. The new government was now attempting to reform Egypt into a republic.

The students both sounded well educated and very knowledgeable about the current situation in Egypt. The eldest student, a fine looking youth, sounded as if he had republican sympathies and was a great admirer of Nasser. I overheard him say to his friend that he would like to see Britain become a republic, a prospect which horrified me! The other student, a well-covered spectacled youth, sounded as if he sympathised with the people of Egypt, but like me was a proud monarchist and looking forward to the queen's coronation next year.

*

We had at long last reached the outskirts of Bath and we past beautiful Georgian town houses and terraces set in smart avenues of trees and paved roads. Many of the terraces were bare of their railings as so many had been taken down during the war, including my own flat railings. The bus sped down a road of small but productive shops and grocers. Further up was an austere looking bank, a curious chemist and a sparse looking butcher's. The bus turned round to the left and went over a very classical Roman styled bridge, with two box sized gate houses on either side, two at each length of the bridge. There was some gold letters and Roman numerals embossed across the rusty black balustrade, along with a plaque, neither of which I could read for the bus went by too quickly. Our journey to Bath was nearly at an end. We passed a beautiful church and went down another street of villas, looking more Edwardian in age. The court house looked a hive of activity. Shifty and agitated clients were being coached by their well-dressed, heavy laden solicitors carrying bundles of vanilla coloured files tied with pink ribbons. We passed a large green playing field with a rustic looking pavilion in its corner. Then we went over a second bridge which crossed the River Avon. I looked out of my window down into the green and blue waters of the river. I could see well, down through the branches and leaves of an oak tree and the lush green grass and borders of shrubs. The Parade Gardens had changed little, as they were still looking lovely as they had the last time I had walked round them. I observed people sat around the bandstand, still in blue and white striped deck chairs. There was still a refreshment stand and the gardens continued to be enjoyed by the children of Bath, who loved to play ball games across the grass. The sight of the gardens soon disappeared and my eyes came level with the street and square being overshadowed by the Admiralty building, formally the Empire Hotel. The abbey came in to view, looking rather black and grimy after the war and fires. Across the square I saw my old flat set on the second floor of Sheila's Parade Terrace. As I gazed up at the building with old Jane Randle's shop still below, I thought about the happy times I had spent there and the wonderful year I spent looking after Thelma. She gave birth to a perfect little girl named Emma Edith Times. Poor Thelma had had a rather lengthy and difficult labour, but we had a good doctor from the hospital attend, and Jane Randle assisted us brilliantly. That year living with Thelma and the baby had been one of the happiest. We shared so much together, going through our highs and lows yet we came through it all much stronger.

    As the bus turned again round the bend I could still see flattened areas and piles of rubble and concrete left over from 1942. The legacy of the war was still visible even after nearly eleven years. I caught a glimpse of the tennis court busy with two young couples having a productive game. We passed the orchard and my old church, still looking the same as it had when last I worshipped there. The bus suddenly turned to the right and we finally reached the bus station and my temporary break. Soon I would be setting off again to Bristol and then on to Devon.

The bus grinded to a shuddering halt and the charming driver muttered something to us, all of which I did not listen to, as I was too busy reminiscing over the past.

Thelma determinedly, much to my sadness, stuck to her plan. On a rainy, wet August day in 1943, Thelma and little Emma boarded a train to Devon. Alexander my father's loyal clerk, received my letter and months later wrote back with an eventual positive response. The factory did indeed have need of another clerical assistant, and if Thelma was all she claimed to be in the résumé that I had sent him, then the job was hers. Alexander also informed us that a small one bedroom cottage had just become available on Neptune Hill above the harbour. The cottage sounded ideal as it was only a short walk from the factory. It had been an emotional farewell for all of us that day. I really did not want to let them both go as I had so enjoyed having a child in the flat. Thelma was tearful like myself, but was resolved that she was doing the right thing for Emma. I deep down new that she was right. Thelma promised that she would write to me every week and send photos and pictures from Emma which she did. Her letters became a weekly pleasure to read and enjoy.

"Look love! Are you getting off this bus, or do you want to stay here and clean it for me?"

That flipping, nasty bus driver interrupted my thoughts once again. As I came out of my thoughts of parting with Thelma and Emma, I found myself on the now empty bus. My fellow passengers had already departed, leaving only me and the gorilla of a driver. I walked off the bus with my head held high after giving the bus driver a look of pure disparagement. I walked down to the train station to check the departure time of the next train to Bristol. I had a full hour to kill. So with case in hand I walked towards the Red House restaurant. There I knew I could get a good meal, or at least a light lunch to give me some much needed energy before the start of my real journey. Bath had changed little since I left it for my peaceful cottage in Wiltshire. The Pump Room with its huge glass windows showed off a retinue of people enjoying lunch and listening to a fine orchestra. The room's magnificent chandeliers had been re-hung after sitting out the war in the safe basement of the

Guildhall. The Roman Baths still looked popular and the Grand Pump Room Hotel was still standing. As I had feared it did not return to being the hotel it had been famous for. The M.O.D had now thankfully gone, only to be replaced with another load of undertakers from British Rail who had now taken over the building for their offices.

It was so nice to see all the windows cleared of masking tape and to see people looking happier, although I could still see the dreaded ration books about. The shops were looking a little more cheerful but things were still not what they had been. Stones was of course no more and had not yet been replaced. McElroy's ladies fashion shop looked far busier as rationing had ended on clothes in 1949. However, no one had very much money to go out and buy a new frock. Still the window of McElroy's looked eye catching and the dresses and new blouses were elegantly cut.

I continued on my way past blackened buildings before walking into a darkened alley then out into a cobbled courtyard. A large oak tree sat in the middle. I clambered across the square to a red brick building with large red granite steps heading into a porch. A lantern hung in the apex of the porch roof giving adequate light. I opened one side of the double door and banged my way in through with my case. The Red House restaurant had changed little in external appearance but inside had been given a face lift. The black and white tiled floor was still well cleaned and covered the large mezzanine landing, but the wrought iron rail had been repainted and the cherubs removed. A Chinese painted umbrella stand welcomed me along with the tall head waiter's desk and two original desk lamps. The bakery was still to be found at the end of the mezzanine. The counter's top was sparse, with brown wicker baskets tipped forward to show off a few currant and Bath buns, and only a few loaves of brown bread to be had.

*

The whole restaurant seemed much brighter than it had done when I dined with Eileen. All the panelled walls had been polished and cleaned and all the old light fixtures had been removed and replaced by Louis

XVI French style. A smartly dressed waitress wearing a black blouse, black skirt and a brilliantly white apron scuttled up the three steps clutching a black note book. The waitress greeted me and asked if I was dining for lunch. She looked a nice wholesome girl with very small lips and beautiful blue eyes, the colour of the sky. I greeted her with a warm hello and asked for a table for one. My waitress nodded and showed me to a table along the mezzanine just past the head waiter's desk. I was seated in front of two women who were too busy gulfing down buns to notice me.

My table overlooked the whole restaurant below and on the other side of me was a large window looking out into the courtyard. Below in the pit of the restaurant were several neatly proportioned tables. Their elegant chairs stretched down the room to a heavy looking wooden counter set in an alcove where the buffet and grill was. All the cutlery and china looked clean and I could see that standards were still high. I studied the menu set out on stiff vanilla card. I looked to the grill selection, the buffet and finally the cheese section and wine list. I really did not feel very hungry but knew I must have something ready for my journey. My waitress returned with pen and pad poised at the ready to take down my order. The poor girl looked rather disappointed when I asked for just a Bath bun and pot of tea for one. As I waited I looked down in the restaurant, which was not exactly over-run with customers. A very short waitress pushed around a large, heavy looking dessert trolley, her head only just visible over the top. Over in the alcove the chef with his white hat was carving up a little beef, placing the small cuts of meat onto white plates rimmed with blue and gold. The plates were then collected by a waiter who swaggered over to two gentlemen having what looked like a working lunch. There were only five tables along the mezzanine and I dearly wished that I had been sat down in the pit of the restaurant. The two ladies behind me were talking so loud I wouldn't have been at all surprised if the whole restaurant did not hear their entire conversation. The two women were rather thin and gaunt looking. One woman was in an emerald green jacket and matching hat. The other lady, who had her back to me, had a headful of dark brown hair, with a hat that resembled a slice of coconut. The lady in emerald green was talking about the news of Egypt.

"I can't understand why they have got rid of King Farouk! He seemed such a character and these people need a steady firm hand to keep them in order, don't they Margaret?"

The other lady (Margaret) was too busy devouring her bun to answer back but nodded her head in agreement with her little hat bobbing about.

I had to confess I had almost forgotten about Egypt and the revolution since hearing about Lynrock's disaster. I personally thought the people of Egypt were probably tired, angry and fed up of having no say in their own affairs. They had endured enough of having an extravagant king who feathered his own nest whilst the majority of his people suffered.

My own bun and pot of tea came, and I thanked the waitress for her speedy service. I was just about to cut into my Bath bun, which looked lovely and light, when the emerald lady started up again.

"I went to see my doctor last Friday, Margaret. Every evening for the past few days, following my meal I have been getting terribly bad acid reflux!"

I slammed my silver knife down crashing it on to the side of the plate and pulled a face of revulsion at the thought of acid coming up the emerald lady's throat. I tried hard not listen to any more, but emerald lady had the voice and range of a parrot which travelled well across the room.

"I said to my doctor. Now look Dr Clark! Every time I get ready to go to bed, I get this bitter acid come up into my throat. It's shockingly terrible"

Your acid reflux is like your acid tongue, I thought to myself as I sipped my tea, trying not to listen.

"Dr Clark was so nice and recommended that I start drinking a cup of mint tea after my main meal and abstain from food. I will find the doctor's advice hard to undertake, as I do like a few chocolates after a meal or even a slice of cheese."

After consuming her bun Margaret responded rather patronisingly.

"Oh you poor dear! It is an ordeal for you. Oh my dear! Did you hear about all the troubles that quaint little village in Devon is having, after that terrible flood? They don't have any sanitation down there at the moment, or any electricity! I mean I just would not be able to cope with all that now. It was bad enough during the war!"

Emerald lady gave a sucking noise of her lips and muttered something before speaking in a quizzical, gossipy tone.

"Yes...? Lynrock? Was not that the place where Lord... oh what was his name? That Lord Parker? Patterson? Ah! Parfitt! That was his name. Did he not have some big manor on top of the cliff overlooking the bay down there. You must remember Margaret, he was a highly successful publisher before he became an MP. He was very well connected in London If my memory serves me correctly. Of course poor man lost everything in the crash. I think his family had to sell nearly everything to pay off his debts."

Margaret then joined in the conversation while I was beginning to feel very uncomfortable. I began to fidget and move about in my chair.

"Yes I do believe you are right Lucy. Now, was there not some scandal about one of his children?" Emerald lady got quite excited. Her eyes gleamed like stars and she put her cup down in a sudden rush, leaning closer to Margaret. She had a smile of malicious pleasure across her face, the kind of face that enjoys hearing about other people's misfortune and takes pleasure from it.

"Well from what I can remember, my dear, after the old man died, the son suddenly disappeared and broke off all contact with the family. Of course you know why don't you? They said the son was a..."

I could no longer hear the rest of the conversation as their tone became no more than a hushed, shocked whisper.

"They say the shock of discovering that and losing all the money was what killed Lord Parfitt. Well my dear! You can understand it can't you? I mean...! Well, one does not hear of such things being bandied about!"

By now I could not hold my cup steady. I became all of a quiver and I felt a strange unpleasant sensation in my chest. Yet emerald lady had still not finished.

"I seem to remember there being another child. I can't for the life of me remember whether it was another son, or it may have been...? No!

no tell a lie. It was a daughter who was left but even she seemed to vanish. If I had been her I would have moved abroad. I mean the scandal would have got round, you know how servants talk. I expect she ended up a sad old maid in some little room, in the suburbs of Paris somewhere. I mean, having a brother like that! Well it's just disgusting!"

*

By now I had forced myself up from my seat and retreated to the safety of the ladies' loo to hide the fact that I was in tears. My cheeks had gone bright red and flushed. Upon reaching the ladies' I washed and splashed my face with cold water, and let it run over my wrists to cool me down. I must have been in there for five minutes before I returned to my table. Thankfully the two witches had flown off on their broomsticks.

I sat down at the table still feeling uncomfortable. I felt so angry at what I had overheard. If only those two old crows had realised that the very person they claimed had vanished from Devon and gone to live in a small room in Paris, had in fact been sat only just behind them. I wished that I had had the confidence to tell them to mind their own affairs. I could have even told them what really happened. However I did not have that sort of confidence to tackle them. Nor did they deserve or need to hear about my family's private affairs.

I poured myself another cup of tea, leaving black chips and specks of tea leaves in the wire mesh of the strainer. Then I added a little drop of milk and gave it a gentle stir dragging the spoon along the rim of the cup before placing it down on the saucer. I still felt uncomfortable and very on edge over all that I had heard. I felt like everyone, from the nice waitress to the chef carving up the meat, to the waiter and the two dark suited men were all looking at me with cold eyes. I did not know what to do with myself. I must have looked so pathetic sitting on my own with just a suitcase and handbag plonked on the chair beside me. I must have appeared so tragic. I finished eating my bun but even that tasted bland and tasteless now. I decided I needed to look as if I was busy undertaking something. I needed a distraction, something to show everyone I was busily occupied with a task.

I reached over to my black leather handbag and undid the gold coloured clasp. The bag opened up like a frog's mouth to reveal its contents: two letters, ration and identity card books, my purse, keys, hanky, and my flask of brandy which I dearly wished I could have had another drink of. However I did not want people thinking I had some sort of drink problem. I slipped my hand in and took out one of the letters. I studied the front of the creased envelope, now slightly bent and at the edges. The paper's thickness had decreased and become slightly finer. The name and address on the front was mine 'Miss Edith Parfitt, Folly Lane Cottage.' I looked around the restaurant as if to check that there was no one about to see me open the letter, as if I were a school child opening my report card to see my grades and comments before my parents got to look at it. If only this was just a simple school report I was opening. If only I was a little girl again, back with nanny in the nursery or with Miss Miles my governess. Not that we appreciate it at the time, life is so much easier when you are a child. Why is it as children we all want to grow up so fast? Then when we are grown up we want to go back to playing in the nursery again. I opened up the envelope, which had been beautifully cut open by my silver letter opener. I cautiously brought out the pages of the letter that had been so innocently written by Thelma. I flattened out the package of pages and, still feeling trepidation within me, I began to read Thelma's letter again.

Chapter 12
Thelma's Letter

9th August 1952

To my very dear Edith,

I hope this letter finds you well, and hope you are enjoying this lovely summer weather. We have had a super season so far and the village has been overrun with holiday makers. We have had a funny professor from Oxford staying down with us. He's something to do with heathers, or is it ferns? Oh well! I can't remember. I was not really listening to him in Sally's the other day. All he goes on about is plants and wildlife all the time. It does get on your wick after a while.

We also have two Australian girls staying with us on holiday! They are both such characters and such chatter boxes. They are returning home on 17th August so they have a few more days with us which will be nice. Since my last letter to you I did receive some bad news. My job that you got me all those years ago at the mineral water factory has come to an end. I was given notice last week. There is just not enough work for two clerks anymore. Alexander is staying on for now but little old me has to go. I will be so sorry to leave your father's old factory, as it's been such a nice little company to work for. There is always such a lovely atmosphere, just like our old office with Eileen in the Guildhall. Them were the days! Mind you, some of the things the men in the factory say! Well I could not repeat them. Still they're only human and it's all said in good fun. Between you and me, I think things are going very bad for the factory. We haven't taken any orders for ages and when we do, it's only the odd bottle or two from passing walkers. Alexander thinks he's going to get the sack soon, and so do all the other men! I think Alexander's going to be working late one evening, to try and get the books ready to be inspected.

The army are still down here practising manoeuvres, they seem to be enjoying their time down this way. One soldier even winked at me outside the fish and chip shop the other day! I still got it Edith!

Edith, I am afraid I do have some news for you, which isn't easy for me to say. I did think about not telling you but I thought you should be told, and I didn't want you to see it if it gets put in any of the papers. You see, the thing is Edith. There's been some trouble up on Hallowed Hill. Some of the children from the village (not my Emma) but some of her friends have been playing in the ruins of the manor house. They like to go up and play knights and dragons, you know. Not that any of us minded. The old place is just a shell now. But about a week ago, Tim Nelson's boy got hit very badly by some old wall that came down on his leg. Anyway Edith, there's no easy way to say this. After the last council meeting the whole village have decided with the Lord Lieutenant's blessing to have the manor demolished to prevent any further accidents or worse! The army are going to do it for us while they are stationed down here. It's taking place next week I believe. I am sorry to be the one to tell you. Your old home looked such a beautiful mansion from the pictures I have seen in the town hall. Funny thing is, what must have been your old father's study is still standing, and a large bit of the bay window from the morning room you told me about. There is also a fragment of the porch left, but it's now all covered in ivy. The thing is Edith, it's no longer the home that you lived in and loved. It's just a shell now, and your father's misfortune and your brother leaving you, well it all happened such a long time ago now. It's all best forgotten. Best for you to forget everything that happened. You've built your own life now, what with becoming a teacher and moving into your own cottage in the country with your lovely garden you're always telling me about. It's best to let the past go and be buried.

I do have some wonderful news to tell you now. I was wondering how I was going to keep a roof over mine and Emma's head what with no job. Well! Old Mrs Sally who owns the tea room? Well she's finding it all a bit too much now, and she offered me a job as a waitress to help her run the tea room! Best of all, she's also given me two small rooms to live in over the tea room with Emma! Isn't that wonderful! Mrs Sally's even said Emma could work there during the weekends. It is such good fortune for Emma and I. Emma's so looking forward to having her very own bedroom! I don't think either of us will miss our old cottage. Not now I have seen the rooms Emma and I will have over Sally's. Only thing we shall miss is our new friend, the harbour master. He lives in the cottage next to us. He only moved in about seven months ago, but he's been so kind to us and very good with Emma. They both get on really well. They built a mobile of sea shells last week, which they spent hours and hours combing the beach for. He's hung it outside his cottage door. It makes such a jangle when it blows about in the wind. Everyone in the village finds him a bit of a loner but I like him, and as I said he's very good with Emma. I think he's got a bit of a past, but haven't we all! I promised him, Emma and I would have dinner with him one evening after we've moved in to Sally's and got settled in.

I know helping in a tea room is going to be a lot different from being a secretary but it is good money, rent free rooms, and I have to think of Emma. Talking of Emma, she sends you her love and is doing a picture for you. I will send it to you next time I write. Can't believe she is ten now! Only seems five minutes ago I was giving birth to her in your sitting room in Bath with Jane Randle running about looking for towels. Gosh! Where has that time gone Edith? Remember the night the Huns came? How could you forget, you went out like a light for a while. Scared me to death!

I have to sign off now as Emma will be back from the beach with her friend Penny. I hope they won't bring back any more shells or Emma will be making another mobile. Will write to you next week and thanks again for the money you sent Emma. We do very much appreciate it. I am going to start a bit of clearing out tonight while Emma's in bed. Start getting ready for our move. I can't wait! Things for us seem to be looking bright for once. You look after yourself. Enjoy the rest of the holiday. Before you know it you'll be back at school again!

With our love
Thelma and Emma

Chapter 13
It Was Our Own Fault

I closed up Thelma's letter as quickly as I had read it. The Red House was still quiet with little activity of customers. My waitress was busy moving a silver meat trolley across the pit over to the chef. He was still standing behind the counter serving a new family of two parents and their two young daughters.

The sun continued to shine through the large glass window and reflected the light of the gleaming cutlery. I put Thelma's letter into its envelope, and snapped it back into my bag. I still found her letter difficult to feel happy about. The way she had wrote about my old house, as if I had never been there or seen it before. The way she spoke about my father's 'misfortune' and the disappearance of my brother, speaking as if she knew what had happened better than I did. Thelma had written to me as if she had always lived down in Lynrock, and I had never set foot down there. I thought it a rather smug and rather belittling letter. I raised my hand to draw the attention of my waitress and when she acknowledged me from down in the pit I mouthed politely, 'Could I have the bill please'. As the waitress went over to the desk to get the thin paper bill on a plate, I thought to myself how easy it was for Thelma, or for that matter anyone to say to someone *'Let go of the past, move on,'* or as Thelma so poetically put it 'Let the past be buried' as what was left of my former home apparently soon would be.

The pleasant waitress returned to me with the bill. I put the correct amount with a small tip for her on the plate and handed the plate back to her, thanking her for her service. She seemed very grateful for the tip and wished me a good afternoon which I reciprocated. I passed the big, bulky head waiter's desk, noticing a fat ledger full of dining details along with a well-drawn up seating plan of all the tables in the restaurant. My waitress opened up the heavy door and again wished me a very good afternoon. I gave her a warm smile and with my two bags, stepped back out into the square.

*

As I walked along the same familiar streets, I remembered the other many times I had done the same walk. I continued to think and brood of that wretched letter.

I was sorry of course that a child had been hurt up at the house, but why do parents never seem to watch their children? The boy in question was probably far too young to go all the way up Hallowed Hill to play in the remains of the old mansion. Surely anyone with one ounce of common sense must have realised eventually the ruins would become unstable. After all, no human structure can stand neglected for ever.

I was now walking along by the British Rail offices housed in the old Grand Pump Room Hotel. The streets were awash with civil servants or the 'undertakers' as I used to call them during the war. They were once again rushing off to lunch. I continued down past the Roman Baths where a small group of children with their parents were about to enter. One little boy was in fits of tears and screaming that the baths were boring and he wanted to go and play in the park. His father gave him a clip round the ear and that soon shocked his son out of his tantrum. I crossed over the road and headed down a badly bombed area of the city where St Andrews church had stood until it had been pulverised by the Huns. The air seemed a little thicker and dusty. The area looked so depressing and deserted. There were only two other people up ahead walking with cases and heading like I was to the station.

As I walked briskly down the street of crumbled buildings, I felt rather on edge. I half expected a hooded figure to jump out from one of the decaying Georgian porches, or a masked robber to leap down on top of me from the empty broken windows. I still continued thinking about that letter. I of course was pleased Thelma had found new work and a new home, but even that came over rather like her old cottage was no longer good enough for her. My thoughts then turned to the village hall meeting Thelma had spoken of. I could see all the villagers sat down in the meeting, pretending to be so concerned about the children's safety when all they really wanted to do was remove one of the last remaining traces of my father's legacy. I could see how many of them must have been only too eager to suggest having the mansion pulled down. What an enormous cheer and applause must have erupted through the hall when they made the decision to pull my old home down. I could imagine Thelma done up to the hilt, sat down with the rest of the villagers asking questions like 'Who built the house? And how did it catch fire?' No doubt many of the gossiping crows would have only been too happy to fill her in, on how Lord Parfitt had built the house and been their MP for years. That he had been a successful publisher and started up the mineral water factory. They would have told her that he had been such a great benefactor to the village until he lost all his money in the great crash. Followed by his son and heir running away in the night, leaving his sister to pick up the pieces. I could see Thelma's eyes probably now full of facts putting two and two together. How she must have finally sunk into her chair with overwhelming details of my former life. Now she must have finally understood why I never spoke to anyone about my life down in Devon or ever returned to my home. Little did she or anyone else sat in that hall know that the facts they all thought to be true were not really the truth but rather they had been pieced together through gossip.

*

My walk to the station became brisker as I came up to a King George's reign bright red post box. It reminded me to post my letter to Gloucester. I got it out from my bag and pushed it through the opening in the box. The post box seemed to be the only thing in the street which had been preserved from the bombing of '42. Everything else around it had been scarred. The station was now in front of me; a typical Victorian railway station with a cast iron entrance and decorative awnings. The building's entrance was smart and clean, with a wide, long hallway. It had Brown, black and orange tiles covering the floor and heavy looking benches with small polished tables and iron sculpted legs. A huge saucer of a clock ticked above a glazed door leading to the platform. Several doors went off the hallway marked with signs of 'toilets', 'rest room' and 'staff only'.

On the right was the booking office where I went and purchased my ticket for Bristol and then on to Barnstable. The bookings officer seemed very jolly but had a hacking cough. I proceeded along a corridor with a few closed doors until I came out in to the light and smoky atmosphere of the platform. The platform was extremely well appointed with a heavy canopy draped over a cold stone floor and littered with benches sat against a brick wall, along with an occasional wastepaper bin.

The platform was a hive of activity. Smartly dressed men in black suits with gold fob watches draped across their midriffs were scurrying about. There were porter's trolleys carrying baggage including huge dark leather cases and bags. Silver milk churns could be seen in the odd place or two, as well as packing cases and tea chests waiting to be moved off to their destinations. I walked along with my cases towards a bench. I could take the weight off my feet until I heard my train approaching. A few of the young lads moving cases for people gave me a nod of 'a good afternoon' and another man with a long black beard and brown cap said 'Hello'. I walked along past a glazed oak door with a tarnished handle and two smeary windows of the canteen building. The canteen had an old fashioned Victorian counter, with a till and two glass cake stands, with current buns piled up on top. Stacks of plain, unexciting white cups and saucers were placed at the far end of the counter, with a sideboard on the back wall which was cluttered with tea urns and glasses. The room was filled with a few solid looking polished tables with black scrolled legs and clawed feet; each one had rickety chairs huddled underneath them. A charwoman with an impressive bust was cleaning out ash trays behind her counter. Two men were sat in close proximity to her, both wearing trilby hats and reading crumpled newspapers. An old gentlemen was puffing away on a wooden pipe, and a lady with fox fir draped round her neck and shoulders was enjoying a satisfying cigarette, displaying herself rather provocatively in one of the windows. Seeing the lady's fox fir reminded me of that fox that had darted across my garden the other night, when I had woken from my terrible nightmare about Lynrock. How I missed the peace of my garden and the reassurance it gave me. I determinedly walked past the canteen as I did not want to have anything more to eat or drink, or I would need the loo again. Even if I had wanted something to eat or drink I did not like the look of the canteen. It looked run down, depressing and the room's air looked choked with tobacco.

As I walked further along the platform I observed that the whole of the back wall was like an art gallery of paintings. There must have been over thirty bright advertisement boards, all in shining glass frames, which from an angle looked like the hall of mirrors. There was an advertising board and posters recommending International Tea, another for Pears Soap, another one for Oxo, Lions, and Garston's Ales and Stouts. It was an impressive picture gallery and rather nice to see all the war posters removed. I remember on the day the war ended, before Eileen and I went to the banqueting hall for the victory celebrations, I cheerfully tore up the poster of that smug looking lady hovering over her sewing machine with the words 'Make Do and Mend'. I never minded making do and mending but I did object to that smug poster with that silly girl, who looked far too confident, self-satisfied and attractive than was good for her. There had been another poster with a creepy carrot on but I could not for the life of me remember what the posters slogan had been.

Standing on the platform I could almost still hear and see the shadows of our young lads that had gone off to the war; their mothers and girlfriends standing gravely on the platform, trying not to show how desperately afraid they were and doing their best not to break down in tears. So many never came back. I remembered young Bobby, our mail boy at the Guildhall, being waved off by his mother doing her best not cry and upset him. Bobby's mother had prayed and prayed that he would come back alive. His mother had already lost her eldest son yet she was asked once again to make yet another sacrifice. It all proved too much when the news came that Bobby had been killed. After his death she lost all zest for life and never fully recovered. As I approached my welcome rest on a sculpted bench, I passed a dark wooden dresser covered with Bradshaw Railway guides, handbooks, newspapers and tins of post cards with old locomotives on. Speaking of locomotives, I could hear the rumble and whistle of my train coming into the station. Two porters stood to attention with luggage trolleys at the ready. The other passengers' who had been sat waiting quietly, all got up and repositioned their bags, ready to board the train. A rather bunged up, congested voice of the announcer, who sounded like he had a blocked nose, informed us over the speakers that the train to Bristol was now approaching. I advanced a little closer into the centre of the platform and put my case down for a minute as I waited. A conductor suddenly bolted out of his office along with his trusty flag, examined his fob watch and sure enough the slender train came shuffling in with a mass of noise and smoke. As the train halted a mass of carriage doors all seemed to open in unison and passengers departed off in a hurry, whilst I gathered up my bags and went to scramble up in to a carriage along with my fellow travellers. The platform's porters franticly rumbled along behind us, pushing their trolleys of heavy bags and luggage on to the train. A flurry of the undertakers (civil servants) looking like they were desperately running late, full of their own self-importance, dodged and dived the porters and other passengers diving into the first class compartments. As I stepped up on to the train, after nearly being flattened by an undertaker who had pushed past me, I scolded myself and asked the Lord to forgive me for what I had dared not say, but God forgive me what I had thought when I had first received Thelma's letter. Her letter had seemed to rekindle all my bitterness, hate and resentment of what had happened all those years ago. I was so angry with the village for wanting to pull down my old home; the home I had loved so much and had desperately tried to save. It had only been for a split second but I wished that the village would reap what they were about to sow in pulling my home down.

*

As I got into my carriage I felt utterly ashamed that I had wished such harm on the village. It had only been for a moment but it was enough for me now to feel miserable, and I wanted desperately to prove that I was able to turn the other cheek and put my Christian faith into practice. I had been so angry with Thelma, who I am sure had never meant to upset me. It was I who was in the wrong to let hate take over my thinking. I slid open my compartment door and threw my case up onto the luggage rack above my stiff and upright seat. I could hear a few late remaining carriage doors clasp shut, followed by a sharp whistle from the guard on the platform. With a rumble and a sudden jerk, followed by a puff of steam and smoke, the train began to leave the platform. I felt extreme agitation come over me. That whistle had finally announced that all my escape plans to stop this trip were now over and dashed. There was certainly no going back. I had felt such anger when I had got Thelma's letter, but the anger had turned to sorrow and guilt when the news broke about the disaster that had struck my old home. I was determined to try to put the past behind me and do what I could to help Thelma and little Emma, and even the rest of the villagers. I desperately hoped I would be able to let my past grievances cease and do some good for the people whom I had spent all these years apart from. Although I had felt so bitter towards the village and people I once knew, I knew deep down that my family's down fall had not been their fault, but our own.

Chapter 14
They Too Had Been the Last

It was certainly odd leaving Bristol station and heading on my way to Devon. I had never made the return journey before and it seemed extremely strange going back to the place of my childhood. Bristol had looked much like Bath only far worse; it was terribly scarred and defaced by the war. I did not know Bristol that well. I only really knew the zoo, which was only up the road from the college where I travelled to from Bath every morning on the train, to undertake what had been a very intensive teaching course.

When the war came to an end in 1945, both Eileen and I continued in our jobs as secretaries in the education department in the Guildhall. Five years later we were both approached by the emergency training scheme director. He asked us if we would be interested in taking a thirteen month course to train as primary school teachers. Eileen was unsure, but I knew I would love to do it. I had always enjoyed visiting the schools while working in the education department. I had built up many friendships with many of the headteachers that I had met on my school visits. I may as well confess now that my visits had always been much longer than they should have been. This was due to me always going out after my meetings with the headteachers to talk to the children in the playground. Even at Christmas I found time to watch and enjoy the children's nativity services, which I adored. The training director said he had received glowing reports about me from the schools I had visited. Several of the headteachers had made private recommendations to him to offer me the chance to join the training scheme.

So when the government began asking people to take the emergency training, as so many of the male teachers had been killed in the war, I decided to go for it. I attended an interview shortly after completing my application. I soon found myself sitting in front of a panel of headteachers, council staff and the director. I went into the interview dressed to impress. I wore a black tailored jacket and skirt and my mother's pearls. Eileen had helped me with my hair piling it up and flicking it out at the back. I remember sitting down nervously in a green leather swivel chair placed before a polished oak table. In front of me was another long table where the panel sat, peering down at me. It felt at times like a congressional hearing. The panel's questions came quick and fast, and I had to respond with the same vigour to achieve my aim. I recognised many of the faces on the panel, as they were either Guildhall officials, or headteachers whom I had worked with over the last several years. I had kept my hands clasped together on the table in front of me all the time. I only took one sip of water from the glass on the table, and made sure I made good eye contact with each person that questioned me. After two and a half hours I was allowed to leave. I went up to each member of the panel to shake their hands and thank them all for the opportunity to attend the meeting.

    I remember walking back to my office feeling tired but proud. I had given what I thought had been a polished, composed performance. To my delight the training director came in after lunch and offered me a place on the training scheme. Eileen too was offered a place. So every day, for the next thirteen months we attended Bristol College for an exhausting but very interesting course. We learnt about child development, the curriculum, classroom procedures, health and wellbeing of a child. Then we moved on to planning, record keeping and marking; followed by learning and getting a feel for all the individual subjects. All the intensity and hard work was well worth it, for soon after qualifying I found a position in a small Wiltshire village school where I still teach happily now. I also decided it was time to move away from Bath and move to the same village where I was about to begin my new career. At long last after years of spending afternoons walking around the Parade Gardens, wishing and dreaming of a garden of my own I finally had one. I was able to afford a small cottage set in a delightful garden with plenty of room for a vegetable plot. My cottage was in a charming lane with only three other houses along by me. I instantly struck up a friendship with my neighbours Madeleine and Victoria, who lived in the cottage next door. I also had Cynthia living opposite and Farmer Richards up the lane. I had found a new peaceful existence and had just about managed to put the past to rest.

I so enjoyed my first term teaching and then going home to work on my garden, especially during the summer term after school. I would happily potter about, cutting back shrubs and deadheading the roses or digging up fresh carrots and cutting marrows, or picking fresh beans and then spending the evening shelling them. Once a week I would be invited over to Madeleine and Victoria's house for dinner and I would always take over with me one of my marrows or a cabbage. Then after dinner we would have a game of bridge, sitting round Madeleine's table in the bay window sipping sherry and listening to the wireless.

Thinking of my home and garden made me feel rather home sick, and the train had only just left Bristol station. Thankfully I had a compartment all to myself not that I did not like to converse with people but today on this particular journey I wanted some peace and thinking time. I could then fall asleep without having to worry someone was watching me. My carriage was relatively comfortable and cosy. The seats were decorated in a floral red and gold colour, with white head and arm rests which looked like paper doilies. The walls were panelled with soft coloured wood with old fashioned lighting of crooked shades with tassels. There were a few prints of old locomotives on the wall and luggage racks opposite and behind me. A rather pale cream blind was fitted in the windows of the carriage, which I pulled up so I could enjoy watching the scenery rushing past. I was rather fixated with looking at the juddering tassels on the gold embroidered light shades. The tassels kept shaking and moving all along the journey. There was an occasional movement in the corridor of a mother and child passing or a young lady stretching her legs. The conductor came in and clipped my ticket and I spoke a few words with him, but apart from that I spoke with no one else. The juddering train shuffled along out of the countryside of Somerset and then through into Devon and the old landscape of childhood began to reappear again. The rambling landscape of lush green meadows and fields, dusted with cow slips and buttercups, sped past far too quickly for one to enjoy. We passed far off hamlets and villages nestled cosily into valleys looking friendly and tranquil, almost idyllic. Spires of churches and chapels rose out of the roof tops of cottages and old wooden fences and patchwork fields, with thick hedge rows brimming with twittering birds. The fields were alive with production with either corn or barley nearly ready to be harvested. Many fields looked the colour of emeralds with grey metal troughs surrounded by thirsty cattle.

*

After about an hour into the journey, I decided to get my case down from the rack. I opened it and dug about through my clothes moving my cosmetic bag and there safe at the bottom was my novel under my black leather Bible. I took out the book I had brought with me to read and then put my case back up on the rack. I fidgeted about in my seat to get myself nice and comfortable. Once I was happy and comfortable I reached over for my book and picked up the volume, covered and bound in tortoiseshell colour leather. The book was beautifully embossed in each of the corners, with a gold sailing ship stamped and raised into the cover. Along the spine were bright gold letters displaying the title; the book still smelt of my father's bookcase. The smell of polish and rich musty sherry hit my senses and sent me back to reading in my father's old study. I opened up the book, carefully turning the leather coloured page followed by the title page with its exciting words; '*The Last Days of Atlantis* by Edward Roger Flint'. The title spoke to me of a great magnificent city, which unknown to its people and citizens was running on borrowed time. The people of Atlantis had no idea what was about to come upon them. Their diamond of a city would soon be no more. I was always struck with what I suppose some would say was a rather morbid fascination with anything which was the last of something. Whether it was a great empire or monarchy that fell, a ship that sunk or in this case an ancient mythical city that would soon be wiped away. There is, I suppose, something romantic and tragic about being the last of anything, because you know it will never rise or achieve power again.

I began to read the introduction and preface, captivated by the words and letters and the meaning of which they spoke. I was so excited to get to the first chapter and the chapter heading. I looked out of the window to see more sheep grazing on the sloping fields and the buzzards flying low looking for lunch. The sky looked far too perfect; white, soft fluffy clouds set in a pastel-blue coloured sky with a bright sun shining overhead. The train rumbled and jerked as we continued down the track, passing hedges and trees with lush healthy foliage. It rumbled into a small station where we paused to let passengers come and go. The sound of steam gulfed out of the train engine followed by the sound of opening and unlocking carriage doors, then of luggage and porter's trolleys driven along the platform. I looked out briefly onto the platform and noted a row of milk churns were waiting for the milk train to come and collect them. Two men in their Sunday best got out of the train, smoked and stretched their legs. They both were in their early twenties, both were very handsome. They wore light coloured trousers, light shirts and waistcoats, carrying their jackets across their shoulders. One of the men had a light scar across his face and walked with a slight limp. The other had a trilby hat with a bright navy blue band around it. They both looked relaxed and comfortable in each-others company. Seeing these two men enjoying a day out made me suddenly think about my brother. That last time I had seen and spoke with Edward had been in father's study in 1929. Eddie and I had very seriously come to blows and had bitterly argued with each other. Yet up until that year Eddie and I had been inseparable. We had been joined at the hip and shared so much together, particularly a silly sense of humour. Eddie was three years older than me, which would make him now about forty-six. I often wondered what had happened to him. Had he found happiness? Or had that dream of his not been what he had expected.

The two young men quickly re-boarded the train as the whistle blew and we began to get under way again. I decided to put Edward to the back of my mind. He had packed up and gone off to start a new life without me.

The train was on a roll again and the tassels were shuddering and shaking after a brief respite when we had stopped at the station. I continued looking out of the window taking in the view of the countryside. I observed a group of children running across a nearby field, scampering about and looking like they were having a wonderful time, heading towards a dense wood. *Their age was such a lovely time to be a child,* I thought. It was a time of freedom. You are able to run about in the fields, explore the woods for hours, throw on Wellington boots and go splashing down into brooks and streams or do some pond dipping. Each new day meant adventure and exploration with no grown-ups to tell you what to do. Only when your tummy started to groan with hunger would there be the frantic scamper home.

*

I suddenly could feel my book about to slip off my lap, still open at the page where I had paused. I managed to catch it with my hand before it fell. I had been so distracted with all that was going on outside, I had for a moment forgotten my book and the first of its chapters I was about to start and read. The idea of a grand city so powerful and mighty which was to be submerged by a great wave and sunk to the bottom of the sea was one that excited me. Most people of course thought Atlantis was nothing more than a myth. A story that had perhaps become embellished and added to over the centuries, and had now become nothing more than a legend. However I always dreamed and wished as a young child that one day an explorer or expedition would find a city beneath the sea. As the train ran into a tunnel I was plunged, apart from my shuddering lamps, into darkness. The train shuddered from side to side as it ran through the tunnel and then finally out into the light and countryside again. I glanced back over the first chapter heading of Edward Roger's book: '*The last fisherman of Atlantis*'. *What a title!* I thought. It was so captivating and mysterious. It was a rather ironic first title when only a few moments ago I been thinking about my brother Edward, who always said how much he wished he could just jump in a boat and go fishing. The times Eddie and I had sat on the beach or by the harbour wall in Lynrock. We would spend hours looking out to sea watching every boat that passed, observing every gull that flew across the bay. We had often talked about our thoughts and views of the world. We had shared so much like politics, history and social views. We had cried with laughter over silly jokes and things we had heard people say in the village. Little did I realise how little I really knew him. There had been a part of his life that he never spoke about or confided in me, until I stumbled on the truth.

Rather like the book I was reading the days I had spent with my brother the laughter, the conversations we had would never come back again. They too, had been the last.

Chapter 15
A Few Dropped Drawing Pins

As the train drew closer to Barnstable my thoughts and feelings about Eddie had not diminished despite me trying to put him to the back of my mind. As soon as the train crossed over the border into Devon my thoughts of Edward and the past resurfaced. I found myself reading my book but not really absorbing what I was reading. By the end of another paragraph I paused and thought to myself *what have I just read? What's the fishermen of Atlantis been telling me?* I had not taken any of it in.

The weather was still lovely and the view outside grew more enticing as I looked out towards the horizon. I could see the skyline over the blue sea of Devon. Old childhood haunts began to enter my mind. Land masses of great hills and rocks reminded me of a long lost childhood. The train ended its journey in Barnstable station as planned. It was now gone three o'clock and I knew I would probably be late for my check in time at The Chough's Nest Hotel. I closed up *The Last days of Atlantis* and put a book mark on the page I was on, knowing I would have to re-read what I had tried to read later. I gave a sharp sniff of the air and could hear the train calm down and lose its steam after its long journey. The sound of opening doors began again, only greater in number and volume. I saw the two young men whom I had observed at the beginning of the journey disembark, with brown and tan leather cases and jackets in hand. They walked off together towards the canteen. An elderly, rather frail looking lady, somewhat shrivelled up with old age, was helped down by a porter, along with a carpet bag of knitting and a small black handbag. I too got myself together and retrieved my case from off the rack, placing my novel back into it and pressing the lid down tightly. I picked up my handbag and left my compartment ready for the next occupant. I stepped down from the train and followed the frail looking lady along the platform.

The walls of the platform were full of advertisements like Bath station had been. A table of seaside postcards and papers were being carefully examined by a shaky hand from the old lady. She had paused at the stand, having put her carpet bag down and was looking at several of the postcards. Her head was shaking from side to side as she studied them with a glint of pleasure in her eyes. I walked past her and went into a corridor. There I could see the platform clock fixed to the wall on a black bracket. I continued along the corridor and into a dusty, and I had to say rather dirty, waiting room. Old newspapers were left dishevelled on warped benches. A wood burning stove was in the corner, now looking redundant. The windows were covered in grime and dust from the trains, and a collection of bags and trunks had been left abandoned in the corridor ready to be moved by a porter. A few rather tea stained cups and saucers had been left in one of the windowsills, which had terribly bad flaking paint.

I looked around to locate the booking office. It was set in a wooden panelled room with a wire cage grill covering the opening in the wall. A small letter box hole was at the bottom with enough room for tickets and money to be exchanged. A brass bell sat to the left side of the counter and a grimy brass nameplate read 'Mr Posh, booking officer.' I peered in through the grill to the office of bookcases, a filing cabinet, railway charts and calendars. A table was placed in the middle of the office set for a tea break, comprising of a brown teapot and an enamel cup, along with a milk jug and a plate of biscuits. The office seemed abandoned, with no clerk or booking officer present. I pressed the brass bell on the counter and it gave out a merry ring. Suddenly, like a cuckoo, a little man with a black suit with shiny gold buttons, fob watch chain and railway cap jumped up from beneath the counter and appeared on the other side of the grill. I presumed this was Mr Posh. I too jumped with alarm at the sudden sight of this rather red, chubby faced-man with hairs growing from his nose and ears. Black and greying strands of hair strayed from under his cap giving him the appearance of a clown.

"A jolly afternoon to you madam!" Mr Posh began in a rather overdone, upper crust accent. "No need for alarm. I did not mean to startle you. I was picking up drawing pins from off the floor. I dropped a whole tin of them everywhere and I have spent nearly five minutes picking them all up!"

*

Mr Posh had a beaming smile and looked as if he would have been better placed in the Russian circus. He spoke terribly refined tones and his voice matched his name for being posh. He did, however unfortunately, sound a bit of an old woman, but there was a look about him which made me warm to him.

"Oh! That must be tiresome," I said, "having to pick up all those drawing pins. I wonder if you could help me?"

I was just about to ask Mr Posh if he could advise me on how to get down to Lynrock, when he burst out in delight and excitement.

"Have no fear madam! I am here to serve you. Do ask me whatever you wish I will hold nothing back from you!"

I was not sure I liked the sound of that so I spoke very calmly and slowly, hoping that by speaking calmly it may help to calm Mr Posh down.

"I was wondering whether you knew of any buses or means of transport I could take to get me down to Lynrock this afternoon?"

Mr Posh looked surprised. He itched the left bush of hair sticking out from under his cap, causing a shower of dust to fall on to his shoulders. He then removed a pencil from the top of his right ear. He sucked his lips, pursed them and gave out a ticking and sucking noise.

"I am sorry madam, but no transport apart from the army and emergency services will be going down to Lynrock at the moment. We have had a terrible flood down that way! Thirteen dead so far and many homeless! It has been the most shocking disaster we have ever seen."

"Oh yes!" I said, "I do realise that. It's because of the disaster that I want to go down to Lynrock. You see…" I paused and thought it best to stick to the story I told *Mrs Barns about Thelma being a relative and not a friend.* "I have family down in Lynrock and I have not been able to reach them yet. I am very worried about them."

Mr Posh gave another sucking noise and his face looked aghast with shock and worry. He clasped his hands up to his rosy cheeks and held them there on both sides. His mouth opened like a tunnel and dropped open to reveal a huge set of wonky, yellow looking teeth.

"Oh my dear madam! How shocking! How terrible for you! Now let me think. Let me see now." He turned his head round almost like an owl and looked at a wooden clip board. He flipped over a chart covered in what looked like coffee stains. A few drawing pins fell from the board and tapped and bounced on to the counter. He looked in wonder at the chart then spoke to me in an uncertain way.

"It's not what you are probably used to madam but as your journey is of such great importance... Would you mind travelling down in the milk cart with old Billy Bath? He is taking down his load to Hunter's Inn in the valley. Billy will then go onto his next stop which will be Lynrock."

It was not exactly ideal but I was pleased he was trying to accommodate me, and as long as I got there I did not care a hoot what type of transport I went on. Plus it was a nice sunny, relatively mild day and it wasn't as if I would get soaked to the skin in rain. So I agreed to Mr Posh's suggestion.

"Thank you!" I said gratefully. "That would be wonderful. If you're sure that's alright and I won't be causing any inconvenience?"

"Oh golly! No madam. No problem or inconvenience. It is our pleasure to help you. Old Billy Bath's such a jolly soul. He would be glad to assist you. He's heading down to Lynrock anyway." Mr Posh seemed to be a man who may have given one the impression he was a complete and utter imbecile, but he was in fact a very resourceful man.

Mr Posh tiptoed out of his office like a ballet dancer and left me for a few minutes to go and speak with this jolly Billy Bath. He was apparently outside loading up his milk churns on to his cart. I stood in the dusty waiting room observing the clock. A draft of air came in through a hole in the bottom of one of the windows sending flakes of paint sliding off the windowsill to the grubby, grey tiled floor. The draft made me feel suddenly cold and made me slightly shiver. I moved about the waiting room like I was waiting for the dentist to call me in. My wait was soon over as Mr Posh danced back into his office full of excitement.

He flapped his arms about and knocked over a pile of books which he then totally ignored.

"I have wonderful news! Billy has agreed to take you down to Lynrock, if you can be ready to leave at once?"

I was thrilled at this quick action and felt suddenly positive.

"Oh! That is wonderful! Thank you so much Mr Posh you have been so helpful."

*

Mr Posh gave me instructions to go out in to the yard at the back of the station where I would find the charming Billy Bath. Who was just securing the last of his load of milk churns before setting off.

I thanked Mr Posh greatly for his help and assistance and he wished me a good journey. He hoped I would find my relative in good health. He then disappeared again to the floor, and began, I assumed, to take up his job of picking the remaining drawing pins from off the floor. With my two bags in hand I left Mr Posh to continue picking up his pins. I stepped out from the dusty, cold waiting room and out into the bright and sunny enclosed yard. As I had been told I found a tall man with a rather bulbous beer belly loading up a silver milk churn onto his cart. At the front was a sandy coloured horse thrashing his tail about. I walked over to Billy; both he and his horse looked impatient and eager to begin their round.

I spoke in a loud and friendly fashion, greeting the apparently happy-go-lucky Billy Bath with a warm, "Good Afternoon. You must be Mr Bath. I am your passenger for the afternoon. I am so grateful for you offering me a lift. It's so very kind of you."

The warm and cheerful Billy Bath, whom Mr Posh had assured me, would be so pleased and happy to accommodate me must have been the most miserable, grumpy and, God forgive me for saying this, sod I had ever met in my life. Billy had the most downtrodden look and had a sound of doom in his voice when he spoke. He had a large wooden pipe which seemed permanently fixed to his mouth and hand. His hair was grey and the texture of rat tails. His manner of dress was typical country:

he wore cord mustard coloured trousers with a piece of coarse string tide round his waist, a grubby white shirt with a brownish tweed waistcoat and a flat cap perched on his head. I did try to smile at him as I approached, but it did little to change the sullen expression across Billy's lose and grey skin.

"Um. So you're the woman who wants to go down to Lynrock then are you? Aha! I don't know you people from abroad," (meaning not from these parts I guessed),

"You think you can come swaggering down here and think us poor folk can wait on you hand, foot and bloody finger. Still…" He paused and studied me, and puffed away on his pipe. Then he gave the most sickly and chesty cough. "You got a nice face I'll give you that, and at least you're wanting to go my way. The last sod I gave a lift to made me go five miles off my normal route!"

I looked at Billy more closely. I noticed he had the most brilliant blue eyes, and thought to myself *I am surprised anyone can make you do anything you don't want to do.* I decided that Billy was one of life's moaners. Perhaps he had been treated badly by people in the past and was unable to live and let live. Normally I would never have used bribery to get anything done, but as the saying goes 'money talks' so I said, still politely, but with more assertiveness in my voice

"I do assure you Mr Bath I will not cause you any trouble. Your round will be my round for the afternoon. I won't even talk if you would prefer to be left in peace. I only wish to get down to Lynrock by the end of the day that's all. As a token of my good wishes and thanks please accept…" I rummaged in my handbag and located my purse. I undid it to present him with two shillings.

"Please accept this."

I passed up to him the coins and placed them into his hands which felt and looked rough, terribly dry and cracked with over work and toil.

"I believe in rewarding good service and I am sure you and your fine horse will get me down to Lynrock before the end of the day." (*I have often found how a little flattery often goes to a man's head!*)

*

Billy looked at the coins. He twirled them about with his long fingers. A hint of a smile crept over his dry lips. He quickly thumbed the coins away in the breast pocket of his tweed waistcoat, like a naughty little boy stashing away his pocket money. Billy gave another very unhealthy cough and cleared his throat with a snort and grunt, spitting out a flow of white phlegm which he sent a great distance over his poor horse Jacob's head to land on the yard floor. "Um I suppose I better help you up then seeing you is coming with me. Mind you I don't like women that sing! I can't abide women that burst into song all the bloody time. Reminds me of my bloody wife!"

I was filled with relief that my strategy of offering Billy something, seemed to have broken a very fine layer of ice. As Billy helped me and my cases up on to the seat I said in a determined and sure way, "I quite agree with you Billy I can't stand a lot of singing either."

Billy grunted, coughed again and said rather dryly, "That makes a change! A women who agrees with me on something. Must tell my bleeding misses when I get home. That will shut her up for an hour or two."

Billy double checked his smart cargo of milk churns all in neat rows, mumbled something about the blasted wet roads and all the army roaming about all over the bloody place and then got on his way.

Chapter 16
A Ghostly Valley

Billy and I conversed a little more easily as soon as we went a few miles up the road. We had escaped the busy and bustling town centre of Barnstable and were now on the outskirts of the town in more peaceful surroundings. We passed many small but fine looking red brick cottages, all in their Victorian regimented rows. Each had small walled gardens mainly for vegetable growing. In the distance there was a large wall with big impressive gates. A large smoking chimney could be seen behind the wall, along with the sound of activity from busy frantic workers.

"Them's is the factory worker's cottages along there."

Billy pointed and scanned along the row of houses with his fingers as Jacob walked us up the road.

"What do the workers make at the factory?" I enquired, trying to make conversation.

"They's make matches in there. I expect you've had at some stage in your life a box of England's Glory Matches?"

"Oh yes!" I said in a peaceful and knowing way, thinking back to the box that sat in my kitchen, the box Eddie had given me. Billy then continued talking and grunting away.

"Course seeing that war ship on the front of the box always brings back the memories of them bloody wars. Damn wars! They always seem to change everything."

Billy looked rather dower and I was unsure what to say to him. Thankfully Billy removed the silence between us and continued talking. I was more than happy to just sit and listen to him, as it gave me relief from talking about myself or my past. *The less Billy knew about me the better,* I thought.

"I took a lad on who was laid off from the factory a few years back to help around the farm. Good lad he was. Name of Philip. Needed a lot encouragement mind. Not the best of home lives I don't reckon. His mum got on the bottle, knocked him about a bit."

"How terrible! The poor chap," I said, "I expect you gave him a fresh new start and something to enjoy each day. What happened to him your Philip?"

Billy looked taken back and his face fell tragically sad. He gave a clear of his throat.

"He was killed at Dunkirk." Billy cleared his throat again. "Poor lad, I did my best for him but there was too much blown out of him." Billy gave a cough and wiped his eyes.

"So you were at Dunkirk with Philip?" I enquired rather surprised.

"It was a hell of a place! The most bloody marshy ground you could ever wish to walk over. Yeah me and Philip we went off together and we…"

Billy suddenly paused and looked rather crestfallen again. His eyes looked far off as if even now he was seeing and reliving all that went on at Dunkirk. It was as if he could still hear the sound of crying and groaning men, the sounds of bullets flying past and the bombs of the Luftwaffe diving on top of them.

"I hoped, even prayed, we would both get back to the farm together. All the time we were on that bloody beach the Germans were closing in. Mind you the RAF showed the bloody Luftwaffe what they could do. May 30th I got evacuated but had to leave poor old Philip behind. Didn't even have time to bury him. Those sands were turned red with blood by the time I got picked up. Poor sods in the highland division, most of them got taken prisoner. Glad my Philip didn't have that happen to him. He would never have coped with being put in a camp. He was a rather sensitive sort of chap, if you know what I mean?"

I bit my lip and new what Billy was implying. I could see that Philip had been more than just a helper to Billy on his farm. He had become almost like a son. I could see the loss was still there in Billy's eyes. Perhaps that explained Billy's attitude. He had still not recovered from Dunkirk or got over the death of what must have been an adopted son. "You and your wife must have missed Philip very much," I said sympathetically.

"I did yes. Don't know about the wife. My Dotty, she's never wanted children. More interested in her blasted singing and constant baking for the village fair every blasted summer. We did have a nephew!"

Billy sounded rather proud at the mention of his nephew but his pride quickly evaporated and again his expression was crestfallen. "But he died in 1929."

"Oh! I am sorry. I don't think 1929 was a good year for many people," I said remembering what a terrible year that had been for me and my family. There was yet another strange silence between us and, wondering how to brighten the mood I decided to ask Billy about his farm. I knew from Farmer Richards back home how farmers loved to talk shop.

"I expect you have to keep working on your farm all the time, otherwise the management runs away from you."

"Oh err your dead right there. Running a farm is a hard life. It's not for the lily livered. But it's a good life, a rewarding one. The land gives you so much back provided you put the work into it and look after it. Not that my Dotty does much to keep it going. If the land girls hadn't worked on the land the whole farm would have gone to the dogs."

*

Jacob continued on at a steady pace and the factory and cottages soon disappeared. Jacob was a sturdy and good natured horse, and we were making good time along the sleepy roads running away from the station and the pavements of Barnstaple. Devon seemed almost lost in time; as if the war and the changes that had taken place all over the world had not reached this tangible county of England. But of course after hearing Billy's story of Dunkirk and losing Philip and his nephew, I knew that Devon had been affected like everywhere else in England had been. In some ways it must be even worse to lose so many young men and boys to a war in such small communities. The losses must have had an even more profound effect on the village way of life.

As we carried on, the milk churns in the back of the cart made little noise apart from the odd clink now and again, and only when the wheels of the cart stumbled over a stone or into a small dent in the road. The roads curved and meandered gently down hills and valleys, with thick hedgerows of thorns and bushes on either side. The smell of garlic mustard hung in the air coming from its triangular leaves growing in front of the hedge rows. I also observed decorative pale pink flowers of dame's violet dotted about amongst the nettles and cow parsley. The roads were indeed not the best. Many had pot holes and at the moment many were still saturated with rain from the many days of wet weather Devon had suffered. We passed down a very sleepy quiet lane, with a rambling grey coloured wall on one side with thick patches of cracked yellow lichen and climbing ivy. Along the wall were several tall pink foxgloves scattered along the bank with a few bees buzzing about looking for pollen. On the other side of the lane grew a hedgerow about waist height, and beyond that were open pastures of green wet grass. The lane began to slope up and our cargo of milk churns became more noisy, tapping into each other. Up ahead was a rather odd looking sight of a farmer herding some very large Devonshire black pigs down the winding lane. I had seen sheep and cows herded before but never pigs. Billy pulled up and stopped the cart for a few minutes to let the farmer and his five pigs go past. The pigs had rather humorous expressions on their faces one even looked as if he was smiling at me. They all went snorting along, stopping and sniffing the ground for a few seconds before being herded along by their farmer. The farmer looked similar to my farmer Richards back home in Wiltshire. He doffed his cap at me and said 'How do' to Billy, who responded with, "Afternoon to you Trevor. Beauty of an afternoon." The two country gents talked for a few minutes in what must have been farmer's language, because all I could make out was grunts, mumbles and an occasional 'bloody this' or' blasted that' from Billy. As Trevor went down the lane with his pigs, we carried on our journey moving up the lane along the stone wall, which as we moved up the lane began to look as though it was beginning to topple over with erosion. As we grew nearer to our first stop at Hunter's Inn, my watch read four thirty-five. I knew I would probably not get to The Chough's Nest Hotel until gone six. The road began to run downhill again into a dense forested valley. Billy continued puffing away on his pipe and gave a cough and snort. I asked him a few questions about his work and his wife, whom he had been married to for over thirty years. Although according to Billy it felt more like sixty.

Billy asked me a few questions about my life and family. I told him about my life in Wiltshire, my job as a teacher and my garden. But I deliberately kept my answers short and evaded the questions of my family. He asked me why I wanted to go down to Lynrock (what with the flood) and I explained to him about my concern over my friend Thelma. I briefly bored him about the years we had spent in Bath, surviving the Blitz and Thelma having Emma.

"Me and Dotty went to Bath last year," Billy responded grumpily. "We had a look at the Roman Baths and Dotty went round the shops spending my money like it was going out of fashion."

"It is a lovely city," I said. "I never thought so when I first moved there. I hated it. It seemed so noisy and crowded compared to here. I can remember crying for days after the move wishing I had never come, but then I got used to it and adjusted."

I quickly realised that I had let slip that I had come from Devon and scolded myself for being so stupid and careless.

Billy looked at me in a quizzical manner and puffed away on his pipe until he said. "You never said you'd lived down here before! You a local girl then?"

My heart sank. I knew I would have to be very careful. If I gave away too much now Billy might be able to piece together who I was. I thought carefully before giving what sounded like a well-rehearsed response.

"Yes I was born and raised in Devon but I moved to Bath well before the war."

I thought that covered me. I told him all I wanted and needed to. I need not divulge the year I moved away or why. Billy however sounded far too interested than I thought was good for him.

"Um" Billy muttered in a miserable way. "What year did you move away then?"

I stuttered and sounded rather flustered. I did consider telling him a lie but thought it was best to tell him the truth and hope that would curb his curiosity in me.

"It was 1929. I lost a bit of money in the crash and thought it would be sensible to cut my losses and start afresh."

I hoped that by telling Billy that he would ask no more questions. Yet I had told him far more than I had ever meant to and I was not pleased with myself for being so stupid.

"That bloody crash caused a lot of problems," Billy mumbled, "Many a big man went down after that. We had a very wealthy family living in Lynrock before the crash. They were a nice family, did a lot of good for the village. Not snobby like some of the bleeding Aristocracy. But like so many they invested their money in the stock market and of course when the crash came they lost the lot. Perhaps you would remember them, they left same time you did, the Parfitt family?"

I looked straight in front of me focusing on Jacob's large ears and studied his mane. I needed something to distract myself and not give any emotion away. I gave a gulp and spluttered out in a rather small voice.

"No. No I don't think I remember them."

I continued to look out over Jacob's head, trying not to go over the past again. I had come to find Thelma and Emma. That's what I had to focus on. Billy gave another sharp cough and cleared his throat. Our pace had slowed a little now and we moved along the lane in a slumbering fashion. Thankfully Billy changed the subject completely.

"I've always found," Billy said in a light hearted manner, "I gets on better with me pigs and sheep than people these days. You take Jacob here," Billy pointed with his pipe, and at the mention of his name, Jacob's ears turned back and twitched. "He's like a son to me he is. He's very reliable and good company. I'd sooner bring him and me lambs in to the kitchen and sit with them by the fire each evening, than listen to my flaming Dotty go on, about poor old souls in the village. The gossip she hears about them all the time it never ends."

"You don't like gossip then Billy?" I asked in a teasing way. Billy replied in a very determined and definite way.

"No! I don't take to kindly to it, miss. I know you women make an art of it, but I never like to talk bad about folks. Take my poor nephew, he was the butt of other people's gossip and cruel comments. A young man that went off to fight in the Great War to keep those silly fools in the village safe. Yet how did they repay him? They laughed and scorned him. All because he was so very…" Billy ceased his talk of his nephew and looked suddenly worried that like me he had given too much information away. Like me I could tell he was holding something back. He then continued our talk only trying to limit the damage he had nearly caused himself by revealing to much of his past.

"Let's just say miss, my nephew had a hard life after the war and it was a happy release for him when he died."

I decided not to question Billy any further regarding his nephew. I could see in his eyes there was a very deep grief. There was almost a bitterness that I too had seen in myself. I only added how sorry I was that people had treated his nephew so shabbily and said to him how much I admired all the young men that fought in the wars.

"They gave us all so much," I said to Billy "a debt we will never be able to fully repay. Apart from ensuring we never forget them."

*

As we carried on with the weather still improving, Billy continued on chatting to me. Our conversation was easier than it had been and as we continued talking I could see how much Billy loved the land we were passing through.

"I do love this place!" Billy said with what sounded like a deep passion and love. Emotions I had not yet seen or even thought Billy had.

"It's so quiet and unassuming. Tis a beauty of a place this land. It's given me a lot over the years and a great deal of peace. Every time I come out to work in the fields I look about and I know why we fought to keep our freedom. I love the fact that when you're out at work you can be deep in the country one minute and then be facing a pale blue sea in the distance. Tis heaven to me this place."

I later learned that Billy had married young but he and his wife Dorothy had not been blessed with children as he had told me. That's why Billy had treated Philip like a son and why the loss of his nephew had been such a blow to him. I could see why he now valued his animals more than people. I thought that perhaps Billy dearly wished he had children and the fact he was never able to have them, had made him sulky with his wife Dotty and he found his marriage hard to cope with. There was also the farm; with no children who would Billy pass it on to when he was gone? Who would continue Billy's work? If that was the case then I could fully understand his sadness. For we all have at one time or another had ideas and dreams for life that never materialised.

*

As we travelled down into the valley another farmer came along with a flock of what must have been at least thirty black faced sheep. They were all *baaing* and talking to each other, looking at the ground and some were eating something tasty they had found at the side of the road. Some sheep wondered off the track and were brought back by the farmer's collie bitch, gently pressuring them to follow the rest of the flock. The farmer kept his head bowed and only nodded his head at me and Billy as he passed. The sheep surrounded the cart on both sides and for a few minutes we were surrounded by a sea of black faced sheep, all looking slightly simple and vacant.

Within a few minutes the sea of sheep passed us by and the wet lane, now with a few piles of fresh wet droppings left by the sheep, was still and silent again. Billy snorted and spoke with his pipe in his mouth, "That was young Alun just gone past. He's not one for talking nowadays, another man like my nephew, another casualty of the war."

We carried on down the hill with the sheep gone and the path now cleared. The trees to the side of us became less sparse now and doubled in number beginning to overshadow the lane and causing the formation of a canopy over us. The open patchwork of fields that had run along either side of us had now completely vanished. We had at long last reached the bottom of the valley. The valley seemed mysterious, silent with only the rustling of leaves from the trees and an occasional crow calling overhead in the sky. We came over a stone bridge with a very full looking stream of clear water rushing past. We passed two very pretty cottages with gardens full of sweet peas and climbing white and red roses. As we passed the cottages the lane became increasingly more wet and saturated with puddles. We past an old barn with stone steps running along up the side to a door at the top. A family of ducks and geese were waddling about through the puddles; they quacked and chatted to each other as we made our way past their ranks. One of the largest geese outstretched her wings and gave them a terrific flap, quacking away in a sharp tone as if to say to us *how, dare you push past.* An old fence ran along round the perimeter of the barn with the gate being kept propped up and secure with a piece of rusty barbwire. The barn's huge doors were closed and bolted, although great sections of the bottom panels were splintered and broken off, leaving wide gaps at the bottom. A small plain of uncut grass was on the other side of the barn and ran along by the fence. The grass was thick and wet with rain covered in Dandelions and wild carrot that had changed it flowers from powder pink to bridal white. Billy steered Jacob along the road until we finally reached our first stop, Hunter's Inn.

*

Hunter's Inn was a ghostly, colonial styled house, with a wide open porch that ran all along the bottom of the ground floor of the inn. A wooden staircase was located running up to the first floor at the end of the porch and the latter porch seemed to be littered with wooden tables and Windsor chairs. The inn looked as though it had three floors. All the rooms above had large, grubby windows, their frames slowly going rotten. Many of the panes had become rather wonky, with the putty beginning to crumble away. Green shutters did their best to compensate the degraded windows, with one shutter banging gently against the wall in the breeze. The roof was tiled with what looked like grey slate but it was hard to tell as there was so much moss and lichen plastered over it. The chimney stacks looked rather rickety and unsteady and one pot was even missing. Billy pulled up Jacob outside along by the wooden steps going up into the porch. The sun looked watery now and the breeze had really picked up causing more of the inn's shutters to bang about. A rocking chair out on the porch seemed to have a life of its own and was rocking up and down with a grinding squeak. It also seemed incredibly dark in this creepy valley. The oak trees that dominated it had grown tall and mighty; their ancient branches looked rather arthritic, twisted and deformed with years of chilling winds and rain that had blown through the valley like a wind tunnel. Ferns of many varieties covered the ground like a carpet; many were tightly curled up still young and youthful. Billy dismounted and bade me to wait while he checked his order with the landlord. Billy gave a cough and spitted more phlegm out onto the soggy path. It had been a long trip, and my home in Wiltshire seemed a long way away now.

The minutes passed and for a while my thoughts and time were my own. I felt nervous however and I dearly wished we could get underway and get away from the creepy inn. Billy thankfully returned, muttering and ranting about something. I could see that something was wrong with him and had rattled his cage. His miserable expression somehow looked far worse than normal.

"Is there something wrong?" I asked innocently.

"Oh the landlord's just told me that the road down to Lynrock has been closed off. One of the blasted army trucks went flying off the road this afternoon and crashed. It's blocked the whole bloody road! Landlord's just said the road's closed until tomorrow morning now!"

"Oh that is a bloody nuisance!" I shouted then suddenly felt shocked with myself, realising what I had said. I had never openly swore in public before! Spending the afternoon with Billy had not improved my vocabulary or my temperament.

Billy however looked highly pleased with my choice of words, and gave me a sly smile.

"The landlord has said he will put us up overnight. He's a decent chap and he has two spare rooms going. No need to look so worried. It's not a ghost inn."

*

I was really not happy or relaxed about the idea of staying in this inn. I had planned to be in Lynrock that day, not the next and I was having to quickly adjust to the fact that it was not possible. My well laid plans had not come together.

"Is there no other road that runs down to Lynrock? Could we not take another path?" I sounded rather desperate and grasped at the idea of still getting down to Lynrock that night.

"Hum. Not on your life! All the other roads are closed. The flood brought down five bridges. The only safe road was the road we were going down that runs along the top of the valley and that now won't be open until ten o'clock tomorrow morning. So I am sorry my dear you will have to stop the night here with me."

I gave a deep gulp. I was indeed stuck there for the time being. I shakily dismounted from my seat. My joints were stiff and my bottom was numb from sitting down for so long. I gave Jacob a soft pat and smooth. Billy informed me that he was going to clean Jacob up and get him into the barn we had passed after he had unloaded the milk churns. He gave me instructions to go on in while he began to get the first milk churn down. The landlord, a Mr Hunter, would see to me and book me in. I got down my case and handbag and looked around surveying the scene. The valley was desolate with only the sound and sight of Billy manoeuvring round a milk churn, and Jacob snorting and slightly stamping a hoof down. Up the lane towards the picturesque cottages came the sound of the ducks and geese talking and flapping about.

The breeze had now turned into a wind, but the air felt fresh and I could smell the salt and fish of the sea, which Billy said was only down a track which ran down the side of the inn. I still felt tense and was unsure of entering this creepy looking dwelling. I climbed up the wooden sunken steps, which creaked and groaned as I stepped on each of them. My case felt far heavier now; a bit like myself for I was feeling heavy hearted and tired. The floor boards of the porch were painted a dusty white and the pillars holding up the roof were painted in a forest green colour, along with the doorframes and skirting board. All the tables were dry and void of life with only a few beer stains left over from glasses. All the tables had dull silver candlesticks on with white candles left in their holders. I crept in through the open door leading into an open bar full of dark wood, more Windsor chairs and sticky looking tables. The place looked empty like a ghost ship with only the sound of a grandfather clock ticking away (with a menacing chime at every hour) and the still rocking chair outside on the porch. The bar and lounge was dominated by beams and shelves full of model ships and boats; all covered in cobwebs and dead spiders shrivelled up, with their legs crooked and wrapped around their bodies like they had endured hours of torturous pain before dying. I went up to the bar and put my case down by the side of a bar stool. I Placed my hands on the dark wood of the bar, thinking to myself what on earth had I come to. It was not a bad place. It looked well equipped and I am sure was very nice, especially only being a short path away from what Billy said was an old smugglers cove; and rocky beach. But somehow there seemed something dark and mysterious about the inn and the valley it was placed in. It reminded me of the story of *Sleepy Hollow*, as if a hidden spirit would soon appear or the headless horsemen. Then there came a deep depressing voice from behind me.

*

I spun round with my heart beating a little faster, my body now chilled with sudden fright from the sound of the voice. I now faced a dangerous looking man. He was a short, well-built man with a bald head and plump features. He wore dark trousers and a long white apron covering most of his body, stained with what looked like blood. I felt as if I was face to face with an escaped convict. Seeing this man with red stains over his white apron sent me into panic mode. I staggered back trapped against the bar. The man's face was smudged with blood and had dark penetrating eyes with a thick big nose and flared nostrils. My panic increased to the point of me wanting to escape and take flight, when I saw the man stained with blood was holding a sharp knife by his side.

"Who… who are you?" I said in a highly nervous and charged voice, almost wanting to scream with fear. The murderous looking man suddenly gave out a beaming smile and his dark eyes lit up and he spoke with a polite, friendly, soft voice.

"I do beg your pardon miss. I am so sorry at my attire. I have been gutting fish in the kitchen and it's been rather a challenge this afternoon. Please do forgive me."

He wiped his spare hand across the side of his apron and pulled his hand up to shake mine to greet me.

"Welcome miss. Welcome to Hunter's Inn. I am Mr Hunter. I hope you had a good journey? Getting about down here is not very easy at the moment what with the flood last week. I hope Billy's looking after you?"

My panic slowly began to subside and my heart calmed down a little. I shook hands with Mr Hunter. His hands were so much bigger than mine and rather cold and gritty with salt from preparing the fish.

"You must have thought me a murderer coming in with a knife and fish blood on my apron! I do apologise. I hope Billy's not been constantly moaning? He's not the brightest of souls but you get used to him after a while."

"No Billy's been very helpful. I am only sorry you have us both stuck with you for the night. I was so hoping to get down to Lynrock tonight."

"Yes. I am sure it must be most difficult for you. Billy has told me you have a friend down there. It must be a real worry for you. So many people have been affected and the death toll's gone up to fifteen now! They pulled another body out of the Bath Hotel this afternoon. It's hit us all very hard. Plus with so many of the roads blocked and flooded with fallen trees, and bridges swept away its made life very difficult and trying. But you must be exhausted miss. Do come over here to sign in and I will take you up to your room."

I was now feeling a little more relaxed and pleased with my host. Mr Hunter seemed a rather jolly fellow despite his macabre appearance. He gave me the inn's ledger and asked me to sign the visitor's book, and I handed over my ration book to him.

"I will be glad when we can all get rid of these books. I suppose we should not grumble, but it causes such a lot of paper work and fuss. Still at least the war is over now, and we are not having the upheaval Egypt's going through at the moment. I do hope our students won't start up here and want rid of our monarchy."

"I shouldn't think so," I said, trying to brush aside his concerns and put his mind at rest while I signed my name.

"I think most people are very pro-monarchy, and everyone is getting so excited about the coronation next year. Egypt's trouble was it had a king who was too much of a play boy, and lived in luxury while his people lived in poverty."

Mr Hunter look reassured and I smiled at him warmly as I finished signing my name and spun the book round back to him so he was able to read it. Mr Hunter looked up and reached up a hand to the wall by the bar to a set of jangling keys, all with wooden tags with room numbers on them. He chose a room key and put it down on the bar. He then undid his apron and threw it across the bar along next to his sharp grimy knife that he had put down earlier.

"Right then Miss…" He paused and looked worried as he studied my name in the large book.

"Miss Parfitt? Is that correct Miss Parfitt?"

I gave a gulp and new what must be going through his mind. He must have been thinking *I wonder if that's old Lord Parfitt's daughter. The daughter that vanished and ran away after her father went bankrupt and died.* I thought it best to ignore Mr Hunter's curious tone and I asked in an undeterred way.

"Is there a problem Mr Hunter?"

Mr Hunter was a good showman and host. He immediately responded with, "Oh I am sorry Miss Parfitt. I went blank for a few minutes, old age creeping in. Let me take your case and I will show you up to your room. You're in room number five. An unlucky number for some! I remember one poor chap, nice young lad he was. He stayed in your room a few years back. Do you know what happened to him? Found him the next morning, stone cold dead!" Mr Hunter suddenly realised that he was not exactly selling room five to me, and quickly added rather briskly, trying to cover up room five's depressing past.

"Of course there was nothing sinister about his death. We got the doctor but of course it was too late for him to do anything, except to tell me that he was dead. The inquest found the young chap had a dicey heart brought on by a bad case of influenza he had a few years back. It was an accident waiting to happen. Bit of a shock though. I mean poor chap, he had only booked in the day before. He sat on the porch in that old rocking chair most of the time, staring into space and drinking. I always got the impression he was waiting for someone."

Mr Hunter suddenly looked uneasy at the thought of the poor young man who had tragically died on his premises. He seemed almost panicked as if he had spoken out of turn or as if I had known the man and he had caused me offence. His uneasy and panicked face soon disappeared by a broad but unconvincing smile. He could not hide from me the tension in his voice, despite him trying to be light hearted.

"Still I am sure you won't find the room unlucky you have a lucky face. Hope you don't mind sharing it with the ghost though. It has been known to put people off!"

I gave Mr Hunter a grin and tried to laugh off his silly joke. Yet inside I felt once again the feeling of wanting to escape, to take flight and stay anywhere for the night but here. Mr Hunter picked up my case as he carried on laughing, amused at his own humour. I reluctantly followed him and together we made our way up to the ghostly room five.

Chapter 17
A Night at Hunter's Inn

The August sunshine left quickly that evening. The valley grew darker and rather chilly, with even the trees looking more distorted than they had in the afternoon. The darkness crept into every corner. Great shadows draped over the path, encompassing the creaking porch and making the interior of the inn far more gloomy and depressing than it naturally was.

Room five was not exactly a suite based on the interior of the Ritz but it was comfortable. The room was dominated by a brass bed with dull tarnished bed knobs, with a thick bedspread which looked like it had been knitted by Mr Hunter's grandmother. There was a mock Tudor dressing table and a crazed mirror with rather rickety drawers which moved at an angle when they were pulled out. Also available to me was an old chest of drawers with brass sculpted handles and a chipped jug and basin set on its top. A few embroidered prints graced the walls, again looking like they had been embroidered by Mr Hunter's grandmother. Thankfully I sensed no feelings of sadness or despair that you sometimes pick up on when a death has occurred in a room. The room however felt bitterly cold and felt as if it was the middle of winter rather than a day in mid-August. The worst downside to the room was that I unfortunately would have to share a bathroom with Billy who I heard knocking into something in the room next to mine, cursing away and saying something which sounded like 'Oh bloody hang me.'

I washed using my jug and basin filled with warm water, which Mr Hunter had kindly brought up. I dressed in a black skirt and black blouse embroidered with gold coloured thread, replaced my mother's pearls and put her watch back on. Then feeling rather like I was walking to the guillotine, I proceeded down a dimly lit hall of creaking floorboards, closed panelled doors and candle lit lanterns. I could hear the sound of cackling old men and grunting old sailors sat in the bar below me. The wind howled up the stairs and along the corridor and I was absolutely frozen with cold. No wonder my room felt so chilly. Why on earth Mr Hunter had not enclosed the stairs and had the porch glazed in instead of leaving them constantly exposed to the elements was quite beyond me. Like most things in this lost part of Devon everything seemed rather run down, faded and behind the times. I reached the bottom of the stairs that were terribly buckled and slightly leaning and I had to grip the hand rail for dear life. The porch was still full of tables and Windsor chairs with the table's candles all now lit for the evening. The candles glowed brightly at their tips, but appeared slightly transparent as they grew close to their black crooked wicks. I walked and meandered my way around the tables in the direction of the bar. The tables and glowing candles looked as if they were set for a crew of pirate ghosts: as if right this minute every table was full of spirits sat around enjoying old tales of smuggling and long lost voyages, and were about to order meals and drinks. It was as if everyone else could see these invisible beings apart from me. I looked out across into the lane which was covered in shadows of oak trees, with an owl hooting away. A few moths were fluttering about in the direction of a row of flaming torches, lit to mark the path from the bay to the inn. It was indeed a dark night, but the moon was its companion for the evening. I walked across to the door heading into the bar with the rocking chair still gently moving up and down, but with no one that I could see occupying it. I then remembered Mr Hunter's tale of the ill-fated young man who had once occupied room five. He had sat in this very same rocking chair that I was now studying. I could feel my mouth become dry and my throat tighten with fear, wondering what sort of night I would have in the same room.

*

The sound of merry fishermen was now much higher in pitch and brought me out of my depressed thoughts. I could definitely make out the sound of Billy coughing away and clearing his throat and it was, strangely, a rather comforting sound to know he was about. I moved from off the cold bewitched porch leaving the rocking chair to continue in its motion and entered a hot, smoky and almost steamy bar. Billy had taken up a seat on a bench by an open fire that was crackling away. Even though it was August it felt more like November down in the valley, thus the reason the fire was lit. Billy was still puffing away on his pipe, freshly filled with tobacco and had a pint of beer with a whippy top of froth. A few fishermen with caps on and long black and yellow coats were sat around small tables drinking pints and smoking. Four farm hands were all seated in an alcove playing what looked like poker, as there was an expanding pile of copper coins in the centre. The men appeared to be well focused on their game, with half-drunk glasses at their sides and ash trays smouldering. An old heavy sideboard behind them was covered in animal skulls; one of a roe deer with its antlers still attached and alongside what looked like the skull of a fox. A quiet man with glasses was sat opposite Billy reading a book, looking like he was finding it hard to focus, what with all the noise. Mr Hunter and a rather overdressed bar maid were behind the bar. Mr Hunter was at his work, busy cleaning glasses with a cloth with a red stripe embroidered round the bottom.

The bar maid was stooped half across the bar chatting up a shifty looking skipper, showing off her assets to their full advantage. She had a rather excitable laugh and her prey, the skipper, seemed to be lapping up her conversation and other things besides. I walked over to the bar in a shy fashion to speak to Mr Hunter, who greeted me warmly and offered me a drink. I asked for a small glass of sherry and took a seat next to Billy at the other end of the bench. Billy gave me a nod and a 'How do' but he was too busy enjoying his pipe to break off into conversation. I however, was sat in a pub full of old men, smoking, drinking and playing poker and I had to say I did not feel comfortable one little bit.

I decided to try and make conversation with Billy as he was sat on the same bench as me, and I wanted to try and distract myself from feeling so out of place. I turned round to Billy, who was cuddled up in the corner of the bench with his head nestled up against the wooden head rest. The fire crackled and spat away. The other man sat opposite us was now too engrossed in his book to notice us.

"Did you get Jacob settled down for the night in the barn?" I enquired to Billy, who looked towards me and sent a cloud of smoke into my face much to my annoyance.

"Oh ar. Jacob be alright in the barn for one evening. So long as he been fed and got some warm hay he be alright. I think he's got better accommodation than we have."

"At least it's only for tonight and we'll be on our way again in the morning," I said, trying to be cheerful and making sure Billy knew we had to be on our way first thing after breakfast. Billy looked at me with an irritated look and sound in his voice.

"Yes, yes me dear. We'll be going down tomorrow as soon as I had me bacon and eggs."

Mr Hunter suddenly approached us and put my sherry down on a small round table in front of us. "Thank you Mr Hunter," I said, trying to be polite, " That's very nice. Thank you."

Mr Hunter then bent over to us both and said in a very self-satisfied voice. "I have some nice trout that one of the farmers fished from up the river, if you would like that for your meal this evening? Or I have a nice lobster you could have?"

The very thought of a lobster made my stomach churn, so I quickly said before Billy could interject, "I'll have the trout, thank you Mr Hunter."

Billy thankfully seemed more than happy to have the lobster.

"Oh ar, I will have that nice lobster you got walking about in the kitchen. That will do well, thankye, and another pint to wash it down with. That would be grand."

Mr Hunter got out a little black book and wrote down our orders, repeating them back to us.

"Would you like a glass of wine with your meal Miss parfitt?"

Billy suddenly turned and looked at me in a most deep way. His eyes sparkled with intrigue at hearing my surname being mentioned.

"Yes thank you Mr Hunter. That would be lovely." I gave a smile to Billy, who was still studying me in a most strange and rather off-putting way.

"Very good then Miss" Mr Hunter responded, "I have laid up a table for you in the back room where you can enjoy a meal in peace. Will you be joining Miss Parfitt, Billy? I expect you would be happier out here wouldn't you?"

I was well pleased with Mr Hunter for trying to encourage Billy to stay in the bar. The very thought of seeing Billy devour a poor lobster made me feel sick. Plus sharing a meal with him would not exactly be a relaxing affair. We hardly knew each other and had only just been introduced.

"Oh ar. I will be happy here. Let Lady Edith enjoy a meal in peace."

I turned round to look at Billy, in shock at hearing my former title of Lady. It was a title I had not used or been addressed by in over twenty years. I noticed Billy had a wicked smirk across his face, and his eyes spoke to me of what he was thinking; *'I know who you are missy, you can't go fooling me no more.* Mr Hunter thankfully had not heard or chosen not to respond to Billy addressing me as Lady Edith. He departed through a door and into what I presumed was the inn's kitchen. There suddenly came an enormous groan from the alcove and a flutter and slam of cards being thrown on to the table. The man who had his back to me must have lost his poker game judging from the shifty but well pleased gentleman who was gathering the pile of coins and copper from the middle of the table towards his chest. The winner rubbed his hands together and scooped up the coins smirking at the others who all looked rather crestfallen and like they were all in need of another strong drink, (if they could afford it.) Billy had shuffled along the bench up close to me. He continued smoking his pipe and looked towards the wooden panelled wall opposite him, covered in old black and white photos of the inn dating back from 1910, 1917 and 1929, the years in which it had been in its hay day. Billy then spoke quietly, puffing out meandering clouds of smoke which trickled away up into the air until defusing into nothing.

"It's no good missy," Billy said still looking at the wall of past photos, his mouth gaping open like a fish and slightly twitching. "I know who you are! So you don't need to pretend any more. I thought as soon as I saw ye at the station this afternoon you had a familiar look about you. You got your brother's sad eyes. I've seen them eyes before, I said to myself and then as soon as old Hunter said your name I knew it was you!"

*

The game was up. I had been rumbled. There was no good in denying it. It would only make the situation worse. Billy Bath may have had the look of the Village Simpleton but he was a sharp, clever man and obviously never forgot a face. I was about to give him a response, but he spoke again.

"It's alright Missy. No need for you to worry. I'm not going to cause you any trouble. Your secret is safe with me. Mind you!" Billy put down his pipe and a trail of smoke came swirling and trailing down with the movement of his hand. He moved even closer to me, our hands almost touching. "I wouldn't go back if I was you. Best not go back Miss Edith. You only find trouble down there.

"My heart began to beat a little faster. My chest tightened like a clam shell and I could feel my lip slightly tremble.

"What do you mean Billy?" I said sounding worried. "I told you why I had to go down. I have a friend down there who's like a sister to me. She has a ten year old daughter, my goddaughter. I must find them and make sure they are well and safe."

Billy continued to look at me. His wicked grin had gone. His eyes were no longer filled with excitement of discovering my true identity. Instead he looked uneasy, almost afraid.

"I don't mean any disrespect to you Lady Edith. I remember both your father and mother. They were both very good to us farmers. Treated us like proper people. But…"

Billy's voice sounded husky and fearful again. He beckoned me closer to him, his voice almost a whisper, not wanting anyone to overhear us talking.

"You will find more than your friend and god daughter down there Miss Edith! I know what secret you've been keeping all these years. Believe me I do know what went on all those years ago between you and your brother. I know why you left. I can't say I blame you. There's a few small minded people down in that village who love a bit of gossip. They condemn anyone who's not like them."

Billy's words were not said in malice, nor to hurt me, but they were a warning. A warning I could not understand. I felt suddenly cold and my hands felt frozen as if all the warmth and feeling within me had left. The fire continued to burn and crackle but I felt no warmth or cheer from it. Billy reached over and patted my cold hand.

"You must do what you think is right of course. But I warn you. Our secrets have a nasty way of resurfacing. It's best to let the past go."

I gave a gulp and closed my trembling mouth, pursing my lips together. I tried to speak but my mouth felt dry.

My brain was spinning. I could not understand or have any idea exactly what Billy knew or thought he knew about Eddie and I. How had he come by such knowledge, if indeed he had learned the truth? Perhaps one of the servants had blabbed; disgruntled when I had been forced to dismiss them all. Yet I could not imagine who out of all the servants could have been so disloyal. Billy was just about to tell me more but we were interrupted by Mr Hunter; who came over to inform me that my table was ready. I looked over to Billy who was now sipping up the last drop of his pint before Mr Hunter brought him a new one.

I was ushered in through a side door by the bar and into a small parlour. The room enjoyed a Victorian fireplace with its elaborate mantel mirror hung over it. China, Toby jugs, sea shells gathered from the cove along with a few grey ammonites and other fossils lay scattered on the mantel piece. An old black Bakelite wireless was perched on a side table. The walls were covered in a heavy patterned green paper with many old black and white photographs sat decaying in black heavy frames. Two old fraying arm chairs were sat by the fireplace and in the centre of the room under an electric green glass china lamp was a round table covered in a grey table cloth with china, glass and cutlery set for dinner for one.

"Do sit down, Miss Parfitt, I will fill your glass."

Mr Hunter was very attentive. He poured me my wine which splashed into the glass. He lit a candle in the centre of the table and then went out of the room. The parlour was musty with its rather faded décor, but it was peaceful, apart from the buzz of men laughing and the sound of that common looking barmaid drumming up trade, flaunting herself in front of the old sailors and farmers. There was an occasional sound of pints being pulled from behind the bar and the clinking of glasses and beer mugs. I sat sipping my wine; the clear gold coloured liquid refreshed my throat and helped to relax my mind, which was overactive and full of Billy's warning.

*

I wished Mr Hunter had not come along at that moment. I wanted to ask Billy how he knew so much about my family. What had he meant when he said I would find more than Thelma and Emma down in Lynrock? What did he mean about my past resurfacing? More importantly, how did he know about Eddie? I continued to sip my wine and move my fork back and forth until quickly repositioning it when Mr Hunter came in with two plates in his hand.

"Hear you are, Miss Parfitt, can't get trout much fresher than this!"

He placed the larger of the plates down in the centre of the table setting. The plate was slightly oval with a pale blue pattern around the rim. My rainbow trout looked lovely; though the trout's face seemed to look at me with the same expression that Billy had had when he found out who I was. The trout's eye looked terribly sad and forlorn. My fish was garnished with a light summer salad and slices of fresh lemon. The other plate was actually a small bowl of freshly made, crispy golden chips. The smell of the chips was divine! I had forgotten how hungry I felt.

"Is there anything else you would like?" Mr Hunter enquired. "I will go and get you some vinegar for your chips. There is some salt on the table."

I thought for a moment, and then said, "No thank you Mr Hunter Just the vinegar. The meal looks and smells delicious."

Mr Hunter left the room again. I picked up the salt pot and dusted my fish with some sea salt. I then squeezed and drizzled the lemon over both the fish and the salad. Mr Hunter then returned in with a brown bottle of vinegar which he placed on the table.

"I do hope you enjoy your meal. Would you like me to put the wireless on?"

"Oh yes, thank you Mr Hunter. I do like to have some music on during my meals."

"Yes I do too." Mr Hunter agreed as he went over to the Bakelite wireless with chrome detailing in the centre of its circle. He flicked a switch and I could hear the sound of the wireless heating up with a slight humming noise gaining in volume until the ghostly sound of Mussorgsky's 'A Night On Bald Mountain' came on.

"Well I will leave you to enjoy your meal," Mr Hunter announced, starting to leave the room. "Please do ring the bell by the fireplace if you need or require anything else."

"Thank you Mr Hunter." I was desperately hungry and picked up my cutlery as he gave a nod of his head before leaving the room and returning to the noisy bar. My meal was indeed as good as it looked. The trout was cooked beautifully and had been gutted extremely well by Mr Hunter with very few bones. My meal and the experience of dining in this reassuring parlour seemed curiously relaxing. Mr Hunter came in twice during my meal to top up my wine for me and take away my empty plates. I did leave a few chips in their bowl but there were only a few. Mr Hunter returned a little later with a small glass dish of summer fruits with a scoop of golden, Devonshire clotted cream which I very much enjoyed. Having cream was a real luxury!

I then returned to the bar for a brandy before turning in. The grandfather clock chimed ten o'clock as Mr Hunter gave me my brandy which I sipped gently in contrast to when I had gulped the brandy down from my flask back in Wiltshire. The fire in the red brick fireplace was now dying down and there was only just a slight red glow. The poker players had left for the evening, apart from one who was right out of it. He lay sprawled across the bar in a drunken, depressed sleep. The bar maid had gone for the evening and the man who had had his head in his book had also gone up to his room. Mr Hunter was going around the tables collecting his customer's empty glasses. He came along with two of his fingers pinching the sides of two glasses and wiping the beer-stained table up with a wet cloth.

I looked up at him, still clutching my brandy glass in my hand and asked, "Mr Hunter has Billy retired for the evening?" Mr Hunter continued with his wiping and put the two glasses he was clutching onto the bar.

"He has Miss Edith, yes. He said to tell you he hoped to be on his way with you by eleven tomorrow morning, if you are agreeable?"

"Oh yes that's fine. Perfect. Thank you Mr Hunter."

I drank the rest of my brandy and took the glass up to the bar. "Thank you Mr Hunter that was lovely. It has been a most peaceful evening."

Mr Hunter beamed at me and asked if I needed anything else.

"No thank you Mr Hunter. I think I will go up now and get an early night ready for tomorrow."

Mr Hunter removed my brandy glass from the bar.

"Very well then, breakfast will be served at eight-thirty. I hope you have a pleasant night's sleep."

I thanked Mr Hunter and then left the quiet bar, leaving only the beaten slumbering poker player and the busy Mr Hunter to their own devices.

*

Out on the porch it felt very autumnal. Most of the candles were still glowing but their flames were becoming erratic and one or two had been blown out. I crept along the creaking porch, passing the haunted looking tables. Outside an owl was still hooting away and there was the sound of cracking branches and moving brambles from rabbits hopping about. I reached the wooden stairs and went up gripping on to the rail. I finally reached the deserted landing and digging out my key from my pocket reached my room. I put the key in to the keyhole and rattled it around until I heard the lock open with a sharp clicking noise. I pushed the door to room five open with a terrible creak and closed it gently. My room still felt terribly cold and rather damp like a church crypt. I went over to the window to pull the moth eaten curtains. The view outside looked down into the inn's garden which was surrounded with shrubs. A large mulberry tree and the great oaks looked deformed and even more sinister in the darkness. They seemed to enclose the garden like a prison. A darkened shadowy path rambled down out of the garden and past the side of the full rushing stream, which I thought must run down into the cove. It would make a rather nice walk in the day light I thought, but not something I would care to do at night. My imagination would run away with itself.

The lawn of the garden looked like it was covered in mole hills. Great mounds of earth were piled up in various places along the grass, like freshly dug graves. A few splintered old benches and tables were shrouded in secrecy and mystery. The whole garden looked like something out of a dark fairy tale and the bushes seemed to twitch and shiver as if something or someone was watching and waiting, ready for the hour of midnight to arrive before creeping out onto the lawn and scaling the inn's walls. The creatures of the night would first have to battle with the mole army. They were waiting in their dug outs, prepared like troops to protect the inn from invaders.

*

I pulled back the curtains to shut out the darkness and felt my way over to the light switch, which I found and put on. I had not realised how faded and depressed the wallpaper was; all the pink lilies and yellow flag irises had lost their colour and vibrancy. In various places damp had seeped into the room leaving stains the colour of vinegar smudged on the wallpaper.

I went over to the Victorian radiator and pressed my hands along the top. To my surprise and relief the heater was warm and getting warmer. So at least my room would soon warm up. Outside the owl was continuing to hoot and was now joined by what I thought sounded like the flights of bats. I began to prepare myself for bed. I undressed, still shivering, and put on my night dress. I shivered my way to the bathroom and gingerly crept into the room, making sure I would not find Billy sat on the toilet. I was scared enough as it was without seeing Billy with his trousers down!

Thankfully Billy had long departed to bed as I could hear his snoring from the door which led into his room, which I carefully made sure was locked. The Bathroom was like something out of a museum; it still contained its old Edwardian plumbing and fixtures and an obsolete basin covered in cracks and chips longer in use. The toilet roll was just sheets of old newspaper and I hovered over the loo not wanting to sit down on the wooden seat. After surviving the ordeal of the bathroom I crept back into my room to wash my hands and carry out my normal routine of washing and brushing my teeth. I used the wash basin with a new jug of tipped water that Mr Hunter had placed there whilst I must have been having my dinner.

I sat on the end of the bed. It felt a little damp and uncomfortable. I read my bible for a few minutes. I said a few prayers, which I had to shorten as I was so cold and desperately wanted the warmth of sheets around me. I nervously crawled into bed which felt like an ice bucket but the sheets did look clean, so that was something. The room looked so unfamiliar, so full of shadows, apertures and cracks in the walls. The ceiling was a vale of cobwebs with black wooden beams running overhead. My pillow was terribly stiff and felt like I had my head resting on a sack of potatoes. I led in bed listening to the creaking and groaning noises of banging doors, creaking floor boards and shuddering walls below me. I could make out shadows and patches of darkness all around, as if the darkness was enclosing me, reaching ever closer until at last it would engulf me. Had it been on a night like this that that young man whom Mr Hunter mentioned had died? Perhaps he too had crawled into this very bed and lay beneath these very sheets, feeling tense and beginning to feel pressure and pain begin to build up in his chest. Had he tried to call for help, or had he met his death unaware of what was about to strike him, giving him no warning? Outside the breeze had died down. There was only the sound of the hooting owl and bats fluttering about outside my window. I thought of how remote the inn was placed in the valley. I imagined years ago how smugglers and pirates had rowed over choppy moonlit seas in the dead of night to the cove at the base of the cliffs, probably arguing over loot and treasure, before smuggling their bounty and barrels of rum into the cave. I could just about hear the crashing of waves rolling into the cove. My thoughts again wondered back to the former guest in this room, the young man who had only just arrived and had died only a few hours later. Mr Hunter had said how troubled he had been, sitting out on the porch in the rocking chair looking worried. Perhaps the young man was so full of worry and trouble that it had hastened his death quicker than it should have come. I pondered on who he had been waiting for on the porch.

*

Realising that I would get no sleep brooding over this sad story I aggressively adjusted and hit my pillow trying to get my head comfortable. No adjustment or manoeuvre made any difference. My neck still felt incredibly stiff and painful. My hands twitched about, draped across the top of my sheets. I lay still, listening and thinking. I now began to think about the present and what had been said in the bar. I could not understand how Billy knew so much about Eddie and I. How had he known that Eddie and I had argued and that he had run away. Or had he just put two and two together? Perhaps he had heard gossip from one of the servants, or heard tales from the fishermen down by the harbour. Billy had certainly not been in my parent's employment. A tenant yes, but he was certainly not a servant. Mother would never have allowed Billy in the house with his colourful language.

Whatever the case I was determined that in the morning I would get to the bottom of it. As soon as we had had our breakfast and left the inn, and Jacob was safely a little up the road in the valley, I would have it out with Billy. I would find out exactly what he knew or perhaps what he thought he knew. Assuming that I made it through the night and I was not about to be room five's second victim!

Chapter 18
The Last Bottle of Mineral Water

I awoke at seven in the morning with my head feeling like it had been put in the stocks all night. Thankfully however, I had made it safely through the night and had not suffered a heart attack. I still felt terribly tense. I hit my pillow like it was a punch bag as I slithered out of bed, knowing it was the cause of my bad neck. The sunlight was trying desperately to creep in through the fine curtains and outside I could hear the stream rushing past and the sound of chattering birds. I headed towards the bathroom door, feeling bemused and still half asleep with my feet frozen solid. I opened the door of the bathroom and rubbed my eyes to revive them as I tottered in. I was suddenly awoken from my slumbering state, my eyes now wide open with alarm and my ears shuddering by my own frantic scream, as in the bathroom I found Billy half-dressed and sat on the toilet! I rushed out like a frantic moth and slammed the door with such a force that the whole room shook and a cloud of dust and string of cob webs descended from the ceiling to fall on to my unmade bed. I could hear Billy next door yelling out "Sorry missy! I nearly done now. I got trouble with my haemorrhoids again. Bloody things, they get so itchy!"

I pulled a face of revulsion and felt rather sick at the thought of Billy and his bowel problems. I shouted back in an irritated and desperate voice, "I really don't want to know about that Billy! Just do what you have to do and then knock on the door when you're done."

Billy replied with a "Right-O." I sat on the bed feeling stressed, shattered from an uncomfortable night and now traumatised from the sight of seeing Billy sat on the lavatory. I attempted to relax my neck by rubbing it gently and circling my shoulders. I stayed like that for some time, continuing to un-grind my neck and listening to the sound of the birds singing along with the roaring of the stream, full from days of the torrential rain. Listening to the sound of the stream rushing past returned my mind back to Thelma and Emma. If we had not been delayed I would have been down with them by now, looking after and supporting them. I said my morning prayers and prayed that help would be given to all the villagers of Lynrock, but especially Thelma and Emma and that I would be with them both this time tomorrow.

My prayers were then interrupted with a knocking sound from the front door of my room and the voice of Mr Hunter from outside in the corridor. I grabbed my night dress and flung it round me, then checked my hair which was reasonably tidy in the mirror before unlocking the door and peering out. Blinking and looking rather worse for ware, I came face to face with the sight of Mr Hunter cradling a jug of warm water.

"A very good morning to you Miss Parfitt! I hope you slept well? No ghost I hope? Just to say I have brought you up your morning's hot water."

I still felt dazed and was rather taken aback with Mr Hunter's cheerful talk and expression.

"Oh! Oh yes thank you, Mr Hunter. No, no ghost. If you could just pass the jug to me I will take it."

Mr Hunter passed me over the porcelain jug, warm with hot water.

"I can see you want to get on quietly," Mr Hunter considerately said, "so I will leave you to it. Breakfast is at eight thirty."

"Yes thank you very much Mr Hunter, I will see you later then."

Mr Hunter smiled, bowed his head and plodded down the bare corridor sending dust to erupt from off the splintered floorboards. As he walked the most terrible noises of creaks and groans came from the ancient floor, as Mr Hunter navigated his way towards the death trap of stairs leading back down to the porch. I shut the door, headed over to the dresser and poured my hot water into the basin. I opened up the soap dish and prepared my flannel for a refreshing wash. I was however becoming desperate for the lavatory but dreaded entering after Billy. I hopped about on one leg for a few moments in a shivery state and I hoped there was no one listening to me from downstairs as the floorboards sounded like they were buckling due to my activity. I sat down on my bed again and crossed my legs together, praying Billy had finished and any minute would knock on the door to give me permission to go in next. The sound of the stream flowing past seemed to have got louder in these last few minutes and was making my wait to relieve myself even more urgent. In the end I had no option. I rushed over to the bathroom door walking unevenly across the mismatch of cold floor boards, and banged frantically on the door.

"Billy! Billy! Look Billy I am sorry but I must use the bathroom, I have to go now!"

I paused and put my ear to the door but heard not a sound from inside. I readjusted my face and put my ear to another part of the flaking door, trying to gauge if Billy was finished or still on the lavatory. I waited but could hear nothing, only the continuous rush of water from that flaming stream. By now I was unable to keep my patience.

"Billy! I am sorry but you have been in there long enough! I need to use the bathroom." I now was hammering on the door in utter desperation. I called out to Billy in a high pitched squeal, fearing there would be another flood any minute.

"Billy! Billy!"

In the end my patience failed me and I called out in desperation now nearly about to burst, "That's it Billy, I am coming in!"

With that I put my hand round the tarnished round door handle and pushed open the door.

"Oh that wretched man," I thought as I got into the bathroom only to find Billy not there, but banging about in his room next door. I rushed over to his connecting door and locked it. In a flash I rushed over to the lavatory, I had no time to worry about hygiene and check the seat was clean after Billy, (it was much too late for that). I sat down and felt instant relief.

After the ordeal of finally reaching the lavatory the rest of the morning went reasonably well. I had a wash and got myself dressed again in the outfit I had arrived in the day before. I pulled back the curtains to see a bright and cheerful morning. The sun looked a bit watery but the sky was clearing and the dew was slowly disappearing from the grass. A gathering of sparrows and starlings were stuttering about on the benches which were covered in bread. I presumed that Mr Hunter had thrown it out for them. The garden did not look so creepy in the daylight. There was no demon lurking between the spotted laurel bushes and ferns. Only visible were the birds and the mole hills; the moles, by now would have retreated deep down into their tunnels and passages until the sun had gone down and the safety of night returned. I put on a little make up and tried to make myself look refreshed rather than appearing like I had lain awake half the night. My watch read the time of eight-twenty, so I thought I had better head down for breakfast and try and get Billy motivated for moving on after breakfast. I picked up my handbag and collected my key (with the number five painted in a white number on the wooden tag), opened my door and proceeded out into the chilly corridor. After I had closed the door and was satisfied that my room was secure, I walked down the passage feeling the cold breeze swirling up from the stairs. No wonder my room was so cold, with the staircase heading down into an open and exposed porch. All the other doors along the passage were closed and I could hear no sign of life or activity. A few of the doorframes were badly scarred and chipped. Great heavy curtains of cobwebs draped from the crevasses of the doorframes. The walls were scarred from grey, flaking and chipped paint. Old brass candle holders were still secured to the walls. There was one outside every door, although I doubt the holders had held candles for what looked like many years. I reached the wooden stairs and gripped the handrail as I stepped down. With one foot at a time I plodded down the flight until reaching the safety of the porch. The porch, like the garden, looked more inviting today. All the wooden tables had been cleaned and wiped over. The depleted candles had been removed and their silver stands polished. The rocking chair was no longer rocking and sat by the steps heading down to the path looking silent and still. A few terracotta pots full of pink and purple lavender were grouped about in various places by the steps and I had to admit I had failed to notice them when I arrived the day before.

*

In fact the whole inn looked far more pleasing and attractive than it had done late the previous evening. I imagined it had been nerves and the disappointment of being delayed from reaching Lynrock. Plus the fact I was still full of anxiety about Thelma and Emma and not arriving at The Chough's Nest Hotel the day I had arranged with Mrs Barns. I just hoped that she had not given my room to someone else. I looked out over the banister of the porch and surveyed the muddy road that Billy and I had travelled down the day before. I looked up to the barn we had passed, where Jacob had spent the night. He had probably been in more warmth and comfort than I had been. The family of ducks were waddling and arguing down the lane towards the inn. The oak and ash trees swayed gently in the morning breeze, their leaves almost whispering as their branches turned and shifted. The ferns rustled shaking off the morning dew and I was aware of the sound of dripping from the gutters by the side of the porch and the continuous rush of water from the stream. I took some deep breaths, breathing in the clear, fresh sea air which unblocked my sinuses and refreshed my skin. The family of duck's quickly rushed past, all talking and arguing with each other. They were heading down the path, past the enclosed garden, down the winding, uneven lane down to the cove. I could have stayed and watched this sleepy lane all day but I knew I could not. Nor could my tummy stop from rumbling with hunger for my breakfast. I was really craving some salty bacon and eggs, a rack of toast and some refreshing coffee. I quickly went in through the front door of the inn and went into the bar which also looked much brighter and cheerful. Although the daylight revealed only too well the cobwebs and dust covering many of the antiques. I passed an old fashioned copper warming pan hanging on the wall and a shelf full of Toby jugs, one of which I noticed was a rather large mug with the face of Edward III and another rather more carefree face of Charles I. The model ships were still sat in a long row opposite the bar, their rigging and sails were covered in dust and webs, along with an occasional dead, shrivelled up spider with their legs rapped round their bodies. The dead skulls of animals on the sideboard however still looked rather macabre and morbid for first thing in the morning.

*

The bar was reasonably peaceful. I could hear the sound of cooking and activity from behind the swinging door of the kitchen. Mr Hunter's voice was booming out instructions to someone. I went down and sat by the still and dead fireplace. It was covered with brass and copper jugs, kettles, old rusted horseshoes and a long copper hunting horn placed on hooks on the wall above. I noticed an old, sad looking deer head peering down at me from high up on the chimney breast. I hated heads of poor animals hanging on the wall. It always made feel very depressed and I was glad, Mother and Father never had them at home.

I sat in the peace and quiet thinking carefully about Thelma and Emma. I might have to bring them back home with me if their home was flooded out. I wondered how many other villagers had been affected and what buildings had been brought down. I knew the Bath Hotel had been swept away, or most of it had. Cynthia and her husband had stayed there. I could imagine Cynthia moving about the hotel like she owned the place, bossing the staff about. I too had been in the hotel. I had often gone into the hotel's Palm Court for morning coffee and cake with Mother before she died. Later, Eddie always found time to come with me. He would often sit always at the same table by a palm tree, and peruse the papers going through the court circulars and reading bits of interesting news. Sometimes he would bring his unopened post with him from home and read out letters from friends and relations. That time seemed like a life time ago now. It seemed a completely different age it was hard even to believe I had been so carefree and happy. Back then I had been utterly oblivious to matters of money, finance and struggling to pay bills or having to make ends meet like most people did. Mind, I soon made up for it after that. After October of 1929 everything changed.

*

Suddenly Mr Hunter loomed over me with a cloth balanced over his arm.

"Oh I am sorry Mr Hunter, I was miles away," I said apologetically. Mr Hunter was undeterred and smiled warmly.

"That's quite all right Miss Edith. Just to inform you that your breakfast is ready for you. Billy has had his, and he is on his way to check Jacob and get him ready for when you depart. If you would like to have your breakfast at the bar this morning Miss Edith, I am afraid the parlour feels like the Arctic." I was taken back by Billy's swift action and was pleased that he was making an effort to be ready and early to leave.

"Oh that's alright Mr Hunter. That's no trouble, when you're ready lead the way."

Mr Hunter escorted me up to the bar and helped me upon to a high bar stool which thankfully had a back to it, as I never enjoyed sitting on stools even when I was a child. I placed my handbag up on the bar and Mr Hunter passed me a copy of The Times. I took a peak at it while I waited for my English breakfast to come in. The paper was full of the problems in Egypt, with Colonel Gamal Abdel Nasser putting forward statements to abolish the constitution and prepare the way to make Egypt a republic. There were still reviews most of them glowing about some new American Western film, endless political arguments and debates, and news about plans for the Coronation next year.

I found the paper so depressing. There was no cheerful news, always something to worry about. I closed up the paper and neatly folded it, placing it to one side to clear a space for my bacon and eggs, which I was so much looking forward to. I looked ahead at the shelves behind the bar. They gleamed with polish from Mr Hunter's efforts the previous night. A curved mirror was set in the middle of the back wall which was covered in a royal blue wallpaper with gold coloured leaves and foliage, all of which had faded terribly and were peeling off in places, due to an array of old beer mats and wine labels plastered over it. Shelves ran either side and in front of the mirror covered with neatly placed sherry glasses in rows of six and heavy and solid looking tumblers and brandy glasses with delicate looking stems. Several bottles were bracketed to the wall upside down with a pump and stopper on securing their necks. There were bottles and barrels of ales and stout, with old wines in green bottles. A container of Guinness was on the end of the sideboard along with a soda syphon. There was a reasonable array of green, blue, bronze and gold coloured liquids and bottles, along with rows of beer glasses, mugs and tankers hanging from above the bar, with a crazed and rusty bell to ring for closing. A few Toby Jugs decorated the rest of the available spaces on the shelves along with two crystal decanters. As my eyes scanned the shelves of bottles all reflected by the mirror set on the wall behind them, I suddenly spotted one bottle in particular. I knew it very well and it brought back the past to me. The bottle in question, was a curved rather tall and slender bottle of Lynrock mineral water, distilled from Lynrock by my father's old factory which he had built long before Edward and I were born. The bottle looked a bit dusty and almost a bit out of place amongst the other bottles of brandy, liquors and spirits.

*

Mr Hunter appeared tottering in with a large tray of what looked like my English breakfast. It looked too perfect to be true. On the tray was a silver toast rack of brown crusty toast. Next to that was a glass pot of marmalade with a glass domed lid and a spoon, a china butter dish with a small slab of golden butter. A pot of coffee and a milk jug were also present along with a cup, saucer and sugar bowl. The smell from the tray was like heaven. Though it was strange it did not smell like the normal aroma of bacon and eggs. Mr Hunter placed the tray down with a thud on the bar, causing a clatter from the saucer and its cup. I was so excited and my face lit up with delight at the prospect of tasting Devonshire bacon. I was just about to ask him for some HP sauce to accompany my bacon, when he placed a hand on the polished silver plate warmer and removed it.

I looked down at my breakfast. There on the plate was not bacon, eggs and a sausage, but rather a bowl of what looked like wallpaper paste!

Mr Hunter looked proud and delighted. "Your breakfast is served Miss Edith!"

He spoke with such pride and delight. My face however had dropped with disappointment and my mouth had gaped open, rather like that of the trout I had eaten the night before.

"Oh! Mr Hunter It looks…?" I paused and tried to pull myself together and to hide my child like disappointment.

"This does look nice. I have not seen so much toast on a rack before, how nice to have such a nice helping of butter."

"My porridge is the best in these parts Miss Edith, everyone raves about it. I did think about doing you an English fry up but I thought you would probably want something light and warming for your journey today. Billy polished off most of the bacon earlier this morning."

"Did he now!" I snarled back with gritted teeth at Mr Hunter. *Trust bloody Billy to get a cooked breakfast and I get a bowl of wallpaper* paste, I thought to myself. Mr Hunter poured my coffee and then said in a happy manner, "You enjoy your breakfast now Miss Edith. You have a long journey ahead of you."

Mr Hunter scampered through the swinging door back into the kitchen and left me to gulp down my porridge. *How on earth did this porridge become so famous?* I thought. I steered my spoon around the bowl and scooped up some of the lumpy, whitish, gluey mixture onto my spoon. I was about to taste it but let the helping slowly fall off the spoon and plop back into the bowl.

I decided to try and make the best of it. Perhaps the porridge tasted better than it looked. I spooned another helping up and tasted Mr Hunter's most famous tasty porridge. After gulping it down as best I could, I quickly took a slug of coffee to help keep the mixture down. Mr Hunter's porridge must have been famous around these parts for all the wrong reasons. Oh it really was disgusting! Parts of the porridge had great chunks of oats left in which I nearly choked on during my second attempt to try it again. I took another gulp of coffee, spluttering as I drank it so quickly. I realised that it was time to take matters into my own hands. Making sure the bar was empty and I could hear Mr Hunter cracking on with errands in the kitchen, I scooped up my porridge bowl that was still a little warm and carried it over to the window where the poker players had played last night. I looked out into the lane. I could see up ahead the barn door was ajar where Billy was preparing Jacob. The ducks were marching back up the lane. The coast was clear! There were to be no witnesses to my deed. I put down my bowl on the chipped windowsill and pulled the window lock, and managing to un stick the window from the catch. The window gracefully swung open, to reveal underneath outside a bed of thick brambles covered in pinkish, white flowers. A lot of bindweed with its heart shaped leaves and white trumpet flowers also made an excellent camouflage around the remaining spaces of soil and had started to climb up the wall. I turned around and looked back towards the bar to check the coast was clear, before picking up my bowl and shaking it hard outside the window but as close to the wall as possible. The porridge would hopefully run down at the back of the bed and be well hidden by the bindweed and brambles. The lumpy mixture trickled and slid out and off the rim of the bowl and down on to the bed. I shook the bowl repeatedly until only a few little specs and small trail were left along one side of the bowl. I quickly rushed back over to the bar and put the bowl down on the tray, not wishing to leave any evidence of porridge in any place it shouldn't have been. I scampered over to the window and quickly forced the window closed. By the time Mr Hunter returned to me I had cleaned round the bowl so as not to show any sign of the porridge being poured out. I ate all my toast, along with a good quantity of butter and marmalade, and finished all my coffee. My breakfast tray was virtually wiped clean. Mr Hunter looked absolutely delighted at me and gave a heartening glow of a smile. "My word Miss Edith, you look as if you enjoyed that! I told you my porridge was special did I not?"

Mr Hunter chuckled and sounded full of self-assurance.

"Oh yes Mr Hunter" I said in a rather gushing and over the top manner. "It really was delicious. Your porridge… Well I don't think I have ever had porridge like it before. I can quite see why it is so famous around here."

I thought I rather over did the praise but I did not want to upset Mr Hunter even though his porridge was disgusting. He started to pick up the tray, before quickly adding in a pleasing and happy way, "There's a drop of porridge left on the stove if you would like it Miss Edith? It won't be any trouble to heat it up for you?"

I sounded panicky, and quickly said, "No! No Mr Hunter. I am absolutely full. I so enjoyed my first helping. I just can't eat any more."

Mr Hunter smiled, "Oh well you can have some more the next time you stay!"

Mr Hunter picked up the tray and left through his swinging door.

"I can't wait for that Mr Hunter," I said under my breath in a dry, sarcastic tone. I continued reading through The Times again until he reappeared and started tinkering about in the bar. My eyes watched Mr Hunter about his work, dusting bottles and cleaning glasses. My eyes then returned to the bottle that had reminded me of Father and of home.

"Mr Hunter could I buy a bottle of Lynrock mineral water I would like to have something to drink on the journey going down?"

Mr Hunter turned round and scanned his shelves of bottles and glasses like a librarian scans their bookshelf. He finally placed his hand on the bottle I requested and brought it down from the shelf, giving it a wipe and polish with his tea towel. I had not had a drink of my father's mineral water since I had left Lynrock in 1929. I had missed its clear freshness. As Mr Hunter cleaned the bottle he gave a deep sad sigh and looked far away as if his mind was somewhere else.

"It's a terrible shame about the factory isn't it?" Mr Hunter looked suddenly crestfallen and lost. He put down the bottle onto the bar next to my handbag.

"What do you mean Mr Hunter? What's a shame?"

"Oh do forgive me Miss Edith. You would not have heard or seen it in the paper yet!" Mr Hunter inhaled another deep breath trying not to let his emotions get the better of him.

"The whole factory was washed away by the flood! The whole place is completely gone! First thing the torrent swept away. The poor clerk was in his office there at the time, working late apparently."

I slightly shifted in my chair and leaned forward in shock, feeling a little light headed.

"But my friend, the friend I have to find she used to work there as a secretary! She said she had been made redundant and was moving to a tea room to work!"

I felt rather giddy now and I was gripping the polished bar surface, my nails digging into the wood. Yet Mr Hunter gave a reassuring shake of his head and he came a little closer to me.

"You must not worry Miss Edith. It was the head clerk who was working late. He had a wife and a child in the village poor chap. I shouldn't think they would ever find his body. His wife's taken it pretty hard they say."

I was of course so glad and relieved that Thelma had not stayed on to work late before she left the factory, and this probably meant that both Thelma and Emma were safe. Thelma being made redundant had probably saved her. The other clerk had to be poor Alexander, it had to be him! I felt a little teary at the thought of him working late, hunched over his desk trying to sort out the book keeping. To distract myself I reached over to my bag to get out my purse. Mr Hunter carried on talking. "Of course the factory was in financial trouble. It had not done well for years. That's why Alexander was working late. He was asked to stay behind until the early hours to get the books ready to be examined by the accountant. Only thing is I suppose, it would have all happened so fast. Alexander would not have known anything about it."

Sadly I did not think that was the case. Before I had left Wiltshire, the night of hearing about the disaster, I had dreamed of a clerk sat in a wooden office. He had been working away at his books, then all of a sudden he heard a terrible roaring sound. In my dream Alexander had not had time to escape. He had looked around the room looking so frightened wondering what to do, when the wall of his office broke open and a wall of water came rushing in on top of him. As Alexander cried out a distorted cry, I too had tried to cry out. Only somehow nothing came. No sound or word would come out of my mouth, and it was at this desperate moment that I suddenly awoke.

I got out my purse and fingered about looking for the correct money. Mr Hunter waved his hand at me and said, "No Miss Edith. You can have this bottle. Somehow it seems wrong to ask for money for it."

I was grateful for Mr Hunter's generosity and thanked him.

We both said not a word for a few moments, both of us feeling rather deflated and wondering how many other people had been killed. I reassured myself that Thelma and Emma were now safe as their home was high up on Neptune Hill. Thelma had probably not had chance to move into their new flat above Sally's tea room yet, (she was never a well organised person), I did feel very guilty for feeling so pleased that she had been nowhere near the factory, but felt wretched for poor Alexander's widow and her child. Outside I could hear the sound of the ducks quacking away again which broke our silence. A black bird was singing in an ash tree opposite the window where I had disposed of my porridge. Even that I now felt guilty for doing. I should have eaten it and been grateful for it. I then spoke quietly in a tiny voice to Mr Hunter, still feeling guilty for my complaints and grumbles.

"Thank you for the bottle Mr Hunter. It's almost like an artefact now."

It also dawned on me that yet another part of my family's history and heritage had been removed. The factory that my father had started up from nothing, which had boomed and been so successful up until the war, was now all but gone. The only comforting thought I could muster was that at least my father's factory had not been declared bankrupt. That was one piece of shame that my father and indeed I had been spared. But that was no comfort for Alexander's wife.

Mr Hunter also came out of his slumbering thoughts and moved along the bar to the till and gave it a dust, trying to find something to distract him from his own depressed thoughts, until he suddenly said, "It's the last of its kind that bottle. There won't ever be another made again. Not now with the factory destroyed. You have the very last bottle of mineral water."

Chapter 19
A Hurled Lobster

By nine-thirty Billy and I were ready to leave Hunter's Inn. Billy had prepared Jacob and got the cart ready to go again which had been sheltering in the 'lean to' around the back. Mr Hunter kindly brought down my packed case from my room and placed it on the porch next to the rocking chair which was once again strangely rocking.

I was relieved that we were finally about to get underway. The delay had been unexpected but it was just one of those things. I only hoped the army vehicle that had crashed and blocked the lane down into Lynrock had been removed, or once again we would be delayed. Mr Hunter and I shared a few parting words while he handed back my ration book and I settled the bill with him, which I thought was reasonable.

"I expect you will be glad to be at your journey's end to day Miss Edith?" Mr Hunter said as he passed me my bill. I neatly folded and placed it in my handbag. "I would think by the now the road would be clearer. Mind you I have told Billy to take extra care, as there are so many trees down in a place or two and still a remarkable lot of water on the roads."

"Don't worry Mr Hunter, I am sure we will be kept safe. Jacob seems a very steady and capable horse."

"Oh indeed he is," Mr Hunter warmly agreed. "Billy treats that horse like a child. I think he greatly misses his nephew. That was a sad business. Then of course he lost his farm hand Phillip, he became the son Billy never had you know?"

My conversation with Mr Hunter was then abruptly halted. Billy came thumping in with his heavy boots clogged up with mud and wearing army green socks which went up over his trousers nearly reaching up to his knees. Billy had his cap on and his pipe was once again glued to his hand.

"You ready then missy? We'd best be off and try and get you down for lunch time."

Billy muttered and grunted a few words to our host then plodded out on to the porch and down up into the cart. I turned back round to Mr Hunter and stretched out my hand to thank him for his service. He took my hand and shook it limply.

"Do come again Miss Edith. It would be a privilege to welcome you back and accommodate you. I hope everything was to your satisfaction."

I thought for a few moments, and would have loved to have said that if I came next time I would love a cooked breakfast, but I thought better of it and decided to be polite.

"Yes thank you Mr Hunter. Everything has been very nice. You have a lovely spot here. If I come again I should love to walk down to the cove."

Mr Hunter seemed delighted and sounded rather astonished that a customer wanted to come back.

"You would? Oh well Miss Edith you say the word and I will prepare your room for you. It would be a privilege to escort you down to the cove next time on your return. It would be no trouble. I would be glad of the company. Although this inn looks like it's the most wonderful place to live in it can be very lonely and desolate during the winter, when all the trees are bare and roads so quiet. The dark evenings draw in so quickly. Plus the constant storms and sea frets that come in are quite depressing. Do you know this winter I went for nearly two whole months without hardly seeing a soul apart from Billy and the farmer up the road."

So it was agreed that I would indeed return to Hunter's Inn whether I really wanted to or not. Hunter's Inn would be perfect if a little money could be spent on it. If one did it up. But with so few guests and with constant hikes in prices I imagine that Mr Hunter was only just able to get by and keep going. We said our farewells to Mr Hunter and I wandered out of the bar with my handbag and clutching the bottle of mineral water under my arm. The sun was still rather watery and the sky looked a bit overcast overhead. It was still relatively mild and not cold. The whole valley seemed still and void of activity. Even the ducks no longer spoke out. The stream was still running past and the rocking chair to the side of me was still gently rocking away up and down. I looked up and down the porch, observing the lonely tables and Windsor chairs. From above I could hear water trickling down a drain pipe and the sound of a closing window from upstairs. I looked down to the rough floorboards to locate my case which seemed to have been moved. I looked out into the lane where Jacob was standing to attention, swinging his tail from side to side and giving a few snorts. His coat looked like gold silk all beautifully brushed with a shine to it, Billy certainly took great care of his horse.

Three empty milk churns were placed in the back of the cart along with my weather beaten case which Billy must have placed in the back for me. I stepped off the porch and onto the path which was a little muddy but mostly dry, due to the protection of the porch. Billy was sat up on his seat with the reins in his hands looking paused ready for the off. He offered me a hand up, with the familiar pipe placed in his mouth. I took Billy's wiry hands, still rough and rather dirty looking, and propelled myself up on to the seat. I was careful to pass Billy my bottle first, which he placed down by his feet of all places. I sat down on the seat and shuffled about before putting my handbag down and then leaning my bottle against it to prevent it from getting broken and also to get it away from Billy, who knowing him would probably stand on it and smash it.

"You took your time! What on earth kept you! Thought you said you wanted to be off quick?"

Billy sounded rather disgruntled and impatient with me.

"I am sorry Billy," I said, "I had to have a few words with Mr Hunter and thank him for the room and meals. I was only being polite."

Billy grunted and gave out a heavy cough and mumbled, "You women you're all the same. Talk, talk, talk, I can't be doing with it. I likes to get on and get on me way."

"Yes I am sure you do Billy," I said, in a domineering tone. "But manners cost us nothing, and Mr Hunter was very good to accommodate us at such short notice, don't you think?"

Billy grunted again and chuckled.

"I should think the old goat would be able to put us up at a moment's notice. He's not exactly over run with customers is he? If he had one customer a week I should think he would be doing well."

Billy then gave the reins a tug and grunted to Jacob to "Gid up" and walk on. Jacob's diamond shaped ears perked up and he plodded up the lane back towards the barn where he had spent the night.

"I know Mr Hunter is not exactly running the Ritz but he was very obliging and did the best for us with what he had. Anyway I don't know why you are complaining?" I barked back at him. "At least you had a nice cooked breakfast out of him! Scoffing down all that lovely bacon and eggs. I only got a bowl of lumpy porridge and some toast!"

Billy looked undeterred that I had challenged him, and looked as if he was quite enjoying my spirited counter argument.

"Well I didn't see you not knowing what to do with that bowl of muck that old goat calls porridge!"

I looked out at the hedgerows thick with brambles and long soggy grass. My eye caught a flicker of a red admiral fluttering about a pinkish flower from one of the brambles.

"I don't know what you mean?" I said indignantly, still admiring the red admiral.

"Needed a bit of fresh air during breakfast did we?" Billy asked slyly.

I gulped hard, but held my nerve and moved my head to observe the dilapidated barn we were just passing.

"I needed a bit of air yes," I said calmly but firmly, "It seemed very stuffy in that bar. I thought some nice sea air would do the pub some good."

Billy grunted, paused and then said curiously, "How's then you needed to take your bowl with you up to the window?"

I felt a little flustered and shuffled about on the seat.

"I was so enjoying my porridge, I took it with me to open the window! Why is that a crime?" I spoke rather firmly and tried to speak in a defiant manner to put a stop to his silly questions. A silly rather mischievous look came over his face.

"If you's were so enjoying it how comes you tipped the rest of it out the window then? You tell me that?"

Billy turned and looked at me with a rascally look on his face. We stared at each other for several minutes, while I tried to think what to say and give an account for my actions. It was no good however, Billy had seen me. I had been found out. I felt highly irritable with Billy for leading me up the garden path once again, making me squirm.

"Oh! You insufferable man!" I shouted at him my voice full of irritation. "Alright you saw me then? Yes alright! I threw the rest of that bloody wallpaper paste out the window. It was revolting! I would not have had to if you hadn't eaten all the bacon! I too could have had a nice breakfast!"

I felt so mad with Billy. Trust him to have seen me, of all people. *I will never live this down* I thought. Billy spluttered out his pipe with an eruption of laughter. He spit and spluttered and his eyes watered up. His face went bright red with pleasure.

"You did look a sight creeping about in the pub like an old hen! I nearly was going to tap you on the shoulder as you were mucking out your bowl!"

I sighed in disgust with him. He really was an old difficult swine. But the very thought of me heading over to the window like a hen and throwing my porridge out the window with Billy, who must have come in to the bar at that very moment watching me brought a smile across my face. I too erupted with laughter.

"Oh you are an old fox Billy Bath!" I said, fighting back tears of laughter and clutching my tummy with the pain from laughing so much.

Billy coughed and spluttered out with laughter. "If you thought your porridge was bad you should have tried that bloody lobster! Like old leather boots it was. Bloody terrible! I picked the poor old crustacean up in my Pocket, went outside and threw it into the stream! Good job no one saw me do it or been outside. They may have been hit over the head with a dead lobster! Billy erupted like a fog horn of laughter again, as did I at the thought of Billy creeping about in the dark and hurling a lobster across the garden into the stream.

"You see?" I said composing myself "You're just the same as me. You didn't want to upset Mr Hunter either."

"Aha! Yes alright missy you're right there. I'm not one to go upsetting folk deliberately. Keep me own council, that's what me father used to say to me when I was a lad. It served me well that piece of advice."

*

Jacob steadily went up the lane with the red admiral butterfly fluttering past. We went on up towards the gloomy hill ahead. The road sloped up and then went into a fork, one path going up and over the valley, the other was the one we had come by yesterday afternoon. The oak and ash trees thickened as we went up the hill, leaving the slumbering valley and Hunter's Inn far behind. Along the banks and ditches grew bugloss and common lungwort. I always thought the lungwort looked prettier with its dusty green leaves covered in white spots and the clusters of pink and purple flowers. Wild carrot also dominated the banks, along with the brambles which had made excellent cover for birds and insects along the paths. Jacob came to the fork in the road and Billy turned the reins to the left. Jacob plodded up on to the steep road that turned sharply up and round. The road ran parallel to the top of the bottom lane that we had come along yesterday afternoon. It was strange how I had never looked up to notice this steep road running along the top of the valley, all shrouded in greenery. The banks were submerged with male ferns and harts-tongue, all like giant green hands. I did spot a few adder's tongue, or at least I thought they were adder's tongue. The banks and cliffs were covered in large grey rocks, many of them becoming covered in thick moss and surrounded by the variety of ferns. Jacob did exceptionally well considering it was a steep and in places narrow road to go along. Billy often praised him and gave him either instructions or encouragement where the road narrowed and went steeply round tight bends. The path had become drier and it was higher up and protected with the canopy of trees but more stonier in places. The cart jumped about and rocketed a little, causing the milk churns to clatter about and me to grip my seat.

I was desperately wanting to now talk to Billy about Eddie and what he knew about him. The road however still looked rather hazardous and difficult both to Jacob and Billy, so I kept quiet and allowed them both the time to be peaceful and to concentrate. As we moved up higher, now well above the valley of Hunter's Inn, the canopy of trees and ferns became more sparse. The rich soil which the ferns loved gave way to more rockier ground. After turning another sharp twisted bend, with the sheer drop down into the valley below, even Billy commented that he was always grateful to pass that point. The path began to become less steep and gently became more level. We began to leave the canopy and corridor of oak and ash trees. The sun came trickling through the branches and shadowed our path in mysterious shapes. Up ahead the corridor disappeared; the darkness and shadows retreated and we came out into an open plane of lush green fields dotted with tall horse chestnut trees; their massive umbrellas of branches and leaves, spread out in all directions. The sky looked no longer overcast, but was a pale water colour blue, with the sun shining ahead. Jacob's golden coat gleamed like a lion's mane and his pace quickened slightly. Perhaps even Jacob was glad the darkness of the valley and the dangers had passed and was behind him for yet another day. The road was much clearer and for the moment was heading down hill. Starlings flew about in the sky disturbed by the sound of a barking dog in the field being inspected by its farmer to the right of us.

The air too had changed. It was a smell of freshness; heady with salt and minerals from the sea up ahead. I took in the smell of hay being harvested, the call from starlings and crows flying in the sky above with no cares about them. A young girl passed us walking with a large wicker basket in her hand. It was full to the brim with grey, white and cream mushrooms. All different shapes, sizes, some with caps and some with tactile textures. The girl gave Billy and I a warm smile as she went through a gate and into the next field.

"The trick with mushroom picking," Billy said, "is you got to look for them in the morning and look for them in several different locations and directions. Tis no good just walking straight through a bloody field in a straight line. I used to go mushroom picking when I was her age. Me mother always used to get me up at the crack of dawn, shoved a basket in me hand and tell me not to come back, till basket was full."

I thought perhaps even then Billy had been a trial, and his poor mother sent him off mushroom gathering just to have a morning of peace.

As we travelled down the open countryside towards a built up belt of hills on the right covered with grazing sheep, the road became wider. The grass on either side of us grew thick, bright green in colour and dotted with bright yellow dandelions. On the left, in the nearby field a group of about five farm labourers dressed in white shirts, braces and dark trousers were picking up straw for the harvest. The lads threw it up into a cart piled high with a mountain of straw with two younger looking men forking it in. A couple of strong, large, well-built working horses were saddled up in front of the cart having a few moments of rest before moving on up the field. As we continued two young and attractive women walked past us carrying a basket each of ploughman's lunches. The baskets contained large Granny Smith apples that looked juicy and sweet; cheese sandwiches I presume were covered up in brown paper and there were small bottles of ale and stout with a few glasses. The girls, dressed in plain summer dresses with pale cream scarves over their hair, rushed past us and hurriedly headed towards the party of farm workers. A great masculine cheer went up from the team of farm hands at the arrival of the girls. Lunch time and rest had finally come!

Billy continued puffing away with his pipe. I thought that now would be a good time to question him about what he knew of Edward. I was just about to speak when Billy took out his pipe and looked over to the right. We were passing the belt of hills and the land sloped down a little, he then mumbled through his pipe. "Just you wait and see. You're about to glimpse the best view in the country!"

As we finally passed the last stretch of hills the whole landscaped changed. The rolling fields of lush green and golden yellow, all neatly regimented with hedges and pockets of farm buildings and cottages, gently fell down towards the bright, sparkling blue Devonshire ocean. It was extremely beautiful and a sight which paused all conversation and heavy thoughts. Billy puffed away on his pipe proudly thinking to himself that this view had remained unchanged and unaltered for years and all for his personal pleasure and enjoyment. The sight of the sea did indeed give one a calming and relaxing mood. All my thoughts of Eddie and concern over what Billy knew had depleted. All I could do was enjoy this glorious sight of delicate land stretching down to the clear blue waters. The only sight of human activity was a tanker moving along the sea in the distance and the sound of laughter from the farmers we had passed enjoying their lunch. The road now went round a bend and passed some wind swept trees deformed by the gusts that had swept through them from off the sea. The view of the sea could still be seen and I kept my eye on the tanker, now looking like just a dot on the horizon. As Jacob continued along the road I decided it was now or never. Raising myself up from my relaxed slouch I asked the question I had been dying to ask Billy all morning.

"Billy? I wondered if you would mind telling me what you know about my brother?" Only you gave the impression last night that you knew something about Edward. Some secret that you knew about him. I can see you are a man of high principles and I know you don't like gossip, but you obviously know or think you know something and I would like you to tell me so I am able to put the record straight."

I inhaled an intake of air and studied Billy closely. He had not moved or adjusted his head to see me, nor flinched in anyway at my questioning him. He paused his pipe and let out a puff of smoke.

"Look Miss Edith! All I know is that it's best for all concerned not to go raking up old ground. It's not my place to condone or condemn your Edward. After you and your brother left Devon none in public spoke about what happened. It was not right to speak about such things in public. After all it was different days back then. Even now you wouldn't speak of it. Many old crows and a few of your younger servants blabbed what they knew, but I think one should never speak ill of a man without knowing him. We are all human. We all makes mistakes. I meant no offence to you or your family. Your parents treated us farming folk well and proper. I only meant to warn you last night that when we get down into that village there are bound to be people who will put a face to you, like I did. I don't want you to come to grief. I should think you had enough of that in your life already. Ah…!"

Billy suddenly paused and pointed his hand towards a newly restored white painted sign post. "Here we are then! Not far to go now?"

Billy pointed a long nodular finger out towards one of the arms of the post which was pointing straight ahead in our direction. Another road went off to the left and another to the right, which must have been the coastal path. As Jacob brought us past the sign post and carried straight on ahead, I looked up to see what was written in smart black letters along the arm.

"*Lynrock 4 miles*"

Billy carried on puffing away on his pipe and Jacob snorted, swinging his head gently back to remove a fly that had perched on his head. I still did not understand what Billy meant. Apart from Thelma and Emma who else would I find? Edward had taken off. Father and Mother were both dead. The rest of the villagers were either too young or too old to remember me and what went on. Those that perhaps would recognise me or see something of the past about me would probably be too full of worry regarding the flood to question me. One thing was certain: that sign post had marked that the end was in sight. After what seemed days of weary travelling and worry I was nearly at my journey's end.

Chapter 20
The Chough's Have Flown the Nest

Jacob walked along the widening road still at a good steady pace. Billy seemed quieter and continued puffing away on his pipe. He handed me the reins only once when he needed to replenish his pipe with some tobacco, which he had produced from his pocket in a dented and tarnished tin. Jacob showed no fright or change in mood while I was holding the reins steady. He trotted along happily at the same pace and speed, and only thrashed his head up once and snorted to remove another blue bottle that was buzzing around him.

    The road turned slightly to the left and we passed a few more ash trees adorned with lush green leaves. Across the road was a full ditch of rain water and beyond it another large group of farm workers with their wives and children. The gathering sat on golden bales of straw in a dusty yellow field. The rustic looking community all looked relieved to have stopped to enjoy their ploughman's lunches. Many of the younger workers were sprawled about on the grass drinking from flasks, so parched from their mornings efforts. Their pinkish coloured Marshall's threshing machine linked up to a shiny green and black steam engine, were both now paused and given a break. A cart and grazing horse was parked a little way off in front of the thresher which already looked half full with heavy sacks, filled up with wheat waiting to be taken along to the granary at the end of the day.

    At the other end of the thresher box was a large bank of golden wheat ready to be processed down the large, wide elevator. The ground was covered in golden coloured dust, straw and wheat. A few large, tall forks were propped up against the silent and still thresher along with empty sacks not yet full with wheat. The sound of the shrill steam engine whistle and chattering of the mechanics of the thresher and elevator had been replaced by the merry banter of the farm labourers. They all appeared glad to be sharing their work with their families. Some of the children were grouped about in huddles, laughing and playing with stray pieces of straw and wheat. As we passed the field a cry went up from the party of farmers. I turned round to spy what they were doing and observed many of them now staggering up to their feet, throwing their caps and hats back on their dusty heads and preparing for a hard afternoon's work. As we went gradually down the road, which was now beginning to fall away down another steep hill, we heard the sound of the steam engine's happy whistle and the sound of a puff and funnel of smoke burst out of the engine's tall chimney. As Jacob began carefully descending the hill we could just hear the slight murmur of an old country song being sung by the farmers, all no doubt happy that the rain had gone and Devon had enjoyed three full days of August sunshine in which to start bringing the harvest in.

"There's nothing better than the sound and look of the harvest being brought in. It's going to be good this year."

Billy spoke through his pipe in his mouth, sending out smoke that swirled around his head and then was left behind us as we travelled deeply down the hill. The sea to the right of us disappeared for a few moments as we went further down. Then suddenly it reappeared right in front of us and again we could see the white sparkling waters of the kidney shaped bay of Lynrock.

"There you are my dear!" Billy said rather cheerfully. "That's a view you've not seen for some time is it not?"

I looked out over the green fields and thick hedgerows to see the cliffs emerging out of the sea on the other side of the bay, rising up high above the village. They were bathed in sunlight which showed off the pastille colours of orange, browns and purplish grey rock. At the bottom of the cliffs lurked black mysterious looking caves with white sandy beaches, all deserted and only approachable by a sailing boat. Majestic peaks and eroded stacks of rock now only the home to seagulls and fulmar birds. The view of the sea grew more blue in colour as we went nearer the cliffs but sparkled like glittering crystal further out in the middle of the bay. A few boats were out in the channel sailing past the far off coat of Wales, but there were no fishermen out in the bay as there normally would be. Nor any tour boats off the coast. All looked tranquil and still on the waters.

As we moved away from the edge of the volcanic shaped cliffs the land became fertile again. The hills were covered in lime green grass and grazing sheep. The vegetation by the cliffs was dominated by thick grasses, sharp and straw like, blowing in the wind. It was rather amazing to see how many plants could live and thrive in such exposed and at times stormy conditions. Primroses, no longer in flower of course, but with their leaves still visible were scattered all over the place along with giant clumps of gorse with its bright yellow sunny flowers. The air was so fresh but much breezier and I did feel slightly cold as we came nearer the bottom. I shivered slightly, and pulling my jacket tighter around me, adjusted my jacket collar up to protect my already stiff neck.

Jacob and Billy did extremely well to drive down such a steep ravine. I would not have wished to have driven down in a car on my own, let alone a sturdy and controlled horse like Jacob. The road meandered down the cliff like a snake, running off into emergency parking spaces in case one lost control of a cart or car. Overhead, two seagulls glided over us and swooped down into the bay ready to dive bomb some poor fish swimming and basking in the sunshine. The further we went the more lush and green the landscape became. The oaks and ash trees became thicker once again and we descended deeper down into a steep shadowy lane, enclosed on either side above us by hanging branches. Ferns and ivy hung and clung to the banks that had now risen up with great rocks and boulders spread along the sides where the road had been channelled through the cliff many decades ago.

Jacob became a little more flustered as we turned and then went up another fairly steep road. The road had now changed to a harder surface but was covered in dishevelled leaves and twigs. To the sides of the road great thick branches had been prised off in the recent storm. In some places torn down branches had fallen out into the road, and Billy navigated Jacob away from the splintered and sharp branches where the wind had cracked them down. Many branches had become precariously caught up in neighbouring trees. They appeared to be just hanging there ready to fall with another gust of wind or when the branches holding them could no longer do so, sending them hurtling to the road below.

We thankfully came out of the dark tunnel of trees and shrubs, and out into the fresh air and light of the sea and sun again. The whole of Lynrock could now be seen stretching down from the highest pinnacles of the alpine forests, with the River Lyn running down through its centre, on through into the village and out past the harbour and beyond to meet the sea. High on the channelled cliffs was Upper Lynrock with grand looking Victorian villas and guest houses, along with more modest cottages and shops for the locals. Quite visible were the spires of three different churches spread out along the cliff top, but there were no grand turrets and spires of my former home which had once dominated the landscape high up on Hallowed Hill. The house, what was left after the fire that destroyed it, was now overrun and covered up by forest. I noticed the whole landscape had been taken over with vegetation. The terraces of fields that had once been allotments and gardens, and which had been so productive with fruit and vegetable gardens, had now all been abandoned and covered over by nature. Down from Upper Lynrock was a steep path that only the brave and adventurous took to get down in to the bay and harbour. The main way to get from top to bottom was the famous cliff railway. In various spots on the forested hills were a few attractive cottages and hotels with what must have been the most impressive views over the bay. To the right of us was the calm blue, shimmering waters of the bay and channel, and beyond at some considerable distance was the coast of Wales.

Looking at my former home one would not think there had just occurred the most devastating storm and flood that Britain had seen in recent times. Not that one could observe the lower village and harbour down in the bay, for we were still not low enough, though Jacob was advancing closer to it.

"Not the same Lynrock you remember is it?" Billy mumbled to me. "When you were last here the cliffs were all smartly kept terraces, with allotments and gardens, but course the war saw the end to all that."

"Yes," I said, scanning the cliffs covered with a thick jungle of forests and shrubs. "I remember there had been trees in my time but not so many as there is now, and not so dense!"

"After you left your old estate was abandoned. I mean no one wanted to buy an old gutted ruin did they? Only the children went up there to play. None of the adults wanted to venture up. They said the whole land and the ruins were haunted!"

Billy sounded so matter of fact about my old home and house being haunted as if I was some tourist excited by an old landmark.

"Haunted!" I gasped with amazement! "How terribly unhealthy. Who on earth did they think was haunting the place?"

Billy gave a sudden cough with surprise and spluttered.

"Who do you think lass? Your poor old father of course! Folk used to say that every night in October they could hear your father moan and wail with such despair in his voice. Some said that after dark a light would appear at your father's old study. Many in The Rising Moon swore blind they'd seen him, and these weren't touched people. They were as sane as you or I."

My head was lowered the whole time Billy was talking and ranting on about the ghost of my father. *How terribly wicked* I thought *for people to make up such silly stories. How un Christian.* But I also felt a chill down my spine and a shiver that went right through me. With all that had happened in October 1929 I suppose I was not surprised that people felt such an atmosphere up on Hallowed Hill. But I hated the thought of my father not being at peace. Not being happy in a better place, but wandering on through the ruins of the house, in utter despair and desperation, that life had so utterly turned against him.

I bit back a few tears at the thought of all Billy had said and for a good while our conversation and the ease of the journey had gone stale. Until I asked the question that had never fully been answered:

"How did the fire start Billy, up at the house? I had left before it happened!"

Billy looked very uncomfortable, almost rather startled at my sudden curiosity in the house. He looked suddenly guilty and shifted in his seat, giving off nervous puffs of smoke from his pipe.

"Oh... I... don't know miss. They said it was a communist cell that did it. There was a lot of bad feeling after the crash. As I keep telling you miss, don't do to look back."

Billy sounded rather aggressive in his final words and I decided to ask no more questions. However I could see that Billy was hiding something. As we continued, still looking over at the hills covered in woods Billy, following a long silence, resumed talking of the old days.

"Most of the gardeners never came back when they went off to war. Those that did make it back weren't in much of a state to go back to doing gardening again. Both those bloody wars, they changed everything. I expect you remember many of the gardens? They were just getting back on their feet after the first war, the war that was supposed to be the war to end all wars."

Billy's morbid talking made me think of my old home. I looked up towards Hallowed Hill where I remembered home to be, now covered in dense wood. I could make out no sign of bricks or walls. The woods had become too thick. I wondered whether the army had demolished the ruins by now just as Thelma had pre-warned me in her last letter. Or had the army been delayed by the flood and the clear up operation.

I agreed with what Billy had said about the war and the gardens gone to ruin and how badly scarred so many of the men had been. The men we called the 'lucky ones,' the ones that came back.

"Yes that's true," I said in agreement, "I remember we had a young gardener working for us while we lived here. He was a nice chap. He always spoke to me when Edward and I were growing up and had such a nice, caring manner about him. But when he came back after the war he was never the same man. I have often wondered what became of him?"

I looked over to Billy, taking in his wrinkled face with deep frown lines over his forehead. Billy looked heavy pressed, with no sight of joy in his face. He suddenly looked deeply pained; a pain that was cut deep within him and had been his companion for many years. Billy sniffed, let out a puff of smoke and wiped an eye with his hand removing the dust or perhaps a tear. He strangely changed the subject.

"Last I heard lass, the army were on their way up to your house to pull it down. Mind I don't think they got too far. Your old drive is impassable in some places. No good for the army trucks to get up there. I remember the days when it had been lined with hydrangeas that your mother had planted. They're all gone now. All brambles and thorns up there now."

I smiled. The past, the look and smell of the drive and how it had been, came back into focus within me. The drive had been one of the most beautiful in the county. All lined with blue, purples and pink hydrangeas; along with pine trees and dark red and pink rhododendrons.

I fought back another tear. To think all that was now gone.

"It don't take long for nature to take over do it?" Billy continued.

"No it certainly doesn't," I said looking over to Wales so as not to look up at Hallowed Hill anymore. "I know from my own garden back in Wiltshire that you have to keep at it nearly every day, or it soon gets away from you. Mind you I so enjoy gardening. It's a labour of love really. I always think you're very close to God in the garden."

I did try to sound cheerful but Billy's ghost stories and his evasiveness about how the house burnt down, as well as hearing my former home was utterly lost and nearly forgotten, deflated me greatly. Jacob finally reached another steep leafy spot with thick ferns and shrubs on either side. To the left side of the road the bank of grass, ferns and soil had been churned up and great tyre marks had cut through the vegetation and crushed many of the plants. An old wooden fence that marked the grounds of the Imperial Hotel set high on the cliff above, had been broken down and splintered into pieces. Billy slowed Jacob down to a gentle slow trot as we passed a broken down tree, completely snapped in two with all its branches and twigs pushed up against the bank and partly hanging into the ditch. Finally from the corner of my eye I saw the culprit of the devastation. An army vehicle had smashed into the side of the bank and gone straight over the ditch, made contact with the cliff resulting in a landslide and sent the truck back into the ditch. Soil, rocks and stones had piled up over the truck and some had spilled out into the road. The whole accident had been roped off and a bright sign with white letter's read 'Danger.' It looked like the landslide had been much worse when it had occurred but now it had been tidied up and made safe. This must have been the obstacle that had prevented us from getting down the afternoon before.

Jacob walked past slowly, swaying his head about. Both Billy and I looked out at the wreckage of the army vehicle, now looking like a right off.

"Poor sod" Billy said as we went by, "How he got out of that with just a few cuts and scrapes I'll never know. Mr Hunter told me this morning before we left."

*

We finally came down low enough to see on the left more signs of devastation; only now much worse than just a freak traffic accident. Flattened trees broken down, some uprooted, greeted us as we came down into Lynrock. Many of the trees had lost their leaves, those that were still standing that is. Looking through the trees that were still standing I could see what looked like the old row of fishermen's cottages though it was hard to tell as there was so much damage to them. It was the same type of damage I had seen walking round Bath the morning after the Blitz. Piles of bricks, timber, rubble and boulders were lying in great heaps between broken cottages. One of them had it's front room and porch intact but the rest of the terrace's frontage had become a gianthole, with gutted floors above. It looked as if a train had driven through the building and brought half the roof and upper floors down as it had torn through the terrace.

We came along to the church of St John the Baptist which was still standing and looked remarkably intact, apart from its storm shutters blown off and few broken roof tiles and torn down guttering. God had spared his house of worship. *Thank goodness he had*, I thought *for the village will certainly need its church and its faith in the coming days*. We arrived to the bridge over the River Lyn. From this point the road continued up to a junction. One could either go up to the upper village or round through the attractive rows of cottages, hotels and gift shops which ran below Neptune Hill and along to The Rising Moon and the harbour. Somehow remarkably, this one bridge had remained intact and safe to go over. Yet the flood waters must have shot straight under it although it looked like the deluge had flown over the top of the bridge and indeed all the remaining roads were saturated with puddles of water, sand, mud and silt along with branches, rubble and dotted with boulder's. Jacob went cautiously over the bridge and I did say a silent prayer, willing it to remain intact while we went over. Both Billy and I looked down into the cold and fast moving waters, still filled with branches of broken down trees, wood, piles of rubble and metal. As we crossed we observed that two other bridges further up the river had been demolished with only a middle column of stone being buffeted by the river, which was all that was left to tell us there had been a bridge there at all and we realised we could go no further towards the harbour.

Billy turned Jacob sharply to the right as the main road that lead along through the high street was closed off. The road was impassable: a dam of fallen trees, splintered drift wood, parts of fallen brick walls, bistro chairs from a café, along with scraps of twisted metal and great chunks of rubble; all engrossed in thick, sticky red mud and soil. The scene was accompanied by a smell of sewage. It was clear from the sight that was in front of us that the road through the high street had still not yet been cleared, despite a number of tractors and bulldozers stationed nearby, which I assumed would be used to clear a path through along to the harbour and down past the Victorian dance hall where the lime kilns and cliff railway station were situated.

Jacob carried on along opposite what had been the golf course and the old Victorian gardens where the village enjoyed cream teas and summer concerts. The golf course displayed a few drenched looking palm and monkey puzzle trees, the only plants left standing. The whole area was awash still with flood water and debris. The flag pole that had always flown the Union Jack so proudly in the centre of the gardens was still there, but the flag was torn and ripped to shreds. Opposite the gardens had been a path that lead to the lifeboat house, also a casualty of the flood. It had been left with three of its walls down and its roof had collapsed.

Two men in dusty boots and trousers, wearing nothing but dirty white vests and thick gloves over their hands, crossed the road in front of us. Both men were smoking like it was going out of fashion. They were the first people we had seen for hours since we went past the two gatherings of farmers in the fields enjoying their break from thrashing.

*

Neither Billy nor myself spoke or said a word to each other, such was the awe and sight of the devastation. The vision of this village looking like it had been bombed and not flooded, left one unable to say anything. I looked above the bay slightly over to Neptune Hill that lorded itself over The Rising Moon tavern. On the hill top were perched two attractive looking cottages one of which I knew belonged to Thelma and Emma. The cottages looked undeterred and unhampered by the flood. This must have been a good sign. It meant Thelma and Emma must have survived! What remained of the main high street now resembled stacks of cards that had collapsed down on each other like dominos. Sally's tea room was completely gone, and I could not even quite work out or remember where it had once stood. Nor could I see the Bath Hotel. There was the most terrible stench of sewage that made my stomach churn, but thankfully as we travelled further up towards the upper village the smell became less and less pungent. Overhead in the pale blue sky a seagull flew across the bay and called out a shriek, piercing the peace of the afternoon. There seemed to be a great deal of flies about too, swarming over the wreckage and red mud that had covered every surface.

We suddenly spotted a group of army personnel all dressed in boiler suits and heavy black boots. They appeared to be working hard to clear the remains of a damaged cottage that had collapsed into the street further up the road. As I looked down from above at their faces becoming less visible as Jacob brought us higher up the cliff road, one face caught my attention. The face was of a young lad with a cigarette in his mouth, his face covered in dust and mud. He looked up at me yet gave no expression or emotion at observing me. He almost looked as if he was dead. After a pause he resumed his drudgery, pushing a wheel barrow filled with bricks, mortar and rubble away from the wreckage. I finally observed the group heave what looked like an old kitchen table out of a hole in the cottage's wall. The men threw the table out into the street, adding to a pile of wrecked furniture that had once been someone's pride and joy. It was like watching the clear up of the Blitz all over again.

Almost standing up I peered down into the road trying to see what had happened to the harbour. I could see neither tower nor the pier. There seemed to be a lot of activity going on down there. I was aware of the rattle of a bulldozer readjusting itself. It was being carefully guided by a tall, thin looking man. The man directing the group was dressed in a long black waterproof coat, and had relatively long hair, that was blowing about in the wind. There looked as if there was a terrific amount of debris down in front of the harbour and work was only just beginning. A large group of men with several policemen looked as if they were receiving instructions and guidance from the tall, thin man with longish hair.

I was struck with the fact that there was no fishermen about. No lobster pots. Nor any scampering children enjoying the summer holidays. Neither were there any families or holiday makers. There was in fact no sign of any women or children, nor for that matter any sign of civilian life. They had all by now been evacuated to the upper village while the army tried to secure the area, and bring some sort of order to the chaos. A few workmen had downed tools and were sat along a sandy coloured stone wall drinking from white enamel cups. They all looked tired and exhausted, covered in dust and dirt. Two of the men's overalls appeared utterly drenched. I thought that if it was the case that all the villagers had been evacuated to the upper village, then Thelma and Emma would be with them. Billy still said not a word and he seemed highly shocked by the carnage. As we went round a bend and started making better progress to the upper village the workers gathered by the harbour were busy once again. They appeared to have received their guidance from the tall gentleman, who towered over them all and looked as if he had some sort of authority among the group. As conversation with Billy had all but dried up and trying to think of something to say, I mentioned the wild, tall looking figure to him.

"There's a very tall man down by the harbour giving out instructions to the other workers. He must be the foreman. Or an army officer do you think?"

Billy looked slightly uncomfortable again and shifted in his seat. He cleared his throat and even took out his pipe from his mouth, which had been a rare occurrence during our journey together.

"I expect that's the harbour master you've spotted. He's assisting the clear up operation in the harbour."

Billy shifted about in his seat again and looked slightly nervous and uncomfortable. He seemed very agitated; his face looked tight and his lip looked as if it was trembling. Jacob followed the bend round and we began to climb even higher now, well above the harbour and remains of the lower village, until the sight of it was nearly too hard to see. The road continued to bend and zigzag round as we went up towards the upper village. We could see to the right the whole bay now deep below us. We were given a glimpse of the enormity of the disaster. A mass of broken wrecked vessels and ships were piled up in the harbours walls, along with cars, trees and great boulders. The lighthouse, which at one time had a brazier on its roof, had been utterly destroyed along with the pier.

On the last stretch of the steep road up we passed a few peaceful cottages and guest houses with attractive gardens. I pondered on the state the harbour was in and suddenly became thankful that Eddie was not here to see the harbour so badly damaged. He would have hated to see all its boats destroyed with a mass of tall masts all either snapped or left looking limp and cumbersome. It would have so upset him. He had loved this harbour so much, as had I. It had been a special place for us both. Now however it no longer looked like the utopia where we had rushed to sit, relax and watch the world go by. Knowing and remembering what Eddie had been like, if he had been here he would have been down by the harbour lending a hand and mucking in with all the dirty work.

The sound of bulldozers, army vehicles and tractors all being operated by the hard working men reverberated up to us, along with the calls of men shouting instructions to each other and the odd shriek from a seagull. Billy suddenly broke the strained silence between us, taking his eyes off the road and looked upon the depressing scene below us.

"What a bloody mess! Looks more like a bomb went off than a freak flood. Not many people about is it? Suppose most of the locals are up at the top."

"Yes it is a mess," I replied, "it reminds me of Bath during the first night of the Blitz. You should have seen the city, the first night of the bombing"

Billy still looked terribly strained. He had the look of a man who was carrying a great secret or weight on his mind. Billy returned his attention back to the road. He called out to Jacob "Good boy" as we turned another difficult bend, thankfully the last.

*

Jacob had finally brought us up the hill to a road and avenue of ash, pine trees and thick bushes of rhododendrons and tall buddleias. Down the road a group of army Personnel all walked along with a local policeman who was wearing a long blue police anorak. His uniform was complemented by a large silver belt buckle and silver coat buttons, matching the silver from his hat. The policeman had thick, wet looking wellington boots on and looked as if he had been assisting the army officers with directions. No one in the official looking group acknowledged us or stopped to question us as I feared they would do. I heeded the warning Mrs Barns from the Chough's Nest had told me that civilians were not allowed down to the disaster zone or the affected area. We finally reached the top of the road and were now high above the bay. Along this quiet coastal road on the left, overlooking the sea, were the former grand villas of the rich and powerful. Now turned into Bed and Breakfast establishments.

The lane was peaceful with old, green, Victorian iron lampposts looking rusty and unloved. On the right side of the lane was a long wall of sandy coloured stones, slightly eroded in places by the elements over the years. Looking over the wall I could see the steep overgrown slopes of the former gardens and allotments, all completely forgotten and submerged by years of weeds, brambles and overgrown with trees and bushes. Every now and then as Jacob brought us down the lane we passed old, rusting, wrought iron gates. The gates were covered in ivy and blocked by weeds, grasses and years and layers of leaf litter. Some of the gates looked rather grand and elaborate, with heavy stone pedestals on either side, with remains of iron stumps of old lanterns and lamps. These gates, which no one had opened or stepped through for years, told me of sad forgotten stories. I could see their former gardeners packing up late on a sunset evening, carrying their trug and tools, feeling heavy hearted. They knew that as they shut the gates to their manicured plots they would never re-open again. Tomorrow they would be wearing a different uniform and preparing to use different tools. They would put away their gardening waistcoats and fob watches, and wear instead their army uniforms. They would lock away their cleaned spades, forks and watering cans and be given training on how to hold and use a gun. The wars did indeed change so much for so many.

Jacob by now was beginning to flag. He looked tired and in desperate need of a drink. Billy said he would drop me at the end of the lane as The Chough's Nest was the last hotel before the road narrowed and went down a small track along the coastal footpath. Billy was still quiet and had barely said two words to me. He pulled Jacob up by a small border of summer flowers and a long slope marked on both sides with ferns and wild strawberries growing into the walls. The Chough's Nest was set up high above on the top of the cliff. Above the hotel was Hallowed Hill all overgrown and wild with vegetation. I glanced up at the slope and observed a set of five steps that went up to a terrace to the three story villa of my hotel. I was so thankful to have arrived and could not wait to set off and find Thelma and Emma. I climbed down from off the cart, as too did Billy. He gave Jacob a pat and then turned round to fetch my case from the back of the cart, extracting it from between the three milk churns. Billy passed me my case as I was soothing Jacob and thanking him for getting me down to Lynrock safely.

"Well then Miss Edith, I suppose I had best be on my way."

Billy looked rather crestfallen and I think he had enjoyed the company and was surprised by how well we had both got on and tolerated each other.

"Thank you Billy for all you have done. I am sorry it was a longer journey than we had originally planned. But you and Jacob have both been superb. I am so grateful to you both. Are you going back to your farm now?"

Billy sniffed, "No not yet. I got to get rid of these." He pointed to the three milk churns in the back of the cart. "Then I shall go and have a pint and something to eat and get Jacob some water and rest. We will both set off for home later."

Billy then came over closely to me to the point where our noses were almost touching. He took my hand and gripped it. He looked worried and concerned as he had done the night before in Hunter's Inn. "Remember. Please remember what I said now Miss Edith. Be careful round here."

Billy looked behind him over the wall on the right to the sparkling waters of the sea.

"You will find more than Thelma and Emma down there. Things that are best kept quiet will come out if you're not careful. The past always comes back to haunt us. It never leaves us for too long."

I waved to Billy. He had turned Jacob and the cart round in the parking space a little further up the lane before one reached the bridal gate along the exposed costal path. As I started to walk up the sloping path up to the front terrace of the hotel, I paused to see both Jacob and Billy pass the hotel. I still did not understand Billy's warning, nor what he was so scared of. Billy was hiding something I was sure of it. Some secret he knew, or had discovered about my family, about Eddie and the house.

Billy and Jacob soon disappeared along the lane of forgotten gates and gardens, passing the other neighbouring hotels on the left of the road. I waited until I could no longer hear the clatter of Jacob's hooves, or the juddering noise of Billy's cart with the clanking milk churns inside. The lane was now peaceful again with only the sound of chattering birds in the hedges and the sound of the sea gently moving below. With my case in hand, my bottle of mineral water and handbag, I staggered up the path. I brushed past a few bright pink hydrangeas and wild delicate fuchsia plants with dark pink and purple flowers. The slope turned a sharp corner and turned into some sagging stone steps that were rather steep. I managed the three steps and went a little bit further up a slope lined with borders of yet more fuchsias. On the left side of the path was a newly planted box hedging. At last I reached some wide, newly built steps with an iron handrail painted in white down the right side to prevent any one falling down the bank into the lane. When I reached the top, a wide tarmac terrace greeted me. The terrace was cluttered with old yellow tea pots potted up with pale and dark blue lobelia. Several stone bird baths were dotted about and a long bench was set against the wall of the terrace with the seat back facing the sea. There was also a tall wooden bird table with great quantities of nuts and stale bread, along with a black metal wind mill with the compass points on.

The hotel was certainly well positioned: it was cut into the cliff with the great steep banks of Hallowed Hill behind it and to the side. The Barns family looked as if they had been trying to clear some of the trees and shrubs. Many of the trees had creamy splintered pieces of wood showing and the banks were covered in stumps of felled trees. A leafy and hazardous path went up along the bank and round the back and top of the hotel through the maze of trees and shrubs. I took in the impressive view of the bay and the cliffs that were lit up with sunlight. It felt rather odd to be looking over a view I had been absent from for so long. I put my hand up to read the time on my gold watch. It read three thirty-five. I turned round and headed over to the hotel. All the bay windows were large and had the look of a captain's cabin windows on a ship. Through the main front window I presumed must be either the dining room or the lounge. It looked deserted. A light shined from within the room coming from a brass chandelier with cream coloured lanterns over the bulbs. Under the window was a dry stone walled border in a semi-circle filled with cottage garden plants.

I went round to a circular porch with an empty Greek wall planter fixed to the wall. An iron lantern hung from the roof of the porch. A heavy door with glazed glass panels was slightly ajar. I pushed my case forward and pushed open the door, and entered the hotel lobby.

*

The lobby was long, carpeted in dark red, gold and brown swirl pattern. The walls were of a white and cream colour, cluttered with old paintings and pictures of war ships and battles, along with old general's portraits all dating back from the Napoleonic wars. As I advanced down this long passage I came into a wide and well lit reception. An old Viennese desk covered in silver platters, salvers and a pile of warn leather menus was in the corner to the right of me. A classical music stand was stood next to this with a closed door opposite, which lead into the lounge. Another door was then located on the other side of the desk with its door also closed. Opposite, a large window with a grotto like wall outside covered in ivy revealing the cliff wall which the hotel had been built into. The windowsill was cluttered with old china barrels and blue and white oriental vases and plates. Under the window was a stiff and uncomfortable looking sofa. A small heavy table was next to that with a visitor's book and guest post box. I put my case down and walked over to the white panelled reception desk. A grand old clock was ticking on the wall behind it with a bookcase filled with files, ledgers and account books.

There seemed to be no one about. I rang a brass bell with a sign next to it that said *'Please ring for assistance.'* I tapped the bell lightly and a shrill ring went out and echoed down through the hall. I waited for a few minutes, sniffing some bright red roses placed in a glass vase on the desk with some white heucheras intertwined. I stood listening to the peaceful ticking of the clock and sound of chirping birds from outside. Then a door from behind the desk swung open and out came a little girl with long golden hair, tied up with a bright pink ribbon. The girl must have been about seven. She had a sweet rather doleful look, with a few freckles on her cheeks.

The young lady came alongside the desk looking rather unsure of what to do or say. She looked at me with beautiful blue eyes for a few minutes before saying briskly, "Which number do you want please?"

I was a little unsure of the question. However understood she must be unaware that I had only just arrived and not been given a room number or key yet.

"Hello," I said, "What's your name?"

The little girl looked surprised with my question. She rubbed her eyes with her tiny clenched hands. "It's Hannah miss. Which number do you want?"

I could see she was itching to give me a key and get back to whatever she had been doing. "It's my job to give out keys. I do the keys. I'm very good at giving out keys. Now what room number are you?"

Hannah suddenly went quiet after informing me of a her role for giving out keys. She spoke in a rushed, dramatic tone rather like an old dowager than a child of seven.

Hannah looked rather disappointed that she could not thrust a key into my hand. She gave a deep theatrical sigh and said, "If you've just come you will have to wait for my mother and father. They have just gone down to try and get some potatoes in the village. They left me and my brother Alfred in charge."

"Oh. I see. Oh well, that's alright. The Chough's have flown the nest have they?"

I gave out a laugh and chuckled away like a school girl, then looked at Hannah who was not impressed by my joke or silly sense of humour.

It had been a long day, I thought to myself.

Chapter 21
So What's the Drill in Here Then?

Afternoon tea consisting of warm plain scones, fruit cake and a large pot of tea was served in the hotel lounge. It was the first meal I had had since leaving Hunter's Inn with Billy. I was extremely glad of some refreshment and I had already drank four cups of tea from the white china tea pot that Mrs Barns had brought in to me, after they returned from their visit to the village.

The lounge was a most bright, sunny and cheerful room. One could almost say it was a room of utter relaxation and tranquillity. It was a fairly large room with French doors on one wall and a large curved bay window, which overlooked the hotel front terrace and steps that I had staggered up when I had arrived only an hour or so before. A brass chandelier hung in the centre of the room with ten bulbs all lit, apart from one, and all hidden with pale pink shades. The room was typically Georgian. It featured a picture rail, dado rail, a panelled built in cupboard and, a sideboard to the right of a red brick fireplace, which looked a bit out of place. A small bookcase covered with old books, many of them old biographies of political figures from the past. There was a very large gentleman's set of dressing drawers covered in brass locks and keys, with pull down drawers and shelves. At one time this attractive piece of furniture would have been used to store ties and collars. The drawers were made of a dark wood with two large Japanese Dresden vases placed on the top. White painted Georgian shelves were covered in blue and white plates depicting oriental scenes, along with old perfume bottles, polished silverware, porcelain jugs, plates and vases. The walls of the lounge displayed several framed pictures of navel and sailing scene's, many of them ships. There was a rather nostalgic watercolour of the Regatta at Cows on the Isle of Wight painted in 1920. The picture comprised of two elegantly dressed ladies with light flowing garments, hats and parasols in the arms of a smartly dressed gentlemen dressed in navel attire. As I sat drinking tea and scooping up thick Devonshire cream, placing it on to my last scone followed by sweet strawberry jam on top, I thought, *how strange to think that only twenty four years ago I was dressed like those girls in the watercolour. Looking carefree, elegant, with my only worries of what to wear for dinner in the evening.*

The lounge was highly cluttered with several different styled sofas and seats, all with different fabrics, designs and colours. The only matching items were some faded vanilla cushions embroidered with yellow and blue roses, all terribly bleached by the sun, but somehow they looked attractive. There were several side and round tables covered in old newspapers, articles and sketches. The smell of sweet roses came from a display in a clear vase on the table in the bay window. Thanks to the French doors being open to the side terrace, the fragrant room was complemented by the sound of the sea. The lounge was indeed a place to relax, unwind and a jolly nice place to indulge in afternoon tea and to read a good book. The best thing for me was that all the other guests had either had their tea, retired to their rooms for the afternoon before dinner, or had not returned from their day out. Indeed I had the whole lounge to myself, hearing only the sound of the sea gently flowing and turning. A ticking grandfather clock by the fireplace made up for the lack of conversation and the sound of silver cutlery being manoeuvred about in the dining room accompanied by the tinkling of wine glasses. After finishing my high tea and dragging myself up from my low seat, I walked back into the hall to the reception desk. Mrs Barns was busy scribbling something down into a fat ledger.

"That was a most delicious afternoon tea, Mrs Barns," I said happily and full of praise. "Those scones where so light!"

Mrs Barns appeared tired. She was a classic looking woman: her hair was jet black and swept back off her face; she had a pleasing bone and cheek structure, with pale complexion and light pinkish lips. Mrs Barns looked rather tired most of the time and never looked the sort of woman you could approach with ease. However once you got to know her, she was gracious, charming, well-mannered and a devoted wife and mother. She was however not a woman to suffer fools, as later in the evening I would soon discover.

Mrs Barns looked up from her work and gave me a pleasant smile.

"I am glad you enjoyed it Miss Parfitt. My second eldest daughter cooks the cakes, scones and deserts, (rationing permitting of course). She has a real sweet tooth!"

I smiled, "I'm the same. I always think desserts are the best part of a meal. Although I don't think my dentist would agree with me!"

Mrs Barns huffed and said in a cut and dry manner, "Teeth, they are a pain in the neck and it costs the earth to have anything done these days. My old nanny, she had them all out at age thirty. Said it saved a lot of agony and money at the end of the day! Now then Miss Parfitt, I had better give you your room number. I have your ration book and I checked your identity book. I don't think you're a Russian spy!"

We both laughed and Mrs Barns handed me back my pale brown identity book, which I placed back into my handbag while she continued chattering away.

"We wondered what had happened to you last night when you did not arrive but John my husband, the man you met when we both came in with the potatoes, said he thought you had been caught up with that army lorry crashing down Bottle Neck Hill. It is a terror of a hill to drive down. A bus went down it a few years ago, tumbled into the bank and rolled over! Thankfully no one was killed."

I too remembered from years ago how steep Bottle Neck Hill was. My father always told our chauffeur to take the village road, as he was terrified of going up or down it. Mrs Barns fetched a key from off a pigeon hole unit hanging on the wall. A wooden tag was attached to it. She slammed the key down on the desk and then carefully jotted down my room number key in the ledger.

"We have put you in room twelve Miss Parfitt, on the top floor, if that is agreeable to you? All the other rooms are full with our guests. The three spare we did have we have had to put survivors from down in the bay."

Mrs Barns' mention of the survivors immediately brought me back to the purpose of my coming down to Devon and I felt terribly guilty and fearful once again about what had happened to Thelma and Emma.

"Mrs Barns?" I said rather weekly and cautiously, "I don't suppose you know if a woman and her daughter a Mrs Thelma and Emma Times, have been rescued from the flood? Only they lived in a cottage on Neptune Hill above the local tavern. I've heard no word from them and I wondered if there was a list of survivors yet?"

Mrs Barns looked rather crestfallen. She closed her ledger shut to reveal a bright red leather cover with black binding along the spine of the book.

"Most of the survivors are along in the village. I think the Tea Pot Hotel next door to us, along the lane, has about seven," Mrs Barns pointed with her hand, gesturing towards the front door of the hotel, "I think another ten are staying in the old coach house and most are in the Valley of Rocks Hotel at the top of the village. As far as I know there is an officer stationed at the Town Hall giving out information about survivors and the missing. I can't say I know the name Times? There are so many newcomers to the village these days and so many comings and goings. Not like it was before the war when everyone stayed put and never moved."

Myself and Mrs Barns pondered on this fact. Villages and communities had changed. Many people no longer stayed close to their roots like they used to. Mind you I was guilty of that, but it had not been of my choosing. I had never wanted to leave Devon. I had loved it too much, but the situation after the crash was untenable. I had been given no option but to leave and start over again. Mrs Barns broke off my train of thought by adding:

"If I were you, first thing tomorrow morning, I would pop along to the Town Hall. It has become the G.C.H.Q of the disaster relief work. Someone there is bound to be able to trace your friend and her daughter. In the meantime here is your key. My son Alfred has taken up your case for you."

Mrs Barns passed me the key. The cold brass of the key and tag slid into my palm and felt rather cold to the touch. Mrs Barns leaned over the desk and looked towards the stairs, turning to the right under an arch.

"You go up the stairs, turn to the right and walk along the first landing. Then you will see the stairs going up to the next floor. Follow them up and turn right again and your room is directly in front of you at the far end of the corridor. Please do mind your head when you reach the second landing. There's a terribly low beam that runs across it and I don't want you knocking yourself out on your first night."

"No, that would not be very pleasant," I said, pondering on Mrs Barns warning. "Thank you for your help Mrs Barns, and thank you again for that splendid tea. I had forgotten how tired and hungry I was, and it was so lovely to have some cream!"

I began to move towards the steps looking up at the bright rich carpet and pale walls covered in pictures and artefacts.

"I'm glad you enjoyed it Miss. I do hope you will be comfortable up in room twelve. It's not one of our best rooms of course but it does have a comfortable bed and you do have the best view. There's a bathroom on your floor at the other end of the hall about three doors down from you."

"Thank you Mrs Barns," I said reassuring her, "It sounds very nice, room twelve. I am sure I will be very comfortable."

"Dinner is served from six-thirty until nine. John, my husband will be looking after you and my eldest boy Alfred will also be serving tonight in the dining room. Myself and the girls will be cooking. We have a very nice roast pork tonight! Not easy to get I can tell you! What time may we expect you down?"

I thought for a moment before deciding on venturing down to the dining room at six-thirty, as tomorrow I would be busy searching for Thelma and Emma. Mrs Barns said six-thirty was fine and that I would be able to sit in the lounge for a sherry before being seated. With that I thanked her and headed up the stairs to my room.

After navigating my way up the stairs along a wide carpeted landing full of shut closed doors, I found the next set of stairs up to my floor. I heeded Mrs Barns advice and ducked low down when I reached the top floor which indeed did have a very low, penetrating beam which one did not realise could knock you out for six. The top floor was not so well kept as the first landing was. The carpet up there was frayed and nearly bare in places. The walls looked dirty and grimy with only a few cheap prints of wildlife to grace the walls. Two bulbs from the light fixtures were not working, and one was blinking on and off. An old china chamber pot, half full of rain water from a slight leak in the roof, was placed along the corridor. This reminded me, with surprising delight, of the old corridors of the Guildhall in Bath during the war, when they had been neglected from lack of care and maintenance. The only difference was there were no war posters of 'Keep Calm and Carry On' and that other poster of the scary looking carrot, the slogan of which I still could not remember. I finally reached my room, passing the door of the communal bathroom on my way. I put the key in the lock and turned it to open the door. As I stepped inside I feared my room would be another Hunter's Inn experience. To my surprise and relief the room was rather pleasant. It was an impressively large room for such a small hotel. A nice large bed dominated the room, with two night stand tables complete with lamps either side. A dressing table gleaming with fresh polish was in the corner with a small jug of the same pink roses I had seen down in the lounge, and there was an old wardrobe, clean and tidy with a few wooden hangers hanging on the rail inside. There was a small Victorian fireplace with decorative tiles surrounding the grate, and with two high backed arm chairs sat in the large bay window. The room's best feature was the glorious view. The bay looked idyllic from my window; sparkling sea was to the left, with the view of the cliffs and hills across the bay. I had rather greater appreciation of how steep Bottle Neck Hill was and it was hard to think that Billy, Jacob and I had gone down it only a few hours ago. I found my leather case sat neatly by the bed and my bottle of mineral water on the dresser. The room even had a wash basin! Thankfully the bathroom was only down the hall so I would not have too far to go if I needed to spend a penny. Everything was just as Mrs Barns had promised.

*

After half an hour of slumbering sleep in one of the comfy armchairs, I awoke at six to make a hasty wash and change for dinner. I had unpacked all my clothes earlier and hung up most of my garments in the wardrobe, including my evening dress, which I was planning to wear that evening.

I put my toiletries by the washbasin and got out my *Last days of Atlantis* to read after dinner, along with my Bible. I thankfully found the bathroom down the hall vacant so I was able to run myself a bath which, believe it or not, still had the hint of the black painted line around the inside of the tub: a common practice during the war to save water. I never was extravagant with water, but I did need a good soak. So I ran it a little way over the line. I was so glad for a wash and soak and to feel clean again. The hotel's soap was basic but so long as it made me clean I did not mind what brand it was. After my bath was completed I got back to my room and slipped into my midnight, blue, silk evening dress. The garment well covered my knees in length, with a decorative bodice slightly decorated with a trail of blue flowers, embroidered with sparkling silver beads running along the line of the bust down to the left side of the bodice. Two wide straps ran off along my shoulders to secure the outfit. I added my mother's pearls around my neck to complete my look for the evening. The dress had been my one extravagance last year, and at the time of buying it I had felt a little guilty, but now seeing it on made me realise it had been well worth buying. It was elegant without being too fussy or over the top. Even when I was younger and money had been plentiful for clothes, I always chose something simple and tasteful. Less is always more, as my mother used to say.

I had also packed a blue evening clutch bag to go with the dress. In it I placed just my purse, key, hanky and identity card. The rest remained in my normal handbag. After checking my appearance one last time, I closed up my room and headed down to the dining room (being careful not to bang my head on the beam going down). As I got down to the first landing, and the smarter well-kept floor, I could hear the sound of classical music coming from the dining room. An aroma of apples baking in sugar with a dash of nut meg caught my senses. I could also smell roast pork drifting along the passage from the kitchen, where I knew Mrs Barns and her daughter's would be busily cooking away. As I went down the stairs into the hall I could see the lounge door was open, with only one man visible, sat in one of the pink sofas reading a green, leather bound book.

I headed down across the hall past the still closed door of the dining room over to the lounge. I walked past the desk, full of gleaming silver and the music stand with the evening's menu spread open across it. The lounge was rather quiet with only Mr Barns adjusting one of the curtains, and the gentlemen I had seen as I headed down the stairs. The man was dressed in a tweed suit with several gold lapel pins. He wore a gold fob watch and rather grubby looking brown shoes. His hair was thinning and sat like a wave across his head. His glasses were perched over his nose, which looked rather red and inflamed as if he had a cold. As I walked in he looked up from his book and jumped up to greet me. Mr Barns turned round from the French doors, now closed up for the night and came over to me. Mr Jonathan Barns was a tall man; well-built with a round, moon shaped head, he had a beaming artful smile with eyes to match, accompanied by light framed glasses.

"Good evening Miss Parfitt. How are you this evening?"

He greeted me warmly and shook my hand and gestured with his hand for me to take a seat opposite the man who had been reading and he greeted me with a shy smile.

I placed a hand around the bottom of my dress to prevent it getting creased at the back as I sat down. Mr Barns presented me with a warn, soft leather menu and asked me how I was.

"I hope you have recovered from your journey? I was sorry that neither I, nor my wife were here to greet you when you arrived."

"Oh that's alright Mr Barns. It was not your fault. Your daughter Hannah gave me a warm welcome. I hear she is in charge of all the keys!"

Mr Barns gave an artful smile and laughed.

"Oh yes, our Hannah is a proper little jailer! Even if the guests want their keys or not, she soon demands they are handed in or alternatively she thrusts them into their hands."

Mr Barns suddenly turned to the quiet man who was now sat back down opposite me.

"Where are my manners, Miss Parfitt. Please let me introduce you. This is Professor Norman Phillips." Professor Philips held out a hand to me which I took and shook lightly. "Professor Philips was staying down in the Bath Hotel before the flood last week."

I could see Professor Philips looked visibly shaken by the mention of the Bath Hotel.

"Professor Philips is a professor at Oxford University." Mr Barns added.

"Oh!" I said, rather impressed. "What department do you teach in?"

Professor Philips looked suddenly more relaxed at the mention of Oxford and my interest in his work. He closed up his green book and shifted slightly in his seat. He spoke in a peaceful, rather dull voice with no rise or fall or expression in it. It was a voice that could easily send one to sleep.

"Well my department is the botanical department. I have particular interest and expertise in ferns and wild tropical plants. Before the war I went all over the world on university funded research trips. I carried out research in Brazil and the Amazon. I discovered some fine orchids, and carried out extensive research on heliconia. They are extraordinary looking plants, over 450 specimens of them. I did also get to see the good old Pitcher plants!"

"Well it does sound highly interesting, Professor Philips… "

"Oh please do call me Norman Miss, Miss?"

"It's Edith," I said rather timidly to Norman. "You have chosen a good place to carry on with your research. The valleys and hills around here are full of ferns and are rather diverse in places I believe."

Mr Barns suddenly excused himself and left me and Norman to chat.

"Oh yes it is a lovely place to carry out research. The beginning of last week I collected over ten specimens, as well as cramming my journal with drawings and observations for a paper that I am currently working on for the university. I was rather smug with my week's work, when Mother Nature reminded me about the sin of complacency. I lost all my research and papers that I had brought down, along with all my specimens! Even my lovely green Humber car which I had parked down by the harbour was washed off the road. They found it a few days ago. I have been told it's a right off."

Norman did look rather crestfallen at the thought that all he had worked on, studied and collected over the last week had been destroyed. As well as all his clothes and even his car. I could appreciate what it felt like to lose so much, so quickly.

"I am so sorry, Norman," I said, trying to comfort him as Mr Barns returned with a silver grog tray of two sparkling decanters of sherry, ginger wine and some glasses. He served me first offering me a sherry and Norman had a glass of ginger wine. I sipped my sherry quietly, thinking about all that Norman had gone through.

"At least I got out of it alive," Norman added, putting down his glass on the polished table with a tap. "So many poor people have been killed several women and children and two young girls from Australia. I believe they were on holiday."

*

The mention of the two girls from Australia struck a chord with me as if I knew them, or had heard of them. Even Norman somehow seemed familiar as if I already knew information about him. I sipped my sherry whilst glancing at the menu balanced open across my lap. Mr Barns suddenly appeared with two other menus and a notepad, followed by a young lady and gentleman. They both looked rather shy and nervous. Norman stood up and greeted the couple, and I too also said good evening to them both. Mr Barns sat the young couple down in the sofa in front of the French doors. The young lady, a rather pretty and attractive girl with brown hair slightly blond in places, was dressed in a ruby red dress with gold thread and a glittering gold broach. The man, rather muscular and broad shouldered, with fine cut, jet black hair and a strong chin and thick neck, looked rather dapper, dressed in shirt and tie, and a smartly cut black jacket and trousers. The couple looked so natural together; both so happy and devoted. The lady was laughing, I assumed at her husband for puffing up one of the faded cushions as if he was sat in his own front room. Mr Barns came scampering back into the room carrying another tray with two glasses of chilled white wine. He came over to me and went through a list of specials on tonight's menu and then paused to see what I wanted. After a few moments deliberation I chose the mint pea soup, followed by the roast pork. Mr Barns then went over to the young couple and gave them their two menus. He went through the specials with them and then asked them about their day and what they had done.

"I am having the same as you Edith!" Norman interjected, breaking off my thoughts and admiration for the young couple looking so full of life, so happy and comfortable with each other.

"Oh well, they say great minds think alike don't they?" I said to Norman as I put my sherry glass down on the table.

Within a few minutes I had begun chatting to the young couple, who had introduced themselves as the newly wedded Mr and Mrs Pelican. They were down in Lynrock on their Honeymoon. Nigel Pelican worked for the admiralty in Bath and Elizabeth Pelican was a secretary for one of the top brass, which is how they met. The three of us chatted about Bath and they were both interested to hear that I had lived there during the Blitz. They were both very warm and hospitable people, and extremely well mannered. Poor Norman also introduced himself and started talking about the seven hundred species of tree in the rainforest and the many hundreds of species of flowering plants to be found in Brazil. Elizabeth listened carefully and smiled and gestured at various intervals. Nigel however looked rather bored with Norman's conversation and fidgeted a little in his chair. He took great gulps of his wine every few minutes. In the end we were all saved by the next couple to enter the lounge.

*

A tall and rather hoity lady, with blond bleached hair cut aggressively short, swayed into the lounge wearing a long, black silk evening dress, rather pre-war style, blowing out puffs of smoke from a long cigarette holder. I know one should never judge a book by its cover but I thought that if Hitler had ever employed a woman to work for the Gestapo, then this lady, would have fitted the bill. Her face looked aggressive, pensive with pencilled in eyebrows, pursed square lips and deep smoker's lines around her mouth and terrible crow's feet around her dark eyes. Trailing behind her, with his balding head bowed low and a vacant, rather touched expression across his face, wearing a shabby jumper over a shirt and tie and trousers that looked too short, was her husband. The poor man looked like a walking corpse. We were all about to greet the couple when the lady gave out an elegant swish of her cigarette holder and suddenly erupted with an air of hawkish superiority in her voice:

"So what's the drill in here then? Do I speak to you people or do we all just sit down looking uncomfortable at each other, reading our menus until we can recite them out loud?"

Nigel and Elizabeth gave a little silent laugh and looked over at me with the look of 'we have a right one here.' The lady and her downtrodden husband took up the sofa in front of the dresser. After a few rather uncomfortable moments Nigel and Elizabeth introduced themselves to the Gestapo lady who introduced herself and her husband as Brenda and Richard Warwick.

I heard Brenda say to Elizabeth that Richard, or as she called him 'the old fool,' had just suffered a stroke and that's why they were both down in Lynrock taking the sea air. Brenda and Richard had been booked into the Bath Hotel, in one of the most expensive suites. They had survived the flood by staying up in the bar until two in the morning, and Brenda being such a strong swimmer had pulled the old fool to safety. She went on to say that all her clothes and jewellery had been washed away, hence why she was wearing the pre-war style dress which was donated from St John the Baptist's last jumble sale, along with Richard's ensemble of unfitting clothing. Mr Barns told me later in the peace of the dining room that Mr and Mrs Warwick had been originally evacuated up to the Valley of the Rocks Hotel but the management there apparently could not cope with Mrs Warwick and diplomatically transferred them here. Mr Barns dryly added, "The Valley of the Rocks Hotel's loss was our gain!"

*

By seven o'clock Mr Barns escorted me out of the lounge, through the hall and into the dining room. The dining room was a well-proportioned room with three large windows, the middle one was French doors, leading out onto the side terrace. The walls were red under the dado rail and cream above, architrave created large frames in the middle of the walls, in which old warn folded out maps and charts were displayed, along with Georgian gilded porthole mirrors. The room was filled with Chippendale chairs, like the Pump Room in Bath surrounding round and oval tables covered in starch white table cloths displaying spotless silver cutlery, delicate glasses and neoclassical, Regency style condiments. All the tables had a small vase of red and pink roses, and crystal candlesticks with blood red candles, all lit and flickering. A sideboard was covered with silverware and glass decanters with silver tops and handles. A small mountain of fruit was piled up in a brass basket, along with spare condiments and glasses, silver sugar sifters and coffee pots. A few of the tables had elegant bottles of wine with impressive labels placed on them and one table had an ice bucket, with a chilling bottle placed in its middle. With the sun beginning to go down, and with the calming sound of Handles Messiah playing on the wireless in the background, the room was full of candlelight and a glow from the three chandeliers gleaming with crystal, cut in the shape of crocodiles teeth and suspended along the stretch of the ceiling. Mr Barns pulled out one of the Chippendale chairs for me, which I slid into and tucked myself in at the table. He undid a well styled napkin which he handed to me. The room looked like a family's dining room ready for Christmas all full of red, gold and sparkling colours. Mr Barns poured me a glass of water from a jug placed on the table with a slice of lemon treading the water in the middle of the jug. Professor Philips was then escorted in by a young boy who looked the spit of Mr Barns, with the same artful expression on his face. I took the young boy to be Alfred, the Barn's eldest son. Norman, to my amazement, came and sat down at my table, which was set for two but which I assumed was solely for me. Even Mr Barns looked a bit embarrassed by the presumption of Professor Philips. Alfred looked over to his father with a worried expression on his face, as if to ask his father what he should do with this change in the seating plan. Mr Barns gave his son a reassuring look and sent him along into the kitchen to collect the soups. Norman twiddled about moving and shifting his cutlery and not even bothering to put his napkin across his lap.

"I thought as you were on your own, I would sit with you during your stay to keep you company."

"You're too kind Professor Philips," I said in a dry dim tone, drinking a sip of water.

"Not at all Edith, not at all, and you must call me Norman now!"

Mr Barns came over and asked if I wanted a glass of wine. I immediately said yes in a rushed, charged voice and requested a bottle. Mr Barns gave me a sly smile and went off to fetch it, passing Alfred carrying in the soup.

Norman poured himself a glass of water, took a slurp and then continued talking. Going on and on about endless ferns, plants and orchids and rain cycles. I sat trying to enjoy my sweet, very refreshing mint and pea soup, watching Norman rip open a bread roll, while I cut through mine with a knife and spread a thin amount of butter across it. I was relieved when Mr Barns brought me my bottle of wine, which I splashed into the glass and drank a great gulp down trying to numb my mind from the endless chatter of ferns and plants. Norman never really asked me anything about my life or why I was down in Devon. Nor was he interested in the fact that so many people had lost their homes and some even their lives in the flood. All he was interested in was his research and fern collecting. After we had finished our soup the conversation suddenly turned and I found myself beginning to listen and to hear more of what Norman was saying.

"The morning of the flood! Oh my Lord did it ever rain hard! All day it went on, like being back in the rainforests again it was. It had that same intensity. Well anyway, I went into this charming tea room which I had gone into nearly everyday for a bite to eat while I was studying and cataloguing the ferns. Run by an elderly looking lady. She was a bit sharp like an old dragon, but you could not fault the cooking and it was beautifully clean. A lovely waitress served me each time I went in, nice girl, she was too, well I say girl, she must have been in her late thirties. She had a lovely young daughter about ten I should think. Maybe bit older I suppose. Lovely little thing, very polite, hair in bunches."

I suddenly interrupted Norman.

"Wait! Wait, a minute," I suddenly put down my wine glass and readjusted myself in my Seat. I almost began to hover over the table. Could he really be talking about...?

"Norman! You must listen and think very carefully about this." There was an air of urgency, almost nervous excitement in my voice as I tried to get Norman to concentrate on what I was about to ask him.

"This tea room you went in each day. What was its name?"

Norman looked puzzled for a few minutes then suddenly said, "Oh it was Sally's tea room. A charming place it was too. Mind you not as grand as this but… "

I cut Norman off from his ramblings, "Now Norman listen! The girl you saw. The girl with bunches. The young one," I gave a pause and gulped, "Was her name Emma by any chance? "

Norman looked puzzled again and tilted his head to one side like an owl, before a hint or realisation came over his face.

"Well now you come to mention it. Yes! Yes I think… " He paused and then went on, "Yes she was definitely called Emma. I would state my office of Professor on it. Yes the young girl was called Emma. I remember she brought me over my bill and she seemed very excited and happy, and her mother, at least I think it was her mother, explained that she and Emma had only just moved into the flat above the tea room as it went with the job. Emma was excited about sleeping in her new room at long last."

I collapsed back into my chair and suddenly realised why Norman and the two Australian girls that had been killed had all sounded so familiar. They had all been mentioned in Thelma's last letter that she had sent me. A wave of panic suddenly crept into my mind. I had assumed so far that Thelma and Emma had not yet moved into Sally's. That they had still been living in their cottage on Neptune Hill. Norman then added in a sombre voice, "Poor things. Fancy, a young mother and daughter going like that! They were both so young. So full of energy and plans, and it's all been cut short. I don't know. Life does change in ways we don't often see or ever expect."

I sat in the chair feeling rather sick and frail. Mr Barns and Alfred came in to clear away our soup bowls ready to bring in our roast pork.

"What! what do you mean Norman?" I said in a small, terribly worried voice, half dreading what his response would be. I thanked Alfred who gently picked up my soup bowl and went over to Norman, who seemed oblivious to him. Alfred was doing his best to remove Norman's dish off the table with some difficulty, as Norman's hands were sprawled around it.

"Well poor old Mrs Sally's tea room was completely washed away, did you not hear? Went down like a house of cards. The lady in the post office told me this morning. I think the elderly lady, the owner, her body was found in the wreckage on the beach. Badly battered about they say. The young mother and her little Emma they are both missing, presumed dead."

Norman took a gulp of his wine and wiped his lips with his napkin which he unfolded and then threw on to his lap.

"Hey ho hum! That's life I suppose. Here one day, gone tomorrow."

Mr Barns came in, hovered round behind me and presented me with a white plate with a pink pattern round the rim with a beautifully cooked and golden glazed roast pork. The meat looked fluffy and white with crispy crackling on top. A drizzle of light gravy and an apricot stuffing by the side. Alfred then came with a silver salver with a dish of bright orange carrots, golden crispy roast potatoes, deep green beans, a little cabbage and a little onion. I thanked Mr Barns and directed to him the quantity of vegetables I desired. My voice sounded rather croaky and I spent a few seconds trying to clear it as my words wouldn't come out. The pork looked lovely, but my appetite had left me. Norman opposite was throwing on salt and pepper and asking Alfred to serve him another roast potato, as he only had two. He had forgotten we were still in rationing I thought. I tried to pick up my cutlery but my hands were not eager to work. They had become a little shaky, like I had trapped a nerve in my arm. I glanced at the plate, wanting desperately to go up to my room. My eyes were blinking and trying to hold back tears. It surely could not be true? Surely, surely Thelma and Emma had not been in Sally's on the night of the flood. Thelma had only just been offered the position of head waitress. She could not have moved in that quickly could she? How did this post mistress know so much? Yes the owner may have been killed but she was elderly. Thelma and Emma were both young and Thelma had told me years ago she was a good swimmer. She could have survived. She must have. Thelma and Emma could have got out in time, I'm sure they could have. They could not be dead. Not now. They just had not been accounted for yet. I could not contemplate them being dead. It could not be true.

*

The dining room, which had looked so cheerful to me only a few minutes ago, now looked so much smaller and dimmer. Even the golden glow of the lights and candles, which reflected and beamed the light and reflections from the silver and Georgian mirrors could do nothing to inspire me. I forced myself to pick up my knife and fork and began to tuck into my pork. Norman was already well away eating his dinner, but he paused his eating, put his cutlery down, raised his glass of wine in the air and bid me to do the same.

"Cheers Edith!" Norman said rather smugly, "Now tell me Edith. What brings you down to Devon. On holiday? You could not have chosen a worse time to come down!"

Chapter 22
Among the Missing

After dinner coffee and brandy was served in the lounge. I left my table in the dining room, with Norman trailing after me. He nearly crashed into the wooden dessert trolley, with a few of Mrs Barns famous meringues left. They were the size of shot putts, all sandwiched together with whipped cream and fresh, sweet strawberries.

I quickly darted into the lounge and took a seat with Nigel and Elizabeth who were talking about their walking plans for the next day. Norman then shuffled in and clumsily sat down opposite us. We were later joined by Mr and Mrs Warwick but they sat down on the sofa by the door and hardly said anything to us, nor to each other. I observed Mr Warwick had clearly not recovered from his stroke. His head seemed permanently bowed down and he just sat staring at his hands. At one point he shakily picked up his coffee nearly spilling it down him, much to the annoyance of Mrs Warwick who muttered to him "Oh you are a wretched nuisance." Mrs Warwick seemed to have little patience or sympathy with her husband, and I wondered why she was so hard on him. After all, he was clearly not in good health.

Norman rambled on and on about botanical plants and bragged about some of his successful students who he had taught over the years. By half past ten both Elizabeth, Nigel and myself had all pretty much had enough of Norman and his constant bragging with endless details of ferns and trees. I made my excuses to the room saying how tired I was from my journey. Norman looked rather sad that I was leaving and offered to escort me to my room. I quickly put him off that and thankfully Elizabeth came to my rescue by rising from her chair along with Nigel to inform the room that they too were off to bed. Norman stood up and kissed my hand and nodded his head to Nigel and Elizabeth.

"I will see you at breakfast tomorrow then Edith. I would be pleased to escort you to the Town Hall so that you can make enquiries about the fate of your friend and her daughter. It would be no trouble." Norman looked highly pleased with his suggestion but my face must have looked terrified at the idea of having him walk me to the Town Hall.

"Your too kind Professor, I mean Norman. Shall we see how we both feel in the morning?"

"Very well then Edith. We will make our plans for the day over breakfast tomorrow!"

With that both Elizabeth, Nigel and myself walked out of the lounge, leaving Norman to bore the Warwick's. Poor Mr Warwick looked a little panicked as Norman walked over to him, and promptly introduced himself and sat down. Mrs Warwick gave him a look of pure revulsion and her lips were tightly pursed together. I wondered how Norman would be able to interest Mrs Warwick about his university work. She hardly looked like a woman who enjoyed gardening or plants. I thanked Mr Barns for a lovely meal, he then proceeded to wheel the desert trolley out of the dining room back down the narrow corridor, behind the reception desk to the kitchen.

*

I headed up to the top floor just remembering in time the low beam on the landing. I avoided smacking my head on the beam and went along the slumbering passage to the door of my room. I retrieved my key from out my blue clutch bag and opened the door, discovering it had a most irritating squeak. I walked into my room much relieved that I could retreat for the evening and shut out the world. For the next few hours I spent most of the time sat in the armchair, looking over the darkened lane and orange glows of lights from down in the village. The sea was rippled with a sparkling silver glow, but with no activity of late night fishing on its waters. Eventually I pulled myself up from the chair and got myself ready for bed. I staggered about like a drunk, feeling so warn out from the journey and what seemed like days of travelling, but without seeming to get any further forward. Wiltshire seemed like another planet compared to Devon. I wasn't just drained from travelling, I still had no idea of how Thelma and Emma were, or where they had been evacuated to. Just some vague information from a gossipy post mistress who had passed on information to Norman, who knowing him had probably not taken in what the she had said and got all the information wrong.

Most probably Thelma and Emma were both safe and alive in one of the hotels. Both traumatised of course, but alive. Soon, by this time tomorrow, Thelma and Emma would have me to look after them. When I found them tomorrow I would be able to bring them home, with me, to Wiltshire. Thelma and I would be able to sit through the dark evenings of winter in front of the fire, telling Emma about our years in Bath. Emma and I would be able to play the piano together, and I would at long last be able to play the 'Moon Light Sonata. Thinking of all the good times still to come reassured me as I climbed into the unfamiliar bed, and wrapped the cold sheets over me. I read a little of my Bible, and then opened up *The Last days of Atlantis*, but only got as far as the second page before I could feel my eyes becoming heavy and wanting to close. I shut up the book and placed it on top of my Bible and then turned out the light. I snuggled down into the bed, nestling my head into the pillow.

I tried to pray for a few minutes remembering Thelma and Emma along with all the other villagers who had either lost their homes or been bereaved like Alexander's poor widow and child. I then prayed for the people of Egypt and all the turmoil and changes they were going through. I never did finish my prayers, for I soon drifted off to sleep. My sleep had begun well, but later on in the early hours of the morning I felt twitchy and began to slip into dreams and nightmares…

*

The village was grey, white and bleak, like a black and white film. All the colour from everything I observed was drained. The high street was long, deserted and void of life. No one was about. No person came into view. Nor did any bird or animal breathe. All looked dead. I could feel myself being pulled along, like on a factory conveyer belt, drifting through the grey streets past the flower shop, bank, chemist and endless hotels, guest houses and tea rooms. Then I came up to the large building of the Town Hall with the war memorial in front of it. A mountain of poppies surrounded the monument all blood red, the only objects that were of any natural colour. The amounts of tributes placed around the memorial somehow seemed unnatural. There seemed to be so many of them. Some were piled up on top of each other in high peaks that almost reached the middle of the memorial. The wreaths carpeted the pavement and went out into the road. I was abruptly pulled sharply to the right of the Town Hall, levitating up a steep road, passing a few cottages to an abandoned lodge house. The house was all boarded up with an overgrown garden and aggressive ivy covering its walls. By the lodge house were a pair of obelisks marking the entrance to a drive all shadowy and dark like a tunnel. I tried to stop myself from entering this tunnel. It seemed a place of sadness; a place of a deep unhappiness that seemed unable to find peace and be made well again. But as I resisted my momentum of travelling increased and I was pushed up through this dark and gloomy avenue. In places the drive was blocked by dead rotting trees, fallen down across the path. Brambles and sharp bushes reached out at me, trying to grab and trap me. The drive winded up and round then moved sharply to the left. On both sides of the drive were dense forests, having grown wild and become old and ancient. The air seemed thick now with fog and mist, which became more dense as I went up the drive. Then through the gloom I could hear a noise, like that of a bear or wild animal, screaming in torment and pain. The voice was deep and painful and sounded full of emotion, as if crying from an injury. As the noise became louder, I became more frightened. I desperately wanted to turn back and flee back down the lane. As I tried to pull myself back round, the speed of my levitation through this grey and white world increased. Then suddenly, through the mist and protruding trees I could see high up on the top of the summit a wreck of a once fine grand manor all burnt out and gutted. Its walls of brick and cement were slowly crumbling and overrun with climbing ivy. Every window was dead of life, with no glass in their centres, only gaping holes scarred and transparent. The house seemed surrounded by forest with great shadows drenched over its walls.

High above, in a curved and circular turret with ivy bushing out through its former arched windows, an orange glow of light eroded through. As I looked up a cloaked and darkened figure appeared at the window, their face hidden and deep in shadow. It was like the figure of death; still and forlorn, groaning out in pain like that of a dog pining for its master. I could suddenly feel myself drifting up towards that top window, gliding up and along the walls and ivy, up to the window bathed like that of a light house. Finally I became level with the goblin like figure. The figure wore a deep black coat and matching black slanting hat, both looked shiny and were dripping with wet like that of a fisherman. I seemed to float in the air hovering in front of this window, with the unknown and secretive figure watching me through a black veil of darkness across its face. I tried to speak, wanting to ask who or what they were, but my voice seemed trapped inside my throat and no sound came out through my gaping mouth. Then suddenly the figure at the window stretched open both hands, which were as white as bones, thin and wiry. As I focused on the hands I did not realise the blackness across the spectre's face had cleared. I looked at the face. It was that of a young man, pale, gaunt almost dead looking. I could feel myself become panicky. I tried in vain to scream out at this man. His appearance distressed me. It stared at me with a dull, almost questioning expression across the face. His outstretched hands reached my own which seemed possessed by some unnatural force, for I had no control over them. The man placed a small box into my palm and then wrapped my hand around it, like an oyster shell enclosing a precious pearl. I looked down at my hand wrapped up around this small object, and slowly began to open up my fingers.

There, sat in my hand, was a small box. The box like the poppies, was natural and bright in colour. The box was actually a match box, with an old steam boat sailing on a blue aqua sea with a mustard sky behind it. Above the picture were the words: 'England's Glory Matches.'

I suddenly tried once again to speak. Yet my voice seemed

imprisoned within me, as if it was trying to break through a wall. I struggled to speak, managing to smuggle out a few words yet my voice became distorted. It sounded very high in pitch like that of a quacking duck, and my words did not come out properly.

"W-a you want?" I desperately tried to scream out at the man. Realising my voice and words were distorted. "W-you want! Why you here?"

The man just stared at me with a deadly look on his face. He showed no concern for my fright or upset. As I screamed out like a dying or trapped cat I thankfully awoke from my dream, rushing up like a ballista in my bed. My whole body was shaking and my head and face were wet with perspiration. The dream must have only been for a few minutes, yet it felt as if it had gone on for hours. Its effects made me feel highly strung and I found it difficult to get back to sleep again.

*

I must have eventually drifted off for I awoke to find my bedside clock reading seven-twenty. A hazy sunshine was attempting to seep through the curtains, and I heard the sound of seagulls calling out to each other while gliding over the bay. I detected the sound of movement, as the other guests were also beginning to stir in their rooms. I noticed too the faint sound of a wireless from the room below me. Then the rushing about of Mr and Mrs Barns' children, who were no doubt up ready to assist their parents with the preparation and serving of the breakfasts. I crawled out of bed, rubbing my eyes and feeling gritty sleep dust in their corners. I looked out through the curtains to the view of the sparkling water of the sea, with a clear morning of sky above. Down in the lane a dog walker was sprinting along with his dog at his heels heading along towards the coastal path. I too wanted to be up and about early this morning, if only to escape having Norman escort me down to the Town Hall. The beautiful view outside cheered me up from my disturbing dream, and I felt rather optimistic and slightly cheerful thinking that today I would finally find Thelma and Emma. I went over to the wardrobe and got out a green skirt, yellow top and matching green jacket. After washing and going about my toilet routine for about twenty minutes I dressed and headed down the stairs to what I thought would be a quiet dining room. As I arrived down in the hall I noticed a quantity of neatly stacked linens were sat on the chair opposite the dining room door ready to go up to the linen cupboard. A pile of black and white newspapers tied up with coarse frayed string were sat on the reception desk, along with a bundle of letters and cards left by the post man. Mr Barns suddenly span through the front door, carrying a wooden box of vegetables en route to the kitchens.

"Oh… Good morning Miss Parfitt. I won't be a minute. Please do go in and sit at your table and I will be with you shortly."

*

Mr Barns sounded highly strained from carrying such a heavy delivery and rushed down behind the reception desk, down the passage to the kitchens. I did as he said and sat down at the table I had sat at the night before. The dining room seemed so full of light thanks to a warming summer sunshine drenching the room. The pristine white table cloths covered the tables along with the breakfast china and cutlery. Each table had a terracotta pot with a variety of sweet jams and marmalades in little glass pots, along with small vanilla breakfast menus, and a silver vase containing a bright yellow Astor. My fellow breakfast companions comprised of a shabbily dressed man sat at one of the corner tables by one of the end windows, staring out into space. He looked very pale and rather depressed. I had not seen this man before. He certainly had not been in the dining room last night, and by the way of his dress and demeanour, I took him to be one of the evacuees from down below in the bay. By the sideboard of spare cutlery, silverware and two large jugs of orange and grapefruit juice, were sat a middle aged couple both eating through rounds of toast. The husband looked about fifty. He had a nasty darkish bruise across the right of his face as if he had been hit by a plank of wood, or had a brick thrown at him. His wife looked rather wind swept, her hair rather out of place, due to the lack of a brush. I could not see her face for she had her back to me. She had some sort of splint on and looked as if she was struggling to pick up a cup of coffee without spilling it. This couple also looked like another pair of victims from the flood.

The other tables were bare of activity but ready and set for breakfast. Elizabeth and Nigel were still not down yet and most probably would enjoy a lie in as they were on honeymoon. The Warwick's had not yet come down, nor thank the Lord had Norman. I studied the breakfast menu, but knew exactly what I wanted to eat. I needed no menu to recommend what I should have. Mr Barns came back into the room and presented the solitary man by the window with a silver rack of brown toast. He then headed over to my table and greeted me, asking if I would like a glass of orange or grapefruit juice. I chose orange, which he poured into a glass.

"Have you decided what you would like for breakfast yet Miss? I can come back in a minute?"

"No, no," I said happily, "I would like the full English breakfast please. Could I also have a small round of toast and a pot of tea."

I thought I would make up for lost time after my disappointing breakfast at Hunter's Inn. Mr Barns rushed the order down on his pad and then hurried off out of the dining room. A few minutes later the Warwick's came down; Mrs Warwick looking as severe as ever and telling the 'old fool,' her poor long suffering husband, to sit down. They did look such a strange couple, both looking so depressing and dower.

Alfred came in smartly dressed in pale cream trousers and a light blue shirt. He brought me my pot of tea, which I thanked him for and asked him how he was this morning.

"Very well, thank you Miss. I will just go and get you your toast." Alfred turned to go when Mrs Warwick abruptly shouted at him.

"I say Merlin! Merlin come here!"

Alfred of course looked taken aback, Merlin not being his name, and looked about the room thinking she must be addressing someone else. Alfred was extremely polite and went over to the Warwick's table.

"Please madam. My name is Alfred not Merlin. Is there something I can get you."

Mrs Warwick looked at him pouting her lips, then said rather briskly,

"Oh! You're not the mystical one then. You're named after the one who burnt the cakes or something. You have a good Anglo Saxon name. It all went downhill after 1066. Yes, now. I would like a pot of coffee for one please, and my husband will have a pot of tea, won't you!" She barked at her husband who just stared down at his empty plate and made no sound or movement. Mrs Warwick looked back to Alfred and briskly said, "That will be all for the present. You may go."

Alfred nodded his head, shrugged slightly and left the room. The room fell awkwardly silent again with only the sound of toast being buttered, glass jam pot lids being lifted up and coffee and tea being poured into cups. Mr Barns then returned to the dining room and put down my white plate with a fat pale brown sausage, a pinkish rasher of bacon with the fat, a little crisp at the edges, a large white discus of egg with a golden yellow centre, a pile of grey mushrooms and a red tomato with its golden nugget seeds still enclosed inside. I was salivating! Never had a breakfast ever looked more appetizing, nor smelt so good.

"That does look good!" I exclaimed.

The breakfast did indeed taste as good as it looked. I got up from the table completely full and ready to start my walk to the Town Hall. I thanked Mr Barns and Alfred for the wonderful meal and then headed up to my room to spend a penny, brush my teeth and collect a coat in case the weather changed. By ten I left my room, avoiding the low beam and handed in my key to Alfred who was managing the desk. As I handed my key in I could hear the sound of a door slam from up on the first landing along with the sound of an annoying humming and the shadow of a man about to step down the stairs. Fearing it was Norman I quickly said to Alfred I would be dining in tonight. I then rushed out through the front door, out into the fresh air of the terrace.

*

I had escaped the torment of another boring conversation with Norman. I could quite see what Thelma meant when she wrote in her last letter, that he was a pleasant man but a real bore to talk to. I did not pause to take in the view from the terrace. Nor wait to watch the squirrel that was being very cheeky hanging nearly upside down from the bird table. He was munching on a few peanuts for his breakfast, with his curled up tail hanging down, causing the table to shudder. The squirrel soon scampered across the terrace into a hedge on the bank as I headed towards the steps.

I got down into the lane and turned right towards the village. I did feel a little cold. The temperature had not yet risen much but the weather looked like it would be promising and certainly judging from the blue sky appearing, we would be in for a nice sunny day. I walked rather briskly just in case Alfred had inadvertently told Norman I had had my breakfast and left for the day, and he was now running down the lane behind me, trying to catch up with me. I passed three other hotels on the right, the neighbours of the Barns. They all looked as if they were full with either guests or displaced residents from the lower village. The lane on both sides was full of hydrangeas and wild buddleias many of them already covered with cabbage and red admiral butterflies. On the left were the forgotten gardens, all overgrown and neglected, their stone stairs and terraces barely able to be seen. The lane went over a bridge which passed over the steep slope and track of the cliff railway.

I carried on over the bridge, looking down on to the destruction of the harbour and bay. How terribly damaged it all looked. There was no sign of villagers or fishermen. The army and emergency workers had just clocked on and looked as if they were going to try and concentrate their efforts on getting the harbour area and road outside the Rising Moon cleared. I imagined that the work would take on more urgency soon, as the village would need some new sea defences put in place, or the lower village would be defenceless against the winter storms. After crossing the bridge I reached the crossroads with the steep winding road that Billy and I had travelled up with Jacob the day before, which went down to the harbour and lower village. The other road went straight on up into the village high street. I carried on up the steep road and by the time I got to the top I was puffing and panting. I walked along the side of the Valley of the Rocks Hotel, a great Victorian building with an impressive porch and Apophyge pillars. The hotels windows were large and substantial with elegant wooden balconies and window boxes.

Opposite the hotel was St Mary's church with its mighty bell tower and clock, and a long gallery and vestry. A neatly kept graveyard surrounded the church with a dry stone wall enclosing it, with a few benches overlooking the sea. Directly in front of me was a curved row of small shops. They consisted of a flower shop, WH Smiths, and a gentlemen's outfitter. Along the curve towards the Town Hall was the main bank and arch way leading into the courtyard of the Valley of the Rocks Hotel stables.

PC Daniels was out on his morning beat. He passed me and the sturdy looking army vehicle which was parked by Mathews Garage and Motor Cycle shop. The streets seemed peaceful with only an occasional man clutching his morning newspaper under his arm. The gift shops all looked rather desperate for visitors but were bright and welcoming, with blue and white sun blinds at the windows and doors. Racks of postcards were displayed outside, along with wicker baskets swaying gently about hanging from hooks. There were also a few displays of beach and summer shoes, all ready and waiting to be tried and tested by holiday makers. A shifty looking young man rushed past me. He continued through the arch into the cobbled courtyard of the stables belonging to the hotel where a sharp grumpy voice erupted from within the compound greeting the young boy with, "Where the hell have you been?"

Up ahead of me along the high street was the grand Victorian building of the Town Hall. Two monkey-puzzle trees stood tall directly in front of the hall, with the war memorial placed in the middle between them. The main road ran past, with the pavement on both sides cluttered with old lampposts, once painted black but now repainted with a forest green, which were now chafed and rusty. A busy chemist's stood opposite and the village children's favourite sweet shop with a bakery next to it; its windows displayed iced buns with bright red cherries sat in a bed of white icing. There was a selection of current buns and seed cakes, accompanied by rows of freshly baked cottage loaves and bread rolls. I could put on weight just looking at the bakery's window so I ignored it and kept heading towards the Town Hall.

It was nice to see the Town Hall in colour and looking more friendly than it had in my dreadful dream. I still was rather on edge thinking about the dream and the man I had seen in the ruins of the house. The Town Hall was like Cynthia's house back in Wiltshire, only considerably larger and grander. The building was made up of mock Tudor front with two stone turrets, like that of a castle on both sides. Under them was a gaping arch and porch with a balcony over the top, which disgruntled councillors often wondered on to, after heated debates and meetings (probably contemplating the meaning of life after a council meeting). Two flag poles were on either side of the building, standing in the middle of the turrets with Union Jacks hanging at half-mast in respect for all those that had died in the flood. I went along the road passing the entrance to the upper cliff railway station and past a steep and sleepy looking road which ran along the right side of the Town Hall. The road went up well above the village to an abandoned lodge house all boarded up and covered in aggressive ivy.

I walked over to the Town Hall with its big heavy double doors left slightly open. Two army officers, both with clipboards bulging with lists and papers, were stood talking in the door then departed back inside. An army vehicle was stationed outside packed with equipment and heavy containers of medical supplies and blankets. A temporary help desk had been set up and was manned by what looked like a disgruntled army officer. The officer appeared to be going through yet more papers, and shifting clipboards up on to a pile, which were then scooped up by a younger corporal who rushed them through into the hall to where the army relief centre was based. I went confidently up to the desk and greeted the officer who was sat down with his pen jotting down directions. The officer looked smart, well groomed and was decorated with a few tabs, he was very good looking. The officer looked up from his stream of papers and pens.

"Yes Madam, how can I help you?"

"Oh um, good morning. I'm trying to find the whereabouts of a relative of mine and her daughter. They were both living and working in Sally's tea room down by the harbour. I know you must be so busy, but I so much want to see if they are both alright. I wondered if you had a list of where they may have been evacuated to?"

The officer looked at me as if I was dense.

"What are their names please? I will check the survivor's list."

I gave him Thelma and Emma's names and with that he quickly scanned the lists he had in front of him. One after the other he scanned the lists of names carefully, checking each name with the tip of his silver pen. He then turned the page and went on to the next one returning then to the first one to double check. The officer looked perplexed.

"Um… they don't appear to be on any of my lists. We have made a list of all the locals who have been evacuated from the lower village up to here, and neither Mrs Thelma Times nor Miss Emma Times are accounted for."

I shifted about awkwardly, putting my weight on my left foot and then moving over to the right. The officer then moved to the left of his table and pulled out a clip board from the pile.

"I'm just going to look at all those villagers who are on the missing list." Where did you say they were living? Sally's tea room wasn't it?"

"Yes that's correct," I said rather nervously.

The officer studied the list and got down half way to the bottom before making a tutting sound and swallowing hard. His Adam's apple moved aggressively up and down. He suddenly rose from his seat and slid back his bistro chair, borrowed from one of the tea rooms. "If you would just wait there madam, I will go and check your relative's details with my commanding officer. He will know what's happened to them."

He gave me a pitiful smile and walked under the porch and in through the double doors. I waited in front of the table. It was immaculately tidy and organised. I turned round to observe the road becoming more busier with villagers and locals. Two people well wrapped up in blankets, were being escorted along the road with an army medic. Two ladies in summer dresses were carrying baskets full of groceries and entered a small tea room to enjoy a pot of coffee and catch up on village gossip and scandal. They both had the look of being highly inquisitive, but no doubt both had been absolute bricks to the community during the last few days, handing out cups of tea, and wrapping blankets around people. I thought how little the village had changed. It looked a little older; aged with time (like us all) but it was mainly how I remembered it.

The minutes ticked past and I walked about a little from one end of the table to the other. I opened up my hand bag and rummaged about in it, finding the envelope containing the donations Madeleine had given me to pass on to the minister of St John the Baptist, down in the bay. That would be my next job as soon as I found out the whereabouts of Thelma and Emma. I closed my bag and the clasp shut again with a high-pitched snap. The officer suddenly crawled through the gap in the door of the Town Hall. His head was lowered. He came over to me not bothering to retake his seat behind his desk. His warn face looked crestfallen and he stroked the end of his regimented and well-trimmed moustache.

"Well officer?" I said trying to sound cheerful to match the sunny weather. "Have you found where they have been evacuated to? Is it a hotel?"

The officer looked rather uncomfortable and when he spoke his voice sounded pained.

"I do very much regret to inform you madam, but I am afraid that both your relatives Mrs Thelma Times and Miss Emma Times are both missing. There is no shadow of a doubt that they were both drowned in the flood. I have spoken to both my commanding officers and they both have agreed that there is no way either of your relatives could have survived. Sally's tea room was completely swept out to sea. We did find the elderly owner's body on the beach a few days ago. If it is of any comfort to you we may yet find your relative's bodies and be able to give them a burial. I am so very sorry madam. It's been a dreadful thing. So many other people are like yourself, with missing relatives. So many of the bodies were washed down with the flood waters."

I found myself sinking, feeling a little faint; a raw, sudden desperation began to creep over me. The officer, tying to be kind, added, "Why don't you go over and have a cup of tea in the tea room opposite madam. You have had a great shock. Madam? Madam!... Please wait!"

*

The officer's voice faded away as I staggered down away from the Town

Hall with tears streaming down my face, with a hand clenched over my mouth to prevent myself screaming out with pain. I could no longer hear the officer, whom I had not even thanked for taking the trouble to investigate what had happened to Thelma and Emma. He had probably sat back down at his desk, looked at me rushing down the road, with my back slightly hunched over like a lady of seventy, and felt sorry for me. Pitying me for not being able to keep a stiff upper lip and for letting myself down in public.

I had no idea what direction I was going in, nor where I was headed. I could feel myself turn to the right, leaving behind the war memorial and went up the road that went up the side of the Town Hall. My tears stung my eyes and caused my eye makeup to run down them like lava from a volcano. The tears were becoming more extreme and I had to put my hand tighter across my mouth to prevent an eruption of mournful wails. I had awoken from a delusion and false hope that Norman had got it wrong. I had tried to convince myself that somehow Thelma and Emma had escaped the flood and got to safety. Thelma had been through so much, through the difficulties of her pregnancy and the eruption that it had caused with her parents; being hated by her father who blamed her for her mother's death in the Blitz. But she had come through all that. She and Emma had made a new life for themselves down here, but it had ended for them both so quickly and cruelly. The tragedy of it was, if only Thelma had stayed in her old cottage on Neptune Hill for another day or so, she and Emma would both still be alive. She had exchanged her safety and her daughter's safety in the hope of improved prospects, and in doing so it had cost them their lives.

*

I finally reached the end of road and came to a forgotten and abandoned lodge house. Its porch had nearly collapsed with rot and its stone walls were a maze of ivy, with all its slatted windows boarded up. Two elaborate stone obelisks by the side of the house were all that was left to mark the entrance up to Hallowed Hill. The grand iron gates that had once hung with the help of the obelisks had been removed, taken down years ago during the last war and never replaced. The drive ahead was dark and black with a cave of trees and branches on either side, looking like the entrance to a grotto. The gate obelisks were of a pastel red colour, the stone was slowly being weathered away, and was soon to be enveloped by the dark green ivy that was advancing from the lodge house. The left obelisk was already covered with a head of ivy, and part of its base was beginning to crumble away. The drive ahead was still and there seemed to be no one about to enquire or observe me. Still crying and sobbing, walking about in a stiff, haphazard way, I advanced into the grotto of trees and vegetation looking back one last time down into the village. No one was walking past to see me. No traffic past. No person went by. With a deep breath, feeling frail and fraught with loss I began the crawl up Hallowed Hill and towards my former home.

Chapter 23

The Path that Lead Up Hallowed Hill

Although I was hesitant I began my advance into the wide dark mouth that lay ahead of me. As I entered the gaping hole, where once stood the handsome iron gate's I noticed the change in atmosphere. A darkness that caused haunting shadows upon the grey stony path. The milky sunlight had disappeared. The sun completely shut out by the stretched out hands of branches of pine and oak trees. A deadly hush chilled me, for there was now no sound of any kind, not even the creaking of tree joints groaning in the breeze. It was as if the world outside was lost and gone.

My eyes were still wet and smudged with tears. I got out a hanky from my green tailored jacket and dried my eyes a little with a quick dab and then blew my nose trying not to let out any more tears for the time being. I was still rather breathless from all the emotions I had tried to suppress after that officer had told me the news that could not be argued with. I had not believed Norman when he had told me as he was only interested in ferns and plants, and I had assumed that he had misheard what the post mistress had said and that he had got the whole story completely wrong. I hoped that he was far to unreliable to convey such tragic news. Yet the officer had taken such time in checking Thelma and Emma's details and had even consulted his superior officers. That's when he had told me I knew it had to be true. After all, if Thelma and Emma had survived they would have been found by now.

I was deeply aware that the vortex which I had willingly walked into had shut out all existence of the world, with no other being able to account for where I was. No one would be able to locate me but despite my isolation, I still found myself walking up the drive, if you could call it that. Where once had been a levelled and skilfully woven drive, there was now little trace of its former self. The path was dusty, the colour of ash. Hairline cracks had spread along the surface, weaving around small chippings and stones. Colonies of ants had now made their settlement following the cracks like an ancient highway. Now and again there would be great ruts and canyons, making my walk more difficult and cumbersome. I reached the first slight bend and came to the part of the drive which seemed familiar to me. I was now slowly advancing upwards as I walked along the forgotten drive.

On every side of me now were colossal walls of stone, which reached up like castle walls formed decades ago. Father had engineered and commissioned his team of builders to blast a channel through the hard rock core of the hill and then channelled a drive through it, thus why the drive was walled and banked on both sides on the first stretch up the hill. The walls of rock to the right and left of me had also experienced the same plight as the drive, for they had now weathered from years of rain, damp and winter snow. Rusty coloured patches and scars were sprayed over their surface like graffiti. Ivy had also scaled down the walls from the wood above, which had formed thick curtains of greenery down the sides of the drive. Jurassic looking ferns and conifers were now ledged in alcoves and shelves, along with green patches of moss and lichen.

I reached the second of the bends as the zigzag drive suddenly turned and the path levelled out. Now the banks lost their mighty height creating just gentle sloping banks, its floors covered in a thick carpet of ferns, with well-established pine trees all in a disjointed procession. The trees mirrored each other on both sides of the drive creating a haphazard avenue. The sunshine was now beginning to recover and pass through the canopy of pines. The once fine banks of grass, that had been so well kept by our gardening staff, had now become wild and choked with ferns and brambles. The brambles seemed to reach out to me, trying to deter me or anyone from advancing any further up the drive. The ferns seemed to grow like weeds. The avenue of pine trees had over the years reproduced and self-seeded, causing the avenue to almost disappear from the numbers of trees which had taken over the entire hill and become a thick, dense wood.

Along this stretch of the drive I could recall beautiful pink, white and purple hydrangeas like the dresses of ballerinas. They of course were all but gone now, choked by the vigorous roots of the pines and the onslaught of ferns and brambles. If any were still growing I could not detect them. I could hear Billy's words, *that it doesn't take long for nature to take over again*. With over a decade of neglect, the landscape that my father and his team of gardeners had so meticulously designed and planted had all evaporated. A stranger with no knowledge of the area and not knowing about my family's history, would never know that there had ever really been a house up here. The drive now changed to a muddier and wetter consistency as the woods and their branches above, became less dense and allowed rain and sunshine to pour through. It was in places a rather slippery affair to steadily walk up. The pot holes and craters, which below, had been bone dry were filled up with murky rain and slushy mud. I managed as best I could to dodge the worst of the mud, but my brown walking shoes were beginning to suffer.

*

After walking a little further and feeling the most dreadful pain in my back and legs, I finally faced the last of the bends in the drive. On the opposite side of the bend to the right of me was a pair of wrought iron gates. They were about waist high and looked large enough to get a car through or even a small trailer at a push. Not that one could drive a vehicle through the opening at present, for the gates were bolted and padlocked and looked like they had not been opened for some considerable time. The chain and padlock had turned a rusty colour and the grass and weeds had grown tall and thick between them. Me being cynical thought that such unimpressive defences of a padlock and chain (both gone rusty) on a waist high gate, would hardly deter any determined trespasser. I carried on and nosed over the gate to observe a muddy track. It passed through a yellowish patch of mossy grass leading to a pile of brown leaves, cut off branches of rhododendron and a few pieces of splintered wood and timber which all looked ready to burn. This levelled track overlooked a steep bank covered in pine trees and rhododendrons that fell away all the way down behind what must be the Chough's Nest Hotel. I must confess I did not recall what pacific boundary of land these gates marked as in my day all the land had been part of my family's estate, but now it looked like these gates marked the back garden of Mr and Mrs Barns' hotel. I walked on and ignored the gates, thinking that I would make a subtle enquiry to Mr Barns that evening at dinner. Thinking of the Chough's Nest with its fine relaxing lounge in which I had so enjoyed my cream tea the day before, and that glorious view of the sea and sunlit cliffs and coves urged me on. I left the gates and went round the bend to yet another very steep and uneven road in front of me. This part of the drive was indeed the worst stretch of the walk.

Every few steps I found myself having to stop with severe pain in my chest and stomach, and my legs felt dreadfully sore. I puffed and panted every time I paused, my breathing becoming rather sharp and painful to cope with. I carried on a little further to what I thought looked like a mirage, but indeed it was a park bench placed about half way up the last stretch of the drive. I parked myself down on the fluorescent green metal bench which had the most uncomfortable back rest I had ever sat on. Even the pews in church back home in Wiltshire were more appealing than this. I sat at the very far end of the bench, as to avoid the middle due to it being plastered with white, sticky bird droppings. I was so glad to sit down for rest despite the presence of bird droppings. I listened to the chanting of a blackbird singing in one of the near pine trees. The sunshine had far more room to filter through the trees and onto the muddy path as the drive was far wider on this stretch with a bigger gap between the banks of pine trees. The woods beyond and behind me, seemed so still. The breeze had departed and the sun trailed through on to the path, leaving shadows of the pine trees draped over the ground. The friendly chatter of the blackbird continued, his cheery voice the only sound to be heard apart from my panting. I suddenly began to feel very tired, as if all the life and energy from my body had depleted. My whole body seemed to ache and my chest still felt rather tight and painful. I continued to listen to the merry blackbird, still singing away safe on his branch. I was so glad of his company. The only thing that helped me to focus on something positive. I looked round, down the steep road I had crawled up, it didn't seem so bad from my uncomfortable position down to the bottom of the bend, where I had passed Mr and Mrs Barns' garden gate. Funny, all the years I had lived here I never really took much notice of any of the trees or enjoyed listening to the birds. Even the rows of hydrangeas that had once graced the drive I had taken for granted and had not really appreciated. It is very true what people say, you never appreciate anything until its gone, and by then of course it's too late. As I sat on my seat pondering I suddenly realised my friend the blackbird had stopped singing. The hill and corridor of wood that I was sat in was silent. There was not a sound from anything or anyone. The woods and vegetation had locked out all the activity from the outside world, even the birds and wildlife had become subdued. I looked up above at the canopy of pine and oak trees; their highest branches were gently swaying about with the returned breeze, that rippled up through the forgotten drive. For the first time in what had been a long time I did feel entirely alone and it scared me. Being alone on this sad uninviting bench, surrounded by crooked deformed woods on a lost and unloved drive, the memories of the past began to resurface. I recalled the many times I had sat perched like an exotic tropical bird in the back of the Rolls Royce, being driven back and forth up and down the drive, from one party after another. I remembered going down to The Valley of the Rocks to watch a game of cricket in the pavilion on warm sunlit afternoons. I remembered rushing down the drive with Eddie when we were younger, playing in the snow with all the pines covered in cardigans of white, and crystal clear icicles would hang down from the gutters of the house. Edward and I became quite a team tobogganing down the drive. We would start at the top of the house by the south porch, sometimes together and other times on separate toboggans to race. Eddie always won our races but I never minded. I never begrudged him winning. I was glad in fact that he did. Eddie in all fairness was never boastful. He laughed off his winning streak and any achievements he made. We often would go down the drive together on his sledge, Eddie skilfully telling me when to lean either to the right or the left when we approached one of the bends. I remember one occasion during a really hard winter Eddie and I went flying through the snow on the toboggan. We navigated the first bend superbly, but we both got a bit complacent and on the second bend went flying off the drive and landed on top of the dormant hydrangeas. In the spring the drive and grass banks would be a bloom of daffodils and then in May covered in a sea of bluebells. I remembered Eddie escorting me to my first ball of the season and then the wonderful mask balls we always hosted in December before Christmas. All our guests dressed up in fancy dress and masks, and the procession of cars would travel up the drive at around seven; the drive would be all dark and mysterious, lined with flaming torches and chinese lanterns leading all the way up to the house. The last Christmas ball we planned in the end never took place. I had spent all the beginning of October planning the event, ordering the food with Mrs Goodwin our housekeeper. The gardeners tidied up the grounds and ordered the Christmas trees for the house, for the servants to decorate in December. The house at Christmas was always decorated with holly and ivy, with huge displays of poinsettia displayed in every room. I had been so looking forward to my first Christmas ball as hostess, as it was the very first ball we had contemplated having since our mother died. I remember being so determined to make Mother and the village proud. I had chosen my costume which I had ordered from London and I had been so excited going for the fittings and taking my maid, Helen with me. However all my excitement quickly evaporated and by the end of October 1929 my whole life seemed to unravel. I was suddenly struck with a thought I had until now never ever considered. Who had been looking after Mother and Father's grave? After over a decade away from Devon, what had become of their graves? Who had been cleaning the stone? The very thought of my parents' grave never ever being visited, never having any flowers or tributes placed at the bottom of the stone under the words of 'Beloved Mother and Father' made my eyes well up. I panted and gave out shattered deep breaths with tears rolling down my cheeks. I could see my parents' grave at the top of the cemetery looking so unloved and forgotten surrounded by all the other graves so well kept up and cleaned. The grass cut around them with bunches of flowers from friends and relations. Yet my parents' grave must look abandoned now as if no one ever knew, respected or loved them. I remembered what Billy had said about the villagers seeing and hearing my father's ghost up in the ruins of the house, calling out in torment like a dog in pain. I began to sob uncontrollably, my eyes and nose streaming.

*

I then began to think about poor Thelma and Emma. They would not even have a grave or a final resting place for people to remember them. There would be nothing tangible to go to. The most awful thing was I had never really seen Emma. Not since she was a baby and then Thelma and she left Bath to come and live down here. They had come to start a new life. A new life I had been partly responsible for crafting.

I felt incredibly hot, tired and rather flushed. My head felt rather dizzy and my throat was as sharp and as dry as sand paper. A queer daze seemed to rinse its way over me. I knew what was coming. I had fainted enough times to know the warning signs. A blackness that made me feel rather numb began to creep over me. I started to sway about in my seat a little. I quickly picked up my handbag from beside me and rummaged through it to find the little brown, heart shaped bottle with a black metal lid, containing smelling salts. I unscrewed the black top and put the little bottle up to my nose, hovering it gently back and forth. The strong reviving shock of the scent floated up my nose, clearing my sinuses and interjecting a stimulant and a little energy within me. I spent a few minutes with the salts holding the cold bottle in my palm, which helped to cool me down and settle me. I got out my little bottle of brandy and took a sip or two of that, pulling my usual face of disgust when downing the dark, amber coloured drink.

I sat on the bench keeping very still, trying to think of nothing. I stared out on to the muddy drive, looking at the churned up path. It had so much texture and colour, like a potter's clay. I concentrated on looking at the bark of one of the nearby oak tree, its branches had lent over part of the seat I was resting on. The bark was so engraved and looked like a Corinthian column from Bath. It was so was thick and worn, with what looked like a woodpecker's hole half way up, near to one of the first branches.

The silence was broken with the return of the blackbird, who once again was singing out a happy song and then fluttered off to another tree, higher up the drive towards the ruins. After a few long deep breaths I put away my two bottles and gave my face a well-earned dab and clean up from my outburst. I shakily stood up, feeling stiff and my bottom rather numb and began plodding up the last stretch of the drive.

What a fool I must have looked, I thought, as I left my dazzling green bench under the protection of the oak tree and started to climb up the last leg of my walk. *What a stupid silly old girl I am,* I told myself. Thank the Lord no young ramblers had come down the path to see me near hysterical on the seat. What a fuss they would probably have made, trying to be kind and yet patronising on seeing a middle aged woman in distress. I could still hear the blackbird calling out up ahead as I followed him. I dragged myself along up the path, which had become a little steeper, requiring a little more determination. I did my best to ignore the pain and pull on my back and the backs of my legs. As I climbed higher up avoiding slushy mud puddles and a few odd stray bricks, and worn red roof tiles, I saw the drive become wider. To the left of me the wood became less aggressive and spread out, leaving much more hazy summer sunshine to drift through. Up ahead there was a number of enormous spotted laural bushes which had grown more like trees, as well as thick rhododendrons, no longer in flower but thick with leaves and wild looking. The drive suddenly turned to the right, round towards a stretch of overgrown grass with a forest of oaks, ash and pines all in a horseshoe formation. I walked over across the grass stung my leg on a nettle and then stumbled over a pile of stones, rubble and tiles. I continued over the grass covered in all manner of weeds and fought my way through brambles. I stumbled over yet more piles of stones, bricks and tiles. I even strode past an old chimney pot, covered in a messy green stain with a deep crack running along the top. As I continued across the area of grass and piles of rubble, I felt suddenly rather cold and shivery.

A black shadow, huge and tall cut across me and over the grass I was walking along. I passed a tall monkey puzzle tree, like the ones I had seen outside the Town Hall, and to the right I finally saw the object that was causing such a long shadow over everything. I had reached my former home.

*

The house was indeed much as Thelma had said it had been in her letter. It was a shell, a skeletal remains of what had once been. The curved tower and bay window of the morning room was choked with a thick bush of ivy that had grown right through the arch of the non-existent window. High above was what had been my room, that too had been taken over by ivy. The coned roof had caved in, leaving only part of a chimney stack, though no smoke from a fire had passed through it in many years. I walked across the lawn going round the perimeter of the house, passing the elegant curved surround of the dining room window. It was burnt out of course. Along from there was a terribly damaged area. It would have been father's study. Its stone arched bay window was intact with the gutted remains of two more rooms above it standing blank and empty with the sky revealed through them. I peered in through the window arch looking into what had once been a carved oak room, full of bookshelves, with father's desk, leather chairs and a large globe. The room had contained a white marbled fireplace with a black fleck in it. All that was gone. The walls were just bare bricks and stone, all charred and scarred with fire. All the wood and plasterwork had gone too. The ceiling had collapsed leaving great mole hill looking piles of rubble, brick dust and cement all over the room. Only the scarred and blackened fireplace remained badly chipped. It was the only real reminder of the room's former grandeur.

The lawn and gardens had all been taken over by brambles and weeds, and new ash and oak trees had self-seeded themselves on to the lawn. I continued walking round the house finding the library all but gone with only more piles of bricks, rubble and dust. The back of the house was more of the same. The billiard room was a little more well preserved, but the drawing room was a mass of old rotting timbers looking like a debris field of rubble on the floor, with only a few pieces of plaster and cornicing left. The main hall and lobby looked like a bomb had dropped on it. The oak staircase appeared to have been long gone. Much of the upper floors including the fine suite of guest rooms and family bed rooms had collapsed, along with the nursery and attic rooms.

*

After completing a full circuit of the house and starting back at the curvature turret of the morning room, I had to admit that I had not expected the house to be still standing. Thelma had been careful to inform me in her letter that my former home was due to be demolished by the army, after one of the children had had an accident in the ruins. I had expected to find just a crater left with just a few foundations. Billy had told me that the army had been delayed with the flood and clear up operations down in the bay. I thought it would be some time before the army made any effort to get all the way up here, and demolish the house. As I looked up at the carcass of the house, I thought it would not take much to pull it down. The fire had done its worst and gutted the place. Years of stormy weather on such a high summit had weathered most of what was left. I was so glad Mother and Father had been spared seeing the house looking like this.

I walked back along past the morning room, father's study and what was left of the Library. I then went further along the grassy bank that had once been a gravelled path a long a more simply styled wing of the house: the servants' quarters, Mrs Goodwin's old stomping ground. Our formidable but extremely pleasant and loyal housekeeper ran the servants' quarters like an Army Major with her counterpart Mr Tucker the butler. Both Mrs Goodwin and Mr Tucker had run a tight ship. Any member of the staff caught slacking would have been severely reprimanded. The servants' quarters were now as derelict as the rest of the house and looking gutted more like an old cow shed. I passed along the labyrinth and network of torched gutted rooms and silent corridors, and meandered my way round to where the kitchen gardens had been. The walled gardens were covered in piles of bricks and rubble. There were fallen pieces of pale vanilla masonry, and old chimney pots from the house. All the greenhouses were still standing, many with their span roofs looking like they had been prized off like the lid of a biscuit tin, and thrown back on any old how. Most, if not all their panes of glass were broken. The staging inside, which at one time had been stacked with fruit and exotic plants like narcissi and alpines, was now rotting away like a pear. Only a few odd terracotta pots were left looking precariously balanced on the staging where the gardeners had left them. Cobwebs covered the remains of the staging, engrossed with vanilla coloured dust from the rotted wood. Weeds and ivy had invaded the inside of the glass houses, and years of neglect and lack of water had killed off the climbing grape vines. The houses' chequered tiled floors had vanished underneath a carpet of leaves, dirt, fallen timber and soil. The main glass house even had an ash tree inside it. The tree had grown right up through the middle of the glass roof and had burst out shattering the glass roof. The cast iron guttering and rending was hanging on for dear life, with years of moss, leaf mould and grasses. The former plots of vegetables themselves were unrecognisable, swallowed up by a jungle of vegetation and new oak and ash trees, which had become permanent squatters. Even the sundial in the middle of the garden was no longer able to be seen, such was the thickness of the weeds and grass. All the paths that had run up and around the sundial were also covered up by a mass of weeds. Only a few diseased apple trees were left in various places around the perimeter by the old path.

Many of the outdoor climbing fruits, like the fan trailed plums and pears that had graced the inside of the east wall of the kitchen gardens, had grown wild and uncontrollable. In a few places one could see the pegs dug into the walls, that at one time had held the wires to train and support the fruits to grow. I eventually walked through one of the perpendicular arches out of the kitchen garden nearly submerged and covered over by a honeysuckle. I was hoping to still find the path that led towards a set of steps and terraces which led to the rose garden and tennis court. The path however had vanished. Instead I had to push my way through a jungle of bushes, weeds and wild buddleias and managed to catch my skirt on a bramble. Thankfully I succeeded to untangle myself and found the complicated set of steps that had started to sink and subside. After a few minutes of trying to get a leg up I started to climb the steps looking as if I walking a tight rope. No step was the same; each was differently cut and cemented at a different angle from the last. It did not help that the steps were becoming thick and slippery with moss and ropes of ivy. After only one minor trip and graze to my knee, I thankfully at last got to the top.

*

I walked carefully along another path following a grey stone wall that reached about waist height to the left of me. The view on the other side of the wall was obscured by a thick hedge of rhododendrons. I reached a small opening and advanced through it. I came into a large clearing of reasonably well cut grass, enclosed on all sides like a courtyard of silver birches and pine trees, with yet more bushes of rhododendrons. I was now at the highest point of the summit. The sun was nearly right overhead now and it looked like it was going to be a nice afternoon. Two seagulls glided overhead and then disappeared from view. The last time I had stood here the hedges and trees had only been very young and well kept, and one could see the sparkling waters of the sea and channel. That view had now been obscured and the tennis court had become like a box surrounded on all sides by trees and thick bushes. I walked out into the middle of the lawn where a scorch mark had blackened the green grass. *Perhaps some young people had had a campfire up here*, I thought. Who could blame them? It was the perfect, most secluded place for a picnic. I stood in the middle of the court and spun round on the spot, stretching out my hands like an angel, taking in the warm sunshine and dazzled by the seclusion and stillness of the place. The grass looked almost lime green with patches of bright yellow butter cups and daisies scattered over it. As I span round, enjoying a few minutes of letting go of all my tension, I suddenly felt something sharp and jagged under my foot, which knocked me off balance and sent me hurtling to the ground. After a few minutes of irritation followed by a little light laughter at how silly I had been I checked that my foot and shoe was alright. I worried that whatever I had stood on had gone right through my shoe, and cut into my foot. After reassuring myself that my foot was not bleeding and relieved that my foot had withstood the jagged object which had sent me off balance, I got on to all fours. I began to search for the object that had sent me flying. After carefully feeling and patting my hand along the grass I discovered the culprit. It was a sharp, rusty dark brown piece of metal, dug deep into the ground. I stood up feeling the warmth of the sun on my head. Intrigued by the piece of metal I suddenly had an inclination of what its purpose might have been. I stepped over a few feet to the other side of the lawn, knelt down again and after a little investigation and pulling at the grass I found another similar shard of rusting metal, almost identical to the other piece I had tripped over. I knew of course what they were, and remembered the times Eddie and I had spent many a summer up here, dressed in our white tennis clothes and enjoying an energetic, manic game (which Eddie mostly won). After battling him on the court, we would walk down to the first of the terraces to drink a refreshing glass of lemonade at a wicker table and chairs, positioned under a canopy of wisteria with the sweet smell of roses below us from the rose garden.

Although the tennis court had become more wild looking and the net long gone, the two rusty remains of the posts that had once held up the net were left as a minuscule reminder of the carefree life I had so enjoyed, and naively thought would never end. The summer optimism had never left me. Even when Mother had died, I kept going. I kept the house running as mother would have done. I kept up the high standards that the village expected of us. I vowed to do my duty. To keep the family united. Up to October 1929 I thought I had done just that. I thought I had kept the family together as Mother had formed it and left it to pass on to me. Yet I had no idea that October would mark the end of a life I assumed would never end. There had been no warning signs that danger was coming. Nor did I have any inkling that something was wrong. The end of October brought down an order and reassurance that I had so treasured and become far too used to. It had been a month that had begun so happily, yet by its close everything I thought I knew about the world and about my family had shattered into pieces. As much as I tried I could not put the pieces back together again.

Chapter 24
'We Had No Secrets'

October 1929

We sat at our usual Mughal etched table under the shadow of our usual tall palm tree planted in a huge glazed ottoman pot, sipping coffee and eating Turkish delight and coffee and walnut cake. The October morning had started rather overcast and we had been concerned that we might get rained on. However, by eleven the sky had begun to clear and across the channel over to Wales the sky was brightening up.

The Bath Hotel was our meeting place every Tuesday and Thursday morning, always at eleven o'clock. Eddie and I always sat at the same silver metal table, in oriental tub chairs next to one of the tallest palm trees that graced the richly decorated Palm Court of the Bath Hotel. This little custom of ours had not changed for years, even when the general strike had been on.

Eddie and I always made sure we met at our table next to the palm tree to catch up, gossip, eat our way through cake and Turkish delight and wash it all down with Arabic coffee. As always water in the black metal fountain placed in the middle of the blue and white tiled courtyard was cascading down into its basin. Surrounding the fountain were clusters of silver tables with iron legs, each table surrounded by tub chairs. Large slender ferns and lemon trees were all positioned around the court yard by highly decorated cloisters and columns which held up the mezzanine gallery. Great bronze lanterns the size and shape of bird cages hung from above the gallery ceiling richly plastered and decorated with Middle Eastern style motifs. From floor to head height the walls were covered with glazed blue, yellow, red and amber coloured tiles all very exotic and enticing looking. The main light came from a glass roof above the courtyard, allowing natural daylight to filter through. All the hotel windows were large and expansive, with dark wooden lattice shutters embellished with the Star of David. My father and mother had both travelled to the Middle East before they had Edward and I. Eddie had planned to do the grand tour of Europe after his time at Oxford, but only got as far as Berlin and then strangely cut his tour short and came home. I however had never been given the opportunity to travel, nor had I ever had the burning ambition to do so.

But after years of coming here to sit in the courtyard of the Palm Court in the Bath Hotel, the Middle Eastern ambiance had gradually made me just a little bit envious of my parent's experiences. I found myself dreaming and desiring to travel to the Far East and walk through a real bazaar or take a trip up the Nile, or walk through the court yard of Alcazar in Spain. Don't get me wrong, I loved and adored Lynrock. It was my home and I would never dream of moving away, but I would like to have done the grand tour of Europe and gone to the Far East.

For the moment however, I had no time to think or daydream about anything other than the 23rd December: the day I was to host my very first ball since our mother had died two years ago. Every December before Christmas, we always put on a masked ball for the whole county. Last year it had been cancelled due to it being the first year after Mother had died and we obviously could not bring ourselves to organise one. This year however, I thought as mistress of the house it was time to revive the tradition. I was planning a real spectacular evening to make Father and Mother proud. Father had been rather reluctant to give me his blessing, thinking that I was still a little too inexperienced to undertake such a task. I managed to convince him otherwise, sighting that since mother's death I had taken charge of all the running and domestic affairs of the house, without any mishap or crisis landing upon us. With a little help from Eddie giving me his backing, Father eventually agreed, and so the December ball was given the go ahead.

I had spent the last two weeks making plans. All the invitations had been sent out, thanks partly to Father's trusted secretary Marcus, who had assisted me with the stationary and writing. Even Eddie had sat down with us in the Library and blotted the addresses and sealed up the envelopes. We had invited all the neighbouring aristocracy as well as a few of Fathers friend's from London. Most of the villagers had also been invited. My next job had then been the ordering of the food and supplies with the assistance of Mrs Goodwin our housekeeper. As it was a costume ball my next job as hostess was to find the best costume possible for me to wear. Eddie apparently had already ordered his! Father always went as himself, as he always stated he was far too old to go plodding about dressed as a dragon, or classical figure from the ancient world. So it was just me who was in a conundrum of who to go as. At the end of September Father, my maid Helen and I, all went up to London. Father was due to speak and read a bill in the Lords, which gave me the ideal time to find a costume with Helen to assist.

After a whole day of searching and rushing about, from Bond Street to one dress shop to the next, I finally found the most wonderful costume in a catalogue which I immediately asked to be made up for me and sent down to Lynrock. I had to attend one or two fittings as the costume was taking shape, but we stayed in our London house for a week while that was being undertaken. Eddie came and stayed with us to catch up with a friend from Oxford, who was also in town. When we arrived back a flood of invites had already been sent back and nearly all were acceptances.

*

I carried on sucking the icing sugar off my pink cube of Turkish delight and then plunged my teeth into its smooth and delicate surface. Dusting my fingers off from the white powder of icing sugar, I hastily got out my little black notebook from my clutch bag. The book contained all my plans, receipts, and endless lists of things to do and I would be sunk without it. I readjusted my oriental cream shawl back around my shoulders as I could feel a draught coming through the lattice shutters. The Palm Court was rather strangely void of activity. Most of the tourists had gone leaving only the locals and fishermen, but there seemed to be an uneasy feeling in the hotel today. There was a strange atmosphere of tension almost a constrained panic. I wondered if this slowdown in the stock markets that everyone had become increasingly worried about all week was making everyone uneasy and was causing the wealthy regulars that visited the hotel to stay away.

I think it was Eddie and I that kept the Bath Hotel going during the quiet months out of season. The only other people seated, were a middle aged couple in their thirties who had come down for a late Autumnal holiday. I believe I heard the lady's name was a Mrs Cynthia Snail, as I overheard her give her name at the reception desk in the lobby when I had walked in. Her husband was apparently an MP and up and coming star in the Labour Party. He was even tipped to enter the cabinet at some point. That information Eddie passed on to me, as apparently Father knew Mr Snail from his work in Parliament. The only other two people about in the court yard, were a bell boy who was rushing back and forth looking highly stressed and the waiter that had brought us our silver tray of coffee and cake.

I started looking through my notebook, re-examining the guest list so far for the ball. Eddie was sat opposite, completely engrossed by The Times newspaper. The news of the death of Gustav Streetman had dominated the newspapers. He had been Germany's Chancellor and foreign minister but had died on the 3rd October from a stroke in Berlin. Now news of nervous jitters and slides about the stock market and the plunge it was taking was making the headlines. I was never that keen on politics, but I was trying to grasp a little knowledge of world affairs and politics, just so I could make conversation with the endless bores that Father insisted we entertain and keep in with. Personally I could not give a hoot who was in or out at Westminster, or which member of the aristocracy had disgraced themselves, or the constant cheers of delight from the buoyant and booming stock markets, and their ever richer and prosperous investors (Father being one of them). But all that buoyancy in the markets had seemed to have gone. There now seemed to be a fear and shock that what had been going up and up, was now apparently going down and down. Still I knew I had no cause to worry about such things. I left that sort of thing to Father and Edward. Indeed Eddie was the complete opposite to me. He had a political view point on every matter and subject. He knew exactly what the political situation was in nearly every country. He often was able to name various ministers in foreign governments, and tell me a little about them. He regularly gave me dire warnings of what would happen if "that Hitler was not tackled" and paid great attention to the stock markets. He had been toying with the idea of following fathers example and investing in some shares himself but now he was not so sure with the rumblings on Wall street. *The Times* suddenly jolted and unmasked Eddie's face for a few seconds. He then turned on to the next page before his face disappeared behind the black and white print, only his long slender fingers could be seen. His gold ring on his right hand with a dazzling red stone in the centre, clutched round the pages. I paused for a few minutes from the checking of my grand plans, to get a glimpse of Edward's face, to gauge whether the contents of the paper pleased or displeased him. On this occasion it was hard to tell what was going through Eddie's mind. I knew when something upset him. Eddie always displayed what he was thinking; he was a transparent man. He was an extremely good looking young man: tall, slender, broad shouldered with excellent posture. His face was of excellent colour and texture, with thick lips, large brown amber eyes (like Mothers') and extremely long eyelashes, which I could only dream of having. He had thick brown hair which was slightly highlighted with blonde streaks during the summer. He was always excellently and classically dressed, and always looked well turned out for whatever the occasion. Despite his good looks, charm, awards and successes at Oxford, his large knowledge of the world, politics and grasp of history and forward thinking, Edward remained unattached. So far he had not shown any interest or desire in getting married settling down and providing Father with grandchildren to carry on the family line. Eddie also had very few friends. He had many acquaintances, people he knew, who he met once or twice a year either in London or Oxford but he had very few friends who he met on a regular bases. It did not seem to bother him. He seemed happy as he was and did not seem concerned or disconcerted with his lack of friends. I continued on looking at the guest list which now covered three pages of my notebook. I quickly totted up the total with my sharp pointed pencil.

"So far we have over one hundred acceptances, and twenty two rejections."

I carried on gazing at the list as I recounted to Eddie the numbers. A young sarcastic voice came from behind The Times, with a little ruffle of the pages.

"I expect the news of your social event of the year will reach even Queen Mary's royal ear soon!"

"Ha ha very funny Eddie. It's all right for you! It's not you who's planning this ball and hosting it and making sure everything goes to plan and runs smoothly."

Eddie put down his newspaper. His amber eyes looking artful, but he was trying desperately to keep a straight face.

"I was only pulling your leg, Edith. I don't think you have anything to worry about. I expect the whole of the Westminster village will want to try and haggle for an invite to see the glamorous Lady Edith in her snow white costume!"

Eddie sniggered like a little boy of five and returned to his paper to look at the financial pages. I too laughed and tapped his paper with my hand, knocking into the broad sheet and denting the middle, causing Eddie to look up and give me a silly grin.

"I'm not going as Snow White! Don't be such a cuttlefish!" (My name for Eddie when he annoyed me).

Eddie reassembled and flattened out his paper, still looking highly artful and as if he still had another joke at my expense.

"Um… We better inform the managers of all the local hotels to be prepared for an influx of guests. Everyone will all want to stay down here for the ball. Also we had better inform the army to patrol the streets to keep all the villagers calm as I expect they will be collapsing with excitement at the thought of being invited up to Hallowed House for the greatest ball ever put on."

I picked up my blue porcelain coffee cup with gold oriental flowers painted on it, took a few last sips, then carefully placed the cup and saucer down on the metal table. I took a peach coloured cube of Turkish Delight and sucked off the dusting of icing sugar.

"So Mr Clever! Who are you going dressed as then? Rasputin?"

Eddie looked up from The Times.

"No I don't think the long black beard would suit me. I thought I would go as Guy Fawkes. If the ball all gets too much I will escape down to the wine cellar and blow you all up. Let your party really go off with a bang!"

"If you do I will come back and haunt you."

"Well on that happy note Lady Edith, I suggest we start heading home. I'm sure the morning room is awash with invites from all over the country all wanting to come."

Eddie gave one last look at the stock market and shares page hummed, and then folded up his paper. He slammed it on to the table with the coffee tray, leftover cake and Turkish Delight.

*

I put my notebook away back into my bag and stood up to attention. I readjusted my shawl covering over my cream jacket with silver buttons and my string of pearls. I collected my folded up umbrella which was perched up against the palm tree. Edward stood up and straightened his grey striped suit, and put on his black trilby hat with a white band around the brim, which had been resting on the vacant tub chair. He put an arm out to me like a chicken wing, which I took and we both meandered past the fountain and endless clusters of chairs and tables. We had a few words with Mr and Mrs Snail, who partially knew Edward, as Father had introduced Edward to Mr Snail at the House of Lords restaurant when we were all up in London during the summer. Mr Snail seemed very pleasant; an unassuming man and, as everyone had said, highly well versed and competent in the world of Westminster and the political arena. His wife too, seemed very nice. She had a quizzical smile and rather rosy complexion but she did have ideas above her station. I got the impression she gave the orders around the domestic arena. After Eddie and Mr Snail had put the world to right, Mr Snail gave Edward some advice about what shares to invest in. He told Eddie all the doom mongering would be over by next week. As he put it "the market would correct its self."

I made a little small talk with Cynthia Snail talking about my forthcoming ball in December. I explained that it was my first social event as hostess since our mother had died. Cynthia agreed on what a huge undertaking it was 'even if one did have servants to do most of the work.' As we parted I did extend an invitation to the Snails but they sadly were both already engaged at a foreign office banquet and would be unable to make it.

As Edward and I walked out of the Palm Court and down into the lobby, Edward muttered under his breath, "Try not to be too upset that Cynthia Amelia Snail can't come to the ball. Come on I will get you home and you can have a good cry over the disappointment."

"I know it is a shame. Oh well we will just have to soldier on as best we can without her. Our loss is the foreign office's gain!"

"I shouldn't think so," Eddie said dryly, "five minutes with Cynthia Snail there and the Russian ambassador will be putting a revolver to his head. There will probably be another world war after Cynthia has spoken to all the diplomats."

*

We both came out of the hotel arm in arm laughing, feeling carefree and truly happy as we always did after our coffee and scandal. We walked along the curved narrow high street with a stone wall protecting the village from the River Lyn. The river ran down the middle of the village out along by the harbour and out to sea. A wooden trellised bridge ran over the river to the other side where the Victorian gardens were landscaped, located next door to the golf course. As always the Union Jack was fluttering about on its white flag pole in the centre of the gardens with a few exotic palms and monkey puzzle trees surrounding it. Cheerful autumnal flowers were displayed in the flower beds. A path ran along past the gardens and golf course towards the beach. It stretched all the way under the cliffs and Bottle Neck Hill. Edward and I meandered down the high street, passing a few gift shops with baskets of sea shells outside, metal buckets and spades and packets of flags and postcards. As Eddie and I made our way down the high street the locals we passed doffed their hats, and the ladies gave a slight little bob. We ran into Mrs Sally who was walking along the high street, towards the post office. Mrs Sally was a lovely lady of about forty six, who ran her very own tea room and Bed and Breakfast 'Sally's'. She was a very small lady but had a strong determination in herself, and a great business head on her small shoulders (so Mother had told me after serving on many church committees with her). Mrs Sally had the look of wanting to knock you over the head with a rolling pin for she had a rather fierce appearance. She was nearly always dressed in black with a long white apron and always wore her famous cameo pinned under her chin on a black blouse. However, despite her severe look, once you got to know her one found her a kind and practical Christian. She would do anything for anyone in a spot of bother. After sharing a few words with her and Edward pulling her leg about her cooking, which she took in remarkable good humour and fun, we carried on up the road passing the large attractive expanse of cottages. Eventually we reached Sally's with its large black and gold sign of *Sally's tea Room* across the front of the door. A few wicker tables and chairs were arranged outside for people to enjoy their cream teas, along with two milk churns waiting to be collected.

After passing a few more cottages and guest houses, with mushroom clouds of smoke billowing out of their chimneys, we passed a huddle of Spanish bayonet trees, their dagger like leaves shivered in the coastal breeze. A little further up the road was the Rising Moon tavern. It was set on the road that gradually climbed up Neptune Hill, towards two miniscule fishermen's cottages, set up high on the remote hill. Further up were well kept terraces of allotments where strawberries were grown and picked during the summer. Alongside were private sloping gardens, with washing fluttering about in the breeze whilst drying on the lines. The weather had certainly improved now. The sun had crept out from behind the clouds and many of the coves and cliffs were losing their shadows and revealing their orange and pale red chalk and rocks.

The Rising Moon and indeed all of the front row of cottages had a glorious view of the harbour and sea, which at the moment was perfectly still and tranquil. The tide had not yet gone out, and a trawler was navigating his way into the harbour. Its sails were down and only a tall mast towered over everything, apart from the red brick light house, perched at the end of the quay, where the elderly harbour master went out every evening to light the brazier. Eddie coaxed me over to the wall overlooking the harbour with a steep and slippery set of steps sweeping down into the murky water of the sea. We leaned up against the cold rough wall, breathing in the fresh salty air. The breeze tapped our faces and caused my shawl to flutter about like the Union Jack flag in the gardens. We must have stood at that wall for nearly twenty minutes just taking in the air, nosing down into the harbour and looking out to sea. Eddie took off his hat and put it down by his side, allowing the sea air to whip up his hair and float across his face.

*

Along the quay a few elderly men were sitting down on sturdy stools up against the red dusty walls, patching up and customising their nets using a needle and spool. Coracle baskets were perched up against the walls, with a few broken willow lobster pots awaiting repair. A robust looking girl was pushing what looked like a porter's trolley along with a cargo of herrings and mackerel, heading towards the ice house located round the back of the white painted lifeboat house. Further along the pebbled beach a wooden construction that looked like the frame of a tent was assembled in readiness to hang the skate (when fishermen were lucky enough to catch the winged mysterious creatures). A few small rowing boats and coracles were moored along the wall off the harbour, bobbing on the relaxing waters, tide to rusty iron chains in the wall or secured by black, metal bollards. Along the road behind us a grumpy looking man, smoking a pipe tinkered along in a horse and cart, stopping by each cottage and guest house to collect the silver milk churns and bottles. The man looked highly miserable and dissatisfied with his job. He flung up the churns with such a force into the back of his cart, causing them to clang together. The man looked far too young to be so grumpy looking, but perhaps he was having a bad day or was suffering a bad time at home. Whatever was causing him to look so downtrodden, it did not deter him from walking on up the lane along the sea front collecting his milk churns, with his horse's head bowed low. Three young lads from the mineral water factory strolled past him, joking with each other and smoking on their way to the tavern for lunch. One of the lads bobbed his hat to a young girl he passed, who was staggering along the road carrying a tremendous basket of washing and linen. The girl gave the lad a shy smile. Her pale brown hair was tied up in a bun with a few odd hairs becoming disentangled and fluttering into her smiling mouth. This caused her to stop her task and put down the basket to retie her hair. It also permitted her time to give her poor back a rub and stretch. The lads meanwhile, waltzed on up the sloping path and entered The Rising Moon. The sky above us was turning a brighter blue, but still had some thick cotton wool clouds about. A few seagulls landed on the sloping run into the water of the harbour, and waddled about on their bright orange webbed feet looking for some lunch. The boat we had watched coming into the harbour was now nearly docked alongside. Its crew of four were organising themselves to unload their cargo of cod. Eddie gazed at the scene as if he was watching an opera. He had the look of utter relaxation on his face, appearing calm and undeterred.

"Oh Edith! What a life it must be hey? To set sail across the sea with the wind pulling you along with, the stars above you at night, and no one about to tell you what to say or do. To be completely free and self-reliant."

Edward spoke as if he was reciting some noble poem. I knew he had always loved the sea; as a younger boy he had been obsessed with all the old story's involving the sea, like *Treasure Island* or *Moby Dick*. All the dangers and perils of the sea never seemed to put him off, or deter him from his love of the ocean. When he had been younger, he had stumbled across all the old crumpled papers and cuttings father had kept of the *Titanic* and *Lusitania* disasters, which he had insisted on reading sat in one of Father's leather arm chairs in the study. I got the impression that somehow he wanted to escape something. That he wanted to almost lead a nomadic existence, and he thought the sea offered him that life. I don't know why he should have felt like that (if he did) after all Eddie had everything going for him. He was a man. All the titles, land and property would pass over to him on Father's death. He was well educated and had travelled. He was extremely good looking and would one day make an excellent husband for someone and provide grandchildren to carry on the family name. Perhaps Eddie felt a little at a loose end; having completed his time at Oxford, he attempted to travel around Europe, but strangely came back earlier than planned much to Father and

Mother's amazement and now he had taken on the responsibility of running Father's mineral water factory. Perhaps once he settled into his role there or found something else to occupy him he would settle down. Eddie carried on gazing over the harbour, watching the rippling water of the sea beginning to sparkle with a golden tint from the sun. I looked at my mother's gold watch to observe the time moving on to nearly one o'clock.

"Eddie we had better make tracks or we will be late for lunch. You know how Father is about being punctual. Plus I have to see Mrs Goodwin this afternoon about tonight's dinner arrangements."

Edward carried on staring out at the docked boat with its name *The Fan Tail* painted in white letters along by the side of its bow. Towards the bottom of the mast was a shiny brass bell hanging from a hook, along with a red and white ring life raft. The crew had secured their large black fishing net, now pulled up with the rigging. The white sails were rolled up like a rug stretched long ways across the ship. Below the bare wet planks of the boat had become the colour of brown envelopes. Puddles of sea water covered the deck with piles of coarse rope looking like the baskets that one stumbled across in the East, used by snake charmers to store their serpents. The son of the captain, a young lad, was holding up what looked like a skate the colour of a speckled quail eggs. The creature looked wet and slippery, with its long tail dangling down along the floorboards of the ship. Eddie suddenly paused from his observations of the romantic looking scene and the activities of the crew of the *Fan Tail*.

"What's so special about tonight?" he sounded highly unsure of tonight's events, even though I had told him three times already over the last two days.

"Oh don't be such a cuttlefish, Edward! You know the vicar is coming to dine with us this evening and the Lord Lieutenant. Plus Father's invited two big wigs from the Lords down. I did tell you!"

"Oh yes. Yes you did tell me. Sorry. It slipped my mind. Can't we just wait a little longer to watch the *Alexandra* go past? Then we can go. I promise."

I looked out over the harbour into the channel.

"I don't think the *Alexandra*'s coming by today Eddie, and if we wait any longer we will…!"

I paused and just as Eddie had said (right once again) out in the sparkling shimmering waters of the channel, the long two funnelled steam ship, *Queen Alexandra*, slowly crept along the waters. The ship's first funnel chuffed out a long mushroom cloud of smoke.

"See! Told you she would be along in a minute. She's always on time. Great sight isn't she?"

Eddie looked so pleased with himself and sounded very smug but I never minded. I was glad he was always right. The *Queen Alexandra* was indeed a marvel. The ship had the look of a White Star Line vessel, all painted white with a black middle and red keel, and two bronze coloured funnels set in the middle of the boat deck in close proximity to each other. A few packet boats cluttered up the deck along with a compass platform. A wheel house was at the bow of the ship, overlooking the forecastle deck, with a foremast and rear mast at the stern of the ship in front of the docking bridge. The *Alexandra* always docked a little way up the coast dropping its passengers off at the pier for either a long weekend or holiday. In recent years it had become popular with day trippers (much to the annoyance of the upper class passengers) The *Alexandra* was always a hopeful sight to the hoteliers and guest houses. It meant that the wealthy and well to do had arrived to spend their money with them. If the tide was favourable many of the day trippers often came over in the packet boats and landed on the pebbly beach. This was often rather amusing to witness. It was funny. I had lived down in Devon all my life yet had not once been on board the *Queen Alexandra*, or gone over to Wales. Eddie took a deep breath and breathed the fresh sea air up through his nose, clearing his sinuses. He stretched out his hands resting his arms and elbows on the uneven wall and leaned over, transfixed with the splendid view. The *Alexandra* glided past leaving a foamy, frothy trail behind it. Seagulls and jackdaws swirled about in the sky. In the harbour the crew of the *Fan Tail* had unloaded the morning catch and were enjoying a quick pint in the tavern before heading off again, ready to sail with the next tide.

"This is the life hey Edith? If only we could stay here all day and watch the world go by, or jump into one of those little boats and sail over to Wales leaving everything behind."

Edward spoke with such excitement and speed in his voice. As if we could just walk down the harbour steps, commandeer the still and silent *Fan Tail* and set sail for Wales. I looked up at Edward rather vacantly and put a hand on his shoulder.

"Course we could Eddie. But why stop at Wales? Let's go all the way to Ireland and then after undertaking some Irish folk dancing, we could set sale for America! "

We both laughed at my sarcastic joke but I could not shake off the feeling that Eddie wanted to get away from something. He seemed happy enough, but there was something lurking in the background that was causing him to feel uneasy and apprehensive. He had got over Mother's death rather too well at the time. Perhaps he was still missing her. Perhaps there was still a gap in his life that had not yet been filled.

"Come on then Lady Edith, we had better get back home or we'll both be in the dog house with Father. Since your mistress of the house you need to make sure the soup is served in the correct terrine or the world will crumble to pieces."

*

I noticed Eddie had to force himself to leave the harbour wall. We both walked quietly away from the harbour, up towards the cliff and sealed entrance of the lime kilns; sealed for the present, while the burning process was being undertaken. Eddie stroked my hand which was tightly curved around his arm. The red ruby stone in his gold ring flashed out a dazzling flicker of blood red colour as the sun's rays caught it. We walked up and through the well-kept gates and entrance of the cliff railway, where I spoke a few words with the ticket collector, who said how much he was looking forward to the ball. Edward seemed very tense while we waited for the railway carriage to glide down from high above us at the top of the cliff in the upper village.

"Eddie is everything alright?" I inquired sympathetically. "You're not worried about anything are you? You would tell me if you had a problem wouldn't you?"

Just then the carriage came hurtling down. It slowed and juddered down to a clatter followed by the rushing sound of water as the carriage was secured in place. Then the controller unlocked the gate and undid the heavy wooden door to let out a trickle of passengers from inside.

Eddie kissed my head, feeling his nose touching my hair.

"Dear Edith. Everything is fine. Nothing to worry about. If I had a problem I would soon tell you. Shall we go up then? After you."

Eddie motioned me to go first and I walked on through the unlocked gate.) We walked through the next gate up into the wooden panelled carriage with Eddie close behind me. As we sat down in the carriage I pondered what Edward had said about how he had no problems and that all was well. Despite Eddie's reassurance I still felt as if there was something he was not telling me. Eddie sat down in the seat opposite me gazing about the compartment which apart from us was empty. He sat with his legs a little apart, with his trilby hat on covering his thick brown hair. He smiled at me warmly and gave his face an itch with his long fingers. The doors to the compartment slid into place and locked. There then came the sharp ring from the bell, followed by the sound of rushing water, the carriage shuddered and then began to slowly move up on its track, up towards the top of the cliff to upper Lynrock.

Eddie shifted in his seat and looked towards the sea that was quickly diminishing away from us as we moved up the cliff. Eddie almost looked as if he was never going to see the view again. He was paying so much attention to the sight of the sea. I too looked back at the sea, still feeling unsure of Eddie's response. But then again, I reconciled myself, Eddie and I had always been close and had only been parted during his time at Oxford, and his month away in Paris and Berlin. Apart from that we had never been parted and were inseparable. We both got on so well and we trusted each other completely. We had never really argued or quarrelled like some brothers and sisters did. The strong bond between us had always remained cemented on the strong foundation that above all we told each other everything. We had no secrets'.

Chapter 25

I'll Go Tell Mr Tucker to Stop His Worrying!

October 1929

I had escaped for the afternoon on a short but pleasant walk along the coastal path. The path had been a little wind swept and was littered with tiny black bullets of goat droppings. I did manage to avoid stepping into them and the enjoyment of walking along the edge of the cliff outweighed the worry over the unpleasant presents the goats had dropped. The edges of the cliffs were covered in grasses, heathers and the sight of yellow moors growing on plunging rocky banks that ran down into shear drops into the aqua sea. It was certainly a pleasing stroll. I had walked along the cliffs for some time until I came to the Valley of the Rocks. The afternoon's stroll had been a peaceful one but I knew I had better make tracks. I could not put it off any longer. Feeling a little apprehensive at the thought of returning home, I slowly made my way back into the village and had come full circle. Home was not far off.

I just had to get out of the house for a few hours. Even in the safety of the morning room, which was my own domain, I could still hear the yelling and shouting from Father. He had called Eddie in to the study as soon as we had both returned from our morning coffee and our relaxing trip to the harbour. We both had been hoping for a peaceful lunch but Father had summoned Edward and delayed lunch by over an hour. I felt highly embarrassed that such a slanging match was carrying on in the house and I knew it was bound to be talked about in the servants' hall. I felt bad for the servants for, with our lunch delayed, it meant they would not get their meal until much later, if at all.

Downstairs was going into action stations ready for tonight's dinner, with Father's fellow Lords from London coming down. At one point I had got so on edge listening to the raised, angry exchanges between Eddie and Father and feeling most anxious I rushed out of the morning room towards Father's study door. I thought I had better try and attempt a ceasefire. After hearing what sounded like a glass being smashed and more heated words between Father and Eddie I ran down the passage up to Father's study door. I gripped the golden coloured door handle about to turn it and enter. However as I prepared to enter I was stopped in my tracks with the heated exchange that Eddie and Father were having. I listened with my ear pressed against the walnut panelled door. Father was shouting rather aggressively with a touch of exasperation in his voice. I could hear papers being flung as if he was waving his hands about with a pile of papers in his hand.

As I listened in, Eddie sounded as if he was pouring himself a drink. I could hear the thud of a decanter stopper being clumsily taken off, and the clanking of a glass next to its neck and the slight pouring of a liquid. There was suddenly another tremendous crash and crack of glass. Something else had been thrown and smashed. My heart was pounding. Never had Father been violent with Eddie or me before. I heard Eddie sounding like he was trying to calm Father down and appease him.

"For God's sake Father, calm down!"

Father however was in no mood to negotiate or start diplomacy and continued his aggressive ranting.

"You sir will do nothing! You have caused enough trouble and damage! What would people say when they realised you had taken flight and left for the continent. People would soon realise there was some truth in it! No! No sir, you will pull yourself together and carry on doing your job, which is running my factory and upholding your station as heir to this estate."

The rest of the conversation became a little muffled and I was unable to hear what Eddie and Father were saying. Then the tone increased in volume and anger again. Eddie had now become more emotional and his voice sounded highly charged and shaky

"You can't do this Father! You can't just send him away!"

Father sounded undeterred by Eddie beginning to lose his composure, something Eddie did not ever do. Even when mother had died he had not cried. Not in front of me or Father. Now however, something had broken Edward's veneer of not showing any emotion. He sounded as if he was close to tears, almost choking back his raw emotions.

"I will never forgive you for this Father! Never! You do this and I will go as well. I warn you! You will never hear anything from me again!"

By this time fearing that Father had perhaps pushed Eddie too far, I turned the handle of the door and began to push it. To my amazement and shock I found the door was locked! Locked from the inside. Father had locked himself in the room with Edward. Why had he done that? Father had never locked his study door, never. What on earth was going on? I tried the handle again and pushed against the door thinking that perhaps I had been mistaken, and the door had just become a little stiff. It was to no avail. The door was most definitely locked. I even lowered myself down to the lock to try and have a look through the key hole but the key blocked the lock and my spy hole was no good. Eddie was sounding highly upset and at breaking point. I desperately wanted to break into the room and comfort him.

There then came a noise of someone walking across from the servants' quarter's door, through the main hall and heading in my direction. Wanting to stay, but fearing I would be discovered eaves dropping by one of the servants' I scuttled back down the passage to the morning room. I rushed into the still and peace of the bright room, leaving the door slightly ajar so I could catch a glimpse of who was about to try and gain entrance into the study. I poked my head out and around the door and glared down the corridor of busts, companion tables, bronzes, portraits, and red velvet chairs, waiting rather nervously to see who else was about to stumble upon the locked study door and hear the crying from Edward behind it. I waited and waited, listening to the footsteps getting louder and louder. Perhaps it was Mrs Goodwin or Mr Tucker coming to collect the grog tray for cleaning and refilling. To my great surprise it was neither of them. It was Marcus, Father's trusted secretary who also looked rather on edge and appeared as though he was suffering from a cold, with rather swollen eyes and his face pale. I observed him walk solemnly up the passage and pause in front of the heavy study door. He listened just as I had done. I thought Marcus would soon realise a family argument was raging and, not wanting to intrude or embarrass Father or himself, he would turn away back to his own office. He would wait there until peace returned to the study. To my shock Marcus did not do what I expected. He did what I had dared not do. He knocked on the door!

Marcus was far braver than I was. I did not dare knock on the door and expect it to be opened to me and be given a warm welcome, and I was mistress of the house! Marcus was a man though and Father's secretary, so I imagined he felt undeterred knocking on the study door and expected to be let in as he often was. Marcus was also very close to both Father and Eddie and had father's ear on most things. I continued to watch Marcus. He was still standing outside the study door, standing as still as a statue, looking and studying the intricacies of the door panelling. After a short pause the study door was unlocked and opened. Light from within the study came rushing out into the passage. Marcus strangely paused for a second before entering, taking a deep breath. Then he slowly walked in to the study and the door was shut and locked behind him. After that the house remained still and fell into a deadly hush. Whatever had gone on between Father and Edward, hostilities had been ceased when Marcus had entered the room.

I continued on along past the Town Hall and the war memorial being cleaned in readiness for Remembrance day in a few weeks' time. I was about to turn up the lane towards the house, but dreaded going back. I wondered what sort of house I would return to. Wanting to delay my return for as long as I could I continued straight on towards St Mary's Church and The Valley of the Rocks Hotel at the end of the high street. I turned steeply down a quiet lane shaded a little with young oak trees and buddleias.

The road went along the back of the hotel's garden. They were immaculately kept and restored after the neglect it, and so many other gardens, had suffered during the war. The gardens comprised of a graceful green lawn sloping down steeply to a stone wall, which identified its end. A few stone steps at various places and intervals were put into entrances in the wall, guarded by elaborate single gates to allow guests to wander down and out into the lane. This allowed guests the option of walking along the lane to the harbour, or to take the walk I had just done. I carried on along the narrow sturdy road, passing the hotel's gardens on the left. The road levelled off now with a row of four posh grand villas further on. The villas all had terraced gardens and spectacular views of the sea opposite. The lane was peaceful and almost forgotten for the afternoon. I had only the birds nesting up in the conifers for company with the sound of the sea softly caressing the shore below. There was an occasional ringing of the cliff railway bell, shuttling up and down with day trippers and locals. The vegetation had grown a little wilder in recent years and the rhododendrons had grown rather thick in places. They made the lane rather secretive and mysterious.

On the right were sloping banks that were ingeniously landscaped to provide narrow but long corridors of plots, which were managed by a decreased number of vegetable growers and gardeners. So many men both young and old never came back from the Great War. During the war, many of the allotments had been abandoned and were not taken up again until their gardeners returned (the lucky ones that is). The lane was full of tiny gates set in the right side of the wall leading down steep sets of steps towards the terraces of vegetables and fruits. Some of the gates had however still not reopened. Their gardeners had not come back from the fighting in the trenches. Thankfully many of the plots were being again restored and no doubt would continue to be for decades to come, as it was unthinkable that there would be another war to send them back into neglect.

I walked over the bridge which ran over the channelled cliff and track of the railway and came past one of the grandest villas along the lane. It was a superb three story villa known as Chough's Nest House owned by Mr Theo Barnaby, a former cabinet minister of the last government, and his wife; both of whom were coming to the ball in December.

As I passed the Barnaby's imposing villa, I came along a more leafier and shadowy part of the path due to the tall oak trees on either side of the lane, their roots dug deep down into the banks of the cliff. I turned a corner and found the north steps that went up a considerable way around the back of the villa, up towards our own garden and tennis court. The stone steps were as normal, swept and cleaned of leaf litter. The steps and paths ran up some way through a sparsely wooded area right up to the rose garden and tennis court. It was always a long and rather labouring walk, and one felt the need for a good stiff drink afterwards. However anything was better than going into the house too early and hearing yet more arguments. Still I had to go in as it was nearly four and I would have to inspect the dining room to check the staff were well on schedule for tonight's dinner. Goodness knows how that was now going to go after all this bad atmosphere and arguing.

*

After a long trek up the series of steps and paths, then through the well managed woods and banks of ferns, I made it up to the tall set of gates and urns which lead into the rose garden. I went with the path passing the wall of the kitchen garden, then back along to the south lawn and side of the house. The gardens were still looking lovely, even though it was now mid-October. We were very fortunate that five of the twelve gardeners we had before the war came back to us. Rogers had sadly been severely shell shocked and every now and again had a sort of relapse, I suppose you would call it a panic attack. But he found returning to the garden and his work a tonic and gradually his attacks became less frequent. I think for Rogers, being in service was a place of safety and reassurance. He knew his place, and knew we would always look after him, and that he would always have a job with us for as long as he wished.

I reached the south porch of the house and went in through the garden room. The room was tiled with a blue and white Chinese patterned floor, with a table full of pink, purple and white orchids and aspidistras. A wicker set of tub chairs were also available around the table, which occasionally we sat at during the summer months to have breakfast. I walked on through into the main hall. The hall had a rather impressive diagonal chequered floor in black and white tiles. A tremendous ornate imperial style chandelier hung from the ceiling, over a richly decorated polished oak staircase. Young Spencer, our under footman, greeted me and took from me my light brown coat with dark brown fur trimming around the sleeves and collar. I placed my leather gloves, hat and pin on the round walnut inlaid table, which was decorated with an enormous vase of white and yellow roses for that evening's dinner. I marched across the hall through the vestibule then through into the morning room. I rang the bell by the white marble fireplace, its mantle covered in china parrots and a mantle clock with a glass dome over it.

I walked over to my writing desk and moved a pile of invitation replies into a pending tray. I would sort through these the next morning. I went over to the window and looked out on to the lawn. It was a lovely afternoon, more like a summer's day than mid-October. Rogers was wheeling a wheelbarrow across the lawn, picking and sweeping up a few brown discarded leaves dropped by a few of the trees. Rogers seemed to be almost his old self again. He was whistling an odd tune now and again, and often gave me a wave and a doff of his cap when he saw me. I never thought of the servants as just underlings, rushing about fulfilling our every whim. I liked to think of them as an extended family. After all they had nearly all watched me grow up and been with me through my days of childhood. They had all contributed to mine and Edward's happy childhood, and now I saw it as my duty to protect them and make sure they were all happy and provided for during their time with us in service. A knock of the door interrupted my maxim. The door opened and in stepped young Spencer, who came in and closed the door softly behind him. I turned back to the writing desk and put away a few letters of correspondence into one of the tiny drawers as I talked to Spencer.

"Ah Spencer. Is his Lordship still in?" I enquired almost dreading to ask.

"No my Lady. His Lordship left for a meeting with Mr Cuss after receiving a telegram, and Mr Edward went out a few minutes after. I am afraid Mr Edward did not mention where he was going."

"I see. Thank you Spencer. Would you bring me some tea please and some of Mrs Goodwin's Victoria sandwich cake. My walk has rather warn me out."

"Very good my Lady," Spencer nodded and was about to leave the room when I suddenly thought about tonight's dinner.

"Oh Spencer! Before you go. Is everything organised and ready for this evening?" Spencer nodded again, "I believe so my Lady. We have laid up in the dining room and Alice has done the flowers in the hall and in the drawing room."

I smiled "Yes I saw the hall flowers they look very nice. Do tell Alice how well she has done for me. I will go and see the dining room before I sit down for my tea."

"Very good my Lady. I will tell Alice how pleased you are. I will go and organise your tea for you."

Spencer left the room as carefully as he had entered it and closed the door behind him. I too left the peace and brightness of the room and walked down the vestibule towards the double doors entering the saloon. I crossed into the dining room with the drawing room door opposite. As Spencer had said the dining room was indeed ready for the evening's dinner. The long walnut table was laid to perfection; the table settings were all in equal proportions (thanks to Mr Tuckers ruler) with gleaming chargers and six courses of cutlery set out. Six sets of glasses were at each setting, all sparkling cut crystal glassware, along with silver condiment sets. All the settings had a tiny, white, stiff place cards with the guests names written on them in scrolled, fluent writing, along with tonight's menu on a separate card. There were fresh gleaming white starched napkins, several silver dishes were left on the table ready for the decanters to be placed on them. The centrepiece of the table was a silver gilt epergne, with an elaborate scrolled base and six slender candle holders with long white candles placed in each one. In its centre was a magnificent display of autumnal flowers of yellow, orange, ginger, red and trailing ivy. At either end of the table were smaller arrangements of flowers, along with two ornate china stands of polished fruit, sat on beds of polished leaves. All the red striped velvet chairs had been brushed. The two chandeliers at either end of the room had been cleaned. The sideboards had been polished with the silver-plated copper hot plates on them in readiness to keep the courses warm. All the decanters had been taken away, down to the butler's pantry; Mr Tucker would have selected the wines, Father had instructed him to decant along with bottles of port.

I went over to the dark, speckled marble fireplace and checked the baroque mantle clock was the exact time with Mother's watch. Flowers had been placed either side of the clock in tall vases to give continuity with the table decorations. Two silver gilt, five light candelabras had been cleaned at the end of the mantelpiece. The staff had made a huge effort for this evening's dinner. Everything had been done perfectly. No detail spared. I walked back into the saloon which also had been cleaned and polished. I then had a quick peep in the drawing room, which also looked splendid. Fresh flowers were placed on the fireplace, and the fire was ready to be lit later on. All the upholstery looked spotless and upright, with not a speck of dust or crumb anywhere. I never doubted the servants, nor did I have any fear that all their efforts would not be well received by our guests. I was however terribly worried about Father and Edward. I had never known either of them to have such a row before. Not to the point of becoming violent and smashing glasses. I only hoped that they had both calmed down. Perhaps Marcus going in had cooled their spirits and there would be no embarrassment tonight.

*

I walked back towards the morning room trying to reassure myself that all would go well. Feeling extremely thankful that the servants had done such a superb job with preparing the family rooms, I decided to pop down to the servants' hall to thank them all for their efforts so far. I would wish them well for the evening ahead and also reassure them that all was well upstairs. They were bound to have heard the argument between Father and Edward. I thought it best to kill any fears they had about the family's unity and to prevent any extra nerves for the evening. I would put on a brave face for them, even though deep down I was extremely anxious about the state of my family's health.

Down in the servants' quarters the staff were in a whirl of activity.

The stone passages were awash of footmen and maids rushing past with piles of laundry from the laundry room, heading towards the linen closet. The footmen were carrying silverware, as well as delicate china and parts of the dinner service. They weaved their way from the china closet towards the dumbwaiter. As I walked down the dim and rather dark passages, the servants no matter what they were doing, immediately stopped and greeted me warmly and politely. I wandered past Mrs Goodwin's room with the door partly open. Her room looked rather cosy and comfortable. There was a roll-top desk with plenty of room for her to run and organise the staff successfully. It had a few mahogany letter racks full of letters, rotas and lists, and a nice little fireplace with white painted surround and sturdy mantle covered with Whieldon Cow creamers and an assortment of other jugs and ornaments. The rooms contents also included a glass bookcase full to the brim of fraying thick volumes of household management books like '*The Laundry maid*', '*The Dictionary of cooking*' or '*Marriage And Home Life*'. In addition there were account books, ledgers and photo albums. A long dark wood grandfather clock, two armchairs and a large table set for Mrs Goodwin's afternoon tea occupied the room. There were no Goodwin family photos on the walls for she had no family left living. There were however a few staff photos of all the servants photographed together but all rather formal looking. As I headed past Mrs Goodwin's room and past the housekeepers storeroom and china closet door, I contemplated that although Mrs Goodwin had no husband or children of her own, she had indeed been married to her job as housekeeper here, and her children and family had become the rest of the servants.

Up ahead was the engine room of the house. The kitchen had the height and length of a church with a vaulted ceiling and double hammer beams. Four tall, high up windows let in the maximum amount of light, but were high enough to prevent Mrs Kier's kitchen maids from daydreaming out the windows, or making eyes at any of the gardeners. Mrs Kier was standing over her long beach table with drawers underneath for utensils and cutlery, that glided out with ease. The top of the table was covered in marble. It bore wooden chopping boards with bread knives, wooden spoons and large mixing bowls with balloon whisks in. A metal chicken wire basket was filled with green apples and a large cider jug stood next to it. A white metal and silver imperial set of scales was being used by Betty (one of the kitchen maids) with heavy black metal weights next to it. A large container of flour was positioned nearest Mrs Kier's station, along with a rack of eggs and a large blue and white floral jug. On all sides of the kitchen were tall dressers and work tops covered in polished coppers, storage jars and pots. Plate racks covered the walls with blue and white china plates adorning them. At the far end of the kitchen was Mrs Kier's famous range cooker which looked well-worn with use. Next to the range and cookers were two tall pan racks, with racks hanging from the ceiling displaying additional copper pots and grey metal saucepans. A Windsor chair was sat in the corner and a wooden box was attached to the wall above to store salt.

I observed the large '*Household Wants Indicator*'. The poster had four columns with thirty six items of food listed like flour, fruit, or rice. A box was found at the end of the item to be marked by either Mrs Goodwin or Mrs Kier when provisions were getting low, and a need for reordering was required. A New Gate clock was ticking gently away on the wall, along with a shelf of fat and fumbled cookery books. A large Belfast sink with draining board and plate rack was on another wall. The majority of the washing up was done in the scullery (next door to the kitchen) close to the larder and still room.

The kitchen was run and dominated by Mrs Kier. A round, small lady; her cap covered her thinning jet black hair which was brushed and swept to the back of her head. Mrs Kier was often a woman who, shall we say, spoke as she found and was not one of life's charmers. She was however a brilliant cook and I had never eaten a bad meal with her. Despite the normal tradition of the housekeeper never hitting it off with the cook, Mrs Goodwin and Mrs Kier were the exception to this rule. They both got on well and often took tea in each other's room (time permitting). However Mr Tucker and Mrs Kier had no love lost between them. There were often a few heated exchanges between the two of them and Mrs Goodwin often had to play the role of diplomat.

*

As I walked into the kitchen, Betty was measuring out flour for Mrs Kier. Mrs Kier was supervising Dorothy, who was busy cooking apples for the apple tart. Gillian, the bane of Mrs Kier's life, as she had an unfortunate gift of dropping things, was carefully separating eggs. James then came rushing in with some marrows from the kitchen garden and carried them off towards the back of the kitchen, ready for Betty to prepare later. I was just about to greet the kitchen staff, when there was an almighty crash and scream from Gillian. She had managed to propel her bowl of eggs off the beach table and on to the tiled floor. Mrs Kier charged round to her like she was on a merry-go-round, only she was not so merry.

"You stupid, silly, clumsy girl, Gillian! Just look at the state of the floor, and all those eggs! I don't know, Gillian. I think you could do with having some electric shock treatment, I really do. I have never known such a girl who's as clumsy as you."

By this time, Gillian (who by the way would have made a good daughter for Mrs Kier, as she had the same miserable expression and the same jet black hair) had her head bowed low and had begun to sob. Mrs Kier's temper never lasted very long and she soon got over her outburst.

"There's no good crying over it now, Gillian. You had better go and get a wet cloth, a bucket full of warm water with a bit of lemon in, a mop from the scullery and clear all that up. Then when you have finished that, you can get to and wash and peel those marrows."

Gillian scampered out one of the side doors, drying away her tears. Suddenly Mrs Goodwin came in behind me and announced to the kitchen that I was present.

"Why Lady Edith! Is there anything the matter?"

Mrs Goodwin was a lovely looking lady, tall and thick set with a kind and rosy face with a thick head of blond hair. She always wore either black or blue with a long skirt and a long set of jangling keys with a tiny pair of scissors completing the bundle.

"No Mrs Goodwin, everything is fine. I just wanted to pop down and say how lovely the dining room looks. You have all done a wonderful job. It all looks superb."

Both Mrs Goodwin and Mrs Kier looked highly pleased. Mrs Kier brushed off her apron and tidied her hair, wanting to look her best now I was in the room.

"I am glad it all meets with your approval, Lady Edith. We all will do our very best for you tonight. We are well ahead of schedule," Mrs Goodwin glanced over at Mrs Kier, "are we not Mrs Kier?"

Mrs Kier looked blank for a few seconds, then suddenly sprang to life with a robust, "Indeed we are Mrs Goodwin! No problems yet to speak of. All is going well… " Mrs Kier suddenly broke off from our conversation and looked over at Gillian, who had come in from the scullery with a cordial bottle of lemonade, which she proudly placed on the table. Mrs Kier looked amazed at her happy face.

"For all that's holy Gillian, what on earth are you doing with that bottle of lemonade?"

Gillian looked most happy and was ready to go and get the mop and bucket of water.

"I'm about to clean up the floor Mrs Kier, just like you said to me?"

Mrs Kier turned to look at me and Mrs Goodwin, with a face of pure desperation.

"So what are you doing with that bottle Gillian?" Mrs Kier shouted.

Gillian, still looking highly simple and undeterred, got on her hands and knees to pick up the broken half of the mixing bowl from off the floor, dripping with the sloppy mixture of eggs. "Well Mrs Kier," Gillian stood up with the broken bowl, dripping with eggs in her hands "You said to go and get the water and mop and put a nice drop of lemonade in it."

Mrs Kier by this time looked as if she was about to have a stroke.

Mrs Goodwin decided to make a hasty exit out of the kitchen, escorting me with her, both of us realising that World War Two was about to erupt in the kitchen. As we walked out of the kitchen and down the hall, passing the collection of servants bells, all for the moment silent, behind us in the kitchen the war sounded like it had begun. Mrs Kier's voice was a voice that carried some considerable distance.

"You stupid girl Gillian! I said a drop of lemon from the fruit! Not a whole bottle of blessed lemonade! We shall have ants in the kitchen if you clean the floor with that. I don't know Gillian. I am beginning to wonder whether you are deliberately trying to push me into an early grave!"

Gillian by the sound of it had now become hysterical and sounded as if she had dropped the already cracked bowl again, into yet more pieces. Mrs Goodwin and I continued along the passage towards the back stairs.

"That poor girl" Mrs Goodwin said, "How she stands it I don't know? Now Lady Edith, is there anything else you need ready for tonight? I know Mr Tucker is in his pantry, decanting the port and wines."

I paused for a moment then suddenly thought about after dinner entertainment.

"Oh could you see that the bridge table is set up in the drawing room for after dinner please Mrs Goodwin. I always find a game of bridge very relaxing after hours of listening about the stock market, politics and reform of the Lords." Mrs Goodwin smiled and made a mental note.

"I will make sure Spencer puts it out my Lady, don't worry." Mrs Goodwin then looked a little awkward and worried herself. "Lady Edith I do hope you don't think I am prying, but is everything alright between his Lordship and Master Edward?"

"Oh yes Mrs Goodwin, everything is fine. Just a little misunderstanding. Nothing to worry about, I do assure you."

Mrs Goodwin smiled in relief, "Oh that's alright then. I expect they are both going to miss Mr McKillop. After all, he's been his Lordship's secretary now for over five years. Good loyal staff are very hard to find these days. I expect too, his Lordship is a little worried about this trouble in the States, with the stocks and shares falling. Mr Tucker seems very worried about it all."

I gave a sharp gulp and tried not to reveal my shock at hearing from my housekeeper that Marcus was leaving without my knowledge.

"Yes. It's going to hit us all hard Mr McKillop leaving so suddenly. It's such a Surprise! I think it's all been a bit too much for his Lordship. Things will be better in the morning. Once tonight's over. I should not worry about this stock market slump, I am sure the market will correct itself," I said (trying to sound as if I knew something of how the stock markets work).

*

I went back up the servants' steps and came back into the main hall, then went across to the study to talk with Father. Why was Marcus leaving so soon with no notice? It made no sense to me. Nor could I understand why neither Father nor Edward had told me. Perhaps the argument between Father and Edward had had something to do with Marcus. Maybe Marcus had been fiddling with Father's accounts or investing in the wrong stocks, and with this slump in the market that's why Father was so agitated. Or had Marcus been secretly drinking or cavorting with one of the house maids, and that's why he had gone into the study and looked so nervous. He must have been summoned by Father to explain himself and Edward must have begged Father for lenience for the years of service he had given.

It all made perfect sense and was the only explanation for today's argument. I knocked on Father's study door, but there was no reply. I never ever went into father's study without his permission, a rule I had kept to since I was a child and never broken. I headed back to the morning room where Spencer was serving out my tea and cake.

"Oh Spencer thank you, that does look nice! Spencer, do you know if his Lordship and Mr Edward have returned yet?"

Spencer looked up from setting out a cup and saucer for me.

"Not yet my Lady. Neither his Lordship or Mr Edward have come back yet."

"I see. Did you say his Lordship has gone down to see Mr Cuss?"

"Yes my Lady," Spencer nodded "I offered to order the car but his Lordship said he wanted to walk."

"I see. That's alright then," I said, feeling more reassured that I knew that Father was sat in Mr Cuss's dingy solicitors office. "What about Mr McKillop, is he in his office?"

Spencer looked at me as if I was mad and frowned.

"Mr McKillop my Lady? Mr McKillop has left! He packed his things after lunch. He said cheerio to us all in the servants' hall and then left."

I sat down on the sofa opposite the table and tray of tea things. I wanted to make some sort of statement like, 'Oh yes that's right, he had to go today, his mother's been taken ill' or something to that effect, to prove to Spencer that I was not in the dark about this strange exit. Somehow though, I did not feel able to do such a thing. Nor could I think of a good enough answer.

"I see. Thank you Spencer, that will be all." Spencer nodded then left the room.

*

For the remainder of the afternoon that was left to me, I spent it trying to work out what was occurring in my household. I was worried for Eddie. It was not like him to be out on his own for so long and not tell me where he was going. Father too, was absent, and none of the servants seemed to know how long he was gone for. I was left to hold the fort and to try and put on a brave face for the servants to show them that all was well, even though deep down I knew things were far from fine. I decided to go to Marcus's office to see if what Spencer had said was true on my way up to change and get ready for dinner. It was now half past five and the dinner was set for seven-thirty. I half expected to see Marcus sat in his office, hunched over his desk typing away at his typewriter. But sure enough, just as Spencer had said, I found his office packed up and vacant; his desk cleared and void of any life, or the hope of further occupancy. I was still no wiser. What had transpired in the study at lunch time between Marcus, Edward and Father? I knew that the mystery of Marcus's departure would have to wait till later. Now all I could think of was the dinner, and putting on a good show for the guests when they arrived, which would only be a few hours away. I went up to my bedroom and rang the bell for Helen to come and run me a bath and prepare me for the evening. I sat down at my Louis dressing table and took off my watch, pearls and earrings. I fiddled about playing with a double ended, cut glass perfume bottle moving it up and down in my hand like an egg timer, watching the perfume move from one end to the other. I moved and removed my silver brush and comb. I always fiddled with things when I was nervous. I looked over at my prints of Degas dance examination paintings, but even they did not seem to calm me as they normally did. I got up from my dressing table and went over to the window which looked out on to the drive. All looked still and silent, no sign of Father nor Edward walking up. I came away from the window and pulled the bell again for Helen, wondering where she had got to.

I flung myself into one of my blue carver chairs and prayed that any minute Eddie would knock on the door and come in, and tell me what on earth was going on. There, then did come a knock on the door. It was, however, Helen who came, in her black and white maid's uniform. Helen was a nice, respectable girl, very pleasant, with long brunette hair that always had a wonderful shine and gloss to it. She was a little taller than me, rather slim, and had many admirers on the staff and in the village. But she was too respectable to do anything silly, and she only had eyes for Father's deputy clerk Alexander, at the mineral water factory.

Helen entered the room rather nervously, as if she was in trouble with me.

"I am so sorry Lady Edith to have kept you waiting. It was not my fault, it was Mr Tucker."

I reassured Helen that I was not worried that she was late and bid her to run me a bath. She went in through to my bathroom to run me a nice warm bath. As I heard the plug go into the hole and water began to gush out of the taps and into the tub I called out to Helen to enquire what had been the trouble downstairs with Mr Tucker.

"So what's wrong with Mr Tucker then?" Helen came back into the room to start undressing me.

"Oh Mr Tucker's been telling us about the markets sliding! Millions of shares have been urgently sold. Mr Tucker thinks it's going to get even worse yet. He said something about a complete crash! It all sounds very worrying, there's up to 10,000 people outside the stock exchange in New York all desperately waiting for news!"

"Well I should not let it worry you Helen. There's not a thing we can do about it. Now tell me, how's that young man of yours?"

Helen began to cheer up a little after my words of reassurance and soon forgot Mr Tucker's scaremongering. I saw no reason for anyone to panic. After all, what goes up has to come down and I was sure that within a few hours all this panic would be over and every one would be back to having a good time again.

Helen chatted away about her Alexander, whom she had been courting now for a about a year, and it sounded as if their relationship was getting more serious. I teased her and said, "I might need to find myself a new head house parlour maid soon then."

(Until a suitable and clean girl could be found, Helen was still acting as our head house parlour maid as well as being my lady's maid.) Helen blushed and giggled like a school girl.

"Oh I don't know Lady Edith. One day I think Alexander's going to go down on bended knee and then the next day he's so caught up in his work he hardly notices me. I don't know my Lady, you know what men are like? They seem to make mysteries of everything, don't they? Men seem to blow hot and cold with you all the time."

As Helen took off my clothes and then handed me my kimono, I agreed with what she had said about men in a dry, sarcastic tone, "Don't they just."

Helen went over to my closet door and put away my hat and clothes, while I headed for the bathroom door. Helen then came back into the room to lay out my dress for this evening.

"I am glad things are going to be alright, my Lady. All afternoon I've been so worried what with all these urgent telegrams going out to people warning them, and what with his Lordship getting a telegram and then rushing off. For one minute I thought something terrible had happened. I thought perhaps his Lordship had lost all his money in this crash!"

My walk to the bathroom door suddenly halted and I froze. I turned round to face Helen, who was back at the closet door putting away my white pleated skirt.

"What do you mean Helen?" I said anxiously, "What about these telegrams that are going out to people?"

Helen turned round, still with my pleated skirt in hand, which she placed on a wooden hanger ready to be hung up.

"Oh Mr Tucker said that the people called brokers had urgent messages for their now... what was the word he used?" Helen paused and thought deeply, trying to remember exactly what Mr Tucker had said. Then suddenly she remembered the word

"Clients! Yes that was it. Brokers have been sending urgent messages to their clients, to tell them things are very bad on the stock market, and that they have made very heavy losses. Mr Tucker said that some people have lost their entire life savings! Apparently the ticker tape machines at the stock exchange are nearly running out of tape! Many of the phone lines keep jamming there's so many people making urgent phone calls."

My legs felt like jelly and my mouth twitched slightly with nerves. It began to dawn on me what had transpired between Father, Edward and Marcus in the study. Helen went on with her task of hanging up my skirt, followed by hanging up my white and cream jacket. She then collected my oriental shawl and flung it over one of my carver chairs preparing to fold it up. Helen then carried on with her chattering.

"Still my Lady, as you said, we don't need to worry about it," she said so cheerfully. "It won't cause us any harm. It was just we all thought downstairs that his Lordship could have lost all his money like all those poor souls in America, being his Lordship had an urgent telegram come. I'm glad things are alright. I'll go tell Mr Tucker to stop his worrying! I best go and see if your bath is ready now my Lady."

Chapter 26

The Trigger Had Been Activated and the Bomb Had Gone Off

October 1929

The warm, soapy water and smell of lavender from the bath helped to calm and relax my tense body. As I lowered myself in and sunk into the warm water, I could feel the stress and tension leave me, even if it was only for a brief pause. I had no more than half an hour before I would have to climb out and face whatever had befallen us.

My skin felt so refreshed in the bath and Helen had kindly placed a warm, soft fluffy towel for my head to rest on. The bottom of the towel had now become a little saturated with the tide of the water, which moved every time I did. I sat lounging for well over twenty minutes, laying in the water as if I was in bed listening to the dawn chorus. I looked around at the bathroom. The clinical white tiles had condensation on them from the heat of my bath along with the pearl lustre, octagon shaped framed mirror. I found myself transfixed by the labels on all the scent and chemist bottles. I studied the bottles carefully which were all placed on an art deco vanity unit looking at them as if they were artefacts from an Egyptian tomb.

I did all I could to deliberately distract myself from my problems and not to think about anything which would send me into a panic stricken state. As I cleaned and washed my skin, I kept going over in my mind the contents of the telegram that had sent Father to flee to Mr Cuss's office. I felt so cross with myself that I had not stayed in and waited after I witnessed Marcus enter Father's study. If only I had not gone on that walk. If only I had stayed in the morning room, I may have learnt what on earth was going on. I kept thinking about what I had told Helen. I had reassured her that the stock market crash was not going to affect us. I now realised Father must have invested a great deal of his money into the market for him to be so angry with Edward and Marcus, and for him to be paralysed with fear to the point of keeping way from the house all afternoon. Surely Father had not invested everything? He had never been reckless with money in the past. Not to the point of taking risks. Father had always had such a sensible and reliable business head on his shoulders. No! I was convinced that Marcus must have advised him wrongly. He must have pushed Father into making too big a gamble. He may have even invested Father's money without Father even realising what was going on. Not until it was too late. Yes, that had to be the answer and the reason why Marcus had been dismissed with such speed and abruptness. There was no other explanation. It had to be the answer. There then came a little tap on the bathroom door and Helen's voice on the other side.

"My Lady! I thought you would like to know, Mr Edward has returned home. He is in his room, changing for dinner."

I leaned forward in the bath, my hand gripped the hand rail. My movement caused the comfy towel, which had acted as a cushion, to slide down the back of the bath and fall into the creamy coloured water. The towel began to absorb all the water it could take until it resembled a creature from the deep. I called out to Helen rather desperately, my heart pounding a little with adrenalin on hearing Edward had returned home. I knew that at long last I would get some answers.

"Thank you Helen! I am getting out now. Would you put out for me my black silk dress, I won't be a minute."

I could have stayed in that bath for hours. I knew as long as I was in there no harm would come to me. All the problems that must be piling up could not trouble me in the bath. I was dreading tonight. How on earth could I host a dinner, not knowing what situation we were facing? How would I be able to sit there in the dining room surrounded on either side by Father's friends, keep a smile on my face and pretend that all was well. How could I keep a stiff upper lip, and not face the facts. I sat up in the bath with my head touching the top of my knees. The grey silky water was beginning to turn lukewarm. I prayed that all would be well when I got out of the bath. I pleaded that not only tonight would go well, but that the situation was not as bad as I thought it must be. Helen, as I instructed, was in my bedroom, my long black silk dress was laid out, stretched across my bed. After drying my hair and Helen had helped me to dress, Helen sat me down at my dressing table and did my hair for me. I chose what jewellery to put with the gown, thinking that I had chosen a rather depressing colour to wear tonight. Black however reflected my sombre mood. The dress fell elegantly on me; my diamond necklace, earrings, and a matching pendant broach to fit at the top of the bodice created a classic evening look. It was not too fussy or showy: simplicity was always best. I handed Helen back the blue, velvet lined tray which the jewellery was displayed on. She wondered over to my jewellery cabinet to replace the tray, chattering as she went.

"Just think my Lady. Very soon your dress will be arriving for the ball! Oh it will look nice with your Ladyship's Russian necklace. It was such a clever idea of yours to choose…"

I cut Helen off from talking about my costume or the ball in December. I could not think about that at the moment.

"Helen. How did Mr Edward seem when he came in?" I enquired impatiently.

Helen came back over to the dressing table and completed combing and fixing up the back of my hair.

"Mr Edward my Lady? Oh he seemed a bit quiet, but then I expect he's a bit nervous with guests coming tonight and what with his Lordship still not back yet."

I looked at Helen through the reflection of the dressing table mirror and stared at her worriedly. "You mean his Lordship is still not back yet? I thought you meant both Mr Edward and his Lordship were back!"

Helen carried on putting the last few finishing touches to my hair. She looked undeterred and oblivious to the fact that Father had been away all afternoon and was not back yet to co-host tonight's dinner.

"Oh no, sorry my Lady! It's only Mr Edward back. His Lordship is still at Mr Cuss's office. Right then my Lady, all done."

Helen completed my hair and looked pleased with her efforts. My hair did look shiny and beautifully styled. I briskly got off my stool and collected a black fan that she had put out for me to go with the dress. I then examined myself in a Rococo mirror with filigree around its frame. I was pleased with my appearance. The dress fitted me like a glove and had a little train at the back. It had long flowing sleeves, open to reveal my slender pale arms.

"Will that be all then, my Lady?" Helen enquired.

I continued studying myself in the mirror. I then discharged Helen for the evening.

"Thank you Helen that will be all. I won't be requiring you this evening. You can have the evening off. Go and have a nice evening with Alexander. I can sort myself out tonight. I will see you in the morning."

Helen looked rather bemused but was not going to argue with having an evening off. She thanked me greatly, wished me a pleasant evening then left the room in excitement, to rush off and surprise Alexander. Once Helen was safely away, out of earshot and sight, I marched out of my room and made my way down the gallery towards Edward's bedroom. I could hear a hive of activity downstairs. The grog trays were being carried down to the study and drawing room. The house maids were by now lighting the fires. Mr Tucker was supervising the lighting of the candles for the dining room before going on one last inspection before I came down to give my seal of approval prior to the guests arriving.

*

I made my way along the gallery landing with the carved wooden banister on one side and all the family bedrooms on the other. Another wing spanned the other side of the house, purely set aside for guests. I briskly walked past the numerous busts and statues along the landing, my dress trailing behind me, with my right hand gripped to the front of the dress, picking it up to prevent myself tripping. After a short journey along the hall I came to Edward's bedroom door. I immediately knocked on the door with a quick tap and gripped the handle ready to go in, as soon as he bade me enter. I waited a few seconds then heard some soft footed footsteps come to the door. The bedroom door swung open, Edward stood in the door way dressed in black tie.

"Edith my dear! There you are! You look stunning. Always go for classic black, it never fails. All tickety boo downstairs?"

Edward sounded full of fun and amusement as he normally did, but he was fooling no one. His face looked pale and stressed. His forehead and eyes looked full of tension and worry. He looked as if he had aged five years during the last few hours. His frown lines looked more penetrating and deeper set. His whole demeanour was extremely agitated and twitchy.

"No Edward, all is not tickety boo!"

I marched past him in to his room, crossing a rich royal blue and gold floral patterned carpet. I perched myself on the end of his four poster bed, with my hand rapped round the nearest post to me. Edward shut the door nervously. He wondered over to the window adjusting his cufflinks in the light. Then he wandered over to his masculine oak dresser to put on his gold ring with the red ruby stone inset in the middle.

"What's up then sis? Mrs Kier and Mr Tucker had another ding dong? Or has Mrs Kier struck Gillian, and Gillian's rushed off in hysterics?"

I gave an irritated sigh and scowled at Edward. He was doing his usual upper crust grit and fooling when a crisis was looming.

"Edward! Please stop all the pretending. I know something's wrong. I heard you and Father arguing at lunchtime today and I know that Father rushed off after receiving an urgent telegram. I have had to organise and reassure poor Helen who seemed to be under the impression we are facing some sort of financial ruin from Mr Tucker. I have had the humiliation of hearing from Mrs Goodwin and Spencer, who both knew that Marcus was leaving before I did, when I was under the impression I was mistress of the house. Father's invited all these people from London which I have had to plan and cater for and who will be arriving at any moment. Plus I have been sick with bloody worry for you and Father, and you have the nerve to ask me if everything's tickity boo! Now what the hell is going on!"

Edward looked rather dumfounded at my outburst. It was a rare event for me to lose my rag with him, or for that matter with any one. Edward went over to the window and dejectedly slumped down in the window seat. With his head in his hands, his fingers ran though his highlighted hair. I felt instantly guilty for yelling at him and turned round on the bed to face him.

"I'm sorry Eddie. I did not mean to shout at you. I know it's not your fault. It's just I've been so worried about you. You sounded so upset in Father's office. What was it all about? What's happened?"

Edward looked up at me. His face looked tired, dejected and warn out.

"Oh Edith! Everything is in such a bloody mess. I don't know where to begin, or how to tell you." He paused for a moment. He then continued with a sound of hesitation in his voice. "How much do you know?"

"I only know you and Father were arguing like a pair of hell hounds. I saw Marcus go in to the study. I know there's been some sort of dip in the markets. That's all I know."

Edward sniggered and coughed a little. He raised himself up, improving his posture. Behind him outside the sky was turning grey and looked overcast with smouldering dark clouds appearing over the bay. I could hear the sound of a wheelbarrow from outside being pushed along the gravel path with a clatter of spades and forks being thrown into the barrow. Rogers sounded as if he was packing up quickly from his day of gardening, before the bad weather set in. Edward turned his head to look out over the garden.

"I'm afraid it's a little bit more than just a blip, Edith. It's a complete crash. A massive slide like we have never seen before. A lot of people have lost a lot of money."

"Just how badly have we been hit, Eddie?" I asked, trying not to sound worried.

Edward gulped. He looked back down at the blue and gold carpet, then turned his head round to look at his dresser. His mouth and lip quivered slightly, and his eyes looked full of fear.

"We have been hit pretty hard, Edith. Nearly all of what Father invested over the last year or so has been cleaned out. Father's broker from London and the one in the States tried to warn him that things were looking bad, but Father would not hear of it. By the time he had got the telegram late this afternoon, it was all too late to do or rescue anything. As soon as Father learnt what was happening he went down to old Cuss to try and calculate the damage. I went down with him."

Edward gave a quick inhale of breath and started biting and clawing at his hands and nails.

"To put it bluntly, sis. Cuss has told us that we are going to be in a pretty bad way if things are as bad as he thinks. Apparently there's a massive crowd of people and reporters outside the stock exchange in New York. The crowd's nearly up to the East River. Poor sods. They're all waiting for news. Charles Mitchell was even seen rushing off to an emergency board meeting. Apparently all the brokers are all yelling and shouting that you can hear them out in the streets. Even J.P. Morgan's been hit hard they say.

I listened carefully to what Edward was telling me, trying not to panic.

"Surely it's not all gone Eddie? Father would not have put all his money in the stock market! We have a few assets to support us don't we? Perhaps things are not as bad as they appear to be?"

Edward shook his head like he had been drinking and swayed a little. He got to his feet and turned round to look out over the south lawn and the sea beyond it. A blackening sky was creeping in overhead with a sea threat obscuring the view of the bay.

"I don't think you realise, sis, how bad things are. Father invested a great deal of his money into shares and stocks. He's apparently given out a great deal of his funds to many of his friends in London over the last two years since Mother died. He's been spending money he could not afford to spend. According to Cuss, Father, like so many has been buying on margin, purchasing stocks with borrowed money. To make matters worse, he's apparently re-mortgaged the London house. We really are sunk if old Cuss is correct.

"I don't understand Eddie? Father's always been so careful with money. Granted he's always been far too generous with his friends. He's always had a streak of adventure about him, but he's never been reckless with money. 'Spend a little, save a little' as he always used to say to us. I can't believe it's Father's mismanagement of his finances that's caused us problems. What has all this got to do with Marcus then? Has he been investing Father's money without his permission or something?"

I felt sure my accusation against Marcus had to be the case. Father must have put too much trust in Marcus and found out that he had been swindling him. That was why Father had dismissed him. Edward turned round from the darkening scene outside and faced me with a look of scorn on his face. He looked deeply angry with me. He took a few steps closer towards the bed, looking as if he was going to hit me.

"Marcus! Marcus swindling Father! Are you bloody mad, Edith! It's been Marcus who's been trying to warn Father for the past bloody six months to sell some of his damned shares, while the going was good. Marcus warned Father that if the market did ever take a dive we would be hit very hard. It's been Marcus who could see the danger on the horizon before any of us did. Yet Father told Marcus he was a fool and should know his place! He told him he did not know what he was talking about. It's not Marcus we have to blame, it's our stupid Father who's sent us up the creak without a paddle!"

I had never heard Edward speak so cruelly about Father. Edward sounded so bitter and angry with him.

"Eddie! Don't speak about Father that way. It's not all his fault. Father did not know the stock market was going to crash did he? Up till now everything has been booming. I expect he thought, like we all did, that the good times would go on for a while longer."

Edward continued looking highly angry with me. He sat back down again in the bay window, frowning and scowling at the floor.

"Oh I might have guessed you would take his side! No its never Father's fault is it! It's always someone else to blame."

Edward suddenly erupted from his seat and was almost on top of me now. Our faces were almost touching. He looked crazed, almost wild, and I could smell that he had already been drinking. His mouth and clothes smelt of brandy. He suddenly started yelling, screaming, spitting at me and wiping away spit and saliva from round his mouth.

"How dare you! How dare you think that Marcus is to blame for landing us in this mess. How dare you! It's father who has spent all our money, throwing it away as if there was no weekend to come. It's Father who's run up terrific debts. Why do you think Father was so reluctant to hold a ball in December? It's because there's no money to pay for it! It's all on borrowed money! Why do you think Father came up with you to London in such a rush when you were buying your dress? He was not speaking in the Lords he was re-mortgaging the London house and not only that, but this bloody house as well! " Edward's anger began to give way to a despairing wail, "Our home Edith! "

I sat on the end of the bed, shaking with fear at Edward's rant. My left hand gripped the left post of the bed as I attempted to lean back trying to shuffle myself further back along the bed to escape Edward's close proximity. I felt so cold and numb. I could not take it in. Edward had still not given up his tirade at me. He continued to cry and scream at me, with all that was left of his remaining energy.

"Edith don't you get it yet! Our fool of a father has brought us to near bankruptcy! All because our foolish, stupid father was not happy with what he had. He wanted more and more! Ever since Mother died, he's been racking up debts and bills, all of which are going to have to be paid. Yet who do you want to blame? Marcus! The one man who could see what was happening and did everything he could to stop it. All the while you've been sat in the bloody morning room playing at being Lady of the manor, planning your stupid ball. You thought you could try and replace mother? Well look what a bad, bloody job you've done of it! "

I slid off the bed on to the carpet. My black dress was crumpled up around me like a deflated balloon. Tears ran down my cheeks. I could not help but sob and cry like a child of five. I tried to counter attack Eddie's cruel words, but I was too distraught and my words were taken over by tears.

"All I have ever done, Eddie is to try and keep the house running and to keep the standard that Mother set. I have tried to look after and maintain our household and family. I know I can't replace Mother, no one can. I never set myself up to do so. I have done my best. I really have. Do you think it's been easy for me having to try and run a household and deal with all the thankless work, without having any guidance or help from Mummy? Do you?"

I found I could not talk any more. I could not get any more words out. All I wanted to do was try and get up and retreat to my bedroom. I tried to pull myself up, but the length of my dress kept me down and I was unable to regain my standing. I collapsed back down into a heap, blinded by tears and eye make-up, feeling flushed and faint. Eddie knew he had gone too far. He could see he had spoken in a fit of anger and not meant what he said. He too was now in tears, crying pitifully, with his nose streaming and no hanky in sight. He sank down on to his knees, still towering slightly over me and pulled me up to him, holding me tightly. He rocked me slightly in his arms like a baby. I did not pull away from him or reject him. He was hurting as much as I was. He had spoken in desperation at our situation. He had been keeping this problem all day, if not longer, and had burst out with it at the one person he had in the world to tell.

As Edward and I sunk into each other, he kissed me on the head, still rocking me gently. My arms were wrapped round him tightly, clinging on to him. I could feel and hear the thumps of his beating heart under his black dinner jacket and white shirt. The beating of a heart that sounded highly agitated, worried and anxious. Minutes past with Eddie and I not saying a word to each other, apart from listening to each other's sobs and sniffles. We continued clinging to each other, as if we had been sculpted together, and sunk down into the rich pile of carpet. My black dress draped to the side of me, looking like an oil slick.

*

For a while neither of us said anything. We lay huddled together, knowing that our lives were about to suddenly change, and all our plans and hopes for the future were now looking very doubtful. Life had unexpectedly shifted and not in the direction we had wished. Edward's room was so silent. The only sound came from the copper clock by his bedside table. It was ticking away at a fast speed sounding like a clock wired to a bomb. At any minute I thought time would run out, the trigger would be activated and the bomb would explode and shatter the room to pieces like it always did in a melodrama.

The room was slowly losing its light. The darkening sky outside grew worse; the black rain clouds in the distance had plunged the room into melancholy shadows. Birds were twittering outside, warning each other that the heavens were about to open. I could hear from down on the gravel path some footsteps, those of Rogers probably. However it sounded more than just one man, at least two. Edward gave a quick and erratic breath. He sounded as if he was still feeling overcome from the worry of the day. Added to the shock and guilt of his outburst at me. The silence between us was finally broken.

"I'm sorry Edith. I'm so sorry, I didn't mean it, I really didn't."

His apology was unnecessary. I knew he had not meant what he said. Edward had never been one to be vindictive or deliberately hateful. He had been trying to tell me just how bad things were. I had not understood or realised how bad the situation was until he erupted in desperation at my stupid questions and my naivety about Father's handling of his money. Yet somehow it was more than that. Eddie had got angry with me for blaming Marcus for the mess we were in. From my point of view, I had come to a logical conclusion. Father and Eddie had come to blows. Marcus had been allowed in to the study, then he was dismissed with immediate effect. I naturally assumed that Marcus must have been partly responsible for some sort of crime. As it turned out I apparently had been wrong. Marcus had not been stealing and embezzling Father's money. Quite the reverse. He had tried to warn Father that the course he was on could only end in disaster. Yet if Marcus had not played a malignant hand in this, why had he been sacked? And why had Father and Edward been arguing about him? The window panes on the outside began to be pelted by droplets of rain. The droplets meandered and trickled down the panes of glass slowly and in no hurry, until the amount of rain falling from the sky increased and hit Edward's bedroom window like transparent bullets. The room had not only turned dark but also cold. The room looked so depressing shrouded in shadows with Edward's standard lamps not turned on nor the art deco light on top of his writing desk. I cleared my throat a little and sniffed back, preparing myself to ask him the question that was now perplexing me.

"Eddie? If Marcus was trying to warn Father and hasn't been stealing or doing anything bad, why did Father dismiss him?"

*

The rain continued to hit the window. I could hear the sound of nervous birds outside flying to the safe cover of the trees until the rain passed over. Edward shifted uncomfortably and detached himself from me. His face was shrouded in shadow, his features unable to be seen. He moved from off his knees and turned to sit next to me, with his back rested against his bed. His long legs were stretched out in front of him, with his immaculate black trousers beginning to look creased. His shoes were as shiny as the top of a polished coffin lid. I noticed one of his laces had become undone and dragged down the side of his left shoe touching the carpet. He rested his head against mine at an angle. The two of us sat against the bed. Our heads knocked together, both of us were looking up at the window being slashed by the rain and Edwards round, fast, ticking, copper clock continued to tick… tick… away.

"It's complicated, Edith. It's not easy for me to explain to you."

Edward began to look crestfallen up at the window. I put a hand on his knee and rubbed his soft black trousers, trying to reassure him that whatever else was wrong he could tell me.

"Eddie, why do I get the impression that something else happened in that study this afternoon? Something you're not telling me. I know there's something else wrong. Why was Father so cross with you? It has something to do with Marcus doesn't it?"

Edward turned his head and faced me. His large, crestfallen eyes looked directly at me.

"The thing is Edith… "

Edward gulped and gave a pause. He then went to speak. He was suddenly interrupted when there was a large urgent knock on the door behind us. My heart leapt as the peace and darkness of the room was jolted. Just when Eddie was about to tell me something, something important to him, that had been playing on his mind and caused him so much unhappiness, there was someone at the door!

The rain was now hammering down outside. It dawned on me that the footsteps I had heard must have been those of Father wondering slowly into the house, perhaps along with Cuss. They were both by now confining themselves to the study. They were probably pouring brandy and smoking, slumped over Father's desk, franticly going through papers and financial statements. Edward sprang stiffly up to his feet. He brushed off his trousers from the carpet and assisted me to my feet. He then rushed over to his writing desk to put on his lamp and then blew his nose. He staggered over to his bathroom to wash his face. I was amazed how quickly he had got up and recovered from his collapse. I was still feeling very dazed. My eyes were sore and blinking from the sudden light that filled the room. The room looked so much more cosy than it had done. The desk light showed off the room's imposing fire place and Edward's watercolours that he had done of the harbour and the house. The knocking which had paused for a moment suddenly came again. Now the knocking was much louder and the voice of Mrs Goodwin could be heard on the other side of the door. She sounded rather panicked herself, which was a rare thing, she was always so calm and never one to panic. Yet now with her frantic knocking and calling she sounded as if something terrible had occurred.

I went over to Edward's mirror and straightened my hair. I checked my make-up to see if it looked alright (which it did not). From the bathroom Edward sounded as if he was giving his face a quick wash to hide the fact that he had been crying. It never did for a man to look as if he had been crying, even if Edward had good cause to cry. From outside in the passage Mrs Goodwin was still knocking and calling for me franticly.

*

"Lady Edith! It's Mrs Goodwin! My Lady are you there? My Lady I have to speak to you urgently!"

I knew it had to be some problem with the evening's dinner

arrangements. Gillian had probably dropped all the canapés or dropped the apple tart all over the kitchen floor. I had one last look in Edward's mirror, hoping Mrs Goodwin would not notice I looked such a state. I then called out to Mrs Goodwin to come in. Mrs Goodwin looked pensive and rather gaunt. She tiptoed in and shut the door. She came over to me rather closer than was normal for she was never one to come up close and invade your own personal space. Knowing something must have happened down stairs and feeling guilty that I had neglected my duties as hostess for the evening, I re-assured Mrs Goodwin.

"It's alright Mrs Goodwin. I am on my way down. You don't need to worry. We have plenty of time before the firsts guests arrive."

Mrs Goodwin looked highly uncomfortable as if I had said something wrong or personal to her. She clutched at her skirt with her twitching, stubby fingers causing her chain of keys to jangle about.

"My Lady the Lord Lieutenant is here, and... "

I interrupted Mrs Goodwin, somewhat annoyed.

"Oh golly! The Lord Lieutenants here already! He's a little early isn't he? It's not even seven o'clock yet. He's always normally here at seven fifteen. Don't worry Mrs Goodwin, I will be right down directly. Is his Lordship back yet? I had better go and warn him."

Mrs Goodwin took a step forward. Her hands clasped together and then unclasped again. She looked terribly worried and on closer inspection, I would have said that even she had been crying. Edward then came flying out of his bathroom, his dress and appearance looked refreshed. Mrs Goodwin looked even more anxious when Edward stepped back into the room. He did his best to appear like everything was normal. He joked with Mrs Goodwin that he had asked me to come and help him with his tie and cufflinks. Mrs Goodwin leapt into Edward's banter, looking as if she was about to burst into tears.

"My Lady! The Lord Lieutenant is here and needs to see you and Mr Edward at once! It is very urgent. Would you both please come! "

Edward looked over to me as if to say 'Mrs Goodwin's cracking up over tonight's dinner.' But he gave Mrs Goodwin a reassuring word and said he would go down straight away. We both left Eddie's room leaving the desk lamp on and the urgent sound of ticking from Edward's alarm clock behind us. Mrs Goodwin trailed urgently behind us with her bunch of keys jangling around. I instructed Eddie to go down first and hold the fort along with Mrs Goodwin. I rushed along back to my own room. I needed to freshen myself up and re-do my make-up before going down myself.

*

I observed Edward and Mrs Goodwin rush down the front stairs. I went along the galleried landing to the safety of my room. I went to wash my face, being careful not to splash my dress, then went over to my dressing table to apply some fresh make-up and apply myself with some perfume from my double-ended, cut glass perfume bottle, the bottle that only a few hours ago I had fiddled with while waiting for Helen to come in and undress me. I wished I could get back into that warm bath again and stay in there all night. I felt so cross with Father. Here we were hosting a meal for the vicar, the Lord Lieutenant, three Lords from London and their wives, whilst facing bankruptcy and pretending that nothing was wrong. I left my room with my dress trailing behind me and went along down the gallery to the stairs. I half expected to hear the pompous laughter from the Lord Lieutenant, helping himself to cocktails and pushing down as many cheese swizzle sticks and fish canapés as possible. Knowing Father he was probably down in the saloon all dressed in his black tie, drinking a sherry and pretending that this crash was none of his concern, that it could not possibly affect him. Outside, through the large landing window that overlooked the stairs, the rain was battering down. It even looked like we might get some thunder. The sky had that black angry look about it, and the rain had become heavy and unrelenting.

    I got to the bottom of the stairs and down into the main hall. My hand slid off the polished handrail back to my side and the cold silky sides of my dress. A warm and crackling fire was lit in the grey stone fireplace, throwing out sparks of red and orange into the grate. I crossed over to the middle of the hall, my heels loudly clicking and echoing in the vast space of the hall. A pair of well-worn black leather gloves had been thrown on to the large round table with Alice's flower arrangement in the centre. A silver salver was pushed to the side. On a companion table another silver salver containing a crystal brandy decanter and glasses had been abandoned and forgotten. It appeared that whoever had left it there had been interrupted in their journey to the dining room and quickly left it on the table. They had never come back for it.

As I passed the main hall table I observed the left side of the glazed doors into the lobby had been left open. Traces of large muddy footprints which lead through the open lobby door were plastered over the diagonal black and white chequered floor. There appeared to be two sets of footprints; both appeared to be male, belonging to professional dynamic owners. The gentlemen had entered into the main hall, then had scattered into two different positions. They had turned and paused by a Louis chair, then apparently had been helped off with their coats and then escorted through the vestibule up into the saloon. Two heavy bulky coats, saturated with rain and damp were hanging up on a coat stand next to a Louis sofa. *Probably those of Mr Cuss or Father, I thought.* I followed the footprints until they disappeared and became undetectable up through the carpeted vestibule. The vestibule was wallpapered in a Chinese red and oriental pattern, graced with gold wall lights and French mantel mirrors. It was furnished with amber wood armchairs. A black grand piano was placed nearest the two stone steps heading up to the saloon. A few walnut lamp tables and emerald green ferns completed the grandeur. I passed the closed library door on the left and the billiard-room door on the right. I walked along the centre of the vestibule, carpeted with a red and gold patterned rug. A rumble of thunder from outside made me shudder and caused my heart to thump again. As I headed towards the steps in the left hand corner I noticed that the piano had been left in a hurry. A drink had been poured and a gulp of sherry taken, yet had not been returned to. A few pale cream sheets of music had been thrown across the top and one had glided down to the floor. I picked up my dress to carefully walk up the stone steps, then allowed my dress to drop back down naturally again when I reached the top. I walked along a darkened hall towards the doors of the saloon. Both the saloon doors were opened wide.

As I entered the saloon my confident stride came to a sudden halt. I stepped in like a shy young housemaid on her first day in service. Inside the saloon a strange and unsettling tableau of people were paused in what looked like a scene from a murder mystery. I quickly halted my entrance and stopped silently between the two open doors. In front of me in a French armchair sat Eddie. He was sitting down on the edge of the seat, looking like he had been hit by a train. He looked shattered. His posture was slumped over, with his head bowed down as if recovering from a fainting turn. Mr Tucker was bent over him, dressed in his smart butler's uniform passing Edward a brandy. Eddie took the drink from him with a shaky hand and quickly downed the drink. Mrs Goodwin was standing next to Mr Tucker but slightly behind him. She also looked deeply shocked and distressed. On the other side of Eddie was the tall stature of the Lord Lieutenant. He too was clumsily drinking a brandy. In the corner of the room next to a table of canapés, a young vacant looking policemen was standing stiffly to attention. He appeared to be rushing down notes into a thin black note book. He looked up every now and again for directions from the last member of the group. Police Inspector Martin was dressed in a tweed grey suit, his receding hair covered in sparkling droplets of rain. It appeared that it had been him and the young policemen that had been admitted in to the main hall, and not Father and Mr Cuss after all.

I froze in the doorway not daring to move or go any further into the room. I felt too unsure of myself to take part in the scene. Mrs Goodwin was dabbing her eyes with a hanky, then began to fiddle with it out of sheer nerves. Inspector Martin seemed to have been trying to talk to Eddie, but was getting little out of him. I could not help but worry that I had wondered in to some sort of interrogation. I had never had much to do with Inspector Martin. Our paths had never crossed until now. Yet here he was standing in the saloon, on the evening we were about to host an important dinner, conferring with the Lord Lieutenant and putting questions to Eddie. I soon got the impression that Eddie was a suspect in some sort of crime. Eddie made no acknowledgement to any of the questions put to him by Inspector Martin. His head remained lowered. He only nodded or shook his head from side to side at certain enquiries. Inspector Martin sounded as if he was getting a little impatient with Eddie, who seemed completely dazed and out of it.

"Mr Edward," the Inspector began, "I do realise this is a most distressing time for you, but we must try and find out exactly what transpired this afternoon."

Inspector Martin beckoned closer to Edward, slightly bending down and hovering over him rather menacingly. He then resumed his tirade of questions.

"You said your father was highly agitated and in a worried state. This we have established was due to his fear of the state of his finances. This of course is highly understandable after today's events. However was there anything else that may have been playing on his mind? Was there another problem that he was worried about?"

I could not understand! What was going on? Why was the Inspector questioning Edward about Father? What business was it of his? I suddenly wondered why Father had not been called into the room and why he was missing. I looked over to Edward. I desperately wanted him to tell the Inspector what had gone on in the study and to put an end to Inspector Martin's impertinent questions. Edward only shook his head and slightly looked up towards his interrogator, but not enough to observe me in the doorway. When he finally did answer, he sounded warn out and exhausted, his voice almost a husky whisper.

" Look! I've told you Inspector. Father rushed down after half past two to Mr Cuss's office, after he received a telegram from his broker. I went down with him and stayed with him for about half an hour. I then left Father with Mr Cuss. I went for a walk, then came straight home." The young policemen feverishly recorded Edward's statement and looked over to his commanding officer. Inspector Martin looked unconvinced at Edward's statement.

"Mr Edward. I do not wish to question you in a heavy handed way. Nor do I wish to cause you any upset. However. It has been put to me that you and your father had a row well before your father received his telegram. You and your father were in the study, locked in I believe for some considerable time. You were then joined by your father's secretary, a Mr... Mr... " Inspector Martin looked through his notes, as did his sergeant. It was left to Mr Tucker to clarify the name which had escaped the so called professionals.

"A Mr McKillop, Inspector," Mr Tucker said in a well-mannered prompting tone, "Mr McKillop has been his Lordship's secretary for at least five years now."

Mr Tucker then stood back in line with Mrs Goodwin, who was still sobbing. Inspector Martin continued. "Ah yes! Thank you, Mr Tucker."

Inspector Martin then proceeded with his abrupt questions to Eddie.

"After Mr McKillop entered the study, you and his Lordship continued to argue for some time. Then both you and Mr McKillop left the study together. I have been informed that Mr McKillop has left your father's employment after being dismissed with immediate effect. You were overheard saying to your father and I quote, 'I will never forgive you Father, never. You can't send him away.'"

Inspector Martin looked up from his notebook.

"Now, Mr Edward. You have said to me that there was nothing else troubling your father. Yet you were overheard saying to your father that you 'would never forgive him.' The study was also found to be in an upturned state after you left it. A number of glasses had been smashed. We also found... "

Inspector Martin clicked a finger at his young sergeant. He rushed over with his notebook and handed over a torn and warped piece of paper. The fragment appeared burnt and blackened by a fire. Inspector Martin wandered closer over to Edward and showed him the fragment of paper.

"Mr Edward would you mind identifying the person in this photograph. For the record please." Edward took the burnt edged photograph from the Inspector and studied the photo. He handed it back to Inspector Martin. Edward identified the person in the photograph. He sounded tragically sad. As if his heart could take no more.

"The photograph is of me inspector."

Inspector Martin looked triumphant.

"Would you mind explaining to me, Mr Edward, how a photograph of yourself came to be burnt in the study fire? I would also like to know why other photos that we believe to be of you came to be obliterated by your father this afternoon. What on earth had you done to warrant your father to burn so many of your family photographs. Particularly photographs of you?"

Edward spluttered and did his best to evade the question. He seemed highly tense. He shifted about in his armchair, while Inspector Martin continued to examine him. I decided that I had been a bystander for long enough. It was time for me to come to the aid of my brother. As I stepped in Mrs Goodwin looked round to observe me. Her face dropped open with a sympathetic expression across her face.

"Oh Lady Edith!" Mrs Goodwin gasped, as she alerted the room of my presence.

Mr Tucker stood to attention, he also looked highly strained. Edward raised his head and looked up at me. He got to his feet shaking and tipped over a small table with his empty brandy glass on. The glass slid off the table as it went over and fell to the floor, shattering to pieces. Only the stem remained slightly intact. Mr Tucker righted the table and secured it and Mrs Goodwin helped to steady Edward. Inspector Martin advanced over to me. He put out a hand to formally introduce himself and his young sergeant. The Lord Lieutenant did the same and apologised for arriving so early. He explained he was now here in an official capacity having been summoned earlier by the police to accompany Inspector Martin. After the formalities were done with I thought it best to dismiss Mr Tucker and Mrs Goodwin. I did not want the servants to be disturbed any more than they were already.

Mr Tucker escorted Mrs Goodwin out who curtsied as she left, causing her expansive set of keys to sway and jangle. Mr Tucker said that he would return later to pick up the broken brandy glass then asked for directions on what to do about dinner and our guests. I took Mr Tucker to one side. I told him to keep the dinner ready. Any guests that arrived in the meantime should be escorted into the library and offered drinks and canapés. Mr Tucker agreed, bowed and looking terribly solemn, as if his world was about to come to an end. He then withdrew out of the saloon and drew the glazed doors of the room together, giving Edward and myself some privacy. I offered the Lord Lieutenant another drink which he declined, as did Inspector Martin who gave the typical response of "Not when I'm on duty my Lady."

I then turned back to the Inspector.

"Now Inspector, perhaps you would have the goodness to tell me why you are here, and how my brother and I can help you? As I am sure my brother has explained to you our family, like many others I would imagine, have had a bad blow today, due to this meltdown in the stock market. It has naturally greatly shocked his Lordship."

Edward stepped forward towards me. He looked suddenly awake from his dazed and stunned state. As his feet moved so to did the broken fragments of glass shattered on the floor. I studied Eddie closely. He looked now as if he was a broken man. That all his strength and youth had retreated. Inspector Martin turned to me looking rather surprised with what I had just said. His face and head were shaped rather like a tea cosy. He had a thick brown beard styled like His Majesty the King. His tummy was rather protruding, causing his jacket not to fit as well as it could, and looked as if it was three sizes too small for him.

"Lady Edith. I am extremely sorry to have to intrude on your evening, but I am afraid, I have some very bad news for you."

My heart started to beat a little faster. I dreaded what he was about to say. I looked over at Edward, who had walked across the room like an elderly man, reached out a hand to me and motioned me to come with him and sit down in his armchair. I walked over with him; his hands felt as cold as ice. As we reached the armchair, Edward swept away the broken shards of glass with his foot under his chair to prevent me walking over it. I continued to hold Edward's hand, rubbing it gently to warm it and to let Edward know I was there to support him. As I sat down I continued to hold on to Edward. He had now stood up to the right of me, holding my hand tightly, as if I was about to be given some very bleak health news from my doctor. Inspector Martin came over to us. He passed the chess table, which had a plate of cheese swizzle sticks on and nodded his head in a firm agreement to Edward that it was probably best I was sitting down. The Lord Lieutenant took up a seat on the sofa, placed against the Rococo papered wall under a large painting of Venice. The inspector and his sergeant now had the floor and command of the saloon.

"Lady Edith," Inspector Martin began rather sternly, "I am very sorry to have to inform you, that your father Lord Gregory Parfitt was found dead at quarter past five this afternoon. It would appear he had been walking along the pier in a state of shock and deep depression. It appears he must have fallen off the pier and into the sea. A local fishermen raised the alarm, and a party of five locals tried to get his Lordship out of the water. However, by the time they got to him and dragged him on to the beach he was pronounced dead. Doctor Kenos was alerted and rushed to the scene to see if there was anything that he could do, but it was too late." Inspector Martin's grave tone changed to one of pure pity and regret.

"I can't tell you how very deeply sorry I and all the village are, Lady Edith. You have my very deepest sympathy."

I gripped at Eddie's hand and arm, then suddenly clasped my hand over my mouth. My upright posture no longer held and crippled over. I bent over, trying not wail in tears. A feeling of sickness came over me. Edward knelt down and put his arm around me. Our heads touched once again in despair as we had done in his bedroom after our argument. In my mind, I once again could see Edward's copper alarm clock. It sat on his bedside table ticking… ticking away innocently. Then, like in the motion pictures, when all hope is lost the time finally ran out. The clock stopped ticking. The trigger had been activated, and the bomb had gone off.

Chapter 27

My Reserves Had All But Run Out

November 1929

The car pulled up to the front of the house and stopped in front of the porch. The floor of the porch was littered with a drift of brown dry decaying leaves that had been discarded by the trees. All around the house the deterioration and decline of autumn had taken hold of the garden. Coming up the drive in the car I noticed all the hydrangeas had faded and gone nearly transparent; their vibrant colours of pink, purple and blue had been replaced with insipid dull grey tones. The pine trees above them would keep hold of their foliage, while the other trees across the estate were dishevelling their leaves ready for a long winter's dormancy.

I wearily got out of the car, feeling shattered from the long journey back from London. Helen climbed out from the front of the car, clutching my brown leather case in her hands. She carried it as if it contained highly classified government documents. Our trip to London had not been a pleasure trip. It had been a terribly draining week of clearing out and sorting through endless drawers, cupboards and attic rooms, all before the creditors took possession of the London house along with nearly all of its contents, apart from a few photos and personal belongings. While I was in London I had had to undertake another errand. One I had never, ever imagined I would have to do. It had been a humiliating errand to undertake. Combined with the packing up of our London home and the thought of having to return home to Devon and complete the exodus there it left me feeling, by the end of the week, emotionally and physically crippled.

I thanked Neil for his steady driving and for bringing us safely back home. I proceeded solemnly through into the enclosure and tunnel of the porch, hearing the sound of crunching leaves under my shoes. I walked in though the porch and up two steps into the open doors of the lobby, where Spencer and Mr Tucker were waiting to greet me. Helen trailed behind me, looking even more despondent than I was. Spencer greeted me as best as he could manage with a "Good afternoon, Lady Edith. Welcome home." and took my coat and gloves from me, which revealed my black jacket encrusted with silver and jade beads, a long string of jade around my neck, and a black pleated skirt.

*

Mr Tucker, overseeing Spencer taking my coat and gloves from me, said how grateful he was to see me returned safely home, such as it was. The hall seemed so cold and desolate. The table was bare with no flowers on. Several tea chests were waiting by the foot of the stairs ready to be taken up to begin packing. The walls going up the stairs were blank and bare. Only empty hooks and chains were left with grey faded stains of where paintings had been hung for years, but had now been taken down, packaged up and escorted to the auction house to be sold. Helen came in behind me looking glum and startled at the change in the appearance of the house. She scanned the hall, like a cat looking up, down and all ways, gazing upon the bleak reality of the house's sad depressing state. Spencer then plodded outside to collect my meagre luggage consisting of a trunk and two hat boxes. He carried the lot in and proceeded up the stairs to my room, with Helen following behind carrying my leather travelling case. Neil meanwhile drove the car round to the garage and stables. His final job was to polish, clean and tidy it up for the very last time. Tomorrow the car would be sold and gone. As Spencer and Helen wondered up the stairs, Mr Tucker went over to the lobby doors to shut them. He gave Neil a final wave and nod of the head. A few minutes later I heard the sound of the car engine start up. It was the last time I would hear it. Having closed the lobby doors Mr Tucker slowly followed me through the hall and down the rather bare vestibule. We passed Father's locked study door, a room I no longer felt happy to go in. I turned to Mr Tucker as we walked towards the morning room, walking through the vestibule which, like the hall, was looking bare of furniture and homely furnishings. The house seemed so silent and still and as I spoke my voice sounded hollow and empty.

"How have things been this last week, Mr Tucker?" I enquired solemnly.

Mr Tucker coughed and spoke in a hushed and melancholy tone.

"We have managed relatively well, thank you my Lady. Things are beginning to get a little quieter now. Mr Cuss has been in a few times to help catalogue and go through the remaining items to be taken. I am afraid rather a lot of the contents will be going this week, my Lady. Apart from the items of furniture and goods you have allocated that will be going with you to Bath.

"I see. Very good then Mr Tucker. You sound as if you have everything in hand. How are you and the rest of the staff holding up? It must be very depressing for you all."

Mr Tucker looked rather curious at my note of sympathy for him and the rest of the staff. He had a pitying look on his face as if to say 'we're alright, it's you that we are were concerned for.' He leapt forward ahead of me to open the morning room door. The two of us walked in. I put my handbag down and removed my black slanting hat and pin. I put them both down on the walnut table which I was thankful to see was still there.

"Indeed my Lady. It is very sad that our time in service has had to end so tragically as this. For the younger servants, like Mr Neil and Spencer, it's not as difficult for they are still very young and will find new work eventually when the economic times improve. For myself and Mrs Goodwin it won't be as easy, for we are getting on now, my Lady. But the Lord shall provide for us. Don't you worry, my Lady. Our troubles are nothing compared to what you are having to cope with."

I looked around the bright, sunlit morning room. Most of the room's treasures were gone. All the china parrots had vanished as well as the large vases. The walnut étagère was bare of its former contents of china and knickknacks. The sofa and chairs were still present but covered with old newspaper, packing straw and an occasional pile of papers, photos, old diaries and letters. Only the sideboard with all the family photographs in their silver French frames with a veil of dust over the glass were undeterred from the chaos of the room. I went over to the window and clutched at the curtains with two of my fingers, bare of their rings with faint faded marks around each of my fingers. I looked out on to the lawn. It looked already rather wild and over grown. A few dandelions, or clocks as I called them, had invaded the grass, now scattered with leaves from the surrounding trees and shrubs. The monkey puzzle and umbrella tree were unaltered by the changing season; they both blanketed the lawn in shade. The yew trees and holly bushes were all looking very healthy and I noticed as we arrived back into the village many of the hedgerows were covered in drooping elderberries.

All the gardening staff had already packed up and gone leaving only poor Rogers. He was, by all accounts going round the garden in a haze of bewilderment. Apart from his time in the trenches all he knew was his life here. He had no living family that I knew of to take him in or support him. I had a funny feeling that somehow Rogers had not yet accepted or taken in the fact that his position had been terminated and that he, like me, would have to leave soon. As I observed how forgotten and silent the garden looked with all the summer plants now in decay and the grass uncut, and the leaves and weeds already beginning to gain ground, I could not help but think how depressed Mother would have been if she was here now. I finally came back to conversation with Mr Tucker.

"I think this situation that we all find ourselves in is trying and testing for us all. I am hoping that when the last of the financial settlements are completed and I have seen Mr Cuss and gone through the last of the paperwork and all the creditors have been paid, I may have enough money to take you and Mrs Goodwin with me to Bath. If you wish to come that is? After all I will need some sort of domestic support and Mr Edward will need a valet after all."

Mr Tucker looked suddenly relieved and almost cheerful. His face and cheeks puffed up like a puffer fish. His eyes welled up with tears of what I assumed must be joy and relief at the thought of having some security ahead of him, and the fact that I thought enough of him and Mrs Goodwin to ask them both to come with Edward and I to Bath.

"Oh my Lady! It would be a joy to come with you and Mr Edward. I am sure I can speak for Mrs Goodwin when I say we would both be greatly pleased to remain in service with you." Mr Tucker beamed a large smile and gave a slight chuckle, "I have always wanted to go to Bath. I have seen pictures of the city of course that I have cut out and stuck in my scrapbook. I think I have a few postcards in one of my albums, but it's not the same as actually seeing the place with your own eyes and to be able to walk around the Roman Baths and take tea in the famous Red House restaurant. I shall be able to take Mrs Goodwin in there. I hear their Bath buns are truly something!"

I left the window and walked over to my Queen Ann writing desk. A large brown tag was tied to one of the desk's legs with 'Bath' marked on it. I was certainly not parting with my desk. It was in a bit of a muddle however. It was covered in letters, old photos, bills, mourning cards and condolence letters from people that had written to me after Father's death was announced.

"I should think living in a city will take some getting used to. I don't know how I shall cope without seeing the sea every morning. However I am sure we will all adjust." I gave an unconvincing smile and sigh as if even I did not believe my own optimistic outlook of the future.

I looked down at my desk to see my copy of the order of service from Father's funeral, now well over several weeks gone since Father had been put to rest next to Mother in the church yard in the family plot. The funeral had been well attended given the circumstances of Father's death. Many of Father's friends and colleagues from both the Houses of Commons and Lords had come. A number of Father's friends from the publishing world had come to pay their respects, as well as a number of young authors who Father had helped and supported when they had turned to his publishing house to have their work published. Many of them would not have had the wealth and success they had now if Father had not given them a chance. Most of the villagers had attended as well as all of Father's staff from the mineral water factory. Even the engineers and porters from the cliff railway came to pay their respects, resulting in the railway being closed for the whole day in respect to Father. Yet there was one person missing at the funeral leaving me forced to sit alone at the front of the church in the family pew, tugging at a hanky. Edward had been too ill to attend. Thinking back to Father's funeral made me feel terribly low in spirits and I think Mr Tucker realised this as he quickly said he would go and ask Mrs Kier to prepare me a tray of hot tea and sandwiches.

As Mr Tucker was about to leave I quickly asked him the question I had been dreading and had put off for as long as I could.

"Mr Tucker. How has Mr Edward been?"

Mr Tucker looked uncomfortable and pensive. His smile and the colour in his face faded and his posture became a little tense.

"Doctor Kenos has been continuing his visits, my Lady. He thinks there is a little improvement. Mrs Goodwin has been sitting with him and talking to him as you wished. I believe she has been reading some short stories and poems to him, and some light-hearted trivia from the papers. Mr Edward has eaten a little cold meat and he seemed to enjoy Mrs Kier's soup that she did for him yesterday. Other than that, my Lady, there is no real change yet. Doctor Kenos did repeat his suggestion that he thought Mr Edward should be taken in to hospital or a care home where he could… "

I stopped Mr Tucker in his tracks and took a few steps forward. I felt angry at the thought of Edward being taken away into a hospital or worse.

"No! I am sorry Mr Tucker but that is out of the question. I am not having my brother, Mr Edward, going into hospital and being taken away from his home and all his familiar surroundings. Mr Edward needs rest and peace. He has suffered a great shock and loss. He will get better. I know he will."

My tone had been sharp and unequivocal. I wanted to make sure that there could be no misunderstanding of my orders.

"We will continue to care for Mr Edward at home until he is well again and recovered, is that understood Mr Tucker?"

Mr Tucker looked a little uncomfortable at my brisk and sharp tone. I had not meant to sound angry at him, I just wanted to make it clear that I was not going to abandon my brother to the care of clinical doctors and nurses. Mr Tucker bowed slightly and agreed with me that he and the remaining staff were more than happy and willing to care for Edward. He then made a hasty retreat out of the morning room to inform Mrs Kier to prepare some refreshment. I felt instantly guilty for sounding so stern with Mr Tucker. He had after all been passing on a message, nothing more. Yet I had shot the loyal messenger and probably upset him. I sat down at my desk looking dismally at its contents. I knew I would have to go through and sort out all this correspondence at some time or another, but I just could not bear to go through it or even re-read it yet. The desk contained no cheerful letters and no hopeful news for the future. I was about to stand up and go over to my handbag to retrieve from it the envelope which I had received after my errand when I was in London, when Mr Tucker came back into the room with a note placed on a salver. He bowed his head and approached me.

"My Lady I do apologise for disturbing you. A boy delivered this note a few minutes ago. I believe it is from Mr Cuss."

My heart jumped, like a cork in a bottle being pulled. A rush of nervous tension came over me. My heartbeat quickened for a few minutes. I took the note from Mr Tucker and opened the envelope. The note was indeed from Mr Cuss, requesting an interview with me for half past three that afternoon.

I knew full well what the meeting would be about. The last time I had seen Mr Cuss he had informed me that the next time we met, he would be able to advise me exactly what I would be left with after all the creditors had been paid and all the debts were accounted for. I knew that this afternoon I would finally be told what sort of a future life awaited Edward and I.

After eating a few sandwiches and drinking a cup of tea which Mr Tucker had brought in, I attempted to tidy up the morning room and make the room a little more presentable. I cleared away all the newspaper and packing straw from the sofas and chairs. I went through all the piles of photos and papers on my already chaotic desk. I placed my handbag on the desk chair after shutting and locking away the envelope which had been in it. I desperately hoped that I would not have to open the envelope for some time and that it would be a last resort. It may yet be something that may not be needed or used. I looked over towards the fireplace to look at the time, only to find the gold baroque clock and its large glass dome had gone. I put out a hand to observe the time on my gold watch. It read half past three. Like clockwork a knock came at the morning room door. I called out to Mr Tucker to enter. He came in and stood by the open door and announced Mr Cuss into the room.

*

If I was to describe Mr Cuss's look and appearance I would have to say Mr Cuss had the look of a badger. His manner was rather secretive and elusive, and he as badgers do, had a rather burrowing nature of working. His medium build and short stubby legs along with a tall head which at one time had been graced with thick black hair was all but eroded. It had now turned to a grubby grey colour. His thick bushy eyebrows had remained black and gave his dark eyes a rather hooded look. He had an elongated mouth and jaw containing very pointy teeth. His hands were long and rather claw like, with fingers and nails stained with ink. His style of dress composed of a black and white chequered suit, and a long black coat which gave him a rather sinister appearance.

I was partly excited about this interview. I hoped that Mr Cuss would have some good news for Edward and I. The rest of me was dreading this meeting and had been for some time. I knew that I was running on reserves and was becoming very aware that my mind and body was telling me that any more disappointment or bad news would be the end of me. I warmly received Mr Cuss and asked Mr Tucker to bring us in some tea at around four.

Mr Cuss bowed his head and shook my hand carefully. I gestured to him to take a seat on the couch opposite the fireplace. I took up a seat in a single chair to the right of him. After exchanging some pleasantries about how London had been and asking how Mr Cuss and his family were keeping, he cleared his throat lightly and twiddled his long fingers stained with a little black ink. This was the signal that he was ready to begin the formal matters. He opened up a black leather file and displayed some papers on his lap. He handed one to me as he began his brief. Mr Cuss tilted his long head towards me and his dark, almost inky eyes glared at me, making me feel uneasy and uncertain. He crossed and uncrossed his legs before coming directly to the point.

"I am pleased to inform you Lady Edith, that with all the business of the London house now cleared up we can now prepare this house for sale. Most of the contents has now been catalogued and is ready for auction. Apart from of course your own possessions and belongings that you will be taking with you. You will be glad to hear that they have all been cleared with the powers that be. We can now also proceed, too, with the sale of your father's mineral water factory." Mr Cuss handed me all the documentation which I carefully looked at one after the other. Once I had examined all the documents I turned to the matter of mine and Edward's forthcoming move to Bath.

"Mr Cuss have you made any progress in your inquires about the matter of our new home? As I am well aware that time is not standing still."

I had instructed Mr Cuss to investigate and find a suitable property for Eddie and I not long after Father's funeral, when it became clear this house would have to be sold.

Mr Cuss cleared his throat again. He got out yet another piece of documentation which he looked at then handed to me.

"I have indeed, Lady Edith. I have managed to secure for you an apartment in Bath as you desired. The apartment is partly furnished and is in a sought-after location overlooking Bath's Parade Gardens. My understanding is it is located just across the road from the Empire Hotel and Guildhall. My agent informs me that the abbey is only across the road from the property."

Mr Cuss past to me the document containing the apartments specification and plan. It all sounded very grand and spectacularly placed. I looked at the document eagerly, feeling thrilled that Mr Cuss had found such an elegant Georgian apartment with no doubt a suite of rooms containing several small reception rooms; perhaps a study for

Edward with two or three bedrooms and servants' accommodation. There may even be a small garden or terrace area. I imagined Edward and I would be able to go down into the Parade Gardens for weekend walks and attend the abbey service each Sunday. Mr Tucker and Mrs Goodwin would be able to go and take afternoon tea at the Red House on their days off. My spirits had leapt with joy and delight at hearing Mr Cuss had found us a new home. However my new found hopes faded rather too quickly when I read and studied the paperwork with greater attention. After I read the whole specification of the property I plunged the document down on to my lap feeling bewildered.

"Mr Cuss! There must be some misunderstanding! This apartment looks far too small! It only has one bedroom! Plus there seems to be only one reception room with no space or room for servants. Nor does this apartment have a garden as I requested!"

Mr Cuss showed no sign of emotion nor did he show any sign of bewilderment. He simply stared at me with his dark hooded eyes, and with no sound or expression of sympathy for me. He cleared his throat and began to explain to me the situation which, it appeared up till now, I had not fully understood.

"Lady Edith, with all your father's debts and death duties, the unhealthy loans, and all the funeral expenses, solicitors and agents fees, after the sale of this house there will be very little if anything left for you and Mr Edward to live on. Of course your mother left you both a small legacy but that money will be swallowed up to pay for this apartment in Bath. To be very blunt with you Lady Edith, this one bedroom flat is all you and your brother can afford. Many people in these economic times would consider themselves very fortunate to be able to afford such a flat and in such a desirable city. Of course the way things are now, not many people can afford to keep servants. I suppose you have heard the horrific stories in the newspapers regarding American citizens who have lost all their savings? Some have even taken their own lives by jumping out of their office windows."

I shifted about in my chair. I was desperately trying not to dwell on those horrendous stories that the papers had been full of. How I hated Mr Cuss for mentioning such stories. He seemed to almost relish in telling me the most terrible and depressing news. My mind started to spin. I was now trying desperately to think practically of some source of money that I could use to provide a better home for Edward and I. Surely we could do better than a one bedroom flat? There had to be something else? Surely things could not be that bad?

"Mr Cuss what about that sale of the mineral water factory?" I said, almost pleading with him to give me the answer I favoured, "Won't that money not be ours when all the business is sold?"

Mr Cuss looked unsympathetic again. He shook his head and sounded rather exasperated by my ignorance.

"I am afraid, Lady Edith, that the sale of the factory will be going to pay off the rest of your father's bad debt. As well as my own fees."

"I see. Surely Mr Cuss you were aware that I had been hoping to take Mr Tucker and Mrs Goodwin with me to Bath. They have been in service with my family for years, and what about poor Rogers, what will… "

Mr Cuss rudely interrupted me and said in a surprised fashion, "I am terribly sorry Lady Edith, but servants are out of the question for you. You and Mr Edward will barely have enough to live upon yourselves, let alone pay two wages for two servants. As for simple Rogers I would assume that he will be put somewhere out of harm's way."

At this point my Edwardian steel and composure began to slip. I became a little desperate, almost panicky in my reply.

"Then how on earth, Mr Cuss, can my brother and I expect to live? Do you suggest I find myself some sort of occupation to keep this meagre roof of a flat over our heads?"

Mr Cuss gave a sly, almost evil smile. He had the look on his face that betrayed what he was thinking: *How the mighty are fallen.*

"I am sorry to say Lady Edith, but yes. Indeed you will have to find some sort of occupation to support yourselves and save yourself from destitution. As you have no other family and very few friends who would be willing to help you out, owing to the nature of your father's death and the financial scandal of your family finances, I have no other advice to give you. So yes indeed you will have to find some sort of suitable employment. Perhaps as a nurse or governess, or as a secretary. I am sorry that I have crushed any remaining hopes you had of living in the manner you have been accustomed to, but it is the way of the world. Millions are facing this same dilemma as you now. So may I write to the agents in Bath and inform them that you will take the property?"

I looked about the room bleary eyed, wondering just how things could possibly get worse. I looked over at the sideboard with the family photos on. Even with the dust glazed over them I could still make out the faces of Edward and I stood with Mother and Father. I looked at them almost as if I no longer recognised them. They were all taken of a happy, healthy, respectable family; in what now seemed a different world and another time. I looked down at the carpet and back at the sheet of paper sat in my lap, noticing at the bottom of the specification for the flat the words 'this property would be ideal for a single lady or a bachelor, or ideal for a newly married couple.' I then thought back to those poor people in America. The thousands who had lost their savings, jobs, homes and some even their sanity. I then thought of poor Rogers. What life would await him now? I realised I had no other choice. There was no other option. There was no plan B. Desperately not wanting to cry in front of Mr Cuss, I lifted my head up high and gave a half-hearted smile.

"Very well, Mr Cuss. You may inform the agents in Bath I would be very pleased and grateful to take the property. Thank you."

After a few papers for me to sign and a few other items of final business, I agreed with Mr Cuss that the money for the flat in Bath could be transferred when he and agents were ready to proceed. Edward and I would be able to leave for Bath as soon as the sale was complete, and when Edward and I would be in ownership of the flat. Mr Cuss drew up a timetable in line with the creditor's demands. We decided that by the middle of December, Edward and I would be on our way to Bath. I therefore had only a few weeks left for me to try and get Edward to his feet, make sure the servants would be properly cared for and pack up the rest of the house.

*

I was much relieved to see the back of Mr Cuss and had great pleasure in ringing the bell for Mr Tucker to see him out. Mr Cuss did not stay for tea. As soon as Mr Cuss had left the house I left the morning room to go and see Edward. I would have to try and break the news to him. I heard Mr Tucker close the lobby doors after Mr Cuss had departed and could hear Mr Tucker cross the floor of the hall and go through the leather soundproof door towards the servants' quarters. I too made the same crossing. I went across the hall from the morning room and down the vestibule. I walked opposite the door leading to the servants quarters, and turned to go up the stairs. The walls up the stairs were blank and void of the classical paintings and tapestries that father had collected over the years from Italy, Spain and France. Mr Cuss had advised me not to sell off any of the contents until Edward and I were ready to leave for Bath. Yet I saw no point in delaying the inevitable. The creditors demanded their money. I naively thought that the more I sold early on the more chance Edward and I would have of ending up with a small but nice amount of money to pay for a new home in Bath. Yet now I realised that I could of spared myself and the servants a lot of heartache in leaving the house as it was until we were all ready to leave. Instead I was slowly dismantling our home, much to mine and the servants sadness. I reached the top of the stairs and went along the mezzanine towards Edward's room.

His room was the only room left in the house that had not been dismantled. The room looked exactly as it had done on the day of the crash and the evening of father's death. The room was like a tribute; a time capsule, kept exactly as it was on the day everything had changed for us. I crept into the room, my eyes blinking and readjusting to the softer light. The curtains had been drawn and the window left slightly open to let the room air. My eyes immediately fell towards the bed where Edward remained exactly as I had left him a week ago. He was wrapped up under blue and gold coloured sheets with his head nestled into a white plump pillow. He looked like an elderly man of seventy. His appearance was pale, vacant and unshaven. He was in a deep sleep and unaware I was home again.

Ever since we had both been told of Father's death, Edward had been unable to leave his room. He slept most of the time or sat in his gentleman's library chair by his window, staring out into the garden. He showed no life or spark for anything or anyone. He had suffered, what one would call now a days, a complete breakdown. I went over to his bed and kissed him gently on his head. His hair texture was greasy and smelt of sweat. I topped up his water on his bedside table using the jug and tumbler Mrs Goodwin had brought up for him. A few magazines and articles lay out on the end of his bed as well as a leather bound book of short stories from Father's bookcase. I walked over to the window and gently closed it, fearing the November air would cause Edward more harm than good. I turned round to see his mahogany desk looking more dishevelled and in more chaos than my own was in the morning room. Every drawer had been riffled; every letter and scrap of paper had been thrown out. A few letters had found their way to the floor as well as a fountain pen that had rolled off the desk. I turned back round to Edward. He was still deep asleep, his bare arm revealing a few pricks where Doctor Kenos had to sedate him when he had become panic stricken and almost out of his senses with grief and worry. Thankfully he had not had another attack like that for several weeks. I went over to him and gently placed his arm back under his blue silk sheets. He did not wake, nor did he stir. I made my way back over to his desk to tidy it up a bit until Edward awoke. It would give me something practical to do. I closed a few of the desk's small drawers, placed pen lids back on and removed a smudged piece of paper from Edward's silver blotter. I threw it into the empty fire. I then tried to set about putting the many letters and correspondence back into the drawers. I found many of the letters were from me; letters that I had written to Edward while he was studying at Oxford. Other letters were from Mother, all very loving letters, full of news from home and events down by the harbour.

After placing many of her letters into one of the drawers, I came across a letter I had sent to him when he had gone off on his tour of Europe. I had sent it to Berlin where Edward had stopped off. My letter was rather poorly composed. I had had none of Mother's eloquent words and style of writing. I wrote such silly things to him; telling him about the harsh weather, Father's latest speech in the Lords, and more domestic matters like Mother's latest dinner for a few of their friends from Cornwall, as well as Marcus being taken very ill with flu, and all the drama of having to call for Doctor Kenos. I had even put down that Doctor Kenos had told Father that the next twenty four hours would be crucial for Marcus. It was strange that this was the last letter I sent Edward as he strangely cut the rest of his tour of Europe short and came home almost immediately, claiming he was homesick. I pondered over the letter for a few moments before placing it back in its original envelope. I opened up another drawer of the desk, in readiness to slide my letter into it. On opening the drawer I came across yet more letters, all sent to Edward from Devon to Oxford. The handwriting looked large, bold and fluent and had a rather graceful composition. It was a hand that seemed familiar to me yet I could not think quite who the owner of the handwriting was. I opened up the first of the letters and began to read its contents. It became increasingly clear as soon I read the first line of the letter that it was a letter of deep affection and love between two people, one being Edward. As I got to the end of the letter, which was extremely personal, I noticed whose name was to be found at the bottom. I looked at the name. I shot round to look at Edward, still asleep and not aware that the secret he had kept from me for so many years I had finally discovered. Edward had no idea that all he had hidden and kept from me had now been revealed and much more besides. I now knew why Edward and Father had quarrelled so bitterly, and why Father had been so devastated and angry with Edward. I now knew why Marcus had been allowed into Father's study that afternoon, and why he had been instantly dismissed. I understood Edwards desperate feeling of wanting to leave Devon and set sail for a new life. I now realised what had always been lurking and menacing Edward all through his adult life and why he was now suffering with a complete breakdown. For not only had he lost our father, but he had also lost his lover. For the name at the bottom of the love letter belonged to Marcus.

*

I quickly closed up the letter flung it back into the drawer and rushed out of the room towards my own. I went down the mezzanine, my legs feeling like they were no longer working properly. They felt like they were beginning to slowly fuse. I managed to make it to my room and grabbed at the brass handle of the door, turned it and staggered in.

My room was the exact opposite of Edward's. Where as his room had not been touched or disturbed, mine looked like a waiting room at the doctors. All my Degas 'Dance examination' prints had gone, along with my carver chairs. My Louis dressing table and stool still sat in the bay window, with a few glass perfume bottles, brushes and a small empty vase. I ran over to my bed and sunk down on to it, as if it was a life raft adrift in the sea. I could hardly get my head round what I had just discovered. How could I have not noticed or seen what was going on? Everything made such perfect sense now. Part of me wanted to go into Edward's room and slap him. The other half of me felt bitterly sorry for him and wanted to go to him and give him a hug and tell him that everything would be alright. That things would be better. Yet I could not help but feel angry towards both Edward and Marcus. I looked about the room seeing my luggage piled up in a corner by the wardrobe door, not yet unpacked. My bedroom looked so unfamiliar now; as if I was sitting on someone else's bed and looking around someone else's room. I played and fiddled with my black strand of jade mourning beads as if they were a rosary. My eyes fell upon my leather travelling case placed carefully on my chest of drawers with the sturdy handle flopped down, and with the gold coloured lock reflecting the light from the window. Helen had guarded the leather case like she was carrying the crown jewels on the train, giving the impression that my case still contained my jewellery.

When we had left Devon for London the case had indeed held all my jewellery. Yet now the case lay empty. Its contents had all been sold in London and the meagre funds my jewellery had fetched was now sat locked away in the left drawer of my writing desk down in the morning room. I had never felt so ashamed and so humiliated having to go to a backwater jewellers almost begging the fat, pompous man to buy them. I had at first gone to many of the high ranking jewellers that Mother and I had been patrons of for so many years. Back then I had been welcomed like a queen into their establishments being sat down, offered tea and treated like no one else in the world mattered apart from me. Yet now these same jewellers turned their noses up at me as if I was dirt. This forced me to try more, shall we say, humbler establishments. I hoped and imagined that one day I would have been able to pass on my jewellery, to my own children and loan pieces to my future sister in-law when Edward married. That of course would never have happened. I had hoped that I would never have to part with any of my jewellery. Yet there was the case standing empty looking dejected, made redundant and never to be used for its proper purpose again. For all that was left of a collection that had contained a necklace that had once belonged to the Russian Royal Family, and heirlooms that had been in my family for generations, was my mother's gold watch which was still strapped to my hand and her string of pearls that were on my dressing table. Everything else had been sold.

*

Nothing was at it should be. Just when I had prayed that things would not get any worse, they suddenly had. My mind wondered back over that letter I had stumbled across in Edward's desk. How could he have had such feelings for another man? Where did such feelings come from? How on earth would Edward and I ever be able to go back to the way we were? All the trust was gone. Everything I thought I knew about him and what he stood for had shifted and changed. I felt like I was a ship's anchor being slowly lowered into the sea, getting deeper and deeper until I plunged into the sea bed. Yet there was no ship or crew floating above me to pull me back up. Like my jewellery case, I felt suddenly empty and redundant. My reserves had all but run out.

Chapter 28
I Would be Going to Bath Alone

December 1929

They came at eleven o'clock. Spencer had innocently let them in. He had been helping Mr Tucker catalogue and box up the last of the dinner services from the china closet. It was rather a painstaking ordeal considering the number of china and glass services we had. They had been making good progress when they were interrupted by the jangling bell at the back door of the servants' quarters. Spencer immediately suspected it was the staff from the auction house come to take away the grand piano and the other large pieces of furniture. He left Mr Tucker in the china closet and went along through the silent passage to answer the knock at the back door.

He brought all four of them up the back stairs, then up to the morning room. He had no idea nor realised what they were for. I had enjoyed a good morning up till then. I cleared the mountains of papers, letters and photos from off my Queen Ann desk and had gone through everything very carefully. I had been rather ruthless completing the task. I threw out many of the old letters and engagement diaries. I even disposed of a few old photos which I placed into a tea chest as they were going to the kitchen garden to be burnt. I knew space in our new home in Bath would be minimal. I decided to keep the special letters that my parents had written along with photos of family members and legal documents. All the rest had to go! I had felt pleased with my efforts and by eleven my desk was cleared and all the drawers bar one were empty and secured. My desk was ready to be shipped off to Bath at the end of the week. I began pushing the box of sentimental papers and photos over to the sofa so it would not get muddled up with the box I had sorted out to burn, when Spencer entered the room. He appeared to be cradling four boxes. They were all of different sizes and widths; one was extremely wide and long, the other was a little smaller in capacity and length and one was like a small box of chocolates. The last one was a small cube shape. They were all done up in thick brown paper, with yards of string and the king's stamp and London postal mark in the right hand corner. All the packages were written in an eloquent hand and addressed to me, with the senders name and address stamped at the bottom. The sender was 'Natasha's Fashion designs, Bond Street, London.'

I gave Spencer a clear displeasing look as he left the morning room. He left me to look down on what should have been one of the most exciting moments of my life. Yet now I could have attacked the four parcels and carried them outside to the smouldering bonfire in the garden and watch the lot go up in smoke. Why! Oh why had Spencer not checked at the door what they were, before allowing them in to the house. Why had he not shown more common sense? Everybody who had been invited to the Christmas ball knew it had been instantly cancelled after Father had died. I had sat down the next day and written to all the guests informing them that the Christmas ball was cancelled. Mrs Goodwin had been a brick and seen to all the cancelling of the food and catering. I had phoned Natasha's in London and spoke to a girl, who at the time I thought sounded about twelve. I told her firmly to cancel my dress. Yet somehow Natasha's had not understood. My message and instructions had not been acted on. For here now was four packages containing my scarlet satin and goldthread dress with a long train. A black fur rap and a Russian diadem concluded the costume. Now here they were. All packaged up in front of me waiting to be opened. I had planned to wear Mother's Russian necklace with the dress as it would have gone perfectly with the costume.

*

After Father's inquest which thankfully the coroner gave a verdict of death by misadventure, although we all knew it had been suicide, but the village and coroner had given the former verdict to allow Father the dignity on being placed in consecrated ground in the family plot.

I somehow had gone through all those difficult days in a kind of stunned trance. I knew at the time that I had to hold everything together, that I could not fall apart, particularly with Edward in such a dreadful state, and apart from the servants I had no one to turn to. I had to cope. I had no choice. Yet now, seeing those packages reminded me of the time before the crash and Father's death. I recalled the time when I had been content and happy. The packages contained something that I knew had died with Father. They were a stark reminder of how quickly one's life can change. I spent a few moments studying the parcels and walking around them. It was as though they were a museum exhibition. They were like objects that I was not allowed to touch, only look at from a distance. I could not bare to even pick them up or handle them. I knew if I did I would run the risk of wanting to rip open the thick brown paper and reveal what was inside. I instantly went over to the bare fireplace and rang the bell next to it. I pulled it several times until Mr Tucker came quietly in. I briskly ordered him to take all the packages down stairs and to immediately organise for the dress and accessories to be sent back to London. Mr Tucker carried out the task and staggered out of the morning room door with the four packages stacked in his arms. They all towered up to his chin. I knew I would have to ask both he and Mrs Goodwin to pop up and see me later. I would have to inform them that very regrettably I would not be able to take them to Bath with me. I felt so guilty for giving them both false hope. They would both be utterly devastated. I had seen a change in them both these last few days. They seemed secretly happy that they had future employment with me. They had both gone about their duties putting on brave faces. They had been given hope and now I would have to crush it.

Apart from Mr Tucker and Mrs Goodwin the only other servants left were Spencer, Helen and Rogers. Neil had left for Barnstable the week before. He had been offered employment in a garage repairing motor cars. The job offered him a small room to himself above the garage so it was an ideal prospect. Mrs Kier had left for Scotland after writing to her cousin and hearing back with an invitation to go up to live with her on account that her health was declining. Mrs Kier had seemed pleased to go and be needed. I think she was looking forward to living up in the highlands. The rest of the junior staff had left after Father's funeral. Poor clumsy Gillian who had been the bane of Mrs Kier life left to work in the harbour to prepare and fillet fish. Even Mrs Kier shed a tear when she departed. As for Rogers he continued pottering about the garden working at his duties, despite Mr Tucker trying to explain to him that he would have to go soon. Not wanting to antagonise someone who was already highly strung and shocked from after the war, I set Rogers the task of burning all my unwanted correspondence and papers. He had taken to the job with great vigour and excitement. He set up a healthy fire in an oil drum in the kitchen garden in a cleared space by the greenhouses.

Spencer had also been promised work on one of the fishing trawlers. He was due to start as soon as we all left the house. That just left Mrs Goodwin and Mr Tucker to take care of. I wandered over to the sideboard and continued on with my next task of wrapping up all my family photos in the silver frames. I placed them into the same box that all my desk contents had gone in. I had a last few boxes to see to in Father's study and then that room would also be empty. That would be my task for the afternoon. I hated going into the study. It was the one room in the house where there seemed to be an uneasy atmosphere. When I had ventured into it I could almost see and smell the vapours and swirls of tobacco smoke that had always been present when Father was in the room. Despite that most of the bookshelves were now empty but I could still smell the leather and paper from the now vanished books. The room was unfortunately bitterly cold as I had ordered no fire to be lit in the grate. After Father had died I had searched and looked for fragments of the photographs that he had burnt of Edward on the afternoon he had found out about Marcus. It appeared that Father had burnt nearly a whole album full of photos of Edward. He had also destroyed pictures of Mother and me. Photos that could never be replaced. Despite my searching and digging away around the grate there was nothing that could be salvaged. Most of Father's study contents had been sorted but there were still a few more drawers left to clear out in a cabinet. There then came a small tap on the morning room door. Mr Tucker entered looking uneasy. I thought that perhaps now would be a good time to give him the bad news. I thought, he being a man, he would be able to take the news better than

Mrs Goodwin would. This would then give him some warning on how best to tell her that, despite my efforts, neither of them would be able to come with Edward and I to Bath. Mr Tucker shuffled over to me still looking uneasy and a little flustered.

*

"My Lady I am sorry to disturb you. I know how busy you are. My Lady, Helen would like to see you for a moment if it is appropriate?"

I was a little mystified. Why should Helen need to see me when she had had several opportunities this morning? I then thought that with everything in such disarray I saw no need to send off Mr Tucker with a flea in his ear. So I agreed to see Helen, who was apparently waiting outside in the vestibule. Mr Tucker ushered her sternly in to the morning room where she sheepishly came in, clutching and tugging at her skirt. Although she was nervous there was something different about her. She had a bloom about her and a sly shy smile across her face. Mr Tucker remained for a moment until I dismissed him and as soon as the morning room door closed I offered her a seat. Helen however declined the invitation and remained standing.

"I won't sit thank you, my Lady. Not yet. I am very grateful to you for seeing me this morning, my Lady. I know how busy you are. I would have asked Mr Edward but he has only just got up and about these last few days and being that you are mistress, well Mr Tucker said it would be proper to see you first."

"That's alright Helen. I am very happy to see you if you have something on your mind. Now tell me what can I do to help you? If it is a reference you wish me to write, you know I will give you a glowing one."

I knew that had to be it. Helen must have seen a job advertised for a Lady's maid or a house parlour maid and wanted me to write her a reference. Helen looked highly excited as if she could not contain herself. She had the look of a little girl who was sworn to secrecy about a forthcoming surprise birthday party for a relative and was about to spill the beans.

"Oh no my Lady! It's not a reference I need. No my Lady. You see as you know me and Alexander um… I mean Mr Dunn have been courting for a long time now. Well my Lady, last night on my evening off, Mr Dunn and I went for a walk along the harbour. Well my Lady to cut a long story short, Mr Dunn has asked me to be his wife!"

The news jolted me. It was news that I knew one day would come, yet somehow, what with everything else, I had not expected it. I sunk slowly down into a chair while Helen excitedly continued telling me her happy news.

"I do love him very much, my Lady, and we have been courting for well over a year now, getting on for two. We know each other very well my Lady. So I am here my Lady to ask your permission if we may get married."

*

I continued sitting in the chair. Sitting still not saying anything, trying to smile. Yet I found it hard to smile. I was desperately trying not to show my envy. Part of me was so enormously pleased for Helen. She had been my maid for, well ever since I could remember. We had grown up into young women together. I really did want to wish her every happiness. However there was a lingering, snagging, almost bitter resentment coming over me that Helen had so much ahead of her now. She would enjoy so much love and joy, starting a home and would probably have children. Helen had so much to look forward to. I continued fighting very hard to smile and swallowed hard several times to try and hold back my tears of self-pity. When I finally did speak my voice broke with emotion and sounded rather croaky.

"Well Helen!" I gave another very sharp gulp, "If you are sure and you have thought this very important decision through very carefully." I rose out of the chair and went over to her, smiling with much more conviction and gave her a kiss. "Then of course I am extremely happy for you. I give you both my blessing and very best wishes. You will have to bring Alexander round to see me before we all leave."

Helen's little girl look came over her again. She blushed and went slightly shy.

"Oh well my Lady, Alexander is here! He is waiting in the hall! He wanted to come and see you, but Mr Tucker said I had to see you first, as I am still in service with you. May I go and get him, he so wants to see you my Lady?"

I was rather surprised that Alexander was here already. I again felt rather on edge at the suddenness of events. However I could see how excited Helen was and I too partly wanted to see again the young man she was about to marry.

"Oh Alexander's here? Oh you should have said he was here earlier Helen! Yes do go and fetch him, I would like to see him."

Helen rushed out the room as if it was on fire. She fled down the vestibule towards the hall like a galloping horse. For a few moments I was allowed to show how I was secretly feeling. A tear rolled down my cheek followed by another. I looked up at the ceiling and around the room. It was now like the other rooms in the house: it was hollow, cold and unfriendly. I looked back over to the sideboard which was covered in a haze of dust with only a few areas of dark wood showing where the photos had been. Only one photo was left on the sideboard, all the others had been carefully wrapped up in pages of the *Telegraph*. From outside the door I could hear some excited whispering and giggling coming along through the empty vestibule. After clearing my throat again and giving my black skirt a brush off from the dust and packing straw fragments, then quickly wiping away my tears I stood silently still and awaited the happy couple to enter.

*

Alexander was a huge, strong, well-built man. Not fat or overweight by any means. He had terrific muscles and thick, strong looking arms and legs. He was a giant of a man to be a clerk at the mineral water factory, but he was a softly spoken man. He had a kindly manner about him with a very warm, likeable face. His dark hair was cut rather short for my liking but it suited him. Alexander and Helen stood arm in arm in front of me, Helen now showing off her engagement ring that she had been hiding purposely until I had given her my blessing. They both did look highly in love and seemed very well suited. I sat them both down for a few minutes and asked them about their plans. Alexander spoke first with Helen gazing round at him with her hand in his.

"We thought we would have a very simple wedding, my Lady. Not too much fuss. Just family and friends. I am only allowed a day off to get wed, then I have to be back at the factory. We have a prospective buyer looking round soon my Lady so all the books and papers have to be up to date."

Alexander suddenly looked worried. He appeared to be worried about mentioning that Father's factory would soon be in someone else's hands and ownership. I indeed knew nothing about the factory sale. I had left all that to Mr Cuss. Eddie had made it clear he was not well or had any intention to carry on running the factory. He had hated the foreman's job even when Father was living. Father had forced him into the role and Eddie had not made the job his own or a success. Alexander, feeling and sounding awkward, quickly said to cover himself, "I do miss Mr Edward as foreman, my Lady. He was always very thoughtful and kind to me. May I ask how Mr Edward is now my Lady?"

I was grateful for Alexander's kind words but found answering the question hard. Edward was now up and about. I had told him of all that had happened and transpired during his weeks of illness since Father's death. I could no longer protect him from what was coming. Edward was not the man he use to be. He was still very distant and morose in his appearance and his general manner. He seemed resentful and bitter with me and with everything else for that matter.

"Oh he is much improved, thank you Alexander. Mr Edward is up and about and seems much stronger now. It is very kind of you to enquire after him. Now tell me both of you, when will the big day be?"

I wanted to change the subject and not to think or talk about Edward. Helen and Alexander both grinned at each other looking into each other's eyes.

"Well, my Lady" Helen started still holding Alexander's hand as if she was surgically stuck to it, "we thought the week before Christmas. Best to get all this sad leaving business over with first we thought. Then we can really enjoy the day. We are going to be so happy."

Helen's face absolutely beamed and glowed with happiness. Alexander however was perhaps a little more tactful.

"We will be staying with my mother for a while, my Lady,"

Alexander announced turning to the more practical and domestic matters as any good husband should.

"We don't have enough saved yet to afford a place of our own, but my mother has cleared out her front room, so we will have our very own room until we are more financially independent."

I smiled thoughtfully at Alexander, nodding my head in agreement with him. Alexander certainly seemed a highly responsible young man. I thought Helen would do very well with him. Helen carried on talking for a few more minutes. She chatted on about how wonderful life was going to be. She even invited me to the wedding. Alexander added that both Edward and I would be very welcome to attend.

I knew of course it was out of the question. For one thing Edward and I would be living in Bath by then. Secondly it would not do nor would it be healthy for Edward and I to return for the wedding. It would be a hard enough leaving on Friday as it was, let alone return again for a wedding, which after all was a joyful occasion. An occasion which I knew Edward would find very hard to cope with given his personal circumstances. I of course thanked them both for inviting me. I replied I would see what I could do. Before Helen and Alexander left I offered Helen the opportunity to go through the servants' quarters and take any of the remaining linen or china that she would like for her new home. Helen was thrilled and said she would do so. Alexander thanked me and shook my hand.

"Thank you for your kindness to us, my Lady" Alexander said, "I do know what a difficult time it must be for you. I am very grateful for all you've done for Helen. I will always be so grateful to your father, his Lordship I mean, offering me the job at the factory. I will never forget his kindness nor his encouragement."

Alexander let go of my hand and retook Helens. I felt a lump in my throat. I was trying desperately hard not to cry in front of Alexander and Helen. Alexander's kind and genuine words about Father had meant a great deal. I could see that he really meant what he said. No matter what road Alexander had gone on in life and whatever life threw at him in the future, I knew he was a man who counted his blessings and would always be grateful to my Father who had believed and saw the potential in him when no one else had.

*

Helen wanted to go on talking but Alexander could see how I was secretly feeling and made his excuses. He stated that he needed to get back to the factory and Helen would have to get back to her duties or Mr Tucker would box her ears. After a respectful and formal good bye the happy couple left the room. I was left in the morning room to carry on with my packing alone. The rest of the morning continued as most of the days seemed to consist of now. Packing. I carried on sorting and throwing away, then taking the rubbish to the burning box which would go across to the kitchen garden. The morning room was virtually empty now. All that was left was the sideboard. The auction house said it was not worth a thing yet I knew I would have no room to take it with me. The sofa and chairs were being donated to a nursing home and would be collected on Thursday. The Walnut étagère was tagged now ready to go to Bath along with my desk. The rest of the house was looking more like a warehouse. It was full of tea chests, boxes, baskets of linen and an occasional piece of furniture which was deemed worthless and would not sell.

 After a brief pause for lunch which I had on a tray, consisting of a bowl of soup and a roll, I picked up the box of papers to burn and staggered out of the morning room with it. I trotted and stumbled carrying the heavy thing through the vestibule heading towards father's study. The vestibule was like an empty wing in a hospital only without the beds and patients. Mother's grand piano was due to go to auction today along with the rest of the furniture. I dragged the box for the rest of the way relieved when I finally reached the study. I opened the door rather hesitantly as the room was not a pleasure to enter. The study resembled an empty burial chamber. Where once had been books now were wall to wall alcoves of empty shelves covered in dust and an odd cobweb in a place or two. Odd book marks and scraps of paper had been left behind on the shelves by the packers from the auction house, along with old notes that Father had made and placed in certain volumes which had fallen to the floor when the books had been pulled off the shelves, catalogued and boxed and were simply picked up and placed on the dejected shelves. A globe which Father had brought back from Sorrento in Italy before the war had gone, along with Father's chess table with the sculpted stone Roman Gods and Goddess pieces. The study had a musty unlived in smell about it now. Hardly anyone went in to since Father's death. Even Mr Tucker appeared to be disturbed to do so. Every now and again there was a smell of brandy and cigars about the room, now simply fading ghosts of the room's former occupant. Father's abandoned widespread desk opposite the large bay window had not yet been collected. It somehow appeared more like a coffin than the old familiar desk that I had seen Father sat behind most days. The whole study was floodlit with the December afternoon light. The curtains and blinds had been taken down the day before leaving the dark and deserted room to be brought out of the shadows to reveal the empty book shelves and cabinets.

 I placed my box of papers to be burnt on top of Father's bare desk with only his bankers desk light left to adorn it. The lamp's shade was Irish green glass in colour with a tarnished stand below. A small pile of spare name tags yet to be allocated to items and furniture going with us to Bath lay scattered under it. The most valuable object left in the study was a huge bronze *Medic* horse, which Mother had purchased for Father for one of his birthdays. The bronze had been an ornament in all of Father's offices dating back from his early days in his publishing house, to his office in the House of Commons. A scoop back leather chair the colour of sherry was sat dejectedly by the fireplace. Next to that was Father's high back leather chair which he had always sat in after dinner to read a volume, smoke a cigar and drink a glass of brandy. I found the state and bare appearance of the study rather unsettling. I went over to a pile of papers and documents that I had sorted out the day before after the blinds and curtains had been taken down. I scooped up the lot in to my hands and threw the assortment into my box. I walked over to the bookshelves and removed Mother's stamp collection along with Father's volumes and albums of foreign coins and post cards. I went back and forth from the desk to the shelves repeating the same action. By the time I was done a stack of albums and binders were built in a neat tower on the desk. When I placed the last album on top of the newly built pile they stood nearly as tall as the bankers lamp. My task that had sent me into a rather slumbering state of mind came abruptly to a halt. I shuddered and was so alarmed that I nudged the glass shade of the lamp on the desk. From behind me a weak and depressed voice called my name. I turned round in an instant; not that I had heard or seen Eddie enter the room, yet when I turned round there was no one present.

*

The room appeared to be empty. I was still alone apart from the bronze horse sat on the desk. I glanced round the study looking into its four corners. I then glared up to the top of the room and to the side door which lead into the Library. The door was panelled and decorated cleverly, disguised like a shelf of books. The hidden door was, unusually, open and exposed to reveal its secret passage that lead into the cavernous library. Standing in the doorway, like a pale and walking corpse, was Eddie. He was leaning against the door, clutching at it like it was a handrail. He was dressed casually. He wore a white shirt with the sleeves rolled up to mid length, the shirt's neck collar open. A jumper the colour of port was worn over it, the garment's sleeves ending the same length as his shirt. Sandy coloured cord trousers with a brown check completed his afternoon attire. His hair looked clean and washed, blessed with a high shine to it. The length was a little longer than was customary for him and it appeared a little wild looking. Edward remained leaning against the door speaking in a dull far off tone.

"Do you remember when we used to play hide and seek here Edith? And that other game we used to play here after we heard the news about the Romanov's being murdered. We used to pretend you were one of the Russian princesses and I was a loyal Russian officer come to rescue you. We would always escape through here wouldn't we?"

Eddie finally wondered over towards me continuing to scan the room. The change and scarcity of the study must have been rather startling to him for he had not been down in this room since the day of Father's death. I studied Eddie's appalling appearance, *Gosh he looks so thin,* I thought as he got up to the desk and greeted me with a bony hand on my waist and a kiss on the cheek. I nervously replied to his question.

"Yes I remember Eddie. It seems such a long time ago now. In some ways it seems like only yesterday. Our childhood seemed to go by so quickly looking back now."

Edward went round by the desk and caressed the bronze sculpture of the Medic horse. He then turned and went over into the bay window to gaze out onto the lawn. Beyond the overgrown lawn a tower of smoke was billowing up from behind the kitchen garden wall where Rogers was still burning our unwanted papers. Eddie then continued his meek conversation. "I wonder how she ever got over it?" Eddie said with his back to me, still looking out into the garden. Puzzled at his ad hock and vague question I asked, "How who got over what, Eddie?"

Edward sounded rather annoyed at my question

"Empress Maria! Tsar Nicola's mother. Don't you remember? We saw her once very briefly with Queen Alexandra at the Chelsea Flower Show. Mother pointed her out to us. I have been wondering how she coped with the loss of her family. Makes you wonder how she ever came to terms with all that?"

I thought back for a moment and after a few moments racking my brain did very hazily recall the meeting.

"I only vaguely remember seeing Empress Maria at Chelsea. You and I were would have been rather young back then."

I walked over to Edward in the bay window and put an arm around him, rather worried at his question. I joined him in gazing out through the grimy window, my eyes drawn to the looming smoke that was swivelling over the red brick wall of the kitchen garden. "In answer to your question Eddie," I said, trying to keep him talking with me as Doctor Kenos had recommended, " I can't imagine how any one, whether your royalty or a humble shopkeeper, copes with the loss of so many relatives, especially children. The only thing that gives me any comfort is our faith. That one day we will be reunited with our relatives, and all the chaos and changes that we face in this world will be replaced with peace and joy in the next life." Eddie continued looking out of the window staring into space, appearing to ignore my comforting words. Outside a robin had landed on the lawn and was stuttering about trying to find a worm to pull out from the ground. The Robin had the most loveliest red breast that I had seen in a long time. He had the most merry singing voice, and skipped and jumped about looking for a snack. At times he disappeared from sight behind tall patches of wild grass. He would then re-appear and jump onto the fallen piece of oak branch which had gone rotten and fallen to the lawn.

"I don't think I shall ever get to heaven, Edith," Eddie tragically announced. His eyes welled up with the most heart-breaking despair and sadness in his voice. I turned round to face him with my back against the window and felt a slight cold draft on my back. I pulled Eddie into me and held him tight, feeling his ribs and bones which had become so exposed due to all the weight he had lost. He nestled into me like a child unable to stop crying. His body becoming less rigid and more relaxed. The only sound apart from his despair was the sound of the singing robin from outside, jumping about on the fallen arm of the oak tree looking for insects that had taken up residence within its chambers and vaults.

"Of course you will go to heaven Eddie!" I said in a positive and determined manner. I wanted to attempt to encourage him and assure him.

"You have accepted Jesus as your saviour and he loves you. We all make mistakes, Eddie. We fall short. Not one person on this earth is perfect."

I pulled Eddie back a little so he could see my face and I his; he had been nestled into my shoulder with his back looking painfully bent as he was, after all, much taller than me. I decided I could keep my own council no longer. It was time to come clean and now seemed a good opportunity.

"Eddie I know about you and Marcus. I know why Father was so angry with you both."

Eddie quickly stopped his crying and looked at me with a slight look of fear in his eyes. He put a hand to his nose to rub it gently, gave a sniff and wiped his eyes.

"How do you know? Have you seen Marcus! Has he come back? Do you mean he has come back? He's spoken to you?"

Eddie sounded excited almost hopeful at the thought of Marcus returning home. Yet I was about to disappoint him severely and I would accidentally say something which would cause the biggest break up and grief that I had ever known.

"No Eddie! Marcus hasn't returned. Nor will he. No. I found his letters in your desk the afternoon I got back from London."

Eddie pulled away from me, looking startled, and asked me accusingly, "London! But that was over three weeks ago! Why didn't you tell me you knew? Why were you going through my desk?"

I could hear the anger in his voice. I could see in his eyes the agitation of being discovered and having his personal belongings violated.

"I did not know how to tell you, Eddie. You were still not yourself when I got back from London. I only went through your desk because it was in such a mess and I was so worried about you, it gave me something to do while you were sleeping."

I felt a little angry myself now. I felt that Edward had no idea what I had to go through on my own while he was ill.

"I am sorry I went through your desk Eddie. I was not trying to pry or snoop. I was just trying to bring some order to your desk and take my mind off worrying about you."

Edward meandered away from me looking out of the window. He headed back over to the desk with his hand stroking Father's bronze horse. His red ruby set in his gold ring flashed as it caught the light.

"I know he will come back for me Edith! He promised he would come back!"

Edward continued smoothing the dark, cold bronze feeling the contours and sculpted neck of the horse. His hand slivered up the horse's arched neck up to its main. I was a little taken back by Edward's naivety, thinking Marcus was coming back. Even if he did the relationship could not go anywhere. They would not be accepted. Not by anyone. It was not the done thing.

I walked over to Edward and put a hand on his shoulder.

"Eddie even if Marcus did come back for you what would you do? You could not live with him. Society would shun you both. Every door would be slammed in your face. Now with both of us having to find work of some kind when we reach Bath, well your character must be exemplary without a stain on it. If you are going to find an occupation to rise in you will have to accept that this relationship which you had with Marcus is over. It may be for the best. Perhaps in a few years' time you might yet find a nice young girl and… "

*

Edward's hand moving up the horse's neck suddenly went into like a spasm. His hand which had been gentle and soft made a sudden fist and it looked like he was about to try and throttle the horse as if it was alive. He let go of the sculpture and spun round to tackle me. He was looking at me as if he hated me.

"You know Edith, you sounded just like Mother did before she sent me on that bloody tour to Europe!"

I looked at Edward in utter disbelief with my mouth quivering. Edward seeing the shock in my face quickly fired back.

"Yes! Mother knew, Edith! Why do you think I got packed off on a tour of Europe? Mother thought a change of scene and different cultures and people would kill off my strange desires. She even said I might find a nice girl while I was on tour. I agreed to go as long as Marcus was allowed to keep his position. Then of course Marcus went down with the flu which you thankfully told me of in one of your letters, and I knew the deal was off. I came straight back home. The strange thing was, going on that tour only made me more sure of myself and my feelings. The more difference in people you see the more you realise it's alright not to fit into a mould."

I listened as best I could but I felt anger like I had never experienced or felt before in my life. The fact that Mother also knew and had allowed

Marcus to carry on working for Father, and sending Edward away made me mad. The fact that I was the last to be told in the family and that all these secrets, deception and lies had been undercurrent in the house for much longer than I ever expected, made me feel disgusted and defiled. I then thought of Mother and I tried to see the situation from her point of view.

"I'm sure Mother did what she thought was for the best," I said tiredly. I was trying not to lose my temper. "Mother most probably did not know how to help you. I expect she was terrified Father would find out and she must have come to the conclusion that a change of scene would do you and Marcus good."

Edward became even more agitated. He circled menacingly round Father's desk like he was stalking it.

"What the hell do you mean by that Edith? Oh... I suppose you think that my going off to Europe and getting away from home would kill my feelings for Marcus, is that it?"

Edward's prowl round the desk suddenly picked up in speed, like he was on a merry-go-round. He soon came full circle round the desk and got back to me. He now had his back almost touching the ears and head of the bronze horse.

"We'll let me tell you something, Edith. That separation didn't change anything! My feelings for Marcus only became stronger. Of course when I got back Mother convinced Father to give me the foreman's job in the factory to try and keep me out of the house. It wasn't until I did start working at the factory and started examining the books and looking into more of Father's business dealings that I realised what a mess he was making of everything. Marcus eventually let slip how much Father was investing in the stock market. Then when Mother died his love of the stock market only intensified. Marcus and I both went through Father's papers one night, trying to see just how bad things were getting. Marcus had been getting urgent messages for weeks from Father's brokers who were worried that he was taking on too much. Then weeks later on the day of the crash Marcus tried to warn Father while you and I were at the Bath Hotel. Marcus told Father about our fears of his financial management. He showed Father the letters from the brokers, even Mr Cuss had warned Father of the risks of the markets but it was all too late. Later, Father received that telegram and seemed in total denial to start with. He said the brokers were wrong! That it was just a blip again. That the market would correct itself.

I confronted Father. I told him what a fool he was. That if he was not careful he could bankrupt us. I told him he had to act quickly to salvage something. But Father was having none of it. Do you know Edith, he was in such denial he started to blame everything on Marcus and the brokers! It had been them who had badly advised him! Even with the bloody telegram in front of him and all the other pre-warning letters, Father could not accept it. Then when he started tearing into Marcus and said he would dismiss him, that's when I really lost it. I told him about Marcus and I. About how we felt for each other and that if Marcus went then I went too. Father thought I was joking for a while but he soon realised how serious I was."

"So what happened?" I said, my heart pumping faster than normal. In my mind I could almost see the scene that must have played out in the study that afternoon. I looked about the vast empty room as Edward continued on with his recollection of what had transpired between him and Father. I could picture Father at his now empty desk. On that day it must have looked very different. The desk must have been full of warning letters with the all-important telegram taking centre stage. It must have been laid out in front of him just thrown in front of his ink and pen stands. I could see Father bang the desk with his fist, causing his blotter to rock like a child's cradle and his bankers desk lamp to shudder. I imagined Eddie stood in front of the desk with his hands clenched together and his head low, trying to talk reason with Father. The scene must have looked like a school boy about to be caned by his headmaster. Eddie continued with his story.

"Father went mad then! I don't think I have ever seen him or anyone lose their self-control like he did that afternoon. He rose out of this chair and walked over to the study door and locked it. He seemed calm at first but then as I turned around to look at him he hit me round the face. He got more violent after that. He started throwing things at me. At one point he even threw a decanter at me! He said Marcus and I were dirty sods. That we were both queers and he rushed over to the desk and picked up the

horse…"

Edward paused and turned slightly to look back to the now innocent looking bronze. As his eyes fell upon it he looked suddenly worried, recalling those terrifying moments. He must have feared that Father was going to bludgeon him to death. Eddie then came out of his frozen state of terror and continued his story.

"Then Marcus knocked on the door. The rest you already know. After Father told Marcus to pack his bags and leave Father rushed down to see Cuss. I followed him down and sat in Cuss's office hearing the grizzly news until Father told me to go.

"But Eddie you can't blame Father or Mother for not understanding what you are can you? Even if Father and Mother had not found out what future would you and Marcus have had? It's not the…"

I paused for a moment, not really sure what to say or how to help myself or Edward.

"It's not natural Eddie is it? You can't blame Father for being angry with you."

Eddie's face went bright red. A rage rushed over him. He looked as if he was going to erupt.

"Why the hell not Edith! Would you have treated your child in that way?"

"Oh Eddie, don't be such a cuttlefish! I don't have a child. It must be hard work being a parent. All I know is Father and Mother wanted the best for us. All they ever thought about was our future and well-being. I realise it's hard for you Eddie, but this thing, this love you have for Marcus, it can't go on. It's not right. For goodness sake Eddie, you had the same upbringing as I did! What would the vicar say if he knew and the rest of the church?"

My voice had become slightly charged and agitated. I attempted to calm myself down and said in a self-assured manner, "I think our going to Bath may be a blessing in disguise, Eddie. You and I can make a fresh start. You can find a job and in time you may change…"

Edward lurched at me, looking like Father must have done at him.

He became even more angry and emotional again. Only this time his anger had reached a new fever pitch.

"Oh for heaven's bloody sake, Edith! How many more bloody times have I got to say it! This isn't some phase I'm going through. I'm not going to wake up in a month's time in this bloody flat you are moving us to and start liking women in that way. I love Marcus, Edith! Do you hear? Marcus! Neither you, Father or Mother can change that!"

I had been trying very, very hard to keep my calm and not to lose my control like Father had done. However I was slowly simmering inside and Edward was pushing me to boil over.

"All you ever think about, Eddie, is yourself and about how you are feeling and suffering. Never mind me! Who's had to hold everything together while you've been lying in bed feeling sorry for yourself, saying you can't cope with all this? How do you think I bloody well feel! I had to sit in the Town Hall in front of the whole village and hear in graphic detail about how poor Father died. I have had to sit through meeting after meeting with Mr Cuss, hearing how all our money and savings have been thrown to the winds on the stock market. I have had to cancel the Christmas ball that I had been planning and preparing for months and instead plan our Father's funeral, which you conveniently could not go to. On top of all that I have had to sell everything we bloody well have, to pay off all Father's bad debts including all mine and Mummy's jewellery. How do you think all the servants feel having to pack up and leave without getting any financial support? This has been their home too you know. How do you think poor Rogers is going to cope without us and this house to look after him? Who's going to employ a man who's been touched after the war?"

I turned around and started heading over to the window, still not able to let go of all the anger and grief that had been building up for weeks. I eventually turned round to look at Edward. He had appeared to lose his anger and looked crestfallen and tearful. Perhaps he finally realised just what he had left me to cope with.

"You know Eddie, I can quite understand why Father lost his temper with you. I can quite see why he felt so depressed that he had to throw himself into the bloody sea!"

By now there was no stopping me. The flood gates had been opened and I had to let go of the tide. My voice had now become a scream which caused the most terrible echo of my words to reverberate around the silent and empty house.

"Because of you and your sinful, disgusting relationship with Marcus," I screamed almost wincing with the out pouring of tears and grief. My face screwed up and felt bright red and inflamed with anger.

"Father felt driven to drown himself. Do you hear me Eddie! It's because of you and what you are that broke Father's heart!"

*

The study became still again. The dust however was far from settled. Even the robin outside on the lawn had been put into silence. Perhaps he was shocked by what I had said. Edward stood looking up at me, like he had been hit by a bus. All the life and colour had drained from his face. His eyes were trembling with tears which were cascading down his pasty cheeks. His whole body shook from head to toe with fear and shock from what I had said. He looked like he was about to keel over. He swayed a little on his heels. I knew I had gone too far and staggered over towards him to apologise. I wanted to hug him and ask him desperately to forgive me. But as I attempted to go over to him, Edward backed away and put his hand up to prevent me coming any closer to him.

"Eddie... Eddie... I am so sorry I did not mean... "

I tried to get closer to him to make him understand that I had not meant the cruel and wicked things I had said. All the stresses and worries over the last few months, trying to hold everything together had finally proven too much. I had taken my desperate anger out on the one person I had any love or care for. But Eddie was too upset to listen. He simply wondered away from Father's desk and headed towards the door.

I called out to Eddie in a last desperate attempt to tell him how much I loved him. I wanted to tell him that no matter what the problem was or how little I knew or really understood his feelings for Marcus, I wanted to tell him that we would work it out. That I still loved him no matter what. Yet it was not good enough. The harder I cried and the more I tried to say how sorry I was the worse the moment got. As Eddie reached the study door I wailed at Eddie to come back. I almost tripped over by Father's desk not being able to see where I was going, my vision so impaired with tears. As Eddie's hand gripped the scrolled door handle and turned it to pull the door open, I called out one last time to try and get him to remain in the room with me.

"Eddie! Wait Eddie! Please wait! Don't go I didn't mean it. I love…"

Eddie went through the door out into the vestibule. He smoothly closed the door behind him, the door fixing with a click back into place. For a while I could do nothing. I sunk to the floor, grabbing at the desk as I went down. I knocked over Father's bankers lamp with my outstretched hand. The lamp crashed to the floor with me. The green, emerald, coloured glass shattered and broke into pieces. Somehow I knew in that cold silent study that it would be the last time I would ever see Eddie. I had scarred him too hard for him to stay. As I continued to cry in utter desperation and guilt after all I had said, I suddenly knew I would be going to Bath alone.

Chapter 29

A Box of England's Glory Matches

December 1929

I closed the warped and flaking door of the kitchen garden, knowing that I was closing a door I would never open or pass through again. The door's black Tudor handle fell away from my hand and swayed back hitting the door where it had done in the same spot for years. I brushed past the honeysuckle, now dormant for the winter. It had begun to climb over the red brick walls of the garden and had encircled the perpendicular door. The two well-groomed topiary trees stood either side of the door. They would both remain well clipped for a little while yet. I walked sombrely away from the kitchen garden with the smell of the bonfire submerged into my clothes and hair. As I wondered along the gravel path heading back towards the house I wondered where Rogers was. I had expected to see him in the kitchen garden supervising my paper burning in the oil drum. Although I conducted a search around the garden it proved unfruitful. He was nowhere to be seen. I hoped that at long last he had accepted that his time with us in service had come to an end and that he had gone.

I knew that I did not have long either. The car would be here soon. I thought I had heard the lorry leave a few minutes ago. All my things that had been carried out all looked so shabby being loaded up into the lorry. I walked along the gravel path brushing through wet damp, sanguine leaves. I still felt that terrible presence of someone following me. Despite my unease I did not hurry in my return to the house. There was nothing to hurry for now. Everything had been done. A line was about to be ruled through this part of my life. In truth I was dreading going back into the house. I never liked goodbyes even before all my troubles began, but this goodbye would be so difficult. I knew how upset Mrs Goodwin had been when I asked her and Mr Tucker to come up to the morning room. They had both been expecting me to tell them that I had secured for them their positions and that they would be coming with me to Bath. When I confessed to them both that Mr Cuss had told me that it was no longer possible and that the three of us would have to go our own separate ways Mrs Goodwin looked like she going to pass out. Mr Tucker had to take her arm and hold it for a few minutes to steady her. The worst of it was that they both desperately tried to put on a brave face for me. They were both biting their lips trying to hold back their sheer disappointment. They attempted not to make the moment worse than it already was. As I thought of them both and all the years they had been with us serving in the house I felt the envelope in my pocket again. I had quickly managed to retrieve it from the locked drawer of my writing desk before the two men scooped it up and carried it out of the morning room towards the lorry parked outside in front of the house. I patted my pocket with my hand reassuring myself that the envelope was still there and had not fallen out. I looked up along the path to the right of me which headed up along the rose garden and up to the terrace of steps to the tennis court. I would have dearly loved to have gone up there and seen the view of the sea for one last time. There was not the time for such a trip sadly. As I continued on my walk I could hear in the distance the sound of the first car arriving. It sounded as if it had swept up the drive into the space where the lorry had been parked. I could hear the gravel shifting as the moving car's tyres rolled over it. Finally the sound of movement stopped and the car had parked in front of the porch.

*

I reached the side of the house and walked around the perimeter with the overgrown lawn to the right of me and the fallen piece of oak branch still sunk in the grass where it had collapsed. There was no sign of the robin today. Nor could I hear any sound apart from a car door being opened and shut, and the clatter of a bonnet being let open and inspected. The driver was probably giving his car the once over in preparation for the two passengers he had to take to the station. I reached the steps that lead up to the garden room. The glazed door was slightly open where I had walked out of it a few minutes ago carrying my box of papers and rubbish to be burned. On entering the garden room I locked the door and left the key in the lock. The room was empty. The orchids had vanished leaving only a few stray petals on the blue and white Chinese tiled floor. A broken wicker tub chair was left looking sad and unwanted in the corner. Mr Tucker had stood up on it to take down the blinds and his weight and the years of wear on the chair were too much for it. Poor Mr Tucker's feet and legs had crashed through the seat but thankfully he had not cut or hurt his legs. His butler's trousers however had torn slightly on the outside left leg, yet Mr Tucker no longer needed to worry about the state of his butler's uniform. After today he would be free but unemployed, which is why he took the incident so well I thought, without causing a fuss. I walked into the main hall which seemed depressingly dark with a sheet and cover draped over the chandelier. I crossed over towards the foot of the stairs with no large table in the centre to manoeuvre round. Mrs Goodwin and Mr Tucker were waiting for me by the fireplace as previously arranged. Mr Tucker's luggage, a large black battered suitcase, was stood by his feet. Mrs Goodwin's small brown suitcase and carpet bag were stood next to it. Mrs Goodwin was well wrapped up in a tweed skirt and matching tailored jacket, with a brown shawl with long cream tassels draped over her, secured with a cream cameo. Her hair was, as always, neatly piled up in a bun with what looked like a sink bowl of a hat to cover it. The hat could do little to cheer her face which looked terribly pale and blotchy. Dark circles surrounded her round, small eyes. In her hands she clutched at her tiny handbag like it was a kitten, along with what looked like a handkerchief which she was trying to hide. Mr Tucker was dressed in his casual suit that he wore on his afternoons off. Covering his suit was a long, thick black coat which had been one of Father's. After sorting out Father's clothes

I had kept back for him the coat along with a bowler hat which was now anchored in his hand.

I walked over to them both and looked at them longingly. I wanted to savour the moment of looking at the two faces who had been like grandparents to me as a child. Mr Tucker nodded his head on my approach and Mrs Goodwin gave a shallow curtsey. Mr Tucker broke a little away from Mrs Goodwin to address me. He wanted to discharge himself quickly knowing that Mrs Goodwin was bound to get emotional.

"My Lady, the lorry left a few moments ago and is on its way to Bath. Both myself and Mrs Goodwin have made a thorough inspection of the house. All the house is empty apart from the sideboard in the morning room and the chair in the garden room which I unfortunately broke. May I take this opportunity, my Lady, to say on behalf of both myself and Mrs Goodwin… " Mrs Goodwin reached for her handkerchief and began to sob rather deeply while Mr Tucker continued his farewell address.

"It has been a great privilege and a great honour to serve you and your parents for all these many happy years. No family has been more distinguished than yours, my Lady. I know both his Lordship and her Ladyship would have been extremely proud of the way you have coped and conducted yourself through these many months of trials and… "

Mr Tucker paused and his normally formal and elegant way of speaking broke a little with emotion. "And both Mrs Goodwin and I are extremely proud of you and the woman you have become. I still remember when you and Mr Edward were children. You would both come running down to the kitchen and sit at the kitchen table to eat one of Mrs Kier's jam tarts with a scoop of cream. Then Mr Edward would come into my pantry and watch me decant your Father's wine."

I too could recall those children running down to the kitchen, sitting up at the table eating tarts and scones. We would watch Mrs Kier roll out pastry using a jam jar as a cutter. Edward and I would watch poor Gillian, only a child herself then blundering about, breaking one plate after another and driving Mrs Kier mad. Then Edward would run down the passage trying to jump up at the servants' bells. That time went by so fast. Where did all those years go? What happened to those children?

Mr Tucker came a little closer and took my hand to shake it, patting it gently. "I know things are far from right at the moment, my Lady, but our Lord never forsakes us. He is always with us. No matter how bad our troubles and tribulations seem."

Mr Tucker suddenly paused and looked a little afraid. "My Lady, there is something left in the kitchen for you. It arrived while you were in the kitchen garden. Please make sure you collect it."

I let go of Mr Tucker's hand. I gave a nod of understanding to him, thinking that he and Mrs Goodwin had left a leaving present for me. I reached into my pocket to get out the envelope that contained the small amount of money I had gained from the sale of my jewellery. I handed the envelope to Mr Tucker.

"Mr Tucker I have a little something for you too. I would like both you and Mrs Goodwin to have this. It is my way of thanking you both for all the years of loyal and devoted service you have given this house. I really don't know how I would have coped without you both these last few months. I do realise it does not make up for the money you have lost. Nor does it make up for the promise I broke in not being able to take you both to Bath with me. Please take, it Mr Tucker. Mother and Father would have wanted you both to have it."

Mr Tucker's eyes glistened with tears and his chin wobbled a little. Mrs Goodwin continued sobbing as he took the envelope from me and looked at it in astonishment. Mr Tucker put on his bowler hat and then picked up his case. He then turned to me again as if he wanted to tell me something but I interrupted him.

"God bless you both."

Mr Tucker returned the sentiment and gave me a kind smile. He still appeared as though he wanted to say something more to me. The moment passed however and he proceeded to help Mrs Goodwin to pick up her two bags. Mrs Goodwin looked overwhelmed and tired. She dabbed her eyes with her sodden handkerchief. She then came over and kissed me.

"Goodbye, my Lady. God bless you."

The sad couple collected themselves together before trying to walk confidently across the black and white chessboard floor. They opened the lobby door and walked out through the lobby and into the porch and the cold December air. The driver was waiting for them. He helped Mr Tucker load their bags into the back of the car while they unwillingly followed. As they were getting in, I thought how poetic it was that on their last day in service they had both left through the door which they were never normally allowed to use while in service. They left by the front door and not through the servants' entrance. Their time in service was indeed over.

*

After their car disappeared down the winding drive, I closed up the heavy front door and then fixed together the glass lobby doors. I went over to the stairs where my handbag was waiting for me along with a black pair of gloves. I looked about the main hall for a few minutes, wanting to tour the house again. I had looked round the house once already remembering and recalling happier times of childhood. I had somehow made my way up to Edward's room and sat in his window seat for nearly twenty minutes. I had wanted to go over the past few months and the terrible things I had said to him in the study. Eddie had rushed up to his room after our argument and collected in haste a few clothes, books and photos along with all of Marcus's letters. He had sadly left behind the letters from Mother and I. Then he had simply walked out of the servants' entrance, not saying anything to anyone.

I continued standing at the foot of the stairs clutching the scrolled wooden pine cone at the bottom of the banister. I looked up towards the top of the stairs, studying the blank walls. I had no more energy to go back upstairs, even though sitting in Edward's bedroom made me feel closer to him. Sat in his room it felt as if he was still about in the house and any moment he would come through the door and greet me in that carefree, loving manner I had become so used to. It was strange but I could still smell his aftershave in his room even though he had left. I looked back across the hall and saw my exit in front of me. I plodded across the chequered black and white tiled floor and put a hand out to open the swivel leather door of the servants' quarters. I turned around one last time to look back at the hall and the world I had grown up in. The only world I knew. I then pushed myself forward through the door and down the stone steps. I heard the door push backwards and forwards as I went through before it ceased to move and remained still for good. I made my way past the open door of the servants' hall and along the main corridor lined with the procession of servants' bells that Eddie and I had tried to jump up and ring as children. Yet now the bells would never ring again. For no one was upstairs to ring them and no one was downstairs to answer them. The bells had finally fallen silent.

*

In the laundry room the box mangle would never be operated again. The armoires doors were open but with the linen, sheets and towels absent. The Sheila maids still hung from the ceiling yet had no washing hung on them to dry. I pottered past Mrs Goodwin's room, now deserted. Her bookcase was still full of volumes of house keeper's guides and household management books. Her photo albums had been taken and her fireplace was bare. A few of the black and white staff photographs had been left still hanging on the wall; they looked like a museum exhibition of how life used to be. I wondered if the faces of the people in them would ever be remembered. Would anyone recall in years to come the world those faces had worked and lived in? A world that seemed to be coming so quickly to an end.

I finally came to the place that Eddie and I had run to on most afternoons. The place we had sat in at the long ancient table, Eddie helping me up on to a chair to tuck into a plate of Mrs Kier's scones, homemade jam and Devonshire cream. While we tucked into our cream teas we would often watch the rest of the kitchen staff prepare the endless dinners and meals that Mother, Father, Edward and I would consume. The kitchen was now as forgotten as the rest of the house. All signs of life had faded: the table was bare; all the mixing bowls, cookery book, storage jars and scales and weights were gone. All the copper pots and pans that had hung from the racks and had been stacked like the tower of Bable on the pan racks had vanished. The blue and white china which had decorated the dressers and plate racks were also no longer present. One plate however had not been taken. It lay on the floor in several pieces where it had been dropped in haste, when the dressers had been cleared. This time Gillian was not the culprit and there was no Mrs Kier to scold her. At one of the Belfast sinks a tap silently dripped away; the sound had replaced the absence of the New Gate clock that had always ticked away above on the wall. The time piece now lay packed up in the lorry heading towards my new home. I also had taken one of the pan racks and its copper pans. As I went round the kitchen observing the range where all my meals had been cooked on, I looked over at *The Household Wants Indicator*. It still hung on the wall with red tags on various items like bread, milk and sugar. Yet no one was around to check the indicator and see what ingredients were needed. This was the final grocery order. One that no one would ever complete.

*

As I reached the other end of the table, recalling the meals that I had seen prepared on it, I walked round the other side of the table and reached what I assumed was the leaving gift that Mr Tucker had informed me of. The leaving gift however was not what I was expecting. It was practical perhaps, but not what I thought it would be. On the table was a small box of England's Glory matches. A charming picture of an elegant steam ship sailing on a turquoise sea against the back drop of a sunlit sky was painted on the box lid. Underneath the matchbox was an envelope with my name written across the middle. I was somewhat surprised that Mr Tucker and Mrs Goodwin had addressed the envelope to 'Edith' and not 'Lady Edith' as they had always addressed me. I laid my handbag and gloves down on the table and tore open the envelope. As I did I studied the handwriting and letter formation of my name. I instantly knew that neither Mr Tucker nor Mrs Goodwin had written my name on the envelope. I became eager to open the envelope and proceeded to do so. I pulled out the letter on thick, pale, blue paper unfolded it and opened it up. As soon as I saw the beautifully written letters and design of the letter I knew who had written it. As I started to read I looked up at the high set window hearing a noise of a car horn being blown twice and the sound of an engine running. I knew my home would soon no longer be mine and that time was running out on me. The car that Mr Cuss had arranged to collect me and take me to the station had arrived. First I had to read Eddie's letter.

*

To my dear Edith

I know I have caused you much grief and worry over the past few weeks. I realise I have not been the best of bothers to you, nor been the son Mother and Father wanted. I want you to know that whatever harsh words passed between us, I do and always will love you. Which is why I can't stay with you anymore. Nor can I come to Bath with you. If I was to stay with you and go with you the problems and troubles that have caused us such grief would only follow us. I know you will be far better off without me and that no gossip or scandal will be able to hurt you as long as I am absent from you. I have taken everything I wanted from my room and leave you all my other possessions. Apart from you the only other person I love is Marcus and I am on my way to be with him and to start a new life. I hope one day you may be able to think more kindly of me and forgive me for all the pain I have caused you.

I am giving this letter and the box of matches to Mr Tucker before I leave Devon. I have left instructions with him to leave you this letter and matchbox on the kitchen table in the very two places you and I always sat in when we would come and taste Mrs Kier's scones. Tucker's a good man and I know he will get this letter to you before you leave. Enclosed in the box of matches is the one thing I have that I know is of value and may help you financially if you get into trouble. Father brought it back from Turkey and he always said it was worth a bit. It's not left my finger since Father gave it to me for my twenty first. If you need to sell it Edith, sell it, if it means keeping a roof over your head. Its absence on my finger won't be as bad as not seeing you anymore, but I have your photo and will keep it near me always. I have placed my ring in the matchbox as I thought the picture on it would remind you of our happy times by the harbour watching the Queen Alexandra go past.

May you always remember our times by the harbour and the childhood I so loved and enjoyed sharing with you. May your new life be happy.

May God bless you, as I hope he may bless me.

With my love

Eddie.

Chapter 30
Hopes Dashed by a Gold Ring

The light, whispering Devonshire breeze rustled through the hedges and shrubs that surrounded the tennis court. They acted like the walls of a secret room reawakening everything that had fallen silent and still. The breeze seemed to grant the birds permission to begin chattering and singing again. The lime-green sunlit grass also began to stir with the light wind, ushering the sunny yellow buttercups to do the same. The breeze urged the still and slumbering tennis court to re-join the world of 1952 again. For I had, for a short time, temporarily slipped back in my mind to the lost and forgotten world of the twenties and my former home's hay day. I had then turned to the dramatic crash that had brought such an exciting and promising decade to a bitter and pitiful close.

That final letter that Eddie had left for me on the servants' kitchen table had, from that day forward, remained captured and imprinted on my mind. I had read the letter so many times over the months and years that followed that I no longer needed to take it out of its drawer in my desk to remind me of what Eddie had said. His words had never been misplaced by me. They had been my constant companion through the difficult first few months in Bath when everything seemed bleak and unfamiliar. They were my constant companion through the war and the Blitz. Even in my new and peaceful life in Wiltshire I often thought of Eddie. I never threw away the matchbox he had given me. It was always refilled with new matches and never replaced or put into retirement. It remained in my kitchen, always by the kettle, so I could always remember Devon and home.

*

With my mind returned back to the present, I remembered why I had come back to Devon and how I came to be standing on the tennis court of my former home. That murmuring sickly pain of panic crept over me again. That deep feeling of grief and hopelessness reawakened deep within me. Thelma and Emma's names had not been on the list of survivors. They were both missing, presumed dead and that supposition once again caused me distress.

I felt the physical, slight grinding pain in my foot where I had stupidly stumbled over the rusty remains of the tennis net posts. After a few more minutes of taking in the sun's pleasant rays and thinking back to when there had been no wall of trees surrounding the court; when a game of tennis and afternoon tea could be accompanied by the sight and smell of the sea, I decided it was time to leave. It was time to leave these shadows behind. It was time to head back to the Chough's Nest.

*

I left the security of the tennis court and began my problematic and complex descent back down the eroding and subsiding steps. In places the terraces were beginning to disappear altogether under the clutches of bind weed, moss and ferns. After a few difficult moments of navigating safely down, I was back, thankfully, to the security of the ground again. I attempted to relocate myself back towards the wall of the kitchen garden. The vegetation was so thick now and at times along my walk I lost my bearings completely, partly due to the fault of the new ash and fir trees that had self-seeded and grown up in the middle of where I recalled the path to be. After fighting my way through the encroaching buddleias and rhododendrons I rather wished I had a machete with me. I thought how Norman would have been in his element up here with all these varieties of ferns to study and catalogue. Thank the Lord I had escaped him that morning!

Eventually I manage to navigate my way back along to the wall of the kitchen garden and reached the garden's entrance. It had not been easy to locate due to the honeysuckle that had now grown abnormally large and wild all over the wall. It had nearly concealed the opening into the garden where the flaking, creaking door had been. Now it was like approaching a thick stage curtain of growth. The door had fallen off its hinges years ago and rotted away, replaced by a tapestry of honeysuckle.

I knew I had found the entrance into the garden again as the two topiary trees still stood on either side of the door like they had done years ago. They reminded me of the soldiers guarding the entrance of the Pump Room Hotel in Bath during the war. Now the topiary trees looked not a bit like they had done years ago. They had lost their slender spiral figures and had become bloated, over grown and increased dramatically in thickness, height and width.

I placed a hand through the draping curtain of the thick, leafy honeysuckle. I must have looked like I was an opera singer peering through a gap in the stage curtain on opening night to see how many people were sat in the auditorium. There was, however, no orchestra tuning up and I was not about to start singing! I gingerly crept through the curtain and bent down a little entering the arch. There was no audience waiting for me on the other side; only the abandoned and disused kitchen garden with piles and stacks of red bricks, mossy chimney pots and grey slate tiles covered in lichen. All the fragments were sunk into the wild overgrown grass, with only the sound of an irritating cooing pigeon roosting on the roof of one of the geriatric looking greenhouses; the biggest of which had started a new trend in indoor gardening: an ash tree had grown through the roof. Looking about me there was no sign of soil or vegetable plots. They had long ago been carpeted by decades of grass and weeds.

I did try to squint forward and locate the sundial that had stood smartly in the middle of the garden. It too had now disappeared under the vigorous grasses. It may have even toppled over with subsidence. The only thing that was still just about visible, standing exactly as I had left it on that cold December afternoon in 1929, not far away from the greenhouse, was the circular top of a rusting and well weathered oil drum; the same drum which I had burnt all my unwanted papers and photographs in. Remembering that last hour before I, Mr Tucker and Mrs Goodwin left the house made me feel suddenly guilty and ashamed again. How could I have burnt that photo taken by the harbour of Eddie and I. I had done it out of sheer bitterness. I had blamed Eddie for all our troubles, yet of course it had not been his fault. I knew that now. What's more, if I could have been given the chance to see him again I would have told him that whatever he was he was still my brother and that I loved him. That parting in Father's study had haunted me for the rest of my life. I had never really recovered or forgiven myself. The worst of it was I knew I would never be able to take back what I had said.

*

The pigeon that had been observing me from its cumbersome position on the roof of the decaying greenhouse suddenly looked panicky. It fluttered and flapped its wings and took flight into the air, escaping over the wall and out of sight. I looked around behind me towards the darkened and shadowy door leading through the tunnel of honeysuckle. What had startled it? I stood still, with the long grass swaying at my legs, listening to the sound of the chirping birds. A tormented creak and groan came from the greenhouse as the ash tree that had grown up through the roof swayed gently in the breeze. Its movement grinded the broken roof timbers and remaining shards of glass together. The panelled and glazed door to the greenhouse was shut. It had not been opened since the last gardener had left. Grass and shrubs had now grown up to the door and sealed the access to it. I could see no stray cat or animal on the prowl which could have startled the pigeon. Then from behind me came the sound of a sharp snap of a twig followed by another. From the other side of the wall came the sound of another flapping pigeon deterred by something pushing its way through the vegetation, towards the door of the kitchen garden. As the pushing back of shrubbery and cracking of twigs continued I could feel my heart thumping in my chest. I felt a little panicky and sympathised with the pigeons' feelings of fright.

I turned round towards the greenhouses where I knew there was another escape route out of the garden but getting to it would be a nightmare! The snapping of twigs and rustling of the ferns and vegetation continued from behind me. I staggered forward trying to locate the path that lead up to where I remembered the sundial to be. Yet the grass, weeds and brambles were too thick. I could not force my way through in time. *I could try and hide in the grass* I thought and hoped that the intruder would not see me and would leave. As I looked back towards the door in the wall I could see that it was not a cat or fox as I had thought. It was a man! A pair of large brown military boots were moving through the tunnel of honeysuckle and the boots and the person wearing them was coming closer!

*

I looked around the garden in all directions to see if the wall had crumbled down and collapsed in any place which would give me an escape route. To my horror the walls were all intact. They were still solid looking and had not been breached during the garden's years of neglect. The footsteps through the undergrowth came closer and the honeysuckle began to twitch and shift as the intruder began to come through the curtain and out into the light and space of the garden. I was trapped! I had no escape. The garden had imprisoned me. As the intruder ducked his head and bent down as he entered, I felt even more full of panic. I was all alone on a remote and deserted hill in the remains of a walled kitchen garden with an unknown intruder heading towards me.

*

I had, however, no reason to be worried. There was no danger after all. I gave a great sigh of relief when I saw the good looking officer walking purposely over to me. He looked surprised but mainly relieved to have finally caught up with me since I had left him abruptly at his desk outside the Town Hall.

"There you are miss!" The officer said in wonderment. He seemed pleased that he had finally tracked me down.

"I've been trying to catch up with you since you left me! I was rather worried about you. You looked so distraught and upset after I gave you your sad news about your friend and her daughter not being on the list of survivors. I saw you head up this way so I asked my commanding officer if I could be relieved for an hour. I wanted to check you were alright. May I introduce myself, Officer Williams at your service."

Officer Williams looked around at the sad tragic state of the kitchen garden. He had a sympathetic, kindly nature about him. He seemed aware that the garden he was now standing in held special memories for me. The pigeon also returned to the garden and fluttered on to one of the branches of the ash tree and surveyed the scene below.

"You really shouldn't have come up here all by yourself, miss. It's not safe up here on your own. One of the local boys had a bad accident in the ruins not long ago."

Officer Williams sniffed the air, smelling the strong perfume and fragrance from the pink cupped Felicia roses that had continued to flourish regardless of the neglect they had suffered. They had scrabbled up and over the garden walls and taken over the dead remains of the fruit trees. Officer Williams looked around the garden turning his head like an owl to survey it.

"We were meant to be pulling it all down soon! But what with the flood and all the search and rescue operations, and now with all the reconstruction work we will be involved with, it looks like all this will still be here for some time to come."

I too looked around at the garden, beginning to appreciate the beauty that was tucked away in its lost corners. Creamy white roses were beginning to cover up the garden's top wall where the other door out of the garden was located. A bee buzzed round us for a few minutes until I waved my hand gently and ushered it back towards the roses and their golden nuggets of pollen. The grasses and weeds that had taken control of the ground also contained beautiful signs of colour. Cow slips had become well established along with a tropical looking verbascum with its stately towers of golden yellow flowers.

I then turned back to Officer Williams feeling guilty that I had just walked away from him at his desk outside the Town Hall. I had not even thanked him for trying to find out what had happened to Thelma and Emma. I had also apparently caused him a great deal of worry and had taken him away from his duties.

"I am sorry I have taken you away from your duties," I said apologetically. "I did not mean to cause you any trouble. It's just I was very upset after hearing about my friend and her daughter. It came as such a shock. I was so convinced they were still alive. That's why I came up here. I just wanted to be on my own for a while."

Officer Williams showed no sign of irritation. He seemed more concerned for my wellbeing and safety, which I was grateful for.

"It is perfectly understandable miss. You have had a great shock. I am sorry I had to be the bearer of such bad news. It is terribly sad. Especially as your friend's daughter was so very young. Have you come very far to find them or are you local?"

"I've come from Wiltshire," I began, "I heard about the disaster on the wireless. I tried ringing for days to try and get hold of Thelma but could not get through. Luckily I am still on holiday until September so I decided to come down and try and find them. I fear I have had a wasted trip."

*

My words were tinted with sadness. Officer Williams looked genuinely sad for me. A silence came over us for a few moments while he was trying to think of something that would comfort me. We both stood amongst the tall grass, tickling our legs as it swayed about. The afternoon sun had become brighter and even in the coolness of the walled garden I felt rather warm. The bees and other flying insects swarmed about amongst the flowers and weeds. Two blue tits had joined the garden looking for mini spiders and insects on the walls and shrubs.

Finally Officer Williams, feeling awkward at the silence between, us cleared his throat and changed the subject of the flood and Thelma and Emma's deaths.

"You said you were on holiday until September. Are you a teacher then?"

I was always pleased when I was able to inform people that I was indeed a teacher and my face beamed with delight being able to confirm his question.

"Yes I am! I teach in a small primary school in my village back in Wiltshire. I have a slightly larger class next term, so I am looking forward to being able to do more activities with them. I find teaching harder when you only have a small class. You are so limited with the activities and lessons you can undertake with them."

Officer Williams seemed highly impressed. His face swelled with approval and his frown lines expanded. His mouth curved and opened with his pleasant smile. Even though officer Williams must have been in his late forties I thought he was incredibly handsome.

"Yes I always enjoy working with all the chaps in my regiment. It's often when I am alone I find myself starting to dwell on the friends I have lost and the men that never came back."

We found ourselves in yet another silence and we both shifted and readjusted our standing in the grass before I asked him a question.

"I know it is probably not allowed. I dare say it would be highly irregular as I know no one is allowed down to the harbour. But is it possible for me to go down? Just to see if there has been any news of Thelma or if anyone saw them the day of the flood. I think Thelma lived next door to the harbour master before she moved into Sally's."

Officer Williams thought for a moment. He looked pensive and pouted his lips. He looked deeply at me and could see how much I wanted and needed to go down to try and find out what happened to Thelma and Emma. He finally looked at his army watch on a thick brown leather strap before he gave me his answer.

"It is highly difficult to get down there, miss. You do realise you would have to walk as the railway is being used by the construction works and the army."

I could sense and hear the possible yes to my question. I immediately interjected saying I did not mind walking. I even said the walk would do me good! Which was an utter fib as the walk to the house had nearly killed me.

"Well miss. If you are sure you don't mind walking then I could give you a special pass to go down but it would only be valid for two days. We can't have too many people walking down there no matter how traumatic the circumstances are. It is, after all, a disaster zone. The heat is really on for the army to help reconstruct the flood defences before the winter storms set in after the summer."

I was thrilled with his terms. I agreed not to cause any trouble. I only wanted to walk around up to Thelma's old cottage on Neptune Hill and to try and find someone who had seen her on the day of the flood. Maybe I could find this harbour master that Thelma had mentioned in her last letter. Officer Williams continued on giving me further helpful advice.

"If I were you miss, when you get down there you should go straight to the harbour master. He would be the one to ask. He's a very likeable chap. Very nice natured. I am sure he would be happy to oblige you."

*

I was delighted by his suggestions and thrilled that I could do something constructive and proactive. As long as there were no bodies found there was still a slim chance that perhaps Thelma and Emma may be alive. Whatever the outcome for now I was determined to investigate further. I would not give up making enquiries for them. Not yet. Someone had to know where they had been on the day of the disaster. The harbour master sounded as if he was the man to ask. My new found friend in the shape of officer Williams who was so smartly dressed and presented, made another proposal.

"Well miss, if you are happy to leave we had better walk back to the Town Hall. I can fix you up a pass there. With any luck you may be able to get down to the harbour after lunch."

Officer Williams was certainly a man of action and I agreed to his proposal.

"Very well, that sounds wonderful. Shall I meet you back at the Town Hall then? In about half an hour. Or would after lunch be better?"

Officer Williams looked rather artful, as if I was proposing we were going to the cinema or to a dance together. He opened his mouth as if he wanted to ask me something and I thought he was going to invite me to lunch with him. I was already with my answer. I felt suddenly rather excited. My mouth curled up with a silly shy expression and I felt rather flushed. He then suddenly put a hand up to his face to brush away another bee that had taken an interest in us. As he did so and moved the bee away my heart sank and my excitement with it.

"Well miss I would be very happy to escort you back down safely to the Town Hall. If that is agreeable to you?"

Officer Williams spoke with an air of determination and purpose in his voice. It was clear he wanted us to be on our way and leave the ghosts of my former home behind. I tried not to sound disappointed. I replied I would be very happy to have him accompany me back down to the village. As we walked back towards the door of the kitchen garden officer Williams, being the perfect gentleman, pushed back the curtain of honeysuckle with his hand and permitted me to walk through first. I thanked him graciously for being polite. As I passed through the door and out of the confines of the kitchen garden I caught another glimpse of his gold wedding ring set firmly around his finger. The ring which had dashed my hope.

Chapter 31

He Goes by the Name of Mr Cuttlefish

Officer Williams and I crept out through the entrance of the kitchen garden leaving it in peace to remain unvisited and forgotten. We fought our way through the jungle of shrubs and ferns until we fell back under the shadow and gloom of the decaying carcass of the house. We both looked up towards its high peaks of desolate chimney stacks, towers and solitary empty windows. Our walk took us back along to the remains of the garden room; its blue and white Chinese floor had vanished under years of leaf litter, rubble, cement and brick dust. We then came back to the curved walls and window of the morning room slowly being taken over by the green tentacles of variegated ivy. We finally reached the monkey puzzle tree lording itself over the house and tangled, overgrown lawn.

Officer Williams stood well back under the branches of the monkey puzzle to gaze up at the shell.

"Shame," he said in a melancholy way, "in some ways it would be nice to leave it all standing." He sounded rather philosophical but quickly added, "But I suppose if we don't pull it down nature will do the job eventually. It's a real shame. It must have been quite a place in its time?"

I smiled at him and looked upon the remains. I spoke in a whispered, hushed voice. I did not want to give away to him that I had any knowledge of what life had been like in the house so I simply replied, "Yes. I expect it was."

I looked up towards my old bedroom window. A thicket of ivy was growing through it and had trailed down the walls. My gaze followed the procession of empty room windows and crumbling walls to the window of Edward's old room. I remembered the window seat that he had sat in on the day of the crash. Then recalled the weeks that followed after Father's death when he had sat like a skeleton in his brown leather chair, staring out of the window with all his determination and joy of life evaporated away. Thankfully I had never known or experienced again such a feeling of hopelessness. Back then each new day brought a new problem to the pile. When one problem seemed solved another would replace it. Yet the shock of all that had happened never really hit me until I left the house holding Eddie's letter and matchbox in my hand. I remembered stumbling into the car and recalled seeing the 'For Sale' sign on the front gates as I drove past. That's when it had hit me. When the overwhelming grief, the pain of everything that had happened finally sunk in and could not be overcome for what seemed like years after.

I suddenly looked over to Officer Williams who looked impatient and rather restless.

"Well miss, We had best be on our way and get you your pass fixed up or my commanding officer will have me demoted."

After apologising for daydreaming and saying how intrigued I was with the house, I tore myself away from the sight of my old home and we continued on our walk. The road was downhill all the way, which was far easier than going up had been. Leaving the house behind and walking away from memories buried and burnt within it, I noticed I felt less depressed and drained. I knew I was heading back to the village on the start of a mission to try and find out news of Thelma and Emma. On the way down, Officer Williams and I continued chattering about my life back in Wiltshire. He too talked about his time in the army and his service during the war. We discovered we both had a love of gardening and he told me in great detail his plans for his own garden when he was no longer living in army quarters. He never mentioned his wife, nor if he had any children and I did not want to pry or appear interested in his marital status. We eventually got as far as Mr and Mrs Barns' garden gate with the rusting padlock aggressively wrapped round the posts and latch to prevent trespassers. We carried on walking and reached the more muddier stretch of path where both of us tried to avoid the potholes. We at long last fell back into the shadow and darkness of the trees that had grown so tall their branches interwove above us like the vaulted roof of a catacomb. We wondered on a little more and reached the enormous walls of the cliff covered in ivy and ferns that towered beside us like battle defences. As I had found when I had walked up, the noise and activity of the village was shut out. The murky lush passage was utterly void of sound that you could hear a pin drop.

*

As the drive channelled sharply round like a snake's tail, the daylight and world beyond it appeared once again. The noise and hustle of the village welcomed us out of the passageway of the drive and I had to say it was nice to be back in the village again. I was relieved to see people going about their business and not see the images from my past that had rekindled within me when I had been alone on the tennis court. *It is strange*, I thought, *how returning to old places that you knew lived and grew up in have a way of pushing you back to the time you were present with in them. Even the smallest details and smells of childhood, the conversations you had, they all have a way of reawakening.*

Officer Williams marched me down along the side of the Town Hall. We turned to the left and came back into the square with the war memorial placed in the prime position directly in front of the imposing building. Officer Williams took his post at his desk after exchanging a few words with his colleague, who had relieved him during his absence with me. He sat back, readjusting himself and setting out how he wanted the desk to be for the rest of the afternoon. He collected a red covered file with a black spine from off one of the piles of papers he had readjusted. He opened it up to reveal what looked like a tear off sheet of paper with a duplicate sheet underneath. He scribbled in a frenzied manner into the spaces provided on one of the passes. He then ticked a box in the passes corner, ignored another and ticked again the last box. He then asked for my full name which I gave, then made the pass authentic by slamming down a seal and stamp in the right hand corner.

He carefully tore off the pass from its tear off spine, took one final look at it then passed it to me.

"There you are, miss. That's all in order for you. You have until four o'clock tomorrow afternoon to try and find out what happened to your friend. I wish you the very best of luck. I hope you find out what happened to them. I should warn you miss, it's best not to go down thinking you may find them alive. If they had survived they would be up here by now."

I must have looked disappointed for he added, "Please don't think I am being over pessimistic. I would love to be able to say to you that you may find them. Heaven knows we could all do with a boost in morale. I just don't want to give you any false hope."

Officer Williams eyes were full of sympathy. I knew he was just being practical. What he was saying was probably true, but I had to keep hoping that Thelma and Emma may yet be alive. If they weren't, my return to Devon would have been for nothing. Officer Williams, eyes suddenly changed and altered from the look of sympathy to surprise. His face displayed the feeling of shock as if he had seen a ghost.

I looked round behind me, glancing across the road to the bakery and sweet shop and next to it the chemist. PC Daniels strolled past again and then stopped to have a word with a lady and her little girl who were walking sadly down the street towards St Mary's church. The postman walked past and went into the chemist to deliver a quantity of letters, packets and a small parcel. Surveying the scene, all seemed as it should be. I saw nothing that could have possibly alarmed or given fright to Officer Williams. I turned back round to him, thinking that he would have recovered but was surprised to see that he still seemed to be in a daze. He stared in the direction of the bakery with its window display full of neat little brown baskets with fresh clean white cloths inside showing off golden crust pastries, well risen loaves and scrumptious buns topped with white icing and cherries. I thought perhaps Officer Williams was hungry and wanted something to eat which is why he kept looking towards the bakery. PC Daniels was blocking his view of the bakery's right window where he was still consoling the lady and her daughter whom he had bumped into on his beat.

"Is there something wrong?" I asked politely. Thinking I too should be on my way and get something to eat before I walked down to the harbour. Officer Williams came over very apologetic and returned his gaze to me.

"Oh please excuse me, Miss. It is just we were talking about survivors and you hoping to find news about your friend and I saw another victim of the flood over the road."

He discreetly pointed over to the bakery alerting me to the person he was talking about.

"You see that lady there, the one with the little girl talking to PC Daniels outside the bakery? Well that lady's husband was killed in the flood too."

I looked over towards the bakery paying closer attention to the lady and her young daughter. As I studied them more closely, I thought there seemed something familiar about the lady as well. There was something about her manner, the way she seemed to be tugging at her skirt and the way she held herself while she was being spoken to by PC Daniels. Officer Williams got back to looking at his desk and shuffled his papers about. He neatly grouped his two stamps together that he had used to mark my pass with on top of the closed ink pad. He seemed to want a distraction from looking upon the scene outside the bakery. Something that had rattled him. He then rather shakily continued talking while I carried on watching the lady and her daughter. I was trying to think why this mother and daughter should seem familiar to me.

"Yes that's Helen Dunn," Officer Williams continued, "Her husband, Alexander I think his name was, was the first person to die in the flood. He was in the mineral water factory when the flood hit. The whole factory was washed away. We did try searching for him but there's no way he could have survived. I should think he wouldn't have known anything about it, it would have all happened so fast. Shame for his poor wife having to bring up her daughter on her own."

*

I quickly thanked Officer Williams for all that he had done. I thanked him again for the pass and quickly made my excuses. I wanted to try and catch Helen. She had finished talking to PC Daniels and was continuing on her way towards the church. Officer Williams wished me well and said if I had any trouble to come back and ask for him which I appreciated. I briskly crossed the road, trying not to get run over by the army vehicle that had taken off again from Mathew's garage and driven past the Town Hall in a hurry. I safely got up on the pavement and rushed past the lamppost and post-box, trying to get in earshot of Helen. Luckily for me another local stopped and chatted to Helen for a few seconds to enquire how she was, which gave me a few minutes to catch up with her. By the time I got to her the other lady had completed her pleasantries and continued on her way up the road calling into the butcher's. Panting a little from my rushed walking, I took a few deep breaths as I approached Helen from behind and greeted her in a soft tone, not wanting to alarm her.

"Hello Helen. It seems a long time since I last spoke to you"

Helen turned round, I think expecting me to be another local to offer their sympathies. She had a drained, shattered look all over her face. Her eyes looked terribly puffy and sore from crying and she looked terribly gaunt with broken capillaries across her cheeks. Her hair was still as long and golden as ever, but had gone a little more chestnut at the crown. Helen looked at me rather worriedly, trying to remember perhaps where she had seen me before. Knowing the time that had lapsed since we had last seen and spoken with each other, and knowing the strain and grief she was under, I decided to re-introduce myself to her and save her the worry and embarrassment of trying to remember who I was.

"I don't suppose you remember me, Helen. It has been such a long time and so much has happened since our… " I had no time to finish my introduction as Helen's face lit up with a beaming smile, then dropped and quivered with tears.

"Oh Lady Edith!"

Helen flew into my arms with a mixture of joy, surprise and relief in her voice. For several minutes she clung to me like a limpet, desperately not wanting to let go, while her little girl looked rather suspiciously at me. Helen's daughter was like her in miniature. She had taken after Helen for long light coloured hair, huge brown eyes and small mouse-like ears. Yet I could not see her father in her at all. She had not taken after Alexander for being well built or muscular, instead she had a rather thin, wiry look about her. I instantly took to Helen's daughter as she was the kind of child that every time you saw her you thought to yourself what a lovely little girl she was.

Helen remained hugging me in an excitable, rather distraught fashion. Eventually she regained her composure and introduced me to her daughter, Penny, who I imagined must have been around ten in age, perhaps a little older. Helen explained to Penny that I was the lady who lived in the big house on the top of Hallowed Hill and that she had used to work for me. Penny, now realising who I was and knowing her mum and I had been friends, immediately dropped her guard and lost her suspicious face. She smiled with the same smile that Helen had. Helen was just about to speak when Penny started chattering away in the same manner that her father had, very relaxed and polite. She had at least taken after Alexander for that.

"So you're my mummy's friend! How do you do? Mummy's told me a lot about you! She used to brush your hair for you and help you dress, didn't she?"

I laughed. The very thought of Helen or anyone for that matter brushing my hair, helping me to dress and doing everything for me now seemed unbelievable. I had almost forgotten what it had been like to have so much done for me.

"Yes that's right, Penny. Your mum worked jolly hard for me. She was one of my best friends."

Helen laughed a little but I could see she was only trying to be cheerful for Penny's sake. She was finding it a struggle to keep herself bright and normal. I returned to Helen, who now had questions for me.

"It is so wonderful to see you, Lady Edith. We... I mean I have really missed you. I suppose you have heard about Alexander?"

I nodded sadly, "Yes, I was desperately sorry to hear about Alexander. He was such a lovely man. I will always remember how polite he was whenever I saw him. I was always so grateful to him for being a friend to Eddie and asking how he was when you both came to ask my permission to get married."

I realised what a terrible and tactless thing I had said, reminding her of the day she and Alexander had come to see me in the morning room. "Oh Helen, I am sorry. That was very tactless of me." Helen dismissed it and brushed away my fear of upsetting her.

"That's alright. I have to talk about him. I can't get away from the fact he won't be coming home again."

"Even so Helen, it is very early days for you yet. It is under such terrible circumstances. What about your home, is that alright?" Helen gave a deep sigh and looked up to the top of the high street towards St Mary's.

"We've been put up in the Valley of the Rocks Hotel for now. Our home has been flooded out as well. Mind, we were lucky. Some houses aren't even standing now. Least we have a home to go back to. At the moment they are not allowing anyone to return down to the lower village, it is all in such a state and all the drains are broken. I can tell you the smell down there is lethal. I don't think I shall ever get the smell out of my clothes. Have you been down there yet? "

"No. I saw some of the devastation when I arrived but I have not been down there yet properly. From what I saw it looked shocking. It must have been terrifying for you all. I am planning to try and walk down this afternoon. I have just been granted a pass to go down to look for… " Helen suddenly stopped me in mid flow and took my hand as if to reassure me over something.

"Oh don't worry, he's alright Edith! He's safe. His cottage is up on Neptune Hill. The flood never got up that far. I expect he will be so overjoyed to see you again. He's missed you so much over the years. I've been telling him to write to you since February when he came back."

*

I gave Helen an odd and startled look, wondering who on earth she was on about. I thought perhaps what with all she had been through and with all the other villagers probably still looking for loved ones that were missing, she must have me confused with someone else.

"Helen I think you may have me mixed up with someone else," I said, "I came back here to look for a friend and her daughter who I knew when they lived with me in Bath during the war. I think you may know Thelma? She used to work at the mineral water factory as a clerk but moved to Sally's tearoom as head waitress when she lost her job. Who did you think I was looking for?"

Helen suddenly looked highly worried and tried to pretend she had mixed me up with a neighbour of hers who was still looking for her son. Somehow I was unconvinced by Helen's back tracking and I knew she was not telling me the truth. Penny then joined the conversation and asked me what she thought was a highly normal and innocent question.

"Have you been down yet to see Uncle Eddie? He's working very hard down in the harbour clearing all the mess away! It's a bit smelly down there though. Mummy told me that you and Uncle Eddie are brother and sister. So that makes you my new Auntie!"

Penny looked up at her mother and asked with a puzzled look, "That is right isn't it Mummy? If Uncle Eddie and Auntie Edith are brother and sister that makes her my Auntie doesn't it? Well my adopted Auntie that is. Uncle Eddie's not really my Uncle, I've just always called him that."

Penny looked so happy and giggled with her sweet round face full of excitement.

I, however, looked open mouthed at Helen. My jaw quivered from what Penny had inadvertently told me. Surely it could not be true? Surely Eddie had not been living down here since February without any word or trying to get in touch with me. Helen looked as though she had swallowed castor oil. She was utterly berated with Penny, knowing that her daughter had let slip a secret that had meant to be kept from me.

*

Helen continued looking extremely anxious and had the face of someone who knew they had let out something that was supposed to remain unspoken. She started opening then closing then re-opening her mouth, as if she did not know what to say or how best to say it. She looked so flustered and worried, not only for herself but also for me. In the end, after what must have been in reality only a few seconds but what seemed like minutes of stunned shock and silence, Helen finally told me what she had not meant to.

"Edith, I am so sorry you have had to find out like this. I feel so guilty now. It is just seeing you down here I thought you had come down to look for Eddie. I thought that perhaps he had finally taken my advice and wrote to you. I have been on at him since he came back in February to write to you, but he was so sure you wouldn't want to know. He thought you were better off without him. He came back in February just after the king died and took on the job of harbour master. Neither Alexander nor I knew who he was to start with. Well you forget what people look like don't you? It wasn't until Alexander bumped into him by the harbour in March that he recognised him. I am afraid he's had rather a hard time of it, Edith. A lot of the village haven't appreciated him coming back after all these years. Many still haven't forgotten about your Father's bankruptcy and many of the servants after you left spread terrible gossip, the most filthy disgusting rumours about Eddie having some sort of relationship with Marcus! Well you know how people gossip down here and whether it's true or not people have shunned him. Both Alexander and I have looked out for him. We kept on at him, telling him to write to you."

Helen suddenly paused and came a little closer and took my hand. She looked more serious, yet spoke thoughtfully and with great care.

"Look Edith, either way, I don't care if it is true or not about Eddie and Marcus. I have tried talking to Eddie about it but he won't discuss it. He seems to have become very withdrawn over the years. He's very secretive. As I said, I nor Alexander cared about his relationship with Marcus. Your Eddie's a good man and he's been ever so kind to me and Penny since, well... "

Helen looked at Penny, not wanting to talk too much about Alexander in case it upset her.

"Let's just say Edith, I could not have coped without Eddie these last few days. He's been a good friend to us." Helen gave a deep nervous sigh. "Look Edith, Penny and I have to go and see Rev Heath about the memorial service on Friday but afterwards we are going back to the hotel. Why don't we go for a walk tomorrow afternoon? Have a real good catch up? Penny can show you where she likes to go swimming. There's a special cove we like to go to." Helen gave me a brief hug and a kiss on the cheek.

"I can't tell you what to do Edith. I know it is easy for me to say and I don't know everything that went on, but after everything that's happened these last few days losing so much, losing things that can't be put back, well I would hate for you to miss out on a chance to be reunited with Eddie again. Go down to the harbour, Edith. Go and talk to him. Don't pause to think about it just do it. I know if I had the chance to go and see Alexander again I would be down there like a shot."

Helen then turned to go with Penny's hand in hers. The new widow and her child were just starting to walk up the pavement towards St Mary's for her meeting with Rev Heath when Helen suddenly remembered something important that she had forgotten to tell me. She turned back round and shouted out to me.

"Edith! He goes by the name of Mr Cuttlefish now! When you get down to the harbour ask for Mr Cuttlefish. One of the lads will show you where to find him."

Chapter 32
Nostalgic Memories of the Past

I paused, standing silently frozen to the pavement, unable to do anything for a few moments apart from watch the villagers pass me by, all with intense sorrow and troubles written all over their faces.

I glared up towards the top of the high street still able to just about see Helen and Penny walking up past the bank then disappear under the façade of the Valley of the Rocks Hotel. I stood glued to the spot, like a time traveller from the future, watching and observing the population going about their business yet making sure I came into no contact with anyone. I felt like I could see them yet they were unable to detect me. No one seemed aware that I was amongst them remaining still, forlorn and unmoving. I was like one of the rusting lampposts: a permanent fixture that everyone took advantage of and no longer even noticed.

The only other time I had felt remotely like this was when I arrived in Bath after leaving Devon. Everything was so different. I felt so out of place, like a Christmas decoration that had not been taken down after twelfth night and was left to endure the rest of the year alone, without anything else that reminded it of the Christmas holiday season. My first Christmas in Bath I remember I did nothing. I sang no carols. Sent no cards. I did not even go to any of the churches to worship. I felt so utterly alone and angry. I slept most of the day in my new flat and only left the flat to get food or brandy. The brandy seemed to be the only thing that numbed the pain and loss I was feeling. I continued to pray and pray that a new incentive and new thread would appear in my life but for what seemed a long while no new inspiration came to me. For what must have been weeks into the new year my life felt that it had no meaning or purpose. I could not even face joining a new church. I still had my faith but felt it had been shaken to its core. I felt too angry and bitter with what had happened. It was hardly the attitude to have, and go to God's house and take communion with. Until finally, one Saturday evening after praying long and hard, I decided to walk down to the Baptist church and show the Lord I wanted to make an effort. I felt I had to be prepared to make the first move, even though I did not know where this move would take me. That first Sunday I went was the start of my new life. The service could have been crafted for me. The minister's text was the trials of Job and how he was tested to breaking point, until his life was restored again. The whole congregation gave me a tremendous welcome and after the service I met the town clerk who worked at the Guildhall. As we became acquainted he mentioned that his assistant had been promoted and he was now trying to find a replacement. After I told him a little about myself, the committees I had chaired and the events I had organised he asked me to go to the Guildhall the next day to discuss the matter further, which I did and by the afternoon I had been offered the job. My new career as a civil servant began and, like the person I had replaced as the town clerk's assistant, I was eventually promoted to the education department and the rest as they say was history.

*

Looking back on those early days, the one thing that had depressed and upset me the most was the fact that I had driven Eddie away. Not a day went by when I did not wish I could have put that time back to the moment when Eddie and I had been in the study and when I could have offered him kinder, more loving advice. If only I had not judged him or cared what people would have said about him. Helen was indeed right. I knew Eddie was alive, that he was only a few steps away from me, but I felt afraid of seeing him. Would he be glad to see me after all these years? I thought long and hard, continuing to watch the world go by. Finally I decided to discard my doubts. Eddie had been without his sister for long enough.

*

My lack of movement turned now into action. I confidently walked down the high street following in Helen and Penny's footsteps. I hurried past the tea shop and the bank, heading directly toward the Valley of the Rocks Hotel. I past St Mary's in the corner opposite and turned sharply down the sloping lane heading in the direction of my own hotel. I followed the lane which passed an old, no longer used garden entrance with a rusting old gate, overgrown with ivy and its procession of steps and terraces flooded with years of leaves. I continued down, passing another hotel which was well kept and welcoming, and headed further down the lane until it levelled off and continued as the coastal path up past my own hotel and along to the Valley of the Rocks. Instead of carrying on up to the Chough's Nest I turned to the right, down into a walled balcony area shaded by an umbrella of a thick and wizened old oak tree. Another rusting Edwardian lamppost stood directly under it. From this point a tight costal path ran steeply down through the vegetation of shrubs, woods and rhododendrons and on to the harbour. I paused briefly to remain standing on the balcony under the shade of the oak tree. I looked out over the resplendent sea, its colour a glorious turquoise with a shining bright glimmer trickling through it, running across the bay like a sacred trail toward the cliffs. A fulmar glided above and dive-bombed into the shining stillness looking for fish to catch. It then soared again above the waves, heading back into the bay. I pulled myself away from the scene with my bag in hand and my pass safely within it, and headed towards the harbour.

The path was certainly steep! The steepest I had yet walked on and although it was all downhill and not up I could feel the back of my legs begin to pull and ache from the stress of walking down such a steep road. My legs and body wanted to go down faster than my head, resulting in me trying to stop myself from galloping down. I plodded and dug my heels into the path as I walked. Every now and then the steepness of the path and my own momentum became too great and I started gaining speed. Half running, half plodding down, I managed as I continued on the path to control my speed and every time I came to a steeper section or bend I would stop and shuffle down like an old lady. I paused once or twice to view and enjoy the buddleias with the most attractive lilac and purple cone flowers. On one stop I caught sight of a peacock butterfly enjoying the flower's pollen. Dainty red spider fuchsias grew like common weeds in abundance along the walk, with the pines, oak and ash trees all reaching up to the sky, making ideal places for crow's nests and for birds to survey the steep sloping cliffs. I walked over the first sturdy wooden bridge that ran over the track of the ascending and descending railway cars, which for the time being had been commandeered for rescue workers. I suspected they would also be carrying any destroyed cars that had been wrecked by the flood. I paused on the first foot bridge for a few moments to catch my breath and fight the pain of the stitch I had in my side. I watched the silent tracks running like an ice skating track all the way to the bottom where the small station was located next to the dance hall. I still could not see the state of the harbour or village as I was still too high up. Wearily I plodded on readjusting my breathing to compensate and trying to pace myself more carefully. Further along the path were more fuchsias and some tall, erect pink fox gloves with beautiful marbling effect in the inside of each trumpet. The path began to swerve and meander like a stream. It changed course altogether at some points and slinked round narrow bends channelled through great enclaves of giant ash and pine trees. I finally reached the last of the foot bridges that ran over the track of the cliff railway and, looking over the wooden rail of the bridge, I could see that I was nearly at the path's end. The sea seemed much closer to me now. The warmth from being higher up on the path had left and I stood nestled between the trees feeling much cooler and slightly chilly. I also noticed another distinct change. The smell! The lower I got along the path the more my senses became alerted to a most disgusting rank and foul odour. It was the sort of smell that one would detect heading to a cesspit. The most awful smell of rotten cabbage, mixed with human and animal waste. The lower I got the more rank and stale the smell became. I could quite see why the whole lower village had been evacuated regardless of their homes being affected directly by the flood or not. With all the drains broken open, allowing all the sewage and waste to escape, and with no running water the living conditions were deemed too terrible for anyone to remain in the village. There was also now the very real fear of disease spreading with no sanitation available. I knew that whoever I came in contact with until I found Eddie would immediately tell me to leave. They would no doubt tell me that I had no business coming down here and would give me my marching orders. Being prepared for that possible confrontation, I retrieved from out of my handbag my folded pass. I placed the document in the pocket of my green jacket, so I would be able to wave it in the face of anyone who tried to have me escorted back up to the top again. Doing this also gave me another excuse to pause my exhausting walk. After a few moments of puffing and panting I carried on. The path veered round another large bend with a solitary pine tree on its end. Then it gave way to some grey stone steps which lead under an arch by the side of the old dance hall where the victory dances had taken place after the end of the Great War. As I made my way down the steps the smell and odour intensified. I could feel my stomach churn and every now and again I wanted to heave. I was so tempted to put a hanky over my face but knew that would make me a target of work men and army personnel to say what a stupid, silly women I was and that I had no business down there.

As I came under the protection of the arch next to the old dance hall and went down the last few steps onto the main road, I got out from my bag my little brown bottle of smelling salts. I hovered the bottle under my nose for a few moments, hoping the intense aroma would take off the vile putrid smell that lingered in the air.

*

I stepped onto a deserted dusty road with no sign of life about, apart from a loan seagull walking along the flat stone wall on the other side of the road. The main road I had stepped on to ran along to where the cliff railway station was situated. A Union Jack fluttered proudly on top of a slender white flag pole by the entrance. Beyond that was only a few beach huts used to store ships' tackle and only a few old weathered rowing boats. The old crafts and sailor's former joys sat under the shadow of the cliffs with their paint and colours becoming extremely chafed and brittle, now covered in yellowish moulds of lichen. This tiny corner in the recesses and alcoves of the cliff also provided an extra area for lobster pots to be brought to when not in use. Also I spotted the old wheeled bathing huts that I myself had used back in the twenties. In front of me stretched the pebbled beach with a well built up wall in front of it. The beach was considerably lower down than one might have thought, due to the wall being well built up. It was not recommended for anyone to jump off the wall, that came up to about waist height, directly onto the pebbled beach, not unless you wanted a broken ankle. The wall had become popular with children under the watchful supervision of their parents. Many youngsters would climb up upon the flat smooth top to sit on and enjoy the view whilst eating an ice cream, with their legs dangling over the side. The wall also acted as a tightrope for children to walk along with their right hand placed in the reassuringly safe hand of their fathers, while their free hand would stretch out pointing towards the sea to balance themselves. The local seagulls also used the wall to strut along to the harbour, checking if any holiday makers had dropped any mouthfuls of fish and chips. The seagull on the wall today didn't look like he was having any luck scavenging for food, for there had been no locals or holiday makers down here for several days now. I half expected there to be a great deal of noise from all the workmen and army personnel. Yet surprisingly there was no sound of construction and clear up, only the sound of the aqua blue sea and the sound of seagulls flying overhead.

    I crossed the road feeling drawn and enticed by the noise and sight of the sea. I stepped up onto the pavement causing the hoity looking seagull to plod further along the wall in the direction of the harbour giving out an alarming cry as he went. I fell against the wall with my body sluggishly pressed up against it feeling the cold, rather gritty surface against my waist. I bent my back slightly and placed my arms on top of the wall. I allowed my mind for a few minutes to go blank and to forget the reason of my journey. I allowed myself to completely relax and let go, taking in some deep breaths of sea air trying to rid myself from the ghastly smell that had greeted me when I had reached the bottom of the steps. Thankfully this had not accompanied me over to admire the view.

    Slumped against the wall I watched the waves crash and drape on the jewel tray of coloured pebbles laying littered along the beach. Not one pebble looked the same. Every one of them was a different in size, shape and colour: grey, coffee, jet, cream, amber and brick orange, all with a beautifully smooth texture, glistening in the sunshine where the cold waves of the sea had fallen upon them. Delicate cockle shells and sharp looking sword razors were laid scattered along the beach, along with clumps of wet and drenched bladder wrack and purple laver seaweed draped about in various places. In amongst this splendour were large and small pieces of driftwood discarded by the sea. All was being closely monitored and examined by black and white oyster-catchers, with their long orange coloured beaks digging and poking into every crevice and cranny combing for small tiny sea creatures brought in with the last tide. As each new wave crashed on to the beach it dislodged the spectators of pebbles and shells, before retreating back again with a soft, gentle, calming noise, hushing the beach into stillness, leaving only a slight trail of froth and bubbles before they popped, dissolved and dispersed.

The weather was still bright and pleasant with a pale blue sky reflected in the sea and white cotton wool clouds, shaped like giant meringues. It was much cooler down in the bay and more exposed to the costal breeze. As I looked out to sea, admiring the line of where the sea appeared to meet the sky like an artist's watercolour painting, I suddenly realised how much I had missed this view and Devon's way of life. Time somehow seemed to be much slower and smoother down here. Devon has a mysterious quality of having a much slower pace of life and is always sluggish to change and to conform to the rest of the fast moving world. I had forgotten how much I missed the sea and its continuity. Its waves and tide, never ceasing just continually moving in and out. I had missed the wakeup call of the seagulls swooping over the bay first thing in the morning and to hear the horn of the *Queen Alexandra* gliding over the waters preparing to dock.

I was secretly pleased that just for a few moments there was no sound of bulldozers or tractors. Nor the constant mutterings of work men, reconstruction workers and well drilled routines of the army. Just for a few moments I was able to pretend that nothing had changed; that everything had remained just as it always had done. I believed I was a child again, sat on the wall with Eddie, our legs dangling over the side watching the ships and boats go by, enjoying a sweet refreshing ice cream. For a few moments I could remember my Father taking me by the hand steadying me as I walked along the wall up to the harbour until I had to stop and wait for him to scoop me up into his strong trusting arms.

*

For a few minutes the sight and smell of the sea, the sound of the seagulls, the aroma of fresh fish and the taste of vanilla ice cream all came flooding back. I was fooled into thinking that this tiny bay with its small village and harbour, the river flowing through its middle and a track moving up through the valley of forests and ferns to the mineral water factory had not changed. As long as this view had not altered then nothing else could have changed. Yet deep down I knew that the village had not remained the same. If I left the wall and continued on my walk my nostalgic memories of the past would soon fade away to an unfamiliar new reality.

Chapter 33
I'm His Sister!

Although I could have remained by the wall for the rest of the day just watching and listening to the sea, observing the oyster-catcher tiptoeing along the beach and having the reassurance of childhood memories to enjoy, I knew I had to carry out what I had come down here to do.

I tore myself away from the relaxing view of the sea and returned back to the road. It ran down past the limekilns and the large black and white structure of the dance hall. The hall's construction had been blessed with an elaborate enclosed balcony running along the full span of the building's second floor. Large windows and French doors lead off it back into the hall. The building looked much like it had done, though it had aged with the sea air, causing the paint and woodwork to deteriorate, crack and splinter off. Its grandeur had certainly faded. Further up was a tall four story tower building of red bricks and cream walls, with each floor of the tower boasting large bay windows and the third floor had its own private balcony. Another floor was located above that and the tower was completed with a spire and finial on top. The view of the harbour around this enchanting building was partly obscured but the sea view followed me round along with the seagull to the right of me, still plodding along the wall, both of us heading in the direction of the harbour.

The road, which had been dusty and dry along by the railway and dance hall, was now undergoing a change. It became considerably muddy and slippery with giant puddles making walking much harder to do without slipping and sliding about. I noticed that, the terrible smell had returned again, only now, was much, much stronger. It really was unbearable! Once again I got out my smelling bottle and it just about prevented me from heaving. I still could hear no sound of diggers or tractors shifting and clearing the debris. As I looked at my watch I observed it was just gone half past one, and thought that the army and the workers had probably not yet returned from their lunch. If that was the case it would help me enormously as there would be no one to tackle my presence being down here. Next door to the tower the flood's trail of destruction was clear to be seen. The fish and chip shop's whole frontage had been uprooted and now left only a chasm in the wall. Its roof had caved in and its walls too had collapsed like a cardboard box collapsing in on itself. The surface of the road was becoming more and more difficult to walk along. In fact the road and its pavements had all but been buried under a mass of wet, sticky red mud that had mixed together with the waste from all the broken drains. Great boulders and mountains of bricks and rubble were scattered as far as the eye could see. Cottages and shops had collapsed into the road like dominos. Twisted mangles of giant trees, still with their roots attached where they had been completely uprooted from up in the woods lay discarded amongst the chaos. Soil, silt and boulders (some the size of car engines) which had all smashed into the mineral water factory had ended their journey here. Boulders blocked the entrances to many properties, looking like the village had been dropped in a quarry. Wrecked cars lay dented and battered, some like mangles of metal laying sunk into the mud. Huge expanses of the area still lay flooded with a red, wet and sticky consistency of water and mud. The village looked as if it had taken a direct hit from an enemy squadron or even a nuclear bomb. You might have been forgiven to think an earthquake had struck. In some places it was hard to tell where the land ended and the sea began. I began to stumble and slip with the road no longer visible and found myself either trying to climb over the debris or navigate nearer to the harbour. The quay had just about survived but was badly scarred with a litter of bricks, rubble and timber which was all that remained of the red brick lighthouse which had once stood on the end of the quay. Remains of lobster pots lay shattered and broken about, like the remains of an animals' rib cages prized open. The harbour resembled more of a dumping pit. Its contents of boats, masts and rigging had been crushed by colossal size boulders, weighing tons in weight some looked even bigger than cars. Speaking of cars they too had been swept from their parking space taken with the flood and crashed through the wall down into the harbour from the road. A green badly dented Humber lay half up in the air crushing a fishing trawler, the car's number plate still clearly visible. Several fishing boats and crafts lay shattered and sunk in the waters where they had been slammed into the wall by the force of the torrent. Way up ahead at the high end of the street beyond the expanse of rubble, stones and shattered buildings lay the remains of the Bath Hotel. It had been the most prestigious hotel in the county. The hotel had survived the economic down turn after the great crash of 1929 but its surviving streak had now run out. The building was now exposed to the elements, like the open door of a doll's house. An almighty gash in the wall exposed four of the hotels floors, revealing the hazardous looking contents of furniture: beds, dressing tables and wardrobes were hanging precariously on smashed damaged floorboards.

Many of the other cottages, gift shops and tea shops had also been badly damaged by the tide of water that had run through many of them like a train. It had left a trail of mud, sewage, rubble and bricks, along with the personal items of people's homes and businesses. Nearly every shop frontage had been prized open like caves and caverns of a cliff. Those buildings that had been fortunate enough to survive the flood were now covered in what looked like a volcanic dust. As I turned to look out to the sea that too had been effected by the flood. A brown, chocolate, almost gravy coloured river was pouring and mixing into it, with the sea and the dirty flood water beginning to merge together.

*

The diggers, tractors and bulldozers were all parked and stationed further up the high street in a relatively cleared, but muddy area. They were all waiting for their controllers to return from their lunch. Seeing the huge gap where a building had stood but had been totally washed away upset me, for I could remember the building that had originally occupied the space. Trying to distract myself I looked back over to the left to a sloping lane that ran up along the side of The Rising Moon tavern. I left the sight of the harbour and attempted to walk over the debris to the other side of the road to the tavern. The Rising Moon was a long procession of thatched, white washed cottages with tiny cupboard size windows. They were all linked and knocked into one, each section slightly higher up than the other like a procession of steps. Like most of the buildings it had been flooded out but thankfully was still standing, but all its furniture of tables, bar stools and Windsor chairs were piled up like a bonfire outside in the road. I tried to make my way over to the tavern, I nearly fell over amongst the chaos, and noticed the amount of personal belongings from people's homes that lay in the mud and rubble. Battered leather suitcases, dining chairs, a kitchen sink, drawers out of dressers. Even a child's high chair. As I continued to shakily climb over the rubble, bricks, timber and battered furniture I noticed a sign board lying amongst the wreckage. Most of the board's lower writing was submerged in mud and the board's colours and texture had become badly warped, but the main heading was still legible to read. The bold black letters against a gold coloured board read at the top 'Sally's Tea room. Open.' Seeing the sign amongst the wreckage was like seeing an artefact of a lost civilization and it was yet another reminder that Thelma and Emma, who had been living above the tea room on the night of the disaster, were still missing.

*

As I cumbersomely tottered across the mounds of debris and finally reached the start of the sloping lane leading up Neptune Hill, I was suddenly yelled at from behind. The voice was that of a man with a gruff, masculine voice. He sounded most angry and annoyed at me. My heart sank. As I turned round to see who the man was that was yelling, the voice continued to shout and yell, and a grey and muddy stubby finger was pointed at me as the rather under worldly figure approached me.

"You! I say you! Yes you! What the bloody hell do you think you're doing? Don't you know you're not allowed down here?"

My eyes focused on a thin, wiry looking man now hurtling towards me in an unsteady fashion. He was dressed in great heavy boots plastered in silt and mud. His other clothing consisted of what appeared to be dark blue overalls but again, like his boots, they were covered in mud. As the apparition came staggering over to me across the rubble, he appeared as though he was having as much difficulty as I had crossing over. As he made his way across he lurched at me and grabbed me by the arm with a hand resembling a creature from the deep. Despite his disadvantage of being covered in a skin of mud and being much older than myself he had a powerful grip which rather startled me. The force of his grip and posture gave me further worry that he was going to shake me. I don't think I had ever come across such a man before. His face like the rest of him was completely plastered with mud which unfortunately for him had begun to set like a mud mask and gave his face the texture of cracked clay. A checked hat covered his hair, which was as grey as a badger, but I was unable to gauge what age the man was due to his face and features plastered and set in mud. It appeared that the areas of hair visible from under his cap were ground in brick and rubble dust so he may have been much younger than his appearance portrayed. However judging by his gruff grunting voice, I would place him well into his mid to late fifties and, although I do not like nor have ever called anyone by this name before, he seemed to me to be a right miserable sod! His only immediate asset was his cinnamon coloured eyes, which would have been so much more attractive if they had not kept glaring at me. I had not had time to get my pass out of my pocket to avoid an altercation as the man instantly gave me a right ticking off. Just as I had expected him too. His tirade at me was swift and there was certainly no mistaking what he thought of me.

"You stupid, silly, flaming woman! You're not allowed down here! No one is. Don't you realise how dangerous it is down here? Do you realise you've been walking about on raw sewage! Take me, there I was moving a load of rubble up by the Bath Hotel, walking towards where Sally's had been, when I tripped over and went head first into a bloody hole!"

It is a pity he had not stayed in the hole a little longer, I was thinking to myself as he continued ranting on and tugging at my arm like I was some sort of mannequin dummy.

"I was in that bloody hole for five minutes until some snobby fool from the army got me out. I could have been stuck in there all day if he hadn't come along and heard me shouting."

What a shame, if he had not come along you wouldn't be here shouting at me now, I thought sarcastically to myself.

"I expect you thought I had a face cream plastered over my face!" He said in a silly mocking way. His attempt at sarcasm did not become him.

"You modern women, just typical of your lot. You think now the war's over and we men have come back you can keep running things without us and disregard the rules. Well I have news for you lady! The rules do matter! Civilians are not under any circumstances allowed down here. Now I am going to take you up top to see Officer Williams and will see what he's got to say about your little wonder down here."

The ogre of a man attempted to pull me off the foot of the lane and drag me back over the rubble and mud back, towards the path that lead up to the upper village. As he began to pull me off to get a telling off from Officer Williams he gave me a final warning.

"I warn you missy, Officer Williams don't like you modern women. I think he will be giving a you a right ticking off. He's got a hell of a temper!"

My moment had come. I could not wait to whip out my pass and shut the silly troll up and put him back in his hole where he belonged.

"It is funny you should mention Officer Williams," I said in a light hearted way. "When he gave me my pass to allow me to come down here he did not strike me as a man who did not appreciate women and their place in the world. He struck me as a very polite and accommodating man. As a teacher I think rules and regulations are very important and I would not have dreamed on coming down here without going to the proper authority first. Perhaps you would like to see my pass, Mr, Mr…?"

His hand that had lunged onto my arm loosened its tight grip and for a few moments he was silent. He looked utterly dumbfounded and for a few heavenly minutes he was speechless. He at long last regained the power of speech and gave me his name followed by a gruff demand that I show him my pass.

"It's Mr Mathew Bath and yes I would like to see this so called pass of yours. Hand it over."

As I calmly took it out of my pocket and passed it to him, I wondered if Mathew Bath was any relation to Billy Bath? He certainly had all the family traits. Bad tempered, ignorant, rude and had a low opinion of women. All that was missing was a pipe! As Mathew inspected my pass, up ahead in the clearing at the top of the street I could hear the sound of tractors and bulldozers roaring up and I caught a glimpse of a few more workers appearing out of, what seemed, nowhere. The group all headed towards their machines and began what would be an intense afternoon of hard labour. They proved to be a welcome distraction from having to look at the not so charming Mathew Bath. My pass was certainly being well inspected and thumbed. Every box and detail checked and examined. By the time my pass was handed back to me it was covered and splattered with mud and dust, with monster like handprints plastered over the once smart looking documentation. As the roar and juddering of the machines and tractors became louder the mumbles and conversations of workers increased. Mathew seemed a little more civil now. He wiped his right grubby hand on his overall, trying to clean it a little. He then looked down at his palm realising it had made no difference. To compensate he decided to spit into his hand and rubbed his hands together like he was washing his hands with soap. *How repulsive,* I thought. Then, of all things, he brought forward his right hand for me to shake! I gave a deep gulp and felt aghast. I could not bare to shake his grubby hand. Especially now it had been washed with a mouthful of saliva. But fearing if I did not shake it I would never get away from him, I bit my lip and put out my hand. He immediately took it with great gusto and I suffered the firmest handshake I had ever had. I thankfully got the use of my hand back, wanting desperately to wash it with some carbolic soap.

"I do beg your pardon miss. I did not realise that you had a pass. I never would have spoken to you so rudely if I had known but well you can see for yourself it's like a war zone down here. It is dangerous even for us construction workers. I mean you can see what happened to me falling down in that bloody hole! I even lost me pipe too! What with no running water, no power and, as you can smell no sanitation, this is not an ideal place for anyone to be. Do you mind if I ask you why you have been allowed down here? I mean it can't be just to admire the view. I know from experience Officer Williams don't like any one just coming down. Mind you he has a bit of a reputation with the ladies so I hear."

Ignoring his last remark and insinuations I answered his question.

"Not at all. Officer Williams allowed me to come down for a few hours for me to try and find out what happened to a friend of mine and her daughter. They were both living above Sally's tea room when the flood hit. I could not believe they were dead even though everyone told me they were." My voice suddenly became rather depressed and sounded distant. I looked about the destroyed street and continued my answer. "Now coming down here I can see they must be dead. There's no way they could have survived all this. I can't even see Sally's anymore."

Mathew nodded in a dejected way but showed no emotion due to his facial features being hidden by all the mud that had set over his face.

"I am afraid miss that if they had been above Sally's they would have been killed outright. If you see where all the tractors and bulldozers are," He pointed up the road to show me, "well that gap used to be Sally's. It all got washed away very much like the mineral water factory, which was further up the river."

I looked up to where Mathew pointed and saw the bulldozers reversing and turning round, preparing to start clearing the rest of the main road. I knew Sally's had been in the gap they now occupied and it had been that building's absence that had upset me. It had made me finally realise that both Thelma and Emma were dead. There could be no mistake.

*

I tried not to cry. I sniffed back hard, feeling rather sick still due to shock and the smell. I found it hard to take it in or understand that the person I had befriended during my time in Bath and my goddaughter whom I had only seen in the flesh when she had been only a few months old were both gone. That realisation made me suddenly feel very unsure of myself. Mathew began talking again and for the first time sounded rather thoughtful.

"It is always difficult to accept when someone is missing and you never really know what's happened to them. You keep thinking and hoping they may still be alive. Then little by little you realise that there is no hope of finding them or seeing them again. It is a hard knock to deal with."

After a pause Mathew added in a casual tone, "Look I don't know how long you're staying down in Devon miss, but if you can why don't you come along to the memorial service on Friday? We're having it to remember all those that have been killed and are missing. It's at St Mary's church, opposite the Valley of the Rocks Hotel. It may help bring a bit of closure for you. I am sure you would be most welcome. Most of the village will be there. We all need to keep hold of our faith during times like these."

Mathew's kindness and apparent faith touched me and endeared me a little to him. I then suddenly remembered the other person I had come down to look for. Thankfully I knew Eddie was still alive after all these years of absence away from him.

"That's very kind of you. I will certainly try and attend the service if I can. As you say we all need our faith. I am also down here to try and speak to the harbour master, a Mr Cuttlefish. Do you know where I can find him?"

Mathew looked rather surprised that I should be seeking out the harbour master. He looked over towards the wreck of the harbour then turned his head up and down the street. He glanced and squinted then checked again the area where the bulldozers were pushing a trench through the rubble and mud.

"It don't look like he's back yet from his lunch. You can't miss him. He's such a tall chap isn't he? Every time I see him I think he needs a damn good meal, like a bean pole he is. Are you a friend of his?" Mathew asked curiously.

"I'm a relative," I said. I then paused and quickly added in a proud tone, "I'm his sister!"

"Are you indeed! Bless my soul. I didn't think he had any family to speak of. Bit of a quiet one your brother is. But give him his due he's a hard worker and very knowledgeable about anything to do with the sea. I suppose that's thanks to his time in the navy so he was telling me yesterday. Best thing for you to do is go up to his cottage. I expect he's been in there having his lunch, probably dropped off to sleep too, I shouldn't wonder. He don't like mixing with us folk much. Always goes back to his cottage during his lunch hour. If you walk up Neptune Hill, go as far as you can and you will come to two cottages. One's empty now, the other be your brothers, you can't mistake it. It's got a mobile of shells hanging outside by the door."

I looked up towards the steep and rather narrow lane, leading up alongside the sloping building of The Rising Moon. I was just about to ask Mathew if he was a relation to Billy when Mathew gave me a grave warning, sounding like the world was about to end.

"I warn you Miss. Wouldn't stay too long down here. Next few days going to be all go! It is going to be a real nightmare to re-channel the Lyn and get some sort of sea defence up, otherwise this village will become the next Atlantis by the time the winter storms start."

I thanked Mathew for his advice and assistance. I noticed how fearful his eyes had become since I had told him I was Eddie's sister. A note of panic had set in but he was trying to hide it and behave naturally. I ended our talk telling Mathew that I would try and attend the church service on Friday. He doffed his cap and was about to soldier off when I quickly asked him.

"Mathew, you aren't a relation of Billy Baths by any chance?"

Mathew gave a great belting laugh, showing me the inside of his great cave of a mouth and revealing how many remaining teeth he had left and the ones that were left looked pretty dire.

"You're not looking for him and all are you? Oh ah Billy be my brother. How do you know him then?"

"Your brother was kind enough to give me a ride on his cart with Jacob from the station. I must say Mathew, you and Billy are very much alike."

Mathew gave out another husky laugh but his eyes displayed that same fear again.

"That be true miss. We're both a pair of miserable sods! Even our mother said when we were born she'd never seen such miserable looking babies!"

*

Mathew continued laughing as he went on his way back to towards his awaiting bulldozer. He was probably preparing to tell his fellow workers he had just met Mr Cuttlefish's sister. I too continued on my journey, slowly crawling up the mossy steep lane of Neptune Hill. I passed The Rising Moon as I went up, heading well above the wreckage of the harbour and the rest of the village. The lane was rather dark and shadowy with the tavern on the right of me and the back wall of a cottage on the left. I finally reached the top of the lane and came to a plateau with a paved courtyard area comprising of two small, rather poky thatched cottages nestled together. The walls and banks of the cliff rose high behind them smothered with ivy. The oak and ash trees cradled over the thatched roofs which gave the courtyard a rather enclosed dark and secretive atmosphere. A wooden shed stood in the corner of the courtyard, which I assumed had to be the privy. A thick and rather overgrown pretty pink dog rose surrounded it. To the side of the privy a creepy looking path with a sign post on its corner which read 'smugglers trail' wormed its way high up behind the back of the two cottages. Gazing up at the path it appeared to lead along the cliff and through the dense forest of pine trees and rhododendrons rambling back up the cliff. The courtyard's floor had been beautifully paved with flag stone but green thick moss had woven and sewn in between each stone, creating a patchwork quilt effect. A few chipped terracotta pots stood in little groups around the courtyard containing mint, chives and tarragon. An old rowing boat was pushed up against the side of the cliff with its wood and paint looking rather fossilized from the years of being left out in all weathers. It had clearly received no maintenance for a considerable time and now had become home to wild purple geraniums and lavender. My eyes fell upon the second of the two cottages. It was built slightly at an angle and a little higher than the other. This gave it a more appealing appreciation of the view of the harbour. The cottage walls were of a brilliant white with brown sandy coloured window frames and door way. Storm shutters were drawn across the two front windows. The cottage was finished with a triangular porch with two old chimney pots either side. Rambling runner beans grew from out of the pots and climbed their way up the two porch posts. The sound of a light jangling and rustling noise grew as I approached the cottage. The noise came from a mobile of sea shells hanging up by the door sheltered in the recess of the porch. The mobile was comprised of a variety of cockle, clam, whelk and limpet shells. They swayed about, knocking into each other hanging from course white and blue string, with turquoise buttons sewn and linked into each piece of string.

*

I felt extremely nervous all of a sudden. Perhaps knowing that on the other side of the door I was now standing in front of was my brother. This was his cottage and the rowing boat now planted up with geraniums and lavender, and the mobile that was swaying to the breeze was the very same one Thelma had described in her letter. It struck me how, unknown to us all, Thelma, Emma, Eddie and I had all been connected and sewn together yet non us had realised our bond. Thelma had shared a part of Eddie's life that I had been unintentionally excluded from. What I looked upon now was the life Eddie had made for himself without me. As long as I stayed away this was all he needed. The memories of the past and the terrible words I had said to him could not disrupt this peaceful new existence. He had what I had in Wiltshire. A place of calm. A place to shut out the world but he was still able to access the memories of the life we had before. Part of me wanted to turn away and leave Eddie to his solitude. But I so wanted to see him. The need to lay eyes on him after so many years away was too great. I walked softly towards the cottage feeling the carpet of moss and stone under me feet. I nestled myself into the porch and raised my hand towards the door. A great orange embossed star fish was hanging from a simple and uncomplicated brass door knocker. I wanted to tap it yet I felt so worried to intrude on

Eddie's new life. He clearly had not wanted to re-enter communication with me as Helen had apparently been on at him for months since he arrived back in Devon to write. Yet he had not done so. Perhaps he had not been able to. Our parting words must have harboured within him for years, for I had still not been able to look back on that afternoon in Father's study without being filled with guilt and remorse. A lot of pain had rested within me and no doubt also with him. Some words and memories cannot be erased or forgiven, no matter how hard one attempts to retreat away from them. Yet knowing that Thelma and Emma were dead and learning that Helen had lost Alexander, I knew I could not allow this chance to slip away. Life was too short to hold on to regrets. Even if Eddie shut the door in my face at least I would know that I had tried to rebuild the bridges I had unintentionally burnt.

Feeling heavy hearted and very worried about what reception I would get, I grabbed the slender door handle in my hand and knocked it against the door. I looked down at the smooth white tiled floor of the porch and looked again at the mobile of sea shells. Still there was silence. No sound came from anyone coming to answer the door. I looked back at the rowing boat to admire the purple geraniums that had trailed down the starboard side of the hull with the bow of the boat facing Thelma's old empty cottage. If only Thelma had stayed one more day and night in that cottage. If only she had not been so eager to move into Sally's. My thoughts drifted back to the present and back to Eddie's door. I could still hear no movement from inside the cottage. Perhaps Eddie had left and gone back to work already or maybe he was in the cottage and did not want to open the door to me. After a few more seconds of waiting in the porch and trying to distract myself while I waited, I decided to retreat and turned to go. It was no good. There was no use in staying any longer.

*

As I turned my heart and senses jumped with a nervous excitement. From inside the cottage I heard a noise of a bolt being pushed back from the inside of the door. A lock was quickly being turned. Then slowly the door of the cottage opened. From a quick inspection from my view in the porch the inside of the cottage was revealed. A red vibrant rug was just inside the door which drew my attention at once due to the realistic pattern of fish embroidered all over it. A heavy yellow fisherman's waterproof coat lay hanging on the right side of the door along with a black coat next to it. As I peered in through the open door I could see a kitchen table with two cheap chairs at each end. Set across the table was a white porcelain bowl with a silver spoon resting inside, accompanying the remains of what looked like lunch, a brown chubby bottle of ale half drunk and a set of rejected keys. I was just about to call out to say hello, when an impatient, irritated but soft voice called out from behind the right side of the wall where the coats were hanging up.

"I won't be a minute Mathew! I am coming. I'm just trying to find out what I have done with my keys! I put them in one of my coat pockets and now I can't find the blasted things anywhere."

Suddenly, like a supernatural being the yellow and black coats began to move and shift. Their arms swayed out from around the wall as if they were beckoning me in. The voice from behind the wall came again still searching through the coat pockets.

"Oh where are the bloody things? You best go on without me Mathew. I will catch you up in a moment."

With my voice charged with nerves I called out in a fearful, amused voice "Have you tried looking for them on the table?"

*

The ruffling and flinging about of the coats suddenly paused. The coat arms fell back to their silent hanging positions. A hushed silence fell upon the cottage. Very slowly a man crept cautiously round the corner from behind the wall and appeared in the door way. The man was tall and slender, possessing little in the way of muscle with no masculinity about his build. His hair was mid length, the colour of sunlit brown which appeared to be turning grey in the crown and his hair line had begun to recede with its texture light and swirled over his head and draped round his ears. He wore working labourer's clothes comprising of a cream shirt and tanned coloured V-neck jumper with the sleeves rolled up. Dark coloured trousers covered his lower body stained with sea water, sand and mud. Working boots with laces still not tied had also been well worn and over worked. For a few moments neither he nor I spoke. We both stood examining each other, looking deeply into each other's eyes and observing our tense facial features. The mobile of shells rattled and jangled about in the porch as the breeze picked up and swirled up Neptune Hill and enticed the secrecy of the courtyard. Down below us the sound of bulldozers roared closer alerting a group of seagulls who yelled in fright and dispersed after a few minutes of scavenging the wreckage of the village. The noises from behind gave me a sudden momentum to act. I stepped a little a further into the door and approached my brother who continued to look stunned and overwhelmed.

"You always did have trouble trying to find things. Why can't you be more organised Eddie!"

A glimmer of humour appeared in the corner of Eddie's mouth. His large brown eyes looked suddenly artful and rather emotional.

"Yes. I lost something very important to me once. I thought I could cope with out her but I never could. I thought I had lost her permanently but she has just come back to me."

Tears began to fill up in my eyes and my chin felt like it was being pulled down with a heavy weight. Slowly a well suppressed tear left my eye and softly meandered down my cheeks.

"Oh Eddie!"

I propelled myself through the open door and into Eddie's arms where I remained for some time with his thin little arms wrapped round me and his face snuggled into my shoulder. We had finally been brought back together again. I had finally been reunited with my brother.

Chapter 34

A Final Secret Must Remain Buried

Eddie continued clattering about in his open plan kitchen, still rather nervous of having his sister turn up on his door step after all these years. As I waited for him to finish up in the kitchen I sat at his table covered in scratches, tea stains and dents. The poor table looked and felt very ancient, like it had been salvaged from the ark. Its construction was of old drift wood; not very attractive but very economical. I gazed about at Eddie's tiny but cosy cottage which felt surprisingly homely and lived in.

Clear green and blue bottles stood up to attention in every corner of every shelf and of every rafter and alcove. They had all been washed cleaned and dried with their labels soaked off and removed. A row of green bottles lay lined up on the main rafter above us along with several model boats with extraordinary fine details of rigging, sails and even lobster pots, netting and anchors. The wall nearest the wood burner had a paddle from an old rowing boat hanging above a small window with a shelf under it cluttered with more boats, a wooden lighthouse and a few large shells. Opposite the window was an old sea captain's desk with a few well read and fraying books, a pot of pens and a blotter and with a great model steam ship under a glass case. The only comfy looking chair was sat in the corner. The chair had gone black and was fraying on the arm rests with a few sunken and sagging cushions sat in its corner. A crochet blanket was neatly folded up resting on the chair's back. A small round companion table stood next to the chair with an old bush DAC90 wireless placed on it.

A rickety staircase lead up to the one and only bedroom with more mobiles of shells hanging from the banister rail. Opposite the table up a small step was his poky, cramped kitchen comprising of a Belfast sink complete with draining board. Blue and white tiles decorated with silver mackerel protected the wall and windowsill which was cluttered with more bottles, shells and several unpolished candle sticks covered in white deformities of dribbling dry set wax. The view from the kitchen overlooked the chimney pots belonging to The Rising Moon tavern, with a sparse view of the sea beyond them. My attention continued to be drawn to a sagging chest of drawers set in an alcove by the stairs. The chest, like the table, appeared to be bespoke made of whatever wood was to hand. Every drawer was different in size shape and style. They all appeared to be taken and salvaged from several pieces of furniture and assembled into the piece I now looked upon. It was perhaps not the item of furniture itself that drew my attention, though it was a clever construction. It was mainly what sat on its top. The chest top was covered in grey and pale yellow photos, many taken of Eddie's time in the navy during the war. They all depicted smart men in their sailor's suits and uniforms all neatly and formally posing on the deck of a ship. On the other side of the chest were three other photos in elaborate silver frames. One was of Father and Mother and another of our grandparents. The final photo in this collection was of Eddie and I sat together by the harbour, taken around 1927. The last time I had seen that photograph had been in December of '29. I had burnt my copy in the oil drum the afternoon I had left Devon.

A few watercolours, Eddie's own work, lay framed to the walls, along with a ship's anchor. I was surprised by what a relaxing feeling Eddie's cottage gave me. Everything around me had meaning and value. Everything looked like it contained a hidden story and had no monetary value but was compensated by the sentimental appeal.

*

Eddie finally returned to the table and sat back down in the second of the two chairs that fitted each side of the table perfectly. I picked up

Eddie's old army flask undid the lid and poured a woody coloured tea into two well used enamel cups.

"So how long will it be until the drains are up and running again?" I asked.

Eddie pouted and pondered for a few seconds.

"Oh I don't know Edith, It's all such a bloody mess out there. Our top priority is to get some sort of sea defences up before the winter storms start, and channel a new course for the river, but it's all going to take time. It will be a long time before normality sets in again."

*

Eddie gave his cup an aggressive stir with a tarnished spoon, then took a healthy sip with a slight slurp. I carefully swirled my spoon slowly around the cup then carefully edged the spoon out, placing it back on to a saucer that Eddie had provided from off his dresser. As we drank our tea we both studied each other, both of us thinking that the other was not aware that we were examining what time, age and life had done to us during our years apart. Eddie had not really changed. He was thiner certainly; more wiry and a few more lines added to his face. Crow's feet had surrounded his eyes and deeper lines had developed in his forehead. He still however had a distinguished look which set him apart from others. His hands however looked as though they had suffered the worst; years of work and toil had considerably warn and scared his once pristine hands. Worry and labour had ingrained into his skin and nails with nodules on his fingers set in for the long term. His fingers, which were now delicately wrapped round the handle of his cup were still long, but they had lost their graceful look. Mother had always said Eddie had been blessed with 'piano hands'. They were now gone.

I put down my cup onto the china saucer both looking a complete oddity. My face must have expressed what I thought of this strange ensemble of enamel and china together, for Eddie gave a smirk and snorted with amusement while drinking from his own cup. He looked highly artful and I could see he was about to take the rise out of me.

"It's nice to see one of us has kept up with Mother's training of how one should take tea in the proper fashion! I'm afraid navy life has given my table manners a bit of a knock over the years. How I would ever cope if I had to sit down to one of those dinner parties Mother used to host. I wouldn't know what piece of cutlery to use first."

I laughed and put a hand out to Eddie which he grasped and placed my hand in to his.

"I don't think I would know what cutlery to use at a dinner party now," I gave a sigh and became rather lost thinking back to the old days. "Poor Mother and Father. They would never have coped with how the world is now. It's all changed."

"Yes a lot's gone on since we last saw each other, hasn't it old girl? You've built a new life for yourself in Wiltshire and become a teacher. Unlike me. I've not accomplished very much. Not like you have. I'm proud of you Edith!"

Eddie paused. He looked like he was pondering on something very deep for a minute. He looked suddenly crestfallen and rather beaten. Then his smile returned again.

"You've done very well for yourself old girl. Both Mother and Father would be proud of you."

I clutched Eddie's hand tighter and gave him a deep smile of reassurance.

"Mother and Father would be equally proud of you too, Eddie. Look what you've achieved in the navy. All the far off places and people you've seen. Not to mention the service you have given to the country. Just look at all you have done here in such a short space of time and the fact you came back!"

I now paused and felt a lump in my throat. I felt suddenly very inadequate and rather unsettled with myself.

"The truth is Eddie, you achieved the goal that everyone dreams and aspires to. You've done the thing I could never do. You came back home! You've built up this lovely little world for yourself. You did what Father and Mother would have done. You've held your head up high and been dignified. Now with the flood you have the chance to rebuild the harbour and make a fresh new start again. That's far more than I could ever have done."

I sighed deeply, "It's taken all these years plus a natural disaster to bring me back here again! That doesn't say much for me does it?"

Eddie looked down at his worn and dry table top as if he was too ashamed to look at me. His head was lowered with his chin dug into his neck.

"That's not your fault, Edith. That's my fault. You've had to pay a high price for my mistakes and shame."

"It's not your fault, Eddie," I said, "Yes. I admit back then I was angry with you. Very angry. So angry in fact that the day I left here I burnt the photo of you and me by the harbour."

Eddie looked rather surprised and shocked that I had burnt the photograph, but somehow looked as if what I had said to him made him realise or understand something. It was as if a memory or an event that had puzzled him for years had suddenly become clear to him.

"I know Eddie, it was a terrible thing to do and as soon as I burnt it I regretted it. Then when I found your letter waiting for me in the kitchen, well I knew it had not been your fault. I suppose the truth is Eddie, when I found out about you and Marcus I was shocked yes, but more envious of you. You had someone to love and for them to love you back. I've never had that. I felt so alone after Father died and with you being ill, I guess when I found out that you had Marcus, that you would have him after everything was cleared up and we left the house, it left me feeling jealous of you both."

My words were full of confession; I felt guilty of feeling such jealously. I looked about the room to try and find any evidence of Marcus. There was however, none.

"Eddie? Where is Marcus?"

Eddie looked suddenly very upset and anxious. He got up from the table for a minute and stood staring about the room like a troubled youngster lost on the moor. I looked up at him from the table. He just stood there frozen to the spot not able to move or speak. I too stood up and went round to him. I coaxed him to re-take his seat at the table while I knelt down next to him with my hand poised on his knee.

"Eddie, what happened to Marcus?"

His reply came out like a child in torment after grazing his knee.

"I don't really know Edith." He began spluttering with tears. "I received a letter from him just before we both left, saying that he had got as far as Hunter's Inn. It's that small inn up in the top of the valley." Eddie gave a sniffle and his voice began to break a little.

"It was his letter coming that pulled me out of my gloom and gave me the hope I needed to get out of bed. Anyway I got a letter to him saying that I would join him at the inn in a few days. I asked him to wait for me on the porch of the inn with his case ready to go. We agreed that should I not see him there at the agreed time then I would know he had changed his mind and left without me. When I got to the inn a lot later than planned he had indeed already gone. There was no one on the porch. Only bloody Doctor Kenos talking with the landlord. I thought about going up to them and to try and find out if Marcus had left a note or a message, but I could hardly do so with Kenos being there. Not after all that had happened with Father. And what was the point? I knew it was no good. I felt it in my bones that Marcus had done a runner. Not that I could accept it to start with. I searched around the valley for days trying to catch up with him but it was no good. I tried to find Marcus! I really did Edith!"

Eddie's voice was becoming more and more like a whimper and he was crying like a puppy. I stood up and put an arm round him and cuddled him while he continued his story, feeling like I wanted to cry. I felt so desperately sorry for him.

"But the more desperate my search became the more hopeless everything got. I felt like I had nothing left to live for. I had lost Marcus. I had left you. I felt I had nothing. I remember wandering round the valley in a daze, just wandering around until I was so warn out, dehydrated and hungry that I must have past out. The next thing I knew I was tucked up in bed in a farm house being looked after by a farmer and his wife."

Eddie continued crying for several moments. I felt nothing but pity for him and guilt, that I had driven Eddie away. Why had I not tried to be more understanding and not so judgmental towards him? I soothed his head with my hand and tried to calm and hush him. His head was lightly nested on my breast, no doubt feeling my heart pumping while he gasped and sniffled away until he finally said almost broken heartedly.

"I suppose you think it served me right. That I had reaped what I had sown."

"Of course not Eddie!" I said in surprised, sad tone. "I never wanted you to be unhappy! I only wanted the best for you. I know perhaps at the time I did not understand your feelings, but I do understand now." I too now was fighting back the tears and my voice betrayed my feelings sounding rather croaky and full remorse. "I realise now that I was wrong about you and Marcus. I should have supported you and not jumped onto my moral high ground. I'm just so sorry things did not work out for you."

Minutes past. Eddie continued to sniffle. A ship's clock with a merry ting chimed the hour. Eddie then asked me still sniffing back his tears and trying to regain his composure, "What about you? Did you ever marry or meet anyone?"

I went back round the table and dejectedly sat down in my chair and took a good sip of tea before I answered.

"No. There's been nobody. I never really had much confidence to go looking for love and love never found me. So you see Eddie, you've done far more than me. At least you did have someone."

"Looks like we've both been unlucky in that area of life." He said returning to his own tea taking a good slurp and dribbling a little down his chin, before wiping it away with his hand.

*

Trying not to think on the things that had never come in life, I looked around the cottage again to find a distraction. The cottage seemed surprisingly light and airy for a dwelling that was so small. From outside the sound of the sea was blocked by the sound of diggers and bulldozers manoeuvring up and down the road sounding like they were encroaching on the harbour. I looked round at the many photos of Eddie during his time in the navy. I was drawn to a photo in a wooden frame of two sailors posed on the deck of a war ship. One of them looked jolly serious and rather uptight and the other looked more cheeky and had a rascally looking grin over his face. I got up from the table and went over to the chest of drawers and picked up the photograph to examine it more carefully. I smiled as I noticed the sailor on the right was Eddie. Despite his hair shaven in navy style I knew it was him, there was no mistaking it. Somehow though the other man on the left seemed strangely familiar. I felt that somewhere I had seen a younger version of him before. Eddie stood up and came over to the chest. He wiped his face with his hands attempting to refresh himself from his crying. He put an arm round me and gazed at the photograph I was admiring.

He pensively looked upon the photograph remembering in his mind the day and year the photograph was shot. I looked at Eddie in a hopeful manner, hoping and expecting him to tell me about it. For a few minutes he said nothing. He continued to stare at it deeply with a frozen look upon his face. He gave me no clue or hint to what he was thinking and to start with I feared I would receive no explanation to accompany the photograph. Then after a few more minutes and a transfixed thoughtful silence Eddie began to open up.

"That was taken a few weeks before we were hit by the Japanese off Malay. The chap next to me was my best friend, Frank. Funny enough he came from Bath!"

At last the penny dropped. I suddenly knew where I had seen the younger looking face before. I was stunned. I could not believe it! For a few moments I fell into shock while Eddie continued talking.

"Yeah he had a wife and a little boy. Jack I think his name was. Frank had a photo of them next to his bunk. His son was the spit of him!"

We both looked deeply into the photograph staring into Frank's large friendly face. Eddie looked at the photo rather remorsefully knowing he had survived the *Repulses* sinking yet Frank had not. I however looked at the photograph now in recognition. I now knew why Frank looked so familiar to me. I had met his wife in the Parade Gardens the day after the first night of the Blitz of Bath, along with her son, Jack. Indeed Jack was the spit of his father. What a very small world it was I thought. To think that the woman who had been a complete stranger to me then, had been married to Eddie's best friend.

Eddie took the photo slowly from out of my hands. He held it a few moments almost looking beyond the image and back into the past. The sounds. The smells. The lost faces of the dead all began to resurface in his mind. Eddie had travelled back to the moment the attack came, remembering the horror when he realised Frank was missing.

*

The sound of the bulldozers broke Eddie's train of thought and he came back looking like he had been far away. He replaced the photograph back into its position on the chest and returned to the kitchen table. Eddie dejectedly flung himself back into his chair and continued drinking his tea. I continued to study the photograph and could not get over how much Jack had taken after his father. They both had the same round full face and large beautiful eyes. Eddie then continued telling me more about Frank which brought my attention back to the table.

"I did write to his wife. I told her what a good sailor Frank had been and one of the best friends you could ever wish to have. I tried to tell her how much Frank had loved her and Jack and how much he longed to get back to Bath with them. I never did receive a reply from her. I often wondered what had happened to her and Jack. I suppose he would be about eleven or twelve by now. If he survived the Blitz that is."

I sat back down at the table and finished the last few drops of my tea. Thankfully the cup hid my lower face from him, for I feared I would betray what I knew of Jack and his mother and what had happened to them. I thought for the time being it was best not to say anything. I would wait a little while longer before I told him. Fortunately our conversation turned to a more general chat about our war years.

" So what was Bath like during the Blitz then old girl?"

I put down my cup and returned it to its strange saucer and relayed to Eddie of what life had been like in Bath during the war and how everyone had longed for an orange. I briefly told him about my flat and how strange and small it had appeared when I first moved in. I explained how everyone in Bath had been fooled into a false sense of security thinking that every time the Germans had flown over we thought the target was Bristol. Then on that unforgettable night the terror of hearing that piercing slow squeal of the first bombs being dropped and the inferno that followed. I told Eddie about Thelma and Emma and the problems Thelma had living in Bath. I finished by telling him that Thelma had moved down here to make a fresh start where none would know her. Eddie seemed genuinely shocked by what I had told him and it seemed that neither he nor anyone in the village ever suspected that Thelma had had a child out of wedlock.

"But Thelma told me she had been married! That her husband had been in the army and been killed in action and that she moved down here to get away from all the memories! I never suspected a thing!"

Eddie looked considerably taken back. He sat back in his chair his mouth slightly gaping open with his arms up behind his head. He swung on his chair slightly and then put his arms back to the table as his chair moved back level.

"She never told me any of this! As I say I never suspected a thing! If she had only known about my life she need not have worried or feared that I would have condemned her. You know she and Emma used to live next door to me?"

"Yes I did know. Thelma told me in her last letter that you had moved next to her and that you were a very good friend to her and Emma. But of course she referred to you as the harbour master and it never occurred to me who you really were. Not until poor Helen's Penny accidentally lit it slip."

"I thought it was better to change my name and to come back home a different person. I thought it would be easier that way. For a while I fooled quite a few people. I even fooled Alexander and Helen for the first month. But they found out who I was in the end. Thelma knew nothing about me and I never told her anything about my past or you or the house. I thought it was best to let the past die. Not to go raking it all up again. Did you know Emma and I made that mobile outside in the porch. We only made it a few weeks ago. One of the last times I saw her. She was so busy helping her mum with the move down to Sally's I hardly saw her in the last week before the flood. Emma was so excited about having her very own bedroom and not having to share a room with her mum... "

Eddie paused and looked suddenly rather pained. He sounded almost angry for there was a bitterness detectable in his voice.

"The damn thing is that if they had stayed living up here they would both still be alive now! It's so bloody unfair," Eddie paused and looked up at me realising he had gone off at a tangent. "Oh I am sorry Edith. Do forgive me and my language. It's not true is it? The grass isn't always greener."

Eddie sounded rather philosophical as if he too had realised that the dream he had craved of moving away, starting afresh away from Devon had just been a dream. When he had finally moved away and gone off with the navy the reality was somehow very different. Life had not turned out how he had hoped. I could see that the loss of Marcus was still with him. He had joined the navy hoping distance, time and his second love of the sea would cure him. But it had not worked.

Wanting to change the subject and bring some relief to the tension we were both feeling I said, "I can't believe that Mathew, that man you thought I was at the door, is the brother of the man that gave me a lift on his cart from Barnstable!"

"Oh you mean Billy?" Eddie said in a familiar tone.

"Yes that's right!" I said somewhat surprised. "Do you know him as well then?"

Eddie shifted in his chair and started fiddling with his cup, tapping it slightly with his spoon.

"Oh yes Edith," he said in a rather grave serious and cautious tone. "I know Billy very well."

Eddie continued twiddling with his tea spoon and looked rather on edge. His eyes darted about the room like a frightened rabbit. I on the other hand now understood why Billy had been so worried about me returning to Devon and why he had warned me that I would find more than Thelma and Emma. I attempted to try and get Eddie to focus back on me, for his eyes wandered about in an anxious state.

"Well that explains why Billy was so worried about me coming back down here. He was worried about how you would feel me showing up out of the blue after all these years. You have a very good friend in Billy.

Still I wish the old fool had told me. I thought there was something even worse to come out. Something really terrible!"

Eddie was still unable to look at me. He seemed dreadfully worried about the mention of Billy.

"I don't think he was worried about you and I being reunited again, Edith. I think Billy was worried that you might ask too many questions about the house."

*

Eddie paused and at long last looked up at me from across the table which strangely seemed a bigger distance than it had. Eddie had the same expression across his face which he had had on the night of Father's death. He had that same troubled look on his face when he had tried to tell me about Marcus and himself but really wanted to avoid the issue. Eddie had the look of a man who had a secret which was buried deep within him.

"Look Edith, what I am about to tell you must never ever leave this room. You must give me your word that what I tell you must never be repeated. It would damage a person's reputation and would destroy their family's lives."

I could see that Eddie was not being melodramatic. What he was about to tell me was something so terrible that he had been forced to keep it hidden from everyone. With my body feeling suddenly stiff with tension and wondering what on earth Eddie was about to reveal, I swore that I would never repeat or speak of what Eddie was about to relay to me. Eddie got up from the table and stepped up into the kitchen and clattered about in a cupboard, clinking bottles together until he came back with a brown bottle of whisky. After pouring a little into each of our cups already stained with tea, he shuffled the bottle into the middle of the table and gulped his whisky down like there was no tomorrow. I took a gentle gulp, spluttering from the strong drink and the tension rising with in me.

"A little Dutch courage," Eddie said in a husky hazy voice which had gone suddenly numb with the whisky. When Eddie was comfortable and

I had recovered from the harshness of the whisky he began to tell me one last secret that up till now had never been spoken to anyone.

*

"As you know Edith, Billy and Mathew are brothers. However their surname isn't Bath. It's Bath Rogers! Billy and Mathew thought a double barrelled surname sounded far too posh and La De Da for working class men, so when they moved to Lynrock from Cornwall they took off the Rogers and the family's name became Bath. Billy and Mathew came here along with their sister. I don't know much, but their sister was a young flighty, very striking young woman and by all accounts was very beautiful. It was her looks and nature that unfortunately drew the attention of the wrong sort of men. Eventually she ran off with a man who had a bad reputation but could do no wrong in her eyes. This man promised her the moon but shall we say was only after one thing. This one thing resulted several months later in Billy and Mathew's sister landing back on their doorstep one night several months pregnant. Before you ask no she had no wedding band on her finger. The father had got what he wanted and buggered off. Mathew and Billy took their sister in and looked after her. She later gave birth to a healthy boy."

"What happened to their sister?" I asked.

"Their sister unfortunately did not fare so well. She died a few hours later. There had apparently been complications during the birth. Billy and Mathew were forced to bring up the boy until he was of working age when he was then sent off to work as a gardener at a big estate."

Eddie paused and poured himself another drink. I declined his offer for another one. I wanted to keep a clear head and take in everything he was telling me.

"For a few years the young man did well. He learnt his trade from the head gardener and became a hard working member of the staff. The young man became very popular with the other servants and even the son and daughter of the family from the big house liked him and often stopped to speak to him while he was at his tasks round the gardens. Sadly the Great War brought an end to the security of this young man's life and he went off with the other gardeners to fight. The young man survived but returned badly shell shocked. His peace of mind was nearly gone. He continued to work as a gardener at the manor and found returning to his old life began to help him cope with the harsh hell of the trenches."

I shifted in my seat. "Eddie, what was the name of Billy and Mathew's nephew?" I asked worriedly, now leaning forward in my chair desperate to hear his name.

"His first name was Simon. But he was always called by the family's surname." Eddie paused and took another drop of whisky. The name was now on my lips but I was afraid to speak it out loud. In the end Eddie and I spoke his name in unison both of us saying the word in a hushed tone.

"Rogers."

"Mathew and Billy thought at the time that giving Simon the name of Rogers would give him more respectability and a decent name. Let's face it Edith, Mother and Father would never have taken Rogers on if his true parentage had been revealed."

I was rather breathless. This revelation explained so much. I now understood why Billy and Mathew had looked and been so worried with my arrival back in the village. They must have feared that if I became reunited with Eddie or started poking around too much I may stumble upon their family's secrets. I still did not understand what all this had to do with the house. Nor did I understand why after so many years Billy and Mathew were still so worried about what people would think of their sister and nephew. Many in the village who had known the family back then were probably dead or too old to care or remember. Something still did not add up.

"Eddie, what does all this have to do with the house?" I asked worriedly.

Eddie took a deep breath and I knew that the worst was yet to come. "Do you remember the afternoon you left?" I nodded and recalled that bitter day in my mind. "Well that afternoon I came back. I wanted to say goodbye to you and to give you my ring so you would have something of value. Well late that afternoon, around three o'clock I came back into the village and climbed up the north terrace steps up to the tennis court. I made my way to the servants' quarters back door and let myself in. The whole place was deserted, all accept for Mr Tucker. I found him in the kitchen. He'd broken some plate from one of the dressers and seemed very emotional. I arranged with him to leave you my letter and the matchbox on the kitchen table and told him to make sure he informed you where to find it before you left. After saying goodbye to Tucker and convincing him that I could not stay to see you, I left the way I had come. I got back on to the path where I nearly bumped straight into you! I saw you come out of the garden room and head down the path in my direction. I rushed into the bushes and hid there until you passed. I followed you for a time until you got to the kitchen garden door then as soon as you went through I headed back up to the tennis court."

"I knew someone had followed me!" I said with an air of triumph in my voice thinking back to that afternoon now realising that I had not been imagining it. It had been Eddie all the time. Eddie pulled out a hand and stretched it over to me across the table. I took it and held it for a few moments while he continued his story.

"As I came up to the rose garden I saw Rogers. He was rushing through the garden looking crazed and wild like an animal. He had a strange look in his eyes. It was as if he was seeing red and he was carrying an upright black bag. Luckily he didn't see me and I assumed you had given him his marching orders at last, hence the bag he was carrying and why he looked so angry. Anyhow I thought no more about it. I had my own problems to worry about. I had to meet Marcus and I was already late. I made my way up to the tennis court and then down the north steps. By the time I got down into the village it was nearly four. I made my way to collect my bag which I had hidden by one of the coal sheds. As I got to the Town Hall I met Billy in a right old state. After I calmed him down he told me that Rogers had been ranting and raving all-round the village saying he was never going to leave the house and that he would rather die than leave. He then told me that Rogers had been prowling about Mathew's garage a few hours before and that he had ran off with a can of petrol! Of course that's when the penny fell. I told Billy what I had seen up by the rose garden. Billy and I both went and got Mathew at the garage and then the three of us rushed up towards the drive to try and find Rogers before he hurt himself or did something stupid. When we got to the drive the bloody gates were locked and bolted. I knew you had already left and the house was empty. We climbed over the gates which cost us precious time. We could already smell something burning when we reached the first turning in the drive. When we at last reached the house it was too late. The north wing of the house was already a blaze. Mathew ran back down the drive to sound the alarm in the village, while Billy and I rushed in through the garden room to try and find Rogers. We did not have to look very hard to find him."

Eddie took another drop of whisky and slung it back. He clearly needed it before he continued.

"He… " Eddie paused. He could hardly speak. He swallowed hard a few times and gathered himself together. Moisture had gathered across his forehead and was slowly dripping down his face.

"We found Rogers hanging from the banister from the first floor landing. He had just jumped off with a rope round his neck. I had never seen a man hanged before. Not like that. It was not, shall we say, a pleasant sight. Poor Billy was beside himself. I rushed up to get Rogers down hoping there still might be a chance. Again we were too late. There was nothing we could do. I knew I had to act quickly and make a decision. I decided to drag Rogers out of the house and try and hide him in the garden somewhere. Then when everything had died down I would come back up and decide what to do. I only just made it down the stairs after cutting Rogers down when the smoke and flames reached the main hall. The heat and the smoke was just unbearable. Billy nearly collapsed on me, more in shock I think from finding Rogers. I had to drag him out first and leave him on the lawn and then go back in for Rogers. By the time I pulled Rogers out Mathew had returned and told us the fire engine had been summoned. I instructed Mathew to get Billy out of the way and up to the tennis court. I carried Rogers as far as I could along the path. I got as far as the kitchen garden. I wanted to take him up to the tennis court but I thought he may be discovered up there and I was absolutely exhausted from the smoke. In the end I dragged him in to the kitchen garden and hid him round the back of the green houses. By the time that old fool Mr Cuss had unlocked the gates to allow the fire engines in half the house was lost and the fire was spreading to the other floors. Afterward, at around eleven at night when the fire was out and everyone had left the ruins Mathew, Billy and I crawled up the north steps again and we made our way to the kitchen garden. We buried Rogers by the greenhouses. Before I left for Hunter's Inn to meet Marcus now hours late for him, the three of us all agreed that for Rogers' memory and reputation we would say nothing of what had gone on. Billy made it known during the fire and police investigation that Rogers had left hours earlier for Cornwall. But everyone said that they had seen him about the village ranting and everyone knew how unstable he had become. The finger of blame hovered about but was never proven. Poor old Cuss thought it was a communist cell that had burnt the house done, which was rather laughable! A communist cell in Lynrock! The verdict of the investigation was arson by person or persons unknown and with no evidence and thankfully none was able to testify against Mathew or Billy that they had seen Rogers with a can of petrol that afternoon, the case remained unsolved and was closed."

*

I sat in compete silence and shock all the time while Eddie spoke. I was only able to move when I thought I could do with that second drink. I helped myself to some of the whisky from the bottle while Eddie finished his testimony.

"I left the village and headed to Hunter's Inn to meet Marcus thinking that I would never see Billy again. How wrong I was. Do you remember me telling you that when I was unable to find Marcus that a farmer found me at death's door and took me in? Well that farmer was Billy on his way in his cart delivering his milk. Well you can imagine what a surprise I had when I came round and found myself in bed with Billy and his wife Dorothy hovering over my bedside! Even in those days poor Billy was not exactly an oil painting. But he was a good man. He treated me like a son. He gave me work to do on his farm and gave me a reason to get up in the morning. I got up at six every morning to help Billy with the livestock. I mucked out the barns, helped with the milking, you name it I did it. I think Billy was grateful to have some help and for another man to be about the place as he had quickly found out that marriage was not as blissful as he had originally thought. Dorothy and Billy often had an argument twice a day over the most mundane things. About a year later I decided to move on and join the navy. I wanted to try and forget Marcus and everything else and see a bit of the world while I could. The rest you know. When I was discharged from my service in the navy I didn't know where to go so I came back here. I found out the village needed a harbour master and with my knowledge of the sea I was offered the job and moved up here."

Eddie looked about the cottage his head looking up to the rafters examining the world he had made for himself.

"Hard to think I've been here nearly seven months now. In some ways it feels like I never left. I don't know, Edith. Where has all that time gone to?"

I sighed and thought myself where the years had disappeared to. I then thought of Rogers and how terrible it must have been for Eddie, Billy and Mathew to have to bury him in an unmarked grave, now completely swallowed up by weeds.

"Poor Rogers," I said, feeling so sorry for him and guilty that I had not done anything to help him when he clearly must have been falling deeper and deeper into depression. Life had dealt him one to many blows and just when he was beginning to recover from the trenches, his one bit of stability was eroding away from him. Eddie got up from the chair and stood over the table and was about to collect up the cups and saucers when he said in a rather pleading and begging tone.

"Do you think I did the right thing, Edith? I've gone over it so many times in my mind wondering if I did the right thing."

I got up from the table and went round to Eddie and kissed him on the cheek in reassurance.

"Of course you did the right thing, Eddie. You did what you did to save Rogers' reputation. At the end of the day you did the very thing

Rogers wanted. You buried him in the garden he loved and cared about so much. His wish had been to remain in the garden and that's what you gave him."

Eddie still looked fearful. I held his hands tightly and kissed him on the head.

"But you do see Edith, that for Billy and Mathew's sake and for the memory of Rogers' everything I have told you must remain buried. It can never come out Edith. It would break Billy and Mathew's heart. For their sake let this final secret remain buried.

Chapter 35
Three Masts

Eddie and I had continued talking until six o'clock and then we were forced to leave his cosy cottage for the night and return to the upper village. Eddie had been temporarily billeted in a guesthouse in the high street and I returned to the Chough's Nest Hotel hoping the bathroom would be free for half an hour for me to have a good soak and freshen up before dinner.

Thankfully we were allowed to return up to the village with the rest of the construction workers in the cliff railway. I had not fancied having to walk back up the cliff. It had been bad enough going down let alone trying to attempt walking back up. The atmosphere in the carriage ascending the cliff had been surprisingly jolly and good humoured. Eddie introduced me to a few of the team and after the initial weary looks of 'what's a woman doing here' the men treated me with good grace and we even started singing a few of the old Rag Time songs. If there was one disadvantage to our mode of transport it was simply the reek of that terrible smell which had unfortunately left its presence on all of us. On arrival back at the top Eddie escorted me to the Chough's Nest where we said our goodnights and made arrangements to see each other again the next day. I explained to him that I had planned to meet Helen and Penny for part of the day and go on a walk with them along the coastal path to the Valley of the Rocks. We decided that we would meet again later in the afternoon.

*

The sound of the dawn chorus and a shattering cry from the seagulls flying out over the bay awoke me from my good night's sleep. I staggered out of my bed feeling bleary eyed with legs that felt like they were constructed out of concrete. After washing and dressing I pulled back the curtains to reveal a rather overcast dull, grey morning. I grabbed my room key with my handbag and walked on down to breakfast. Very slowly I might add. My joints and muscles had still not recovered from my walk down to the harbour the previous afternoon. Although my body felt shattered my mind and spirits had been lifted higher than I had felt for years. I felt reawakened at long last. As if from years of sleep and constant worry. All my tension and anxiety over the past misfortunes and my mistakes suddenly seemed to have no meaning or hold over me. I at long last had found Eddie again. I had been given a second chance and a small amount of time left for me to put things right. Not many people are presented in life with a such a fresh new beginning. I was determined not to let this chance pass me by.

*

Breakfast was considerably quieter and more private than it had been the day before. The Warwick's had now left much to the delight of Mrs Barns, who seemed a good deal more relaxed now that Mrs Warwick had departed for home, along with her poor long suffering husband. In fact I seemed to be the only guest down for breakfast. I sipped a refreshing glass of grapefruit juice and perused the breakfast menu, while enjoying the smell of a sweet citrus perfume coming from a single yellow canary rose in a miniature white china vase on my table. While enjoying the peace of the room I stupidly assumed Norman had also checked out and returned to Oxford to bore his poor students and comatose his poor wife with his never-ending knowledge of ferns. Nigel and Elizabeth Pelican were still in the hotel as I had had a good long chat with them in the lounge over coffee and brandy after dinner. They also were planning a walk today. Not that the weather looked particularly inspiring for such an aspiration.

I continued to drink my grapefruit juice and glance through the menu trying to decide whether I should have the full English breakfast or to have just some scrambled eggs on toast. Mr Barns came charging in with a pot of tea for me and a silver toast rack of brown toast. A golden tile of butter was presented on a saucer and a glass cut pot of tangy marmalade. As Mr Barns placed the silver tray on the edge of my round table and began positioning my pot of tea, milk jug, butter and marmalade he glanced out through the French doors and glared out over the bay. The view was decidedly grey, dull and murky, with a slight fret obscuring the cliffs.

"Not the best start to the morning is it miss?" Mr Barns commented as he continued with his tasks.

"No it certainly looks rather overcast this morning Mr Barns. It's a shame I was off to the Valley of the Rocks this morning."

"Not to worry miss. I just caught the forecast on the wireless before I came in. It's going to be a dull start but will brighten up towards lunch time. So you should have a nice afternoon, for your walk. Are you ready to order now? Or would you like me to come back in a minute?"

I pondered over the menu knowing that really I should have just a little scrambled eggs. But I had so enjoyed my full English the day before I could feel myself weakening and once again I had a craving for some bacon.

"Yes Mr Barns. I will have the full English again today please. I will have to walk it off this afternoon." Mr Barns scribbled my order on his pad that he had whipped from out of his pocket.

"If you don't mind me saying so miss, you don't need to worry about your figure." Mr Barns suddenly looked rather flushed and artful. He smiled like a shy school boy then turned and walked back to the kitchen.

I poured my tea, feeling contented that the weather was set to improve and my figure was still to be admired and I buttered myself a piece of toast. I felt blissfully happy. I turned round in my seat to look out over the bay, admiring first Mrs Barns' summer flowers of red geraniums planted in long window boxes. I reassuringly returned to my breakfast and placed a scoop of orange marmalade on to my toast. Out in the hall by the reception desk I overheard Mr Barns greet one of the other guests.

"Oh Good morning sir. Your table is ready for you."

My heart suddenly sank and I dropped my spoon of marmalade on to the table. For who should wander in but dear Norman! I madly thought of escaping out through the French doors or quickly darting under the table but it was too late. Norman came bundling in and just as I wanted to make a hasty retreat and go and cancel my breakfast order with the kitchen, Norman, with his great owl glasses and silver greasy looking hair, dressed in a borrowed summer suit, came rushing over to me with his usual sickly annoying greeting.

"Dear Edith there you are! I was rather worried about you yesterday. I could not find you for love nor money. Still never mind here we both are. May I join you?"

My face dropped and my whole body went into panic stations. "Well actually professor, I… "

Norman interrupted my excuse and promptly sat down in the vacant seat on my table much to the joy of Mr Barns who came in with my breakfast and suddenly stopped in his tracks. He too looked highly annoyed on my behalf and disgruntled that his seating plan had been changed yet again. I glanced over at Mr Barns giving him a pleading look of 'please help me' as he strode over to me, placing my breakfast on the table and cautioning me that the plate was hot. He then unwillingly turned to Norman.

"Professor your table is ready for you if you would like to come over?"

Norman did not take the hint.

"Oh don't worry, Mr Barns. I will join Miss Parffit here for breakfast and keep her company. If you could bring me over some cutlery and my pot of coffee I will be most happy over here."

I intervened and quickly turned to the professor and said in a most anxious almost pleading voice. " Really you don't have to sit with me, Professor. I am sure you would be far more comfortable at your own table." My plea fell on deaf ears.

"I would not dream of leaving you Edith, not after the loss of your poor friend and her sweet little daughter. You need company at a time like this. It would be my pleasure to accompany you wherever you go today."

"How kind you are Professor," I said, gritting my teeth.

"Now Edith," Norman put a slippery hand on mine and gave it a weak, limp pat, "You must stop calling me professor. It's Norman!"

The professor turned round to Mr Barns who was looking like he could snap his pencil that was poised to take down Norman's order. Norman spoke to Mr Barns like he was a servant and demanded. "How about some coffee?"

*

And so for the next two hours were spent with me trying desperately to eat my breakfast which gradually grew colder and colder as I paused before every mouthful waiting for Norman to cease from his constant talking of ferns, plants and the workings of cactus in the desert. Then I had to hear all about his latest expedition that his university was funding him to go on.

"Oxford do seem to like me going off all over the world to carry out more research. You know Edith, we've only just scratched the surface. There is still so much we don't know and have yet to discover!"

As he rambled on I wondered when on earth I was ever going to get away and thought to myself that perhaps Oxford could send Norman to a rainforest inhabited by wild tribes that had a taste for human sacrifice. Mind you, even if a tribe captured Norman they probably would send him back or throw themselves into lakes infested with man eating crocodiles. Anything to get away from Norman's constant talking. I was just about to contemplate whether anyone had a gun handy when young Alfred came in carrying a note which he brought over to our table.

"Oh! Good morning Alfred!" I said, relieved and delighted that someone else was in the room for a few minutes to give me a moment's break from hearing about the latest research on orchid varieties.

"Good morning miss. This note came for you a few minutes ago from the Valley of the Rocks Hotel." Alfred passed me the note which I thanked him for. I opened up the sheet of A5 cream embossed paper and read the details enclosed.

Dear Edith

If you are free and the following time is convenient to you, Penny and I will meet you outside your hotel in the lane at eleven o'clock. Warm regards.

Helen.

I closed up the note and folded it up again while Alfred hovered by the table.

"Is there a reply miss?" Alfred enquired eagerly.

"No, that's fine, thank you Alfred."

"Very good miss. I hope you enjoy your day." With that Alfred turned and went back to the kitchen ignoring Norman altogether and giving him a disparaging look.

I threw my crisp napkin down on the table from my lap with a few specs of toast speckling the table. I rushed up giving Norman a start as he was ploughing his way through his own breakfast and thankfully had a mouth crammed full of sausage so was unable to stop me from leaving.

"Well Norman, it has been a most delightful breakfast and extremely interesting one, but I have much to do this morning. I am sure you have a lot more to do too so I won't keep you, cheerio."

I have never spoke so quickly in my life. With my bag in hand I rushed out of the dining room and up to my room. I brushed my teeth, changed into my walking shoes and spent a penny before handing my key back in at reception with Alfred.

*

As arranged with Helen at five minutes to eleven I was on the lane outside the Chough's Nest. I rested against the wall and looked out over the bay. Several people past me. A wiry and brisk dog walker marched past with a golden retriever and two young students sauntered past smoking. But there was no sign of Helen and Penny. I glared down the peaceful narrow lane with birds darting in and out of the shrubs and trees. Further up I detected the shrill sound of the cliff railway's bell interrupting the peace of the lane. I thought that Eddie was probably on board heading down with the other workers for the day. I examined my watch which read five minutes past eleven, and peered down the lane again looking for any sign of Helen and Penny approaching. I assumed that they were on their way down and would be with me shortly. I thought I would probably see them any minute, both hand in hand walking down the lane ready to collect me. Then we would all continue down the lane out on to the open and gusty coastal path. I walked about a bit for a few minutes or more and looked up at my hotel. I noticed how many of the gutters needed a good clean out and that many of the roof tiles looked rather precarious and were covered in bird droppings and yellow crusty lichen. A large black crow was perched on the end of the guttering just over the terrace that ran along the side of the lounge and dining room. He was later joined by his mate and the two gave each other suspicious looks before swooping down to the terrace to see if the Barnes had thrown out any of this morning's unwanted crusts from the toast. I looked at my watch again. It was now eleven minutes past eleven. Where were they? Fearing that any minute Norman might come out on his way to collect more ferns I decided to walk down the lane towards the village thinking that on my way I would probably bump into them.

I set off towards the village with the birds darting from one side of the path to the other. I passed the old overgrown allotments and gardens, with their iron gates covered in ivy and their steps locked behind them almost lost under years of leaves, weeds and grass. I strolled along the imposing old villas of the former rich, now converted into hotels and bed and breakfasts to try and rival the Chough's Nest. I reached the slope leading up along the gardens of the Valley of the Rocks Hotel and the cemetery of St Mary's on the left. I came up onto the main road of the high street. The grand impressive steps and porch of the Valley of the Rocks Hotel hung over me casting a shadow over the road. A few trunks and cases were waiting outside to be collected by the porter. A long wooden ladder was nestled against the wall reaching up to one of the large tall windows. A bucket of water with a cloth and sponge was waiting for the window cleaner to return. The flower shop directly opposite me was being opened up and the sign board to the gentlemen's outfitters had been proudly put out and was generating interest from PC Daniels who was out on his morning beat. He paused his normal clockwork walk to peer through the window of the gentlemen's outfitters. He spent a few minutes admiring a rather smart light summer suit, the mannequin complete with a summer trilby hat. I walked around the perimeter of the hotel passing the glazed but closed door of the bar entrance and walked up to the Apophyge pillars that flanked the porch.

I quickly stopped dead in my tracks. For who should I see standing under the canopy of the porch but Helen! She appeared to be talking with a soldier and she had a rather guilty look on her face.

*

I decided not to approach for I did not wish to interrupt their conversation. I thought it best to wait until the two of them had finished. Helen's appearance and posture looked rather uncomfortable. Her face appeared pained by what was being said to her from the soldier who had his back to me and I was unable to see his face. Their conversation was rather hushed and muted, but what was being said was not of a pleasant nature judging from the look on Helen's face. Over the road PC Daniels had finished admiring his summer suit and was now heading in my direction. He gave me a rather suspicious and pensive glare. He was probably wondering why I was loitering about outside the most prestigious hotel in the village. I knew I had to do something. I decided that I would have to climb up the steps of the hotel up into the porch and hope Helen would see me and end her discussion with the soldier. As I stepped up onto the smooth white stone steps and headed up into the porch I managed to overhear a little of a Helen's words with the soldier.

"You don't have any rights! Now you stay away from me and from her. Do you understand?"

Helen's eyes finally fell upon mine and she looked a little panicked and flustered at me being present. She broke off her disagreement with the soldier and came hurtling down, greeting me with a kiss and a light hug. As she did so the soldier also turned round and gave me a stunned look, which I also returned back with even greater vigour. For the man who Helen had been arguing with was none other than Officer Williams! He looked highly surprised and startled at seeing me again. As Helen apologised for being late Officer Williams slyly crept down the steps and past us both. Helen gave him a rather curt and final goodbye to him as he went.

"Thank you for your concern Officer Williams, but I think I can manage perfectly well thank you. I will not be requiring your services again."

Helen's tone was formal, sharp and unrelenting. She seemed from my point of view to be politely telling Officer Williams never to speak or come near her again. I was about to say hello to Officer Williams and to thank him for my pass down to the harbour, but he looked rather broken hearted and in no mood to talk. I let him go by and he walked quietly away, giving PC Daniels a nod of acknowledgment. He then wondered back in the direction of the Town Hall. Helen meanwhile continued her nervous explanation for being late.

"I am sorry about that Edith. It's just so many people want to stop and ask me how I am and if I need anything. I know people are just being kind and supportive, but I do find it all a bit too much at the moment. Thank goodness you're here now. The weather looks like it's going to cheer up so we should have a nice day for our walk."

Helen looked up towards the open door of the lobby and called out to Penny. She suddenly appeared from around the corner and scampered down the steps with a straw bag and a cuddly toy elephant. Penny greeted me with a hug and a cry of "Auntie Edith!" before the three of us set off back down the way I had come. After passing the Chough's Nest we made our way down a lime green shady avenue passing a gothic looking gate house until the path narrowed considerably. We reached a locked gate which we just about managed to climb over and crossed over the cattle grid which was put down to deter the wild goats from entering the village. The goats had a bad reputation for straying into the village every summer around the time of the flower show. Needless to say the goats put pay to many a villager's gardens and exhibits.

*

We continued along the path passing numerous towers of pink trumpets of fox gloves and sea kale growing wild and rampant around a few degrading benches. Penny held her mother's hand for a time with her toy elephant in the other. I volunteered to carry her straw basket which contained Penny's swimming costume, a flask of tea and wrapped up cake from the bakery. We continued in relative peace with only the sound of the birds in the trees and the roar of the sea down below. The green haze and pale light trickling through the canopy of the trees grew in strength as we left the passage of the avenue and came out to the open fresh air of the sea and the winding narrow costal path. To the right of us was the long, never ending band of the iridescent sea beginning to sparkle as the sun crept ever further out from under its blanket of cloud. To the left of us weaving in and out, stretching like a peninsular and then enclosing in on itself into enclosed bays was the ragged coast line. Great stacks of rocks were piled high above us, rising to terrifically high summits. They then seemed to fall steeply away down to the sea. The landscape was glorified with green grass and thick bushes of pink and purple heathers and sunshine yellow gorse. The coastal path was much smaller and less wider than it had been by the hotel only allowing us room to walk in single file. Penny lead us at a suitable distance with Helen walking close behind her and me holding up the rear. The path veered up and down heading tightly around sudden bends on the end of rocky turrets. Wild thyme grew plentifully along the sides of the path with green sea spleenwort covering the steep banks that fell down to the shimmering sea.

  The sun was now beginning to gain its confidence and sat in a pale blue sky, with faint stretches of white frothy clouds. The weather was deceptive, for a cold wind was hitting into our faces as we walked along the path and I was grateful I had a coat on. Penny waddled along like a penguin oblivious to the wind and eager for us to reach her favourite bay. Helen seemed very subdued and spoke very little. I could not help but wonder whether there was something else troubling her besides the fact that she had lost Alexander. Many people in life through the years will tell you that you will get over a loss of any kind eventually and in some ways people that tell you that are right. But the reality is that when you lose someone who is as close to you as a husband, parent or sibling, you never really get over the loss. You simply learn each day to adapt to their absence in your life. I got the distinct impression that something had rattled Helen. It was something that Officer Williams had said I was sure of it. Despite what she had told me that they had just bumped into each other. That it was one of those chance meetings, Officer Williams paying his respects. It had looked more to me like the meeting that had been a surprise to Helen but had been planned by Officer Williams. He had for some reason gone to see her and Helen had sent him packing.

We paused for a few minutes and sheltered on a narrow bench set against the cliff wall with small piles of black and brown goat droppings covering the floor. The three of us enjoyed a moment of rest and a chance to look out to sea. We took in the splendid view for some time, watching a steamer out in the channel. We were however not allowed to rest for long as Penny excitedly got to her feet with her toy elephant in tow and exclaimed with wonderment and gusto in her voice.

"Come on Auntie Edith! Mummy and I want to show you the three masts!"

*

With that Penny waddled off again down the path and disappeared around the side of the cliff which jutted out like the ankle of a foot onto the pathway. Helen and I got to our feet and plodded along behind her, Helen calling out to Penny not to go too fast and to stay where she could see her. The path stretched gently down the recess of the cliff and then looked as if it parted in two. One track went steeply up and around a mass of rocks. The other fell back down and around into the valley. Penny continued walking straight on. She charged around a another rocky bend and Helen and I followed, continuing along the cliff. We remained on the path we were on for nearly twenty minutes, Penny leading us like the leader of an expedition with me and Helen trailing behind her. I tried to engage Helen in conversation as she seemed unusually silent and had hardly said two words since we crept on to the costal path.

"Well we have been lucky for weather so far," I said cheerfully, "When I first got up this morning I thought we were going to have a terrible day. But so far it's turned out very well."

"Yes I suppose it is nice," Helen said rather tired and faintly with no sound of expression in her voice. "I just hope it will be nice on Friday for the service. Are you and Eddie going?"

"I'm going," I replied. "I don't know about Eddie yet. We talked for so long yesterday about so many different things I forgot to ask him about it. I will ask him this afternoon when I see him." Helen looked straight ahead of her keeping a watchful eye on Penny who was still a few steps ahead of us. She bounded up and down along the path, her head turning to the left and right looking to see if she could spy any of the wild goats and their young grazing on the edges of the cliffs.

"I am glad you came back Edith," Helen confessed tiredly. "The village was never the same after you left and the house caught fire. Did Eddie tell you all about the fire?"

I felt instantly uneasy at the mention of the house and the fire. I quickly said, "Oh yes! Eddie told me all about the house."

Helen continued keeping a close eye on Penny, not bothering to look out at the sea to the right of us, nor turning to me in conversation. She looked like she was in a trance. Her face not daring to deviate but to keep focused on the road in front of her.

"Mr Cuss nearly had a breakdown over it!" Helen continued. "Poor silly man. He thought it was a group of communists who set it alight! I mean really. Is it likely that a group of communists would have been at large in Lynrock!"

"Oh I don't know Helen. There was a lot of that sort of thing after the crash. People felt so let down by the system."

I hoped that would be enough for Helen that she would not say any more about the fire, but she still was not finished.

"Yes I know Edith, in London maybe, but not down here in Devon! Alexander and I both thought it was more likely to be one of the servants who did it in revenge for losing their job. My money was on that Rogers! Well you remember him? He was never quite the ticket was he after the war? I expect you remember, he would not leave with the other gardeners would he? He kept hanging around the house like a zombie. He even caused a scene at Mathew's garage the day you left!" Helen sounded very sure of herself and indignantly added, "No. I reckon it was Rogers that done it."

I knew I had to say something but I also knew that if I categorically denied it, it may look like I was trying to cover up the matter. So I simply said, trying to sound like I neither cared or worried about it, "Well Helen, whether it was a communist gang or a disgruntled servant it's all in the past now. I know my father and mother are in a far nicer place than to worry about it now."

Helen seemed surprised at my carefree attitude and it seemed to shock her into silence. Thankfully Penny helped to alleviate the situation by calling out to us in a excited, shrill voice.

"Look Auntie Edith! We're nearly there! You will soon be able to see the masts!"

*

Helen and I caught up with Penny, who had stopped on another tight bend around the cliff wall, and as we joined her, I could see what she was getting so excited about. The path had now turned into a valley with the cliffs still reaching high up, like the ruins of the great wall of China, with a sunken floor below carpeted with ferns and tall dry, waving grasses. As the valley stretched further on, the rocky land gave way to lush, stretched out green fields, partitioned with wooden fences. A few flocks of sheep lay grazing in the fields with the highest fields giving way to dense, dark green forests shrouded in mystery and shadow. In one or two places there was to be found an occasional pile of rocks but as we walked away from the sea and went further inland the Jurassic cliffs and rocks became rolling hills and pastures. Beech, pine and oak trees stood proudly about in woods. Some stood silently on their own in the corners of fields, giving adequate shading and relief from the sun for the cattle who were either laying down for a nap or were congregating round metal feeding troughs. For all the beauty of this valley and the rolling countryside I still could not see these three masts that Penny kept getting so excited about. All I could see was grass, rocks, trees and herds of either cows or sheep. Intrigued and puzzled I asked Helen, who was now walking tiredly beside me.

"Helen what are these masts that Penny keeps on about? I can't see any masts?"

Helen smiled and softly said, "No you can't see them yet. Penny just gets a bit over excited. You will see them in a minute when we pass over the next hill."

"But what are they Helen? Are they ships' masts? Are there a few boats in the cove now?"

"I won't spoil the surprise, Edith. You'll soon see them, in a minute or two."

*

As Penny ran up ahead with new freedom within her and with no danger of falling off the cliff I thought how wonderful it was to be young and to have that energy and drive of youth. Penny was already well up on to the hill and had nearly reached the top as Helen and I began to walk up. As I looked up at Penny, who was jumping about like a hare, she suddenly leapt off down the other side of the hill and was out of sight. Helen and I reached the top and looked down upon a vast open expanse of fields with the track running through the middle. Woods and forests covered the high hills to the left with a more gentle, softer expanse of hills and banks on the right. A small dusty track ran up a high grassy bank up to a hill slightly eroded in places, revealing dry stony patches of earth. The track up to this hill looked as if it had been well used and walked up and down many times yet appeared to lead nowhere, except to give the climber an excellent view. As Helen and I carefully walked down our momentum quickening, I could see Penny franticly pointing up to the small expanse of hills and she called out in great excitement:

"Look Auntie Edith! Look, there's the three masts!"

As I looked in the direction that Penny was pointing too I could now indeed see why she was so excited and pleased at what lay at the top. Like a picture from out of a child's Bible and very much how I myself still imagined the crucifixion of Jesus to have been. For standing high up on the centre of the hill for all the world to see were not three wooden masts, but three carved crosses. The middle cross represented the cross Jesus was nailed to, and the other two crosses on either side represented the two convicted thieves that were crucified with him. The three crosses placed into the ground dominated the valley and the scene did look like a rural version of Golgotha.

The sight of the crosses and the tranquillity of this almost hallowed valley touched me deeply and I did not care if we went on down to the cove now. All I wanted to do was sit down and rest a while to enjoy the sight of the crosses on the hill. Thankfully, further up the track opposite a field of grazing Devonshire cows was a newly carved seat which was ideally placed to look over at the field and the three crosses. As we approached the bench I gestured to Helen to sit down for a few minutes. Penny sat on the grass and decided to make Helen and I a daisy chain. She scampered about picking daisies with her toy elephant, while Helen and I took the weight off our feet for a few minutes before continuing on to the cove. Helen sat tightly to the corner of the seat as if there was not enough room for the two of us. She still seemed very tense and looked very pensive.

I glanced over to the crosses, desperately hoping that the sight of the them would inspire in me the right words to give to Helen. Penny continued picking daisies. Later she rushed up with a buttercup wanting me to see if she liked butter, which we found out she did, as her chin glowed with a golden reflection from the flower. Penny then rushed off and continued gathering flowers up and began to form her first chain. When I was satisfied that Penny was well absorbed with her chain making and would not come bounding up to us for a few minutes I tried to engage Helen in conversation again.

"I can see why Penny gets so excited about the crosses. They are a very inspiring sight. What a wonderful, lovely idea."

Helen dejectedly looked up at the hill and gave a faint hearted, "Yes they're very nice."

I could see that she was still probably in great shock after the flood and losing Alexander. The reality of carrying on without him was already starting to hit her badly. "Who put the crosses up there then Helen. Was it St Mary's?" I enquired.

"No. I have a feeling it was the abbey down the road. They often are very proactive. I think they acted out the Passion play last year and left them up."

Helen suddenly turned from out of the corner of the seat and rather nervously asked me.

"Edith may I tell you something?"

Helen looked full of worry, as if she was about to make a confession.

"Yes of course you can Helen. You know you can always talk to me. You always used to years go." Helen faintly smiled at the mention of the past. The time when she had been courting Alexander and that reassuring time before the crash. Before everything changed.

"You must have been wondering why I was having some rather stern words with that officer this morning?"

"Oh you mean Officer Williams?" I said trying to make light of it. "That's none of my business Helen. But yes, if I'm being honest, I could not help but notice you weren't just passing the time of day with him."

Helen seemed surprised that I knew who Officer Williams was. I briefly explained to her that he had been concerned for me after I rushed off from hearing about Thelma and Emma. I told her that he found me up at the house and kindly arranged for me to go down to the harbour. I finished by telling Helen how helpful and kind he had been, but she shrugged and scoffed at my praise for him.

"I bet he was." Helen gave a deep scowl. Not aimed at me but more at her. She seemed cross and angry with herself. "Officer Williams always seems to come to the aid of distressed women."

I looked down at my hands, examining my bare fingers and looking at how lined my hands had become.

"Helen, what's the matter? Why were you and Officer Williams arguing this morning?"

Helen seemed to sink within herself. It was as if she had to find the answer to my question, which she had thrown deep within herself for years and up until now had never dug up.

"Officer Williams is Penny's father."

I quickly raised my head back up at Helen with a rather startled look on my face. Helen looked back at me with a crestfallen look. I was shocked and I suppose my face must have betrayed how I felt. I tried not to make any quick assumptions and give Helen time to tell me what had happened.

"Oh Helen. I am sorry. I did not realise."

Helen gave a strange modest smile, one of surprise at my non-judgmental response.

"Why should you know Edith. Like many people I expect you thought that Alexander and I were so blissfully happy and contented even though we could not have children."

I put a hand out to Helen and placed it on hers which felt rather cold for being such a nice day. Helen continued with her story.

"As soon as we were married I knew there was a problem. We tried and tried for years, but nothing happened. Course, typical man, it was all my fault! I was sent to Doctor Kenos and had the most dreadful tests done only to be told that there was no problem with me and that everything was as it should be."

"So what happened when you told Alexander what Doctor Kenos said?" I asked with a slight hesitation in my voice being careful what I asked and how I replied.

"I never told Alexander. I couldn't Edith. I loved him too much. I just told him that Doctor Kenos had said we wouldn't be able to have children together. I just could not bring myself to tell him that it was his fault. Well you remember him. He was such a proud man and I was afraid that if I told him he would walk off and leave me to find someone else. I could not risk that so I said nothing and pretended I was the one with the problem. To start with it was so hard. Every time we had an argument I could have told him that he was the one with the problem and not me. But I managed to keep it together and eventually we found we were happy just the two of us. We accepted the fact we would never have children together. In a way we grew closer. Then the bloody war started and everything changed. Alexander joined up and was posted off to France and I stayed here and tried to keep things running. I missed him so much Edith while he was away. I used to write nearly every day and he used to write me poetry with his letters. I went round the house talking to him all the time while he was gone. I think the neighbours thought I was cracking up constantly talking to myself. I promise you Edith, all the while he was gone I never ever looked at another man."

Helen sounded rather desperate that I understood that fact before she continued and I reassured her.

"I believe you Helen truly." I did indeed believe her. Helen had never been a flighty girl or played up to men. Helen was not that type of girl. She wearily continued on with her story, checking Penny was well out of earshot and busy gathering daisies.

"When the war ended and Alexander came back he was such a changed man. He was so angry with the war and returning home, being treated by everyone as if nothing had happened. All that hate and resentment built up within him and it came out on me. He started going on and on about how he wished I could have given him a son. He took it out on me all the time. I knew it wasn't really his fault, that he was just desperate for a child, for a distraction to help him forget all he had been through. Then one evening it all got too much. He was so abusive and so argumentative that I walked out and got myself truly drunk at The Rising Moon. I met a young soldier in there by the name of Andrew Williams. We got talking had a few drinks, followed by more drinks and one thing lead to another and well I don't need to tell you what happened next. The next day I felt so filthy. I was so disgusted with myself I could hardly look at myself in the mirror. Despite how people are nowadays I took my marriage vows seriously. Later on of course I found out that I was pregnant and Alexander was thrilled. I don't think I had ever seen him look so happy while I was expecting. He treated it like it was some miracle!"

Helen looked over towards Penny who was well on her way to completing her first chain. She seemed so happy and contented with no idea what her mother and I were discussing. She was in blissful ignorance.

"Penny saved our marriage Edith. If she hadn't come along then I dread to think what would have happened between me and Alexander."

I continued to watch Penny absorbed with her daisy chain, understanding now why I had seen no physical resemblance to Alexander in her. Yet she certainly took after Alexander for being contented in the little things of life. She showed that same thoughtful and polite manner that he had possessed.

"And Andrew had no idea about Penny?" I asked rather bemusedly.

"No. He left with the rest of his regiment. He treated it as a one night of fancy, nothing more and I never saw him again. Not until last Saturday when he oversaw the evacuation after the flood. When he saw Penny he looked rather suspicious at her and I knew he was putting two and two together. This morning he caught me on the steps of the hotel just as I was coming to meet you and demanded to know the truth. When I told him that Penny was his he looked so pleased. His wife can't have children apparently and he said he wanted to see Penny and get to know her. But I made it clear that, that was not possible and as far as Penny was concerned Alexander had been her father. He had brought her up and that was how I wanted it to remain.'

"I take it that Andrew didn't take it very well?"

"He got so upset. He spouted off that he was Penny's real father and that he had rights. That he wanted to meet her and be a part of her life!"

I thought for a few minutes, searching myself for the right advice to give. I strangely thought back to the Parade Gardens in Bath during the war where I had stumbled upon Jack and his grief stricken mother. Once again, years later, I was sat again on a bench on a beautiful sunny day trying to comfort another mother who could not come to terms with the cruel blow that life had thrown at her. All the while Penny, like Jack, had been was oblivious and unsure of what thoughts were running through her mother's mind. Penny only knew that her father, likes Jack's father, was now away and absent from her life. Helen looked back and gave Penny a wave then looked back to me. Her face was full of loss and confusion. "How can I go on Edith? How do I tell Penny that her father wasn't really her father and that her mother was… "

I interrupted Helen and took a firmer hold of her hand. "At the moment Helen, you and Penny need time to come terms with Alexander's death. You need time to grieve. At the end of the day, Andrew is Penny's father and like you said to me when I found out that Eddie was living down here, I would hate to think that Penny misses out on the chance to build up a relationship with him. I think you owe it to her and to yourself to give Penny the option one day."

I looked around the fields and looked at Penny who had now

completed her first chain. Her toy elephant was sat in the grass watching her. In the field opposite the Devonshire cows were swishing their tails and walking about, munching on the lush summer grass. High above them on the hill were the three crosses, or masts as Penny had called them.

"We all fall short in life in one way or another, Helen. Not one of us has gone through life without making bad choices. The thing is though, Helen it's never too late to change and to make a difference. You have to ask yourself if this situation was reversed and Alexander was here now instead of you what would he have done?"

Chapter 36
The Bell of Endurance

It was not at all how I had imagined it to be. I had put off coming here ever since I had arrived back in Lynrock. For I had feared what state I would find it in. I had dreaded that the stone would have begun to lean with erosion. That its letters would have begun to fade and become ingrained with years of dirt. I had seen in my mind a stone covered in ivy. Its surrounding grass all overgrown, almost waist high. I had dreamed of a stone never visited. Forgotten. Never having had any floral tributes or marks of respect.

My parent's grave, however, was the complete opposite. The stone was tall, upright and well cleaned. My parent's names, the dates of their births and deaths were still clearly visible, with no dirt, muck or lichen submerging it. The grass around the stone and indeed throughout the entire sloping cemetery was well kept and looked after. The trees and shrubs surrounding three of the sides of the consecrated ground looked respectable. The gates to the cemetery looked smart and well presented with the military plaques and memorials in its arch all well-polished and gleaming.

I stood. Then crouched. Then stood again for a while, reading and re-reading the words and letters on the grave. No matter how much time passes; no matter how long time marches relentlessly on with the world changing and re-shaping and one having to adapt to its changes, I still find myself missing my parent's. I looked upon the grave the way I had done when the ground had hardly settled and before my father's name was carved into the stone next to my mother's. I still could feel that draining empty sense of loss and felt like a stranger in a foreign land. For when one loses one's parents you suddenly realise that you are the next generation to come of age. You begin to look and feel your own mortality pressing upon you. As I crouched down again to readjust one of the pink roses in the tribute that I had arranged at the base of the stone, Eddie wiped away with a rag some white bird muck that had been deposited on the top of the stone. I stiffly stood up again and re-joined Eddie. He was also now looking upon it with a drained expression. I took hold of his hand and together we walked silently away down the mowed path, heading back towards the gate.

"You've done ever so well Eddie," I said softly with a hint of pride in my voice. "Keeping Mother and Father's grave up together. It's hardly changed since I saw it last."

We continued walking down until Eddie opened the solid wooden gate and allowed me to pass through first. Eddie watched me go through then followed himself. He shut the gate again firmly behind him.

"Father and I did not always see eye to eye on everything," Eddie confessed, "and at the time I did blame him for Marcus leaving. But all that's over with now. It's in the past. At the end of the day you can't blame your parent's for everything. They did their best and did what they thought was right at the time."

*

I took Eddie's arm and together we walked silently but contentedly down the road towards St Mary's church. As we approached the rain began again. Spitting at first. Then it became heavy. I pulled up my black umbrella and held it as high as I could over us both, until Eddie, being much taller than I, took it from out of my hand and held it over us both. St Mary's looked as it normally did; sleepy and silent. The only sound came from its bell ringing within its bell tower. A few bright dots of light shone through the horseshoe shaped arch windows revealing windows of stained glass. The Union Jack was flying at half-mast over the bell tower along with the flags at the Town Hall and down in the harbour. For this time last week Lynrock had been unaware of the dangers that were building up high in the valleys. A full week after the flood it was again raining. I imagined many in the village would have felt highly anxious at the sound of the rain drumming down on their rooftops again, those that still had a roof over their heads that is.

Eddie and I crossed the road passing the Valley of the Rocks Hotel unusually silent for a Friday morning. Many of the shops had closed leaving the streets eerily quiet and forlorn. Over the road the men's outfitter's blinds were drawn concealing their window display of summer suits. The flower shop was also closed with its tall metal vases of flowers brought in leaving the shop's frontage looking considerably bare. Over at St Mary's a small trail of villagers were shuffling in, being greeted and obliged to enter by the church steward. Eddie and I walked into the churchyard, and along a narrow path lined with dwarf conifers up into the porch. Eddie suddenly stopped. He pointed out to me an elderly man standing within the rows of headstones and Celtic crosses under the protection of a large yew tree that had created an impressive canopy over the corner of the graveyard. The man was wrapped up and covered in a heavy rain coat, with a dishevelled cap perched over his head. He was smoking a large pipe. Eddie gave an exaggerated nod of his head to him and the man reciprocated, pausing the frantic puffing of his pipe for a moment. I too gave a slight nod of acknowledgement yet the man looked uneasy at my presence and his strong looking posture failed him for a few minutes.

*

Eddie ushered me in towards the dry conditions of the porch where the church steward was waiting to welcome us. As Eddie began to lower the umbrella and allowed me to go into the porch first, my eyes drew back over to the gentlemen standing silently amongst the gravestones. He seemed to be paying close attention to me, watching me like an owl. His gaze never seemed to leave me. I took the umbrella from Eddie and told him to go on in and save me a seat next to him at the back of the church, where no one would pay much notice to us. Eddie seemed surprised at my request but agreed to do as I asked. He proceeded to shake the hand of the steward and he calmly entered the church. With my umbrella in hand, dripping with the rain, I walked over across the damp and slippery grass, manoeuvring my way through the graves and headstones towards the waiting and silent Billy. He still continued to smoke and puff away like a trooper on his pipe. I adjusted my umbrella over the back of my head so I was able to look at Billy properly. As I came up to him he slowly lowered his pipe and licked his cracked yellowish lips.

"I did tell you didn't I," Billy began, sounding like a father about to give his daughter that well known lecture and famous words of 'I told you so,' "I did warny, that you would find a lot more than a missing friend down here. I suppose he's told you the full story now as he? About what really happened?"

I looked up at Billy with the rain hammering down on my umbrella, with the freshness and clarity of rain and damp grass smothering the summer air.

"Yes Billy. Eddie's told me what happened to Rogers and the house. I am sorry about Rogers."

Billy snorted. He took his cap off from his grey and brittle strands of hair and shook off the many droplets of rain. He then flung his cap back upon his head.

"I don't need your sympathy missy. What I need is your assurance that you won't go telling nobody else about my nephew's misfortune. The lad suffered enough while he was alive. At least let him be at peace now. I know what you women are like. You can't never keep anything to yourselves!"

"You have nothing to fear from me Billy," I began. "As you said, Rogers, Simon I mean, suffered enough during his life. I have no wish to cause you or Mathew any more grief. I think for Simon's memory and for your peace of mind it's best we all forget about what we know and allow the secret to die with us."

Billy gave a huge sigh of relief. His eyes that had displayed such tension now looked suddenly calm. "And as for sympathy, I think I owe you far more than that Billy. Both you and Dorothy."

Billy looked suddenly surprised and rather quizzical.

"What do ye mean?"

"Both you and Dorothy took Eddie in and got him back on his feet again after you found him alone and half dead by Hunter's Inn. You were there for him when I was absent and for that you have my deepest gratitude and thanks. I hope I will be able to repay you one day."

Billy gave a weary shake of his head and smiled slightly, revealing a set of blackened and yellow stained teeth.

"You just do as you promised and keep what you know to yourself. That's remuneration enough for me. As for your brother, I was happy to help. Your brother helped me and Mathew with Simon. It was the least I could do."

Billy paused as I lowered my head, thinking to myself how fortunate Eddie had been that Billy had come along in his cart when he did and found him. Billy sounded suddenly more his artful, blunt self.

"I suppose you will be off now and back to your garden in Wiltshire?"

The mention of home and my garden again, and knowing that I had found Eddie, raised my spirit. As I smiled I noticed the rain drops pattering on my umbrella lessen and the sound of the birds began to out way the sound of the summer shower.

"Yes Billy, don't worry, only a few hours to go and you will have seen the last of me!"

Billy grunted and gave a slight laugh. "Well good luck to you. I am glad you found that brother of yours again."

I smiled, "Yes so am I, Billy. Are you not coming in for the service?" I asked with an expression of hope in my voice as I did not fancy going in alone, for the last time I had entered the church it had been walking behind Father's coffin. Somehow that association made me feel rather uneasy, almost uncertain of whether I could actually enter the church and endure the service.

Billy grunted and gave a quick puff of his pipe before answering.

"I'm afraid I lost my faith when I saw our Simon hanging from the top of your stairs. No, I leave the church to me brother. He's still got it but I prefer to stay away now."

"I understand Billy. Perhaps another time then."

I extended out my hand to Billy, which he took and shook rather feebly.

"Goodbye Billy, and thank you."

Billy gave a grunt and muttered in his usual manner and gave me a short thrift of a smile. I walked back to the path still feeling fearful of entering the church. The steward was just about to close the door before he took his seat but saw me coming just in time as if he was expecting me. Part of me wanted to go back to the Chough's Nest. I felt so worried about entering the church, fearing the memories of Father's funeral would return to haunt me. As I approached the triangular Saxon door of the church which was being kept open for me by the kindly timid steward, I told myself to get a grip. That if I could not enter God's church without feeling on edge then it showed a poor reflection in my faith. Still feeling rather heavy hearted but forcing myself to enter, the steward escorted me into the light and cool church.

*

As I went in the steward closed the church door as if to guarantee that I had to stay and could not leave. I stood still, frozen to the stone floor of the lobby. A wooden dresser of Bibles, music sheets and song books was pushed to the back wall of the lobby, and a church noticeboard plastered with leaflets and statements decorated the wall. A fund raising jar was placed on a table nearest the door collecting money for the third world. The steward after sealing the door, bid me to go on through and in a hushed tone informed me that a seat had been reserved for me at the front row of the church. I suddenly felt rather sick and my tummy felt like it had turned round like a tombola. I was about to try and inform the steward that I already had a seat with my brother at the back of the church, but the steward seemed to usher me forward into the nave. The church design comprised of early English gothic styled pillars, with medieval looking mouldings at their peeks. I was forced to begin the walk through the aisle of pews, full to the brim with villagers and a collection of Sunday best hats warn by the ladies. The church was as still and as silent as it had been at Father's funeral. Only an occasional cough or sneeze, or the sound of someone turning the pages of their hymn book broke the peace. As I proceeded down what seemed like a never ending aisle, with my heels clicking along the tiled stone floor, I headed up toward the raised alter with a beautifully carved oak balustrade separating it. Two stone steps lead up to a glittering altar bathed in a white almost heavenly light, which was pouring through the great stained glass window, depicting the resurrection of Christ. A golden cross and candle sticks decorated the altar, with a medieval pattered cloth underneath. I tried to look straight ahead resisting the temptation to observe if I knew any of the seated congregation. Out of the corner of my eyes I could see a mass of turning heads full of surprise as I wondered down the aisle to take my seat. I felt almost like a bride preparing to join her intended at the altar. When at long last I reached the front of the church the steward behind me manoeuvred round towards the steps to the altar and steered me into the front row pew on the right. The pew seemed void of people apart from Eddie who was sat on the very far end nearest a golden eagle lectern. I was so glad to see a familiar face but could not understand how Eddie and I had been put at the front in what was our old family pew where Father, Mother, Eddie and I had sat every time we attended church. I walked down to sit next to Eddie who also looked rather bemused and even more pleased to see me than I was to see him. I adjusted myself in an upright pew with a prayer rail in front of us with prayer cushions hanging below. The steward gave a pleasant smile and took up his seat on the other side of the church and waited for Rev Heath to come out of the vestry. I bowed my head and prayed for a few moments then after I had finished turned to Eddie and quickly whispered to him. "What are we up here for?"

Eddie, trying to look natural and composed, turned his head and whispered, "I don't know. Not my idea. I was just escorted up here like you were."

As we waited for Reverend Heath I looked around the church. St Mary's had not changed. The red leather pew Bibles were the same, as well as the blue leather hymn books. The lectern was still standing where it had always stood, with the war memorial plaque on the wall behind it. Sadly this had changed. For more names had been added to it since I had last seen it sat in this pew. I thought back to Father's funeral. The day when I had sat in this very pew alone. Yet today the pew was not empty. This time I was not sitting alone. I had Eddie with me. The church seemed hushed into an unsteady silence with not even a whisper from anyone. The mood was one of a deep loss and uncertainty just as the service had been during the war in Bath after the Blitz. That same feeling of shock, desperation and a yearning need for reassurance and answers to why the world seemed to be falling into darkness and where God was to be found in all this? Unlike other services there was no sound of the organ accompaniment. Just a simple peace and stillness with the brilliant glow of white light beaming through the arched glass windows and from the old oil lanterns converted for electricity.

*

From a small door on the left of the church came Reverend Heath, along with his counterpart Reverend Wheeler, from the Baptist church. Today both churches, though different in their worship would for today worship and morn together. Reverend Wheeler giving Reverend Heath an encouraging look of confidence, went and sat down in a Cromwellian chair by the lectern. Reverend Heath moved to the front of the church to begin the start of the service. Reverend Heath had, in a former life been Wiltshire born and bread. He had in fact come from Bath and had worked for many years in one of the parish churches. He then moved down here to Lynrock to become the vicar of St Mary's. It had been he who had advised Eddie and I to make a fresh start away from Devon after Father had died and his bad debts revealed. And it had been him who had suggested that Eddie and I going to live in Bath. Reverend Heath had aged as we all had, but his love of God and of Devon had not diminished. He had lived in Devon for many years now but during that time had never yet lost his lovely broad Wiltshire accent. He possessed the type of accent that can be found on a Wiltshire farm and not in a small Devon parish church. He was a somewhat larger looking man than I remembered him to be. His hair had always been thick but had now gone a dark grey. He had a Goliath figure with thick strong arms and a large loveable face, which seemed always to look cheerful and contented even in the bleakest of times. He certainly had the look of a born again Christian and this brilliant optimism and love for Christ always had come through in his sermons. This service was no exception.

"On behalf of Reverend Wheeler and myself," Reverend Heath

began, "I would like to extend to you a very warm welcome to St Mary's church. It is very heartening to see these pews full to their capacity, something I don't think I have seen for rather some time. Not since the funeral of Lord Parffit have we had such a full church. To those of you who are new to these parts or are visiting with us here for the first time, Lord Parfitt was once our local MP and our village's greatest friend and benefactor. It was my very great fortune to know him when I first arrived down here as a somewhat younger, slimmer looking man. In my first interview with Lord Parffit I was most struck by his warmth and his great knowledge and experience of life down here. But above all his love of God which was so easily seen in how he treated his fellow man. For Lord Parffit had a glorious love of Devon and a devotion and service to its people that knew no bounds. I speak with great certainty that if Lord Parffit had been living today he would have been one of the first to open up his home and offer all those who had been affected by this terrible flood a place of shelter. Very tragically his life was cut short, much sooner than it should have been."

Both Eddie and I bowed our heads as low as looked respectable. Both of us found the mention of father hard to cope with. That raw pain of loss came back again and that stormy night in the saloon, when inspector Martin had broken the news to me of Father's death, replayed again in my mind like an old record on the wireless.

"However. I am delighted to say that today sat with us are both Lord Parffit's son, Mr Edward and his daughter, Lady Edith who has come all the way from my old stomping ground of Wiltshire to be with us today."

Both Eddie and I raised up our heads at the mention of our names and as Reverend Heath continued talking he walked slowly down the steps from the raised altar and approached us with an expression of deep affection and warmth.

"We give you both a very warm welcome." Reverend Heath was suddenly halted as a member of the congregation suddenly started to clap. I looked around to try and see who the person was but I was unable to see due to the rows of villagers crammed into the tiny pews. The view was more difficult to study with the row upon rows of heads and hats masking the perpetrator of the clapping. As I turned back round to

Reverend Heath, feeling rather embarrassed, he too looked surprised at the clapping but had a secret delight written over his face. He gave a nod of approval before he to joined the lonely clapper. In quick succession Reverend Wheeler joined in followed by another person in the congregation followed by another and another. With no word or further prompting the entire congregation suddenly joined in and clapped. As I turned to look at Eddie, who looked rather taken a back, the entire congregation got to their feet and continued clapping in a standing ovation, something that had never happened before. I slipped my hand into Eddie's and in that moment I knew that Father and all the good he had done in his life had not been forgotten. No epitaph could have been better to acknowledge Father and our family.

*

The rest of the service was taken by Reverend Wheeler who at the end took the collection and then handed the final address back over to Reverend Heath. He plodded back up to the altar carrying a brown wicker basket in his hand which he put down behind the rail of the altar. Reverend Heath turned to face the congregation and delivered the sermon of his life.

"My friends. As we close our memorial service and we return to our homes, for some of us we return to our temporary places of evacuation. For others we go home with friends who have taken us in during our misfortune. Sadly, for some of us, we go home alone without the company of our loved ones. As I look upon you all now I can see the faces that are not here. I can see the people who would have been here, but who have now gone to be with our Lord. We think and pray especially for the two Australian girls, Jennifer and Karen, who many of us had enjoyed seeing round our village. Both girls had such a warmth about them and no two girls could have been more excited to be on holiday in England. The girls were only in their early twenties and were due to go home on the 17th. I bid you to remember their parents and family in Australia in your prayers. We also think of young Emma and her mother Thelma, who were both so excited to start a new life working at Sally's Tea room. We think of

Alexander, who worked at the mineral water factory for more years than I can remember, who leaves behind Helen and Penny. Many of our dear friends are not here with us. Our little community has been severely weakened and brought to a sudden and unwelcome period of shock, grief and despair. Like many of you during the last few days I have looked upon the casualty list of the dead and the missing. I have seen the destruction that nature has unleashed upon us. I have looked around at the many views and building that have been changed and been brought down. You are not alone when you ask why? Where is our Lord in all this?"

*

The church fell into a silence. The congregation including myself all pondered on that very question. Why? The silence was only broken by the sniffs and pitiful tears of grief. Many tried desperately not to cry in public and to keep their 'stiff upper lip' but in this instance they were unable to do so.

Reverend Heath then went over to his basket and picked it up. He carried it over to the centre of the gap in the rail. He stood at the top of the steps and slowly took out what looked like a smeared and dented bell.

"My friends. This bell was found by one of the army personnel who have been helping to clear away the wreckage down in the harbour yesterday. When the soldier found this bell he thought little of it. He thought it was just a bell from one of the fishing boats that been destroyed. But as he examined the bell more clearly and gave it a clean and removed the dirt and sand, he noticed that there was a word carved into the side. I will turn the bell round for you so you can take a closer look at the word that is engraved on its side."

As Reverend Heath turned the bell round, Eddie and I like the rest of the congregation all shuffled forward in our seats peering and squinted towards the bell to try and read the word. "For those of you at the back who cannot see the word carved into this bell I will read it out to you." Reverend Heath paused. His voice stuttered for a moment before he could continue.

"The word engraved upon this bell is," after another pause and a breath he finally read the name of the bell. "Endurance."

I, like the rest of the congregation felt astonished. Some in the congregation sat back in their pews in utter amazement. Some were full of emotion and continued sobbing even louder than they had done. Reverend Heath crept down the steps still carrying the bell of endurance. He paused his progression and stood level with the rest of the congregation in the centre of the aisle.

"I believe that this bell is a sign to all of us that our Lord has not forsaken us. For those of us that have lost so much I say to you look to this bell and know that you will endure. For those of you who may not have been directly affected by the flood but come to this church full of worries and fear. For those that are suffering in pain whether it be physical or mental, I say, look to this bell and know that with the strength of our Lord Jesus Christ we will overcome. We will endure."

*

Following the service a few hours later, as the afternoon drew to a close, I made my way along a wet path passing once again the abandoned allotments and gardens with my old trusty suitcase in hand. My handbag at long last felt much lighter after I had handed to Reverend Wheeler the donations and words from all the members of my church back in Wiltshire. Reverend Wheeler had been very touched by their kind gesture and said that the donation would be greatly appreciated and would be put to good use. At the Chough's Nest I had paid my bill at the reception desk assuring Mrs Barns that I had so enjoyed my stay with them despite the circumstances. I thanked her for her wonderful cooking and for being able to accommodate me at such short notice. Alfred brought down my case for me and I gave him a tip which he was highly delighted with. Thankfully. I had missed the exodus of Norman. His wife had driven down from Oxford and collected him while we were at the service. Mrs Barns implied that Norman's wife seemed quite a strong character and as soon as she had arrived he was marched out the door like a school boy. Alfred relayed to his mother that he had seen Norman opening the driver's door of the car for his wife and seemed to be in a grovelling and very humble state. Perhaps Norman's life was not what he pretended it to be. I said my goodbyes to both Mr and Mrs Barns and handed the key in to Hannah, remembering my arrival when Hannah had been desperate to give me a key when I had not even checked in. The Barns seemed a very homely and decent family and I had to say I was sorry to part from them. I walked out of the Chough's Nest with my two bags in hand where Helen was waiting for me on the road.

"I thought I had better come and see you off Edith," she shouted up at me as I walked down the steps of the terrace. "I hope I did not embarrass you, clapping like that in the service?"

I reached the bottom of the sloping walk from the Chough's Nest and greeted Helen with a warm kiss as I got on to the road, rather surprised by her confession.

"It was you who started the clapping?" It was very out of character for her to show such emotion in public.

"Well I could not help myself Edith. It was a long time overdue."

"Where's Penny?" I asked. Rather disappointed that she was absent.

"Penny sends you her love. She's spending an hour with her father."

I looked at Helen, somewhat stunned that she was allowing such a meeting between Penny and Officer Williams. Helen must have seen the surprise in my face.

"I know. I was so cross with him the other day and I know I told him he didn't have any right to ask to see Penny. But as you said, he is Penny's father and like Reverend Heath said, no matter how difficult we find life we have to trust that things will turn out alright. I think Alexander would have wanted me to do what was best for Penny."

I gave Helen a great big hug and kissed her again. "I'm glad Helen. I know it can't have been an easy decision. I think in the long run though you will look back on this and know you have done the right thing."

*

After an emotional farewell and a few more hugs and kisses, I walked along the road getting closer to St Mary's church yard wall and the mighty looking building of the Valley of the Rocks Hotel. As I reached the high street the shops were opening up again after closing for the service for an afternoon of sparse trade. I spotted the last and most important person I had to say goodbye to. As I approached Eddie dressed in what must have been his only suit kept for Sunday best, he looked down at my case and teased me.

"You certainly travel much lighter than you used to!"

I looked down at my case and laughed.

"Oh you mean this. Oh don't worry Eddie. I sent my five trunks on ahead!"

I put my case down on the ground and smiled again at Eddie. He smiled warmly back but for both of us they were false smiles and underneath we both knew that once again we were about to be parted. We were trying to make the moment last for as long as possible. I started babbling about how nice it was that the rain had stopped and what a lovely service it had been. My voice became more and more anxious and charged, until tears began to well up in my eyes. Eddie, realising the goodbye was proving too much for me, came over and threw himself round me and held me tightly.

"Hey come on old girl. This isn't goodbye. We shall see each other in a few months. As soon as I have helped things a little bit further on here I will be back with you in no time. It's only a few months away. That time will fly by."

I sobbed into his jacket. "It won't Eddie! The time will drag and seem like forever."

"I will write to you every week, Edith. I promise. I'll be able to tell you all the news and let you know how Helen and Penny are doing. By the time you've got your spare room cleared out for me it will only be a month until I'll be with you."

Eddie looked up at the sound of a horse and cart clattering down the road coming in our direction. Eddie composed himself and bid me to do the same.

"Come on now Edith. Don't show Billy that you've been crying. You know how he is. You don't want to ruin that image of being a Joan of Arc now do you?"

I looked up from Eddie's jacket which had become a little wet and stained from my tears. He got out a hanky and helped me to dry my eyes and encouraged me to take some deep breaths. The noise of a horse and cart was coming closer. I looked round towards the Valley of the Rocks Hotel and saw the familiar sight of Billy smoking away sat up on his cart, with Jacob walking steadily along in front of him swishing his mane. I turned to Eddie who gave Billy a wave.

"I don't understand Eddie? I was going to catch the bus?"

Eddie gave me one of his artful looks.

"I thought you would like to have some happy and cheerful company on your journey back. So I thought of Billy. I know what firm friends you have become."

Billy and Jacob clattered up towards us and paused. Billy looked his customary miserable self. Eddie put my case up onto the cart and did his best to get me off before my departure proved to much for him too.

"Come on now Edith. It's time you were off." Eddie gave a sniff and his chin wobbled. "Come on or you'll get me started!"

Eddie tried to put on a brave face for me but I could see he was as sad as I was, and looked like he was very close to tears. We both gave each other one final hug and kiss and held each other for some time until Billy shouted down from the cart in a blunt and sarcastic tone.

"Don't you worry, Edith! I have all the time in the world! Me and Jacob will just stand here till tomorrow and then will set off again. I don't know you females you can't do anything without making a production out of it!"

"I'm just coming Billy!" I shouted back at him with as much vigour and determination as I could muster. Billy looked down at me, amused that I was able to stand up to him and show some spirit.

As Eddie wiped away tears from his eyes and helped me up onto the cart, he gave instructions to Billy to drive carefully and to take good care of me. Billy replied in yet another sarcastic tone and puff of smoke from his pipe. "You want to bloody drive do you Eddie?"

*

As Billy marched Jacob up the road I looked back at Eddie, waving goodbye to him for as long as possible until Jacob walked past the old stables of the hotel. We went round the tight bend of the bank and tea shop until Eddie disappeared from view. I turned round and faced the front of the cart to look upon Jacob's head and perked up ears twitching away. I wiped away the last of my tears and did my best not to produce any more. As Jacob walked on we past the road that ran along up the side of the Town Hall and up to the jungle of Hallowed Hill, where the ruins of my former home stood in isolation waiting for its delayed but eventual demolition. Somehow the thought of the house being pulled down no longer filled me with dread. Thelma had been right in her letter: *It was just a ruin now. The house I had known and loved had been gone long ago.* Thinking of the house, Rogers break down and Eddie I suddenly thought of one last thing that I still wanted to try and put right. There was still one person who was still missing from our lives and needed to be found. I turned round to Billy who was puffing away on his pipe and looked like he was driving us to be guillotined.

"Billy, I don't suppose on our way to the station we will be passing near to Hunter's Inn?" Billy looked despairingly at me and jutted his head back.

"You see them in the back there."

I turned my head back and looked down at the back of the cart. It was full with silver grimy milk churns. I turned back round to Billy.

"Yes I see them."

Billy puffed on his pipe again and blew out a cloud of smoke. "Well them lot in the back, my dear, don't deliver themselves to Hunter's Inn do they? That's why your brother talked me into taking you to the station as it was on my way. I'm not taking you just for the love of it my dear!"

"And there was me thinking you just wanted to take me because you enjoy my company!" I said in amusement.

Billy grunted "Hmm. The only company I enjoy is this here horse of mine and that's only because he can't start singing or gossiping or bursting into tears at the drop of a hat. Or start yelling at me to tidy up the bloody house. What do you want to go to Hunter's Inn for then? Don't tell me you want another bowl of that bloody muck old Hunter calls porridge!"

I smiled and brushed some dust off my skirt and readjusted myself in the seat.

"No I don't want any more of that porridge Billy. I just have to ask Mr Hunter to undertake a favour for me. It's something very important. I want to try and put something right."

Billy grunted again, coughed and said dryly, "God help him then. Every time I ever lay eyes on you, you seem to want some lift somewhere at the most bloody awful time. Or you want something doing. You women! You're all the same! Never happy unless you're interfering in something!"

Chapter 37

I Thought I Would Come Home Early

Wiltshire's sky seemed smothered with thick towels of grey dull clouds, which had shut out the August sunshine and gave one the impression that autumn had begun in earnest. A sharp breeze had unsettled the trees, rattling their summer foliage and shivering their trunks embroidered with a thick cladding of ivy. The bus drove down into the heart of the village making no hurry past The Red Dragon pub. The chipped and faded sign board swung with the breeze on its bracket high above the door. The Victorian lamps on either side of the entrance were not yet lit to welcome the village regulars and the darts team. The bus continued down the high street, past the terraces of crooked looking cottages and leaning shops, towards my school all closed up and silent. Finally the bus reached the finishing line and swung round to its stop in front of the sculpted bath stone of the war memorial. I continued sitting on the bus for a few seconds, glued to my arched leather seat, preparing to gather myself together before disembarking, but felt reluctant to stand as both my feet felt like they had gone to sleep. I gazed out of the nearest window that I had been fixated on since we left Bath.

The view and surroundings that my eyes now fell upon were all once again familiar to me and gave me no licence to feel undeterred by them. Somehow though, I could feel no overwhelming joy to be back among the comforting surroundings of home. In a way it felt rather strange to be back here again. I often think how odd it is when you leave a place for a few days, perhaps on a holiday, foolishly expecting something to have altered during your absence. Then when you finally return home you are put in your place by realising that life has carried on regardless without you. The world you temporarily left has not ceased to exist. It was the same now. Everything was just as I left it.

I know I had only been gone for a few days, not even a week, yet somehow it seemed more like a month. So much had happened during my return to Devon. The few days I spent submerged back into my past had reopened memories and feelings that I thought I would never have to confront again. A deep penetrating chill had sunk into my skin and bones, as I tensely clambered down from the bus. I retrieved my cases from the boot. The odious bus driver did as little as possible to assist and scowled at me for taking so long. I desperately wanted to cry as I witnessed my cases being manhandled by the dastardly man, who plunged them down onto the pavement as if they were crates of unwanted bric-a-brac.

I looked up towards the high street and the warn stone market cross situated in front of my school. The Red Dragon's windows were now lit up with a jaundice yellow light drawing my eyes to the top of the high street, as Trevor the landlord was preparing to open up for the evening. A little further down the street the post office blinds had been pulled down, with a crooked sign at an untidy angle reading 'closed' in the window of the glazed door. Old Anne Dottie's book shop next door had its shutters encasing the windows with the bound leather books and paper backs kept secured until Monday morning, when Dotty would plod out and open up again.

*

The boot of the bus was suddenly slammed with a bone shattering thud, breaking the spell of peace and stillness of the village. The breeze continued to ripple down the high street and a haze of dust and dishevelled leaves trickled along the pavement heading towards us and the war memorial behind. Several strands of hair fluttered across my face from under the security of my hat, tickling my nose and obstructing my vision for a few moments until I brushed them up behind my ear. I witnessed the driver doff his cap, bark a good evening to me, and then promptly plod back up the steps onto his bus and prepare to get underway. I made little attempt to make my hair look more presentable, it now resembled rat's tails and felt grimy from the journey. I cared little for my appearance this evening. I was far too tired to give a fig what I looked like. All I wanted to do was get home, hide away for the evening in my armchair, and read the letter from Gloucester that I was convinced would be waiting for me on the companion table in the hall where Madeleine would have reliably placed it.

*

I watched the bus disappear back up the high street, yet I had not noticed it depart or even heard the engine start up. I felt in such a daze and motionless, as if I was suffering from concussion. As I looked about my village, I watched curtains being drawn and blinds being pulled down. Lights were switched on, perhaps in preparation for an evening indoors listening to the wireless or playing a game of bridge. In the distance I could hear the chilled moans of Farmer Richards' sheep grazing in the field that climbed up behind the war memorial. Ahead a horse and cart had paused its round and stopped outside The Red Dragon where Slades were unloading their barrels of beer. The delivery was being checked and supervised by a hunched over Trevor, who was always meticulous for checking in orders. Seeing the sight of Slades' horse and cart reminded me of Billy Bath and Jacob.

*

Billy had done as he promised and taken me to Hunter's Inn, then later left me at the station just in time to catch my train home. It had been a better journey leaving Devon than it had been going, and deep down I knew I was grateful to be going home, knowing that Eddie would be joining me in a few weeks' time. Yet my return home had been marred by what I had discovered at Hunter's Inn, and I desperately wished I had never asked Billy to take me back to that remote place.

My thoughts of Hunter's Inn and the journey home were suddenly jolted as the church bell struck, sending a gathering of pigeons up into the sky who flew over the village street and turned to take up new posts on the school roof. Realising that curtains would be twitching, and the pub awash with news of my return; no doubt everyone was observing me looking like a wreck, standing in the road alone. I wearily went to pick up my cases which were still glued to the ground were they had been flung down by the bus driver. I tried to coil my hand around the handle of my battered leather case. It fitted back into my cold, numb hand. I then went to pick up the second case, only this case did not belong to me. It was in my ownership, but it was not mine to open and I would not open it until Eddie came home. It was only right that he should be the one to open Marcus's case and go carefully through his meagre things. I picked up the dated and dusty case, and with my own in the other hand along with my handbag, I began to walk solemnly down past the war memorial towards Folly Lane and home.

*

I walked in a kind of trance, not noticing that I had gone past the thick iron gates of the cemetery with its two impressive conifer trees flanking the entrance. Their top branches appeared to defy the breeze that had disturbed the August evening. A trail of leaves had carpeted the sides of the pavement and began to build against the side of the leaning dry stone wall of the cemetery. As I got past the entrance to that depressing place, full of graves and wonky looking stones with their occupants' names weathered by the elements, I could not help but feel a deep sense of despair, not for myself or my own life, but for all that had happened to Eddie and Marcus and how tragically their plans had all come undone. When Eddie had told me that he and Marcus had planned to meet at Hunter's Inn and then leave from there together, I convinced myself that the inn should be the place for me to start my enquiries. I knew it was a long shot, but I needed to know what had become of Marcus, whether Mr Hunter had any recollection of him arriving in the December of 1929 and if he did, how long had he stayed? Had he left a note for Eddie on how to contact him? Tragically, when Billy and I arrived back at Hunter's Inn and I broached the last month of 1929 with Mr Hunter, he only too clearly remembered what had occurred that month. Marcus had indeed got to Hunter's Inn and booked himself in for two nights. Mr Hunter double checked with his ledger for that year and remembered booking Marcus in. He recalled how troubled his guest had looked. He remembered the gentleman had sat out on the porch in the rocking chair in the evening staring into space. When I asked Mr Hunter how he was so sure it had been Marcus, Mr Hunter showed me the room he had been booked in. The ledger read quite clearly, that Marcus had been booked into room five. It had been Marcus who had died in room five all those year ago, apparently from a heart attack. Mr Hunter had tried to trace his relatives but discovered he had none. All Marcus had known and loved was his life as secretary to Father and of course his love for Eddie. Mr Hunter had kept his belongings in the attic where it had remained lost and forgotten until he had placed it into my ownership yesterday. I had explained that Marcus had been in my Father's employment and that I knew of one relative who would dearly love to have something of his to remember him by. Mr Hunter was most obliging and had handed the case over to me at once. Yet although I had it and was carrying it home, I knew I could not bare to open the case. That difficult task could only be done by Eddie. I realised now, that I had cast a judgement on Eddie and Marcus. At the time I thought it was the correct and proper thing to do. But now the issue seemed so trivial. I realised that I had been wrong. I had made the wrong judgement and I would have to live with that fact and its consequences.

As I continued walking past the walls of the cemetery up to the picket gate that ran into the allotments, I was at an utter loss to what I would tell Eddie. With each step I took I had less energy to keep walking. All I could do was to keep my head up, look straight ahead and plod on carrying my two cases. Yet as I walked I contemplated why things had turned out the way they did. Why could life not have worked out for Eddie and Marcus when all they had wished for was to be happy? Why could I not have given Eddie better support when he needed it? If I had, things may have turned out so differently. With the feeling of hopelessness gaining more space within me and just when I wanted to stop walking, put my cases down and pause up against the wall of the allotments, I found myself doing just that. Not on account of feeling hopeless and tired, but more with a sense of wonderment and surprise! For to the side of me, perched on top of the allotment's dry stone wall, looking like he had been waiting for me to walk past, sat a very well loved brown teddy bear with beautiful eyes. I say the bear was well loved, for its right paw was missing and it had been treated as if it had been a casualty of war, because someone had placed a piece of white cloth around his torn thread and stuffing creating an ideal bandage. I put down my two cases on the dusty pavement and laid my handbag on top of the wall. I picked up the teddy and examined it closely. Then quickly and rather urgently I peered into the enclosure of the allotment. It was a large plot slightly sloping, with a boundary surrounded by thick hedges and apple trees. I looked around in all directions of the garden feeling a little panicky, for the teddy I was now clutching against my chest was well known to me and apart from its damaged paw the bear had changed little since I met him and his owner in the Parade Gardens in Bath during the war. I rushed to undo the latch of the green picket gate and entered the allotment along with the breeze. It rushed through the hedges around the garden and disturbed the family of hens who were all chattering away to each other, scratching at the ground and meandering about with no thought or purpose. I approached the smart regimented row of runner beans near the Victorian span greenhouse and then carefully went on past the terracotta rhubarb pots heading towards the bickering and clucking hens, by now penned into their enclosure for the evening. Suddenly a young excited voice called out to me.

"Mummy! You're back!"

Through the mass of heart shaped leaves and bright red and orange bean flowers rushed out, two young boys dressed as Indian chiefs, wearing brown sacks made into trousers, matching tops and massive headdress in full plumages of white and coloured feathers.

I knew both children instantly. The eldest was one of my old pupils Adam Berry. The other was my own son Jack. Seeing my Jack after what had been nearly a week of absence made both my legs almost give way.

I sunk down towards the grass path with tears of delight and joy welling up in my eyes and then trickling down my face as Jack ran into my open arms. So overjoyed I was to see Jack that I ended up giving Adam a hug too, and both boys were scooped up in my arms for quite some time. Finally, after what must have been only seconds, Adam pulled away from me looking rather sheepish. Jack followed his example a few minutes later although a little more reluctantly.

"Jack what are you doing here?" I asked, wiping up my tears and trying to find out why he was still not in Gloucester with his Auntie Eileen and Uncle Charles, who had been due to keep him until Monday. Jack looked up at me with his large amber eyes complemented by his long luscious eyelashes. His round little face looked full and healthy, but he had a bewildered look upon him.

"I am sorry Mummy. I was feeling rather homesick. I got your letter that you posted to me in Bath and knew you would be coming home today so Auntie Eileen dropped me off with Auntie Madeleine. Auntie Eileen would have stopped to see you but she had to get back to Uncle Charles, as his new restaurant is fully booked until Monday. Adam came round for me only about an hour ago and Auntie Madeleine said we could come and play Indians in here until you got home." Jack looked suddenly worried.

"You're not cross with me are you Mummy, for coming home early? Only I have missed you so much and Auntie Eileen was tickity boo about it." I quickly gave Jack another hug, which this time seemed even tighter and stronger than before. Once again he had that wonderful smell about him that children often have when after their born.

"No my lovely I'm not cross with you at all. I'm overjoyed to see you."

After reassuring him I turned to Adam and had a little chat with him while Jack held tightly to my hand.

"So Adam how are you then?" I enquired, still rather amused to see him with Indian war paint plastered all over his face. Jack did not have any on as he never liked having a grubby face.

"Oh I'm alright, thank you Miss Edith. Glad to have Jackie back again though. I've been all on my own since you went down to Devon and Jackie went to stay with his auntie and uncle. I can tell you Miss Edith it's been dashed boring these last few days."

Adam gave Jack a beaming and rather rascally looking smile which Jack returned and both boys looked as artful as a wagon load. Adam had been in my class last year and was now due to start secondary school next month. He had been a good student and very able (when he applied himself), but he had a fondness for daydreaming, and was constantly talking at the most inappropriate times. And he had made an art form out of distracting Jack. Yet I was quietly pleased that my Jack and Adam got on so well. Adam found it hard to make friends, in fact his only real friend was my Jack and it was a blessing that they would both be starting secondary school together.

"I suppose I had better call you High Chief Berry?" I said humorously.

After a few more words with Adam, negotiating the time when both he and Jack had to be in by, I left the two Indian Chiefs to their own devices for another half an hour. I made sure Jack understood that he had to be home on time and no later, and told Adam that he had to go home to his mother at the same time.

I was so grateful to know that Jack was home and that tonight I would have my son sleeping next door to me. I was also grateful to both Jack and Adam, as children have an uncanny gift of picking you up when you feel down. I picked up my cases along with Frank the teddy bear and, feeling much more assured, I eagerly set off in the direction of home.

*

As the stone wall of the allotment crumbled away and turned to a thick hedge with pink fluffy dog roses growing rampant through it, I heard the chug and rumble of Farmer Richards' tractor up ahead. Sure enough as I passed the entrance to the organised chaos that was his yard I observed Farmer Richards sat on his new Fordson Major Tractor. He was reversing it into its parking space beside the dilapidated barns of junk. I did call out to him, and attempted to wave with my case and Frank flying up with my hand, but he was too engrossed with his parking. I did not want to distract him in case he drove his new love interest (the tractor) into one of his sheds. So I carried on. Having passed a small patch of grass covered in buttercups I reached the hedge that surrounded Madeleine's garden. As the light continued to dim and the sky now turned a milky, water-colour grey I at long last reached the bend into Folly Lane. I was finally home.

*

The sound of an excited tune reverberated out from Cynthia's Tudor house opposite. The curtains were not yet drawn in her drawing room, and the large latticed window had been left wide open to allow the summer breeze in and her music from the wireless to escape out. The open window revealed a cluttered sill covered in elaborate photo frames which contained pictures of the good and the great of Westminster. A large blue and white Chinese Dresden vase was also visible, positioned in the middle of the sill. Opposite I caught sight of Madeleine sat in her wicker chair, surrounded by her prized red and pink geraniums in the sun room. Upon seeing me Madeleine jumped up, adjusted her skirt and rushed out as best she could. She navigated her way down the path that ran along past the sitting room window, amongst colourful borders of flowers, and around the weeping willow in the middle of the lawn.

As soon as I was level with Madeleine I put down my cases almost as roughly as the bus driver had done. I laid Frank down on top of my case and sank into Madeleine's open arms where I received a welcome home hug and a reviving uplift of smell from her lavender perfume. She kept hold of me for a few moments and I felt a frail, wrinkled hand smooth my back almost as if she knew what an emotional time I had had. I kept my head on Madeleine's shoulder for quite some time. The softness of her blue jumper felt as comfortable as my own pillow. Surrounding us was the music from Cynthia's wireless and, rather ironically, of all pieces of music it was now playing, it had to be 'Moon Light Sonata. The music's haunting sincerity soothed me as Madeleine drew me up.

"Oh my dear! I am relieved to see you safely back home with us."

Madeleine sounded rather croaky and frailer than when I had left her at the beginning of the week, and I think she had been worrying about me for most of the time. She seemed genuinely pleased to see me back. Madeleine then remembered the reason I had returned to Devon in the first place. She quickly re-clasped my hands in to hers where I noticed a bad black bruise on one of her knuckles, with a Nile delta of blue pale veins risen all over her hands. The only sign of decoration was her simple gold wedding ring.

"Did you find your friend? Thelma and her daughter? Are they both safe?"

Her question stung me like a bee sting. For a few seconds the shock and grief came over me again and I tiredly wiped my eyes and told her the news.

"I'm afraid they didn't make it Madeleine. They're both gone."

I sounded as husky as Madeleine. I could still hear the 'Moon Light Sonata' gently playing in the background from Cynthia's house.

"Oh my dear!"

Madeleine groaned with a deep desperation in her voice that I could only too well relate to. She gave me yet another hug and smoothed my back again before giving me a kiss with a weak quivering lip, lightly painted a pale pink.

"I am so very sorry Edith. I really am. How terrible for you to go all that way and go through all that hope and search only to find that out."

Madeleine did look as sad as I felt. She was a woman who genuinely understood and empathised with a person's troubles. This is why I got on so well with her. I wanted to tell her that my return to Devon had not all been for nothing. I wanted to tell her all about Eddie and our plans for him to come and live with me, but I felt so drained and empty and desperately wanted to get in and read Jack's letter.

Thankfully Madeleine knew me only too well and instantly added, "You look done in my dear. I'll help you with your bags and get you inside. Then you can have a good rest. I can see by the sight of Frank that you have seen your son dressed up in his Indian outfit!"

Madeleine gave an amused look as she caught sight of poor Frank with his torn paw.

"When Eileen and Jack turned up earlier on, it gave me quite a turn! I thought something was wrong or that you had been hurt."

Madeleine put a light hand on my arm, and then added, "As it turned out there was nothing to worry about after all. Little man was just home sick and missing his mum. I can't say I blame him. It's not been the same without you these last few days."

Madeleine then proceeded to pick up my belongings. She first took hold of Frank, then my case but then her gaze fell upon the second case I had with me. I could see the surprise and curiosity in her face, yet she knew I was in no state to explain and simply said, "We'll get you inside. You can have a good night's sleep knowing your Jack is safe home. Then tomorrow you can both come round for dinner and you can tell me all about your return to Devon."

*

With my case and Frank in her hands and me clutching at Marcus's case, Madeleine quickly opened up my warped gate. The pair of us passed under the umbrella of the oak tree and we both crawled up the gravel path with the smell of lemon balm and Lady Silvia roses filling the air with perfume. From behind us the murmur of 'Moon light Sonata,' slowly faded away. We both stepped onto the tiled logia while I rummaged in my handbag looking for my keys. There was no need. Madeleine used her key and opened the front door. She put my case and Frank down in the hall, then whipped Marcus's case from me. I was then propelled into the hall and given kind but firm instruction.

"You go straight into the sitting room and sit down. I'll bring you in a nice cup of tea and a piece of my fruit cake. I baked it for you and Jack this morning. "

The sound of tea and fruit cake brought about a great sense of relief. I did not argue with Madeleine as she helped me out of my summer blue coat. I took off my hat, picked up poor injured Frank then staggered into the sitting room. I placed my hat and handbag on the chair which was nestled into my Queen Anne writing desk. I quickly observed the smell and sight of a jug on the piano filled with pink and white roses intermingled with a little lemon balm. Madeleine had put together the arrangement to welcome me home. I put Frank down on top of my sewing basket and finally sank into my arm chair, arching my neck and head feeling nothing but relief and gratitude that Jack and I were home. A few minutes later Madeleine tiptoed in with a tray of tea things and a slice of her fruit cake. A bundle of letters were propped up against the tea pot. The most important letter with its Gloucester post mark was at the very front of the pile. I was most eager to open it. Madeleine went about the sitting room, pulling the curtains and putting on the standard lamp by my desk. I ripped open the letter from Gloucester and with the support of my now lit lamp began to read Jack's letter.

Dear Mummy

I was so pleased to get your letter that you posted to me from Bath, and I hope you will find Auntie Thelma and Emma. I have been saying special prayers for them both. I am having a swell time in Gloucester with Auntie Eileen and Uncle Charles and my bedroom has a view of the cathedral! But I am missing home a lot. Uncle Charles' restaurant is ever so busy and seems to be fully booked until Monday. Auntie Eileen has been reading to me at night as that is the time I miss you the most. She has also been telling me about the time when you worked with her in Bath during the war at the Guildhall, and how you both came to meet Uncle Charles when you went for a meal at the Red House on the night of the Blitz! I don't remember much about my life in Bath. I only remember meeting you in the park one afternoon with Frank. Then I remember coming to live with you a few nights after all the bombing had ended. Tomorrow Uncle Charles and I are going swimming! Which I hope will be fun. I do really miss you Mummy and can't wait for Monday to come. Auntie Eileen is going to spend the night with us if that is alright? Then she will go back to Gloucester the next day. See you on Monday Mummy.

Ps Franks paw is nearly falling off again, I need you to sew it back on again for me when I get back.

Love Jack

"So my dear. What did your Jack say in his letter? Not that you really need to read it now, as he's already back home again."

I went through Jack's letter with Madeleine, telling her the history of how Eileen and I had come to meet Charles. I told her that Charles had definitely had a shine for Eileen that night. They got married after the war ended and moved to Gloucester where Charles had been offered a job as head waiter in a new swanky restaurant. He had then worked his way up and eventually opened up his very own place which he had named 'Eileen's.'

Madeleine assisted me with my tray. She poured me a welcome cup of tea and left me with just my other letters and cake on the table beside me.

She then asked hesitantly, "Does Jack ever speak about his real mother Edith?"

"No I don't think he remembers her much," I replied, "Sometimes he asks me about her. He remembers her being very sad in the park when I first met them, and I have explained to him about his father being killed and how badly his mum had taken the news. I told him that on the second night of the Blitz his mother was sadly killed in the bombing. Because I had given her my name and address in the park when I offered to support her if she ever needed anything, the authorities made contact with me and left Jack in my care until after the war when I was able to adopt him."

I suddenly felt rather stunned as I thought to myself how quickly that time had gone since I adopted Jack after the war, and we had moved from out of our one bedroom flat in Bath to Wiltshire. Where had all that time gone to?

Madeleine gathered her thoughts together and prepared to leave for her own home, but before she left she said, "Well Edith. Jack could not have been blessed with a better mother than you. I am sure the Lord had a hand in it all."

Smiling I rose out of my chair, placing aside Madeleine's fruit cake. I kissed her goodbye and thanked her for her kindness and for all that she had done for me.

" Don't be silly Edith, you know I am always next door if you ever get a problem. Will I see you both at church tomorrow?"

"Yes," I said, "We will see you tomorrow morning for church. We have a lot to be thankful for." Madeleine gave me a reassuring smile and kissed me goodnight.

"I am so sorry about your friend my dear, I really am. I don't know, life never seems to quite work out like we expect it to."

"No, it doesn't Madeleine," I replied rather philosophically. I bowed my head and looked down at the floor, pondering on her words and thinking of Thelma, Emma and Marcus and how lucky I was to have Jack, and to have found Eddie again. Yet how would I tell Eddie about Marcus? That part of his return I was dreading.

Madeleine must have sensed my mood, for as she went to go she turned and said, "Still my dear we can all spend far too much time in our lives looking back on our disappointments and all the things we should have said and done. The thing to do now is to look forward, be grateful for each new day and don't keep worrying about the past."

Madeleine then gave me another quick peck on the cheek, apologised for keeping me up on my feet and wished me a good night's sleep and rest. I opened the front door and thanked her again for looking after the house and bringing in the post. As Madeleine stepped on to the logia she suddenly remembered something.

"Oh my dear you left that lovely gold ring of yours in the kitchen on the windowsill under that plant of yours that I can never pronounce. Best go put it back on your finger or you'll lose it. Well I must be off, God bless."

As I reciprocated with a 'God bless' too, I watched Madeleine walk down the garden path and through the gate. I slowly closed the front door then walked into the kitchen and switched the light on. Just as Madeleine had said, there sat on the window sill under the canopy of my streptocarpus in full flower was the ring that Eddie had given me back in 1929. Eddie's ring, with its red ruby set deep in its centre, slid back upon my finger and I thought back to the many times when I could have sold it. But I never could part with it. I had missed its presence on my finger and was grateful to have it back where it belonged.

*

Upon my return to the sitting room I picked up Marcus's lonely looking case from the hall and placed it on the floor by my writing desk. There it would remain until Eddie came home. I glanced over to the polished piano with its top covered in photographs of my Mother, Father, Eddie, Jack and I. Madeleine's arrangement of roses just about camouflaged the damage which the piano had sustained during the Blitz. That old piano had certainly seen and been through some times and it still bore the scars. But it had survived like I had.

*

Feeling still tired and drained I noticed the time on the mantelpiece clock. It was about to sound 7.30 PM I returned to my arm chair and paused for a few moments. I picked up Frank from my work basket and hugged him tightly for a few minutes, reassuring myself that Jack would soon be home. Perhaps I should wait until he came back before I started eating my cake? It would be nice for us to share Madeleine's heavenly looking fruit cake together. However with my tummy groaning and cajoling, making the most terrible noises from lack of food, I put down Frank (who I would attend to later) and gave into temptation. I picked up my slice of cake and was just about to take a bite, with my fork gently pressed into the yellow fluffy sponge when there suddenly came a sharp hammering on the front door. I was bemused. Why on earth could Jack not have just come straight in? Putting my cake aside I forced myself out of the chair and hurried to open the front door. As I reached the hall I could observe Jack's little figure bouncing on the spot through the panes of glass, still dressed in his bright Indian costume. A rush of fresh breeze came hurtling in through the hall as I opened the door. Jack immediately stopped bouncing (a habit of his when waiting for something to happen) but seemed reluctant to come in.

"There you are!" I said, relieved that he had come home on the dot as I had asked. "Come on in little man, there's some fruit cake for you in the kitchen. Then after tea I will get on and mend Frank's paw for you. Well come on then, Jack. In you get!"

Jack still stood frozen to the spot looking rather shifty. His little brown eyes seemed averted to something round the corner of the logia, as if someone was hiding. I knew at once it must be Adam Berry who was probably hiding round the corner, ready to jump and scare me to death in his war paint and chief's costume. I gave him a suspicious glance and was just about to step out on to the logia, and surprise Adam when Jack suddenly said.

"Mummy there's a man here. He asked me if I knew who lived here and I told him I did. He asked if a lady called Edith lived here and I said yes and that you were my mum. He says he's my Uncle Eddie!"

I froze on the threshold of the door jolted by Jack's words. I looked at Jack and my mouth slightly quivered with fear and excitement. Then from around the corner passing the black classic urn of geraniums appeared a tall wiry looking man. He was carrying a large battered suitcase with the gold faded initials of 'E.P' by the frayed handles. The man was dressed in a long coat similar to a fisherman's waterproof. Upon his mid length hair sat a brown trilby hat which obscured his face. He put down his case with a thump on the tiled floor and removed the hat in an elegant fashion. With his face revealed I could clearly see that it was my brother. He had come home.

I hesitated for a moment, stunned and shocked to see Eddie home so early. I observed Jack take a hold of his hand and give it a light squeeze, as if to tell him not to worry. Eddie's eyes quickly fell down on Jack dressed in his chief's costume. He studied him curiously, with a look of familiarity in his eyes. Jacks gaze too was fixated on Eddie giving him a fascinated look and bemused smile. Eddie turned to me and gave me a quizzical look.

" You never told me I had a nephew! Yet, I don't know Edith. There's something about Jack. I feel like I've seen him before?"

I smiled and swallowed with a lump in my throat, " Well in a way you do know Jack. You were best friends with his father during the war and you served together in the navy. Jack is Frank's son."

Eddie looked stunned! He displayed a shocked yet remarkable expression of happiness. His eyes glistened with emotion and he proudly smiled at me. His mouth trembled and stuttered as he took hold of Jack scooping him up in his arms like a proud father. The two men in my life came towards me and I drew my arm round Eddie's waist with Jack snuggled up between us. Eddie looked like a man who at long last had discovered peace. He was no longer searching. He had found what he had been looking for.

Eddie turned to me with tears welling up in his eyes and said proudly, "I thought you had done without me for long enough so I came home early."

Somehow I knew even Marcus was looking down on us and was smiling.

Author's Note
The History Behind the Story

While *Edith's return to Devon* is entirely a work of fiction and its story and characters are utterly fictitious the history and events witnessed and lived by them is not. After the horror and bloodshed of the First World War people wanted to party! So many had not come back from the trenches and those that had survived understandably wanted to enjoy life and seize the day. Young people especially had spent their early years (the years we are told that should be the most happy) witnessing and experiencing the most appalling loss of life and having to cope with what must have been the most overwhelming feelings of loss and grief. With the war over, the promise was that Britain would become a 'Land fit for heroes.' My own personal interpretation to explain the twenties is as follows. We should view the era in the eyes of a fashion designer. The restricting corsets, tight fitting dresses of the Edwardian era were slowly, through the war and into the Twenties updated with new, fresh designs that were lose fitting and flowing. That new fashion was how young people, and people more generally, felt about life. Dancing, vibrant music, clubs, motor cars, films and the wireless was bringing about a dramatic change in attitudes. The old Edwardian guard was having to evolve into something new, exciting and different. People above all wanted to escape from all the trauma they had experienced in the Great War. However this new found optimism and the dream of a 'Land fit for heroes' was overshadowed by high unemployment, low wages and an expensive exports market. It was this gloom against the back drop of parties, music and dancing that lit the spark for the General Strike in 1926. Although the economy was in bad shape in 1926, by the end of the decade events in the United States turned a slump into a depression. In October 1929 the feverish New York Stock Market which had been booming, accompanied by a glutton of speculation went bust. As the old saying goes 'What goes up has to come down,' And indeed down it did go. The Financial Crash of 1929 was a cataclysmic event for America and the world. In one day millions were completely wiped out. People who had been millionaires one day were paupers the next. The crash of the New York Stock Market caused America and the world to enter a deep and damaging depression. Millions lost their jobs, homes and livelihoods. Many found it impossible to gain new jobs. In Britain exports evaporated and unemployment which at the time was already considerably high, climbed to a new summit of 2.5 million. There was hardly an individual who was not immune to the crash.

During the course of my research for this book I have been struck with how little people appreciate the effect the Second World War had on the city of Bath. I have long had a love of Bath as I was born in the RUH there and when my grandmother was alive and during the school holidays I became almost a weekly visitor to the city accompanying her and my mother for her hairdressing appointments. Bath is wrongly imagined by some to have been unaffected by the war compared to London and Bristol. On April 25th and 26th 1942, the Germans attacked the city on a moonlit night in act of revenge for RAF attacks in the Baltic ports of Rostock and Lubeck. The final count of the dead in Bath was 417. The toll must have had a dreadful impact on the city, as Bath is relatively small compared to London and Bristol. Yet while researching my 1942 chapters I was amazed and full of admiration for the citizens of Bath, who by all accounts did what us British do best. They 'kept calm and carried on.'

Finally we come to Devon and the third historical event that is placed within the book. The flood disaster that takes place in *Edith's return to Devon* is based on the Lynmouth flood disaster of 1952. A horrific and what must have been terrifying event that came without warning in the dead of night. Like Bath the residents of Lynmouth showed great courage, determination and kindness to each other in the face of great adversity. As in the rest of my book, the Characters that Edith meets are purely fictional but my desire was to put in as much detail as possible of the beauty and detail of this enchanting part of Devon. *Edith's return to Devon* came about due to me following the golden rule of writing: 'write about what you know.' Although there was much about Devon and Bath that I did not know and had to research, I had the advantage of visiting these places on a regular bases and have admiration and love for them both. In both instances I hope that I have done them and their residents justice in my writing. It seems to me that everything in life seems to come round full circle. We enjoy years of prosperity, economic and political stability and think the good times are here to stay. Then, often when we at least expect it, the pendulum swings back the other way to years of hardship, instability and conflict. The warning for all of us living in an uncertain world is this. When our economies and stock markets are in decline we should never allow them to rise again at the expense of our democracy and liberty to fall. If we do we will surely risk repeating the mistakes of the past.

Daniel Pitt
July 2012

Acknowledgements

Edith's Return to Devon would not have been possible without the support and help from the following people.

Firstly, I would like to thank, Bill Proyer who allowed me to view his archive of beautiful photographs, postcards and prints that reveal a now forgotten age in North Devon. Without Bill's help the book would have been much the poorer for and I doubt would have ever been completed.

I would also like to thank my dear friend, Eileen Rice who sat with me for a four hour interview, while I asked her question after question of what Bath had been like during 1942. Eileen gave me a remarkable account of her life, memories and experiences during what was very difficult years for our country. Very sadly, Eileen passed away on 22nd September 2012 and never got to see *Edith's Return to Devon* published, nor to read about the fictional character who shared her name. I am so thankful that I had Eileen for a friend and I will deeply miss her warmth, kindness and her wonderful sense of humour.

I would like to thank my good friend, Helen Smith who looked at early first drafts of my book and also for her friendship and encouragement. I would also like to thank my friend, Liz Grieves who also looked at early drafts of my manuscript and gave me her honest opinions and encouragement.

Great thanks must also go to my friend, Jane Hickman who did a great deal of proof reading for me during 2011. Jane has a very keen eye for detail and her guidance and support were invaluable.

I would like to thank my former English teacher, Jill Ellis who, in my last year of secondary school encouraged me to really think about my writing and impressed on me how important it is to give a reader plenty of detail about a characters surroundings. Jill is a wonderful English teacher and I greatly valued all her efforts to support me in my last year at school.

My book would have been much the poorer for if it had not been for my dear friend and mentor, Thelma McCrimmon. Thelma completely read the entire manuscript during her summer holidays and then volunteered to completely proof read the manuscript. Thelma gave me a great deal of her time and skills during the last months of 2011 and often came up with suggestions of how I could improve my writing as well as telling me when she thought I had put in far too much detail and left little notes of, 'do you need this Dan' in various places throughout the manuscript. As always I enjoyed working with Thelma and we both enjoyed some good humour and laughs along the way.

I would like to thank all at Troubador Publishing Ltd, with special thanks to, Terry Compton, Sarah Taylor, Jennifer Liptrot, Ciara Reihill and to all those who worked behind the scenes who contributed to the production and publication of my book.

I would also like to thank Christopher Chard Photography, for the photographs that he took to support the marketing of *Edith's Return To Devon* and for his professionalism and good humour.

I would like to thank, Rose, John, Victoria, Kate, Helen, Alfred, Edgar and Laura Hodges at The Chough's Nest Hotel, who all work incredibly hard for their guests to ensure that they have a very special and relaxing holiday. I have great admiration for them all.

I would like to acknowledge the following books and media sources that I consulted to support me in my research for this book and to evoke the historical periods of the 1920s, 1940s and the 1950s.

Martin Wainwright's, *The Bath Blitz*, Paul De'ath, *Images of England: Bath*, Mark Arnold-Foster for his book, *The World At War*, Philip Wilkinson for his book that accompanied the BBC series, *Turn Back Time: The High Street*, Christina Hardyment for her beautiful book, *Behind The Scenes*, and Dan Cruichshank's BBC series, *The Lost World Of Friese-Greene*. For those who like me have a love of North Devon, or for those interested in the history of Lynton and Lynmouth, which became two of the settings for my book, then I would highly recommend, John Travis, for his wonderful book, *Lynton and Lynmouth: Glimpses of the past*. And Brian Pearce for his book, *Lynton and Lynmouth, The Golden Years*.

Finally and most importantly, my thanks must go to my parents, for without their love, support and encouragement, *Edith's Return To Devon* would never have been started let alone finished. They have both always fully supported me in all aspects of my life and my book was no exception. As each chapter was crafted, then printed off the first people who I went for approval and advice from was my parents. They both gave me their frank and honest thoughts and suggestions and always told me when they thought I could either do better, or could elaborate further. They have both been very long suffering coping with the writing process and my, shall we say artistic temperament. My Mum and Dad are not just my parents but my greatest friends and I could not have wished for better parents, nor a better extended family and group of friends. I count myself truly blessed to have them all.